DEEPLIGHT

DEEPLIGHT

FRANCES HARDINGE

AMULET BOOKS
NEW YORK

Cataloging-in-Publication Data has been applied for and may be obtained
from the Library of Congress.

ISBN 978-1-4197-4320-7

Originally published in hardcover by Macmillan Publishers
Limited, United Kingdom, in 2019.

Text copyright © 2019 Frances Hardinge
Jacket illustrations © 2020 Vincent Chong
Book design by Hana Anouk Nakamura
Cover type design by Maria T. Middleton

Printed and bound in U.S.A.

10 9 8 7 6 5 4 3 2 1

Amulet Books are available at special discounts when purchased in quantity
for premiums and promotions as well as fundraising or educational use.
Special editions can also be created to specification. For details,
contact specialsales@abramsbooks.com or the address below.

Amulet Books® is a registered trademark of Harry N. Abrams, Inc.

ABRAMS The Art of Books
195 Broadway, New York, NY 10007
abramsbooks.com

To Ella and the other members of the Young People's
Board of the National Deaf Children's Society

PROLOGUE

THEY SAY YOU CAN SAIL A THOUSAND MILES along the island chain of the Myriad, from the frosty shores of the north to the lush, sultry islands of the south. They say that the islanders are like the red crabs that race along the shores— hardy, unpredictable, and as happy in the water as out of it.

They say that the ocean around the Myriad has its own madness. Sailors tell of great whirlpools that swallow boats and of reeking, ice-cold jets that bubble to the surface and stop the hearts of swimmers. Black clouds suddenly boil into existence amid flawless skies.

They say that there is a dark realm of nightmares that lies beneath the true sea. When the Undersea arches its back, the upper sea is stirred to frenzy.

They say that the Undersea was the dwelling place of the gods.

They say many things of the Myriad, and all of them are true.

The gods were as real as the coastlines and currents and as merciless as the winds and whirlpools. The Glass Cardinal throttled galleons with translucent tendrils. The Red Forlorn floated like a cloud of blood in the water. Kalmaddoth howled with a razor lattice instead of a mouth. Dolor lurched through the water, kicking with dozens of human legs. The Hidden Lady waited in the silent deeps, shrouded by her own snaking hair.

Now and then, one would rise from the Undersea and appear in the pale light of day, devouring schooners, smashing ports to splinters, and etching their shapes into the nightmares of all. Some of them sang as they did so.

For centuries, the gods ruled the Myriad through awe and terror, each with its own cluster of islands as territory. Human sacrifices were hurled into the waters to appease them, and every boat was painted with pleading eyes to entreat their mercy. They were served, feared, and adored.

Then, without warning, the gods turned on each other.

It took barely a week for them to tear one another apart—a week of tidal waves and devastation. Many hundreds of islanders lost their lives. By the end, no living gods remained, only vast corpses rolling in the deep. Even thirty years after this Cataclysm, nobody knows why it happened. The gods are still mysterious, though the fear of them is slowly waning.

They say that a coin-sized scrap of dead god can make your fortune, if the powers it possesses are strange and rare enough and if you are brave enough to dive for them.

This is also true.

Chapter 1

"ARE YOU SURE THIS IS SAFE?" ASKED THE VISIT-ing merchant, struggling up the ladder that scaled the makeshift wooden tower. "I thought you'd arranged me a place on one of those boats!"

"All the boats are full," Hark told him glibly, as he clambered up behind him. "The governor and his friends, and all the rich men who paid for the expedition, and their families, they took all the seats—no room left!" For all he knew, this might even be true. He hadn't actually checked. "Besides, seats in those boats cost more than your eyes. This is a tenth of the price, and the view is better!"

By the time they reached the top, the merchant was out of breath and patting his face with a handkerchief. The man who owned the rickety tower guided the merchant and Hark to two cramped and precarious seats and took payment for both from the merchant. The cold wind blew, making the structure creak, and the merchant flinched, clutching his hat to his head. He didn't notice the tower owner discreetly giving Hark a wink and his commission.

The ten-foot wooden towers were wheeled out only on fes-tival days or markets. They were not in fact particularly safe, and Hark knew they would become even less so when more low-paying customers were hanging off the sides of them later. He didn't feel that this needed mentioning, though.

"It *is* a good view," the merchant conceded grudgingly.

Aloft on the tower, the pair could easily see over the heads of the crowds that crammed every inch of the quays and jetties. The docks had been thronged since dawn, and even the cliff tops and high towers were covered in figures. Everyone wanted a view of the great, scoop-shaped harbor below.

For now, the harbor hardly seemed to merit so much attention. It was just another deep, placid mooring place perfect for submersibles and cluttered with the usual underwater craft. Flattened iron "turtles" with rear propellers skulked next to slim "barracudas" with black iron fins. Diving bells glinted with steel and glass beside small, old-fashioned timber-and-leather "skimmer" subs.

Today, however, all of these vessels were moored at the edges of the harbor. A far bigger submarine would be returning soon, and the way needed to be left clear for it. When it appeared, every eye would be fixed on it, to see what—and whom—it brought back.

"It looks like everyone on the island has turned out to watch!" exclaimed the merchant.

"The Hidden Lady was *our* god," Hark pointed out. "Lady's Crave is even named after her. You might say she's . . . coming home."

Actually, the Hidden Lady had kept several islands in her thrall, not just one, but Hark allowed himself some poetic licence. What did it matter? She had lived long ago, before Hark was born. The gods belonged to the world of stories now, and you could tell stories any way you liked.

So far, the day was clear, but the distant islands on the horizon were already softening and dimming in a haze that promised rain. Hark smelled roasting crab from the braziers on the waterfront and suddenly felt drunk with love for his own island. All of his fourteen years had been spent on the ragged shores of Lady's Crave, but its lessons were all he needed. After all, everyone and everything came to his island sooner or later. Often they turned up broken or lost, but that didn't matter. He loved the island's jumble of accents, the coming and going of the great ships, and the stealthy sale of almost everything. He loved its cunning and its hunger.

Jelt should be here to see this. The thought ambushed him, and a host of worries hurried in behind him. *Where the scourge is Jelt?*

Jelt had asked Hark to meet him by the bellows house earlier that morning to discuss a "job" someone wanted doing. Hark had waited there for him for two hours before giving up. That was typical of Jelt. He was there for you when it mattered, but the rest of the time he came and went like a cat, without explanation or apology.

Hark knew that Jelt had probably just gotten distracted. Nonetheless, a queasy little tapeworm of anxiety gnawed at Hark's stomach as each hour passed without word from his best friend. Jelt had enemies and the sort of past that sometimes came back to bite.

"How will we recognize the *Abysmal Child*?" The merchant was squinting through a spyglass at the harbor.

"Oh, you'll know her!" Like most Lady's Cravers, Hark felt a vicarious pride in the *Abysmal Child*. "She's as long as a schooner—a real Undersea delver. Thirty oars, hull of black withersteel, ten grabs and three rear propellers. The best and biggest salvage submarine yet. The crowd will go mad as soon as they see her."

Usually no boats were permitted in the submersible harbor except a few customs vessels, diver dinghies, and cargo haulers.

Today, however, three luxurious-looking barges were moored by the wharf, allowing an elite few a better view of the *Abysmal Child*'s return.

"There's the governor's boat!" Hark pointed out the simple green and white flag on its single mast. "That's where all the investors will be—all the rich folks who paid for the *Abysmal Child* expedition." He could imagine them, brimful of expensive wine and hope, scanning the waters with the fervor of gamblers. "This day'll make their fortunes—or ruin them," he added.

"Ruin them?" asked the merchant. "Does that happen often?"

"Sometimes." Hark sensed ghoulish curiosity and hastened to feed it. "One great submarine called the *Wish For Naught* got attacked by a giant squid in the deeps and limped back to port with nothing. As it came up, and everybody saw its empty nets, half the investors jumped straight into the water in despair. The governor's guards pulled out most of them, but a few were wearing heavy chains of office and metal armor under their clothes." Hark mimed a downward plunge with one hand, and shook his head in mock mourning.

The merchant perked up at the thought. It is always a consolation to imagine outrageously rich people miserable and drowning. Of course, from Hark's point of view, the merchant himself was very rich. Thus it was hard to feel too guilty about the prospect of making him somewhat less rich. Hark was hoping to do exactly that before the day was out.

"Giant squid?" asked the merchant in tones of hushed fascination. "So there are still sea monsters in these waters?"

"Oh, there are all kinds of perils down there!" Hark assured him enthusiastically. "Razor-toothed fish with white eyes and bullwhip tails with yellow lights on them! Cold surges and whirlpools! Suck-currents that pull you down to the Undersea! Jagged towers of black rock, and great cracks full of redjaws! Sea-urchin spikes as long as your arm! Tides full of yellow jellyfish so poisonous, a single touch would kill a whale!"

These stories were true, or at least true enough for present purposes. Stories were currency, and Hark understood that better than most. What did a few exaggerations matter? The merchant would be dining out on these tales for years, once he got home to the western continent.

The merchant shuddered. He probably thought everything underwater was alien and mysterious. Folks from the continents were weird like that. They seemed to think that the land stopped when you reached the shoreline, as if the islands were just rafts floating on the gray, temperamental sea. Locals like Hark had spent enough time underwater to understand that the islands were just the very tips of submerged mountains. Beneath the surface, the contours of the land descended and continued, in brutal ridges, deep ravines, cliff drops, and secret plateaus. Each had its own inhabitants, landmarks, treasures, and surprises.

"There she is!" called Hark. Out by the harbor mouth he had spotted a bald, troubled patch of water, where the waves were invisibly broken on some long submerged bulk. The gulls that had been sitting on the surface at the harbor mouth took off and rose into great, strident clouds, dipping and daring each other. "There! See that little white wake? Her periscope's up!"

Other people were pointing and calling out now. A few seconds later, a small cannon fired, the retort echoing back and forth across the harbor. A white plume of smoke climbed into the sky and then drifted.

The crowd became exultant, deafening. There was always a festival feel when a sub brought a god home. As a little kid,

Hark had lived for such moments, eyes wide to store every detail. Just for a moment, he felt a twinge of the old excitement and awe.

Then the great submarine's long, black back broke the surface. Foam poured off the short turret and bladelike fins, and the brass rims of portholes glinted in the sun. The pale, entreating eyes painted on the prow were awash, as though weeping.

"She's lost oars," Hark muttered, his words drowned by the roar of the crowd. Eight of the oars now ended in fractured stumps. As the *Abysmal Child* rose higher, he could see that it had lost more than that. One propeller was gone, and a rear panel hung loose, seawater hissing out of the mangled aperture. The tone of the hubbub changed as others noticed the same thing. The front compartment was presumably still watertight, since someone was alive to pilot the sub, but anyone who had been in the rear would be very, very dead.

The merchant was leaning forward now, spyglass jammed to his eye. Since all of this was a story to tell his friends later, a tragedy was as good as a triumph. Better, perhaps. Stories were ruthless creatures and sometimes fattened themselves on bloody happenings.

"Where's her cargo?" he asked. "Why are people running around on the wharf? What's going on down there?"

"The turret's open!" Hark provided a commentary. "Someone's come up through it . . . There's a conversation going on . . . Looks like the governor's ordered diver boats to go in. There must be something strapped under the sub!"

The governor's guards along the waterfront readied their harpoon guns and wind-guns, to make sure that only the permitted diver boats approached. Any unauthorized swimmers, divers, or subs seen heading for the *Abysmal Child* could expect a spiky and fatal reprimand.

The sun gleaming on their diving helmets, the divers lowered themselves into the water and disappeared beneath the surface. After five minutes, a disturbance was visible in the waters. Something was rising beside the great sub, something long and slender in a frothy mesh of fine netting . . .

"It's huge!" exclaimed the merchant. "I've never seen anything like it!"

The thing in the net—no, there were *two* things—were as long as the *Abysmal Child* but no wider than a man's torso. They were bent in a couple of places near the middle of their length, and for a moment Hark thought they must have snapped during the journey. As the foam settled, however, he could see that the spindly lengths were jointed. Beneath the floating net, he glimpsed the mottled red and white of their shell, draped with black weed and studded with limpets. One tapering gray claw poked out through the mesh.

As he watched, the impossibly long legs stirred and slowly flexed.

His heart gave an unexpected flutter of fear and awe. Just for a second, he was a little kid again. He could almost imagine that the Hidden Lady might rear up out of the water, shake off the net, and scream the cliffs into dust as her writhing hair darkened the sky . . .

The moment passed. Common sense returned. He knew that the uncanny motion had been caused by the waves, manhandling from the divers, and nothing more.

"Is that her?" asked the merchant, tugging at Hark's sleeve. "Is that the Hidden Lady?"

"No," said Hark. "I mean . . . yes. A piece of her. Two of her legs." Spider-crab legs the length of a schooner. It was a great find, but there was a tight, disappointed feeling in his chest. What had he been hoping for?

"I thought she was one of the more human-looking ones?" asked the merchant.

"She was," said Hark.

Now she was godware, and godware meant opportunities. The investors would have their cargo jealously guarded as it was hauled up by cranes and dragged to the waiting warehouse. They wouldn't relax until every last ounce had been carved up, weighed, scraped, sold, or boiled for glue. In the meantime, hundreds of other eyes were watching for chances. A shard of shell, a smear of ichor, a spoonful of pulp could sell for more than a month's wages. When he was younger, Hark might have been one of those squeezed among the crowds, hoping to snatch at some tiny dropped fragment . . .

Now he was older and wiser, he knew that there were ways to make money from the Hidden Lady without braving the harpoons. He threw a brief, assessing glance at the merchant, who was still watching through his spyglass, entranced.

"The menders are lucky folks," he lied conversationally. "The ones who clean out and fix the big nets afterward. It's a difficult job, because of the thick cables, but one of my friends does it. He says he *always* finds a bit of godware or two caught in the net. He's allowed to keep them as payment."

"Really?" The merchant lowered his spyglass and stared at Hark. He looked incredulous, but not incredulous enough. Hark had chosen well.

"It's not quite as good as it sounds." Hark shrugged ruefully. "He has to sell it at the Appraisal auction, which means the governor's taxman gets a big cut."

He looked away, as if losing interest in the subject. He had left a baited hook trailing in the merchant's mind. *Oh, come on and bite, you fat fish . . .*

"Do all sales *have* to go through the Appraisal?" The merchant hesitated, and cleared his throat. "Does your friend ever sell his little bits of godware . . . privately?"

Hark let himself look surprised, then thoughtful. He gave a furtive glance around, then leaned toward the merchant.

"Well, the law says all sales *should* go through the Appraisal. If anybody ever found out about a 'private sale' there would be trouble . . . but . . . do you want me to talk to my friend?"

"If you wouldn't mind," said the merchant, his eyes bright.

Got you.

Hark knew people who could make him what he needed. A piece of lobster shell, coated in glass to make it look special, with some blackened limpets glued on. The merchant would probably be three islands further along his journey before he suspected his souvenir wasn't godware. And would he want to believe it even then? Why not hold the faith so that he could tell his friends: *You see this? It's part of the Hidden Lady. I was there when they dragged it up from the deep.* Why give up a perfectly good story?

"Hark!"

The call came from the base of the tower and made Hark jump. It was the voice he knew best in the world, and it filled him with relief. Jelt was alive and well. Of course he was.

A moment later, the wave of relief receded, and a weight settled on his heart. He felt an odd temptation to pretend not to hear, just for a few moments more.

"Oi, Hark!" The tower shook as somebody below slammed his fist into it twice.

Hark turned and looked.

There was Jelt, standing on the wharf. It was strange looking down on him like that. He was two years older than Hark and had always been taller, but over the last three years, life had grabbed him by the ankles and head and stretched him. It had left Jelt lean, raw, and angry about it. Even when he was motionless or calm, you could sense that anger snaking off him. As usual, his expression was distracted but intense, as if listening to the world whisper something that riled him. You always had the feeling that there was a problem, and maybe you weren't it, but you might become it if you didn't tread carefully.

Jelt raised his hand and gave a quick, fierce beckon.

Hark hesitated a moment, conflicted, then gave the merchant an uneasy smile, and waved at Jelt.

"Good to see you!" he called down to his friend. "I'll talk to you later, all right?" He gave a brief, meaningful glance in the direction of the merchant. *Not now, Jelt. I've got a prospect here.*

Jelt shook his head.

"You need to come *right now*."

"You're *joking*!" hissed Hark.

"Come *on*!" Jelt slammed his hand into the wood of the tower again. "We need to hurry!"

There were protests from the other people perched on the tower. Hark gritted his teeth and apologized to the merchant, promising to find him later, then scrambled down the ladder. A moment later, he was shoving his way through the crowd, in his friend's wake. Somehow Hark always found himself neck-deep in Jelt's latest plan. It was as though he'd signed up for it in his sleep.

"I had that continenter hooked!" protested Hark as the two of them hurried up the stone steps of a priest-track to one of the beacon cliffs. "Why couldn't this wait until I'd reeled him in?"

Jelt gave a snort of mirth.

"You're just angry because I dragged you away from your girlfriend!" he said. It was an old joke of his that Hark had a crush on the idea of the Hidden Lady. "Such a romantic. Oh, don't sulk. I *told* you we were doing another job today!"

"Where were you this morning, then?" demanded Hark. "I waited for hours!"

"Staying out of someone's way," Jelt answered curtly.

Jelt was much in demand these days. Cold-eyed people came looking for him—and not to shake his hand. Sometimes it was the governor's men, sometimes other people who didn't give their names. It had been happening ever since that night on the mudflats, the night Hark and Jelt never talked about. Hark sensed that Jelt was almost daring him to ask about it now. He did not take the bait.

"You lost them?" he asked instead.

"Yeah," said Jelt, no longer in a humorous mood. "Hurry it up, will you?"

Events had a current, and Hark didn't believe in fighting currents. Using them, playing with them, letting them push you slantwise to somewhere that might serve your turn, yes. Fighting them flat out, no. The current that was Jelt pulled him along more than any other. Somehow Hark couldn't slip or slide or shoot off sideways and still pretend he was doing what Jelt wanted, the way he could with anybody else.

I don't want to anyway, he told himself firmly. *Jelt is family.* He knew better than to trust anything he told himself, though.

There were four figures waiting near the top of the hill, in the shelter of one of the lookout towers. Hark's heart lurched as he recognized their leader, a woman in her late thirties, with a bitter, thoughtful mouth and a thick mottling of freckles that covered her face and arms, and even the scalp beneath her close-cropped hair. Dotta Rigg's reckless, cutthroat smuggling runs filled Lady's Cravers with both alarm and an odd pride.

13

Her five children, even the younger ones, could get free drinks anywhere on the island, and only partly because people were afraid of them.

Hark had heard older hands talking of Rigg with trepidation and contempt, combined with bafflement at her success. *She's heading for a fall. Too chancy, doesn't listen to anyone. Who the abyss wants to be a* famous *smuggler?*

"Captain Rigg," said Hark, hoping to sound confident but respectful. Whatever madness Jelt had gotten them into, he had better act as if he could handle it.

He noticed the steel and scrimshaw ear-studs worn proudly by a couple of Rigg's companions to signal that they were "sea-kissed." People who spent a lot of their time diving or trusting their lives to submarines often ended up losing some or all of their hearing. It was the mark of a seasoned aquanaut, and generally respected.

Sign? he asked them quickly in sign language, and received a nod. Many sea-kissed could lip-read or retained some of their hearing, so it was always polite to ask whether they preferred speech or sign language.

You wanted to see us? Hark asked Rigg in Myriad sign language. Since there were so many sea-kissed across the Myriad, virtually all islanders knew some sign language, though the signs varied slightly from one island to the next. Hark could manage the basics of the Lady's Crave variant but always felt a bit clumsy with it, compared with the grace of those who used it more often.

Yes, though I'm going off the idea, Rigg signed sharply with a scowl. *We've been waiting nearly an hour! You better not be late tonight.* She beckoned Hark and Jelt closer, and the six of them reflexively formed a huddle so that their signs could not easily be read from a distance.

Tonight? Things were moving even faster than Hark had feared.

We won't, signed Jelt. No excuses, no apology, just a sky-blue stare.

Rigg jerked a thumb toward the beacon tower on the next headland.

It's that beacon and the one beyond it, she signed, fixing Hark and Jelt with an assessing glare. *You'll need to put both lights out an hour after the cannon. There's a route under the lip of the cliff to the one further away . . . You see that ledge under the red streak? One of you will have to climb along that. You can't use the cliff-top path or you'll be seen.*

Hark was catching up fast and wished he wasn't. He gave a silent, dry-mouthed nod, trying to disguise his rising panic. He wondered if Jelt had deliberately brought him in late so he wouldn't be able to protest and back out. Four dangerous people had been kept waiting in the cold—he didn't have the nerve to tell them that they'd been wasting their time.

It has to be done tonight? Hark asked, thinking wistfully of his gullible, abandoned merchant.

Of course, Rigg signed irritably. *The governor's men will be busy, won't they?*

She was right, Hark realized. Most of the governor's guards would probably be on the docks, guarding the *Abysmal Child,* watching the warehouse with the new cargo, and stopping people diving in the harbor for fallen scraps of the Hidden Lady. There would be fewer men patrolling the cliffs and the coves.

They'll hold an Appraisal tomorrow to sell off the Abysmal Child*'s godware, I guarantee it,* continued Rigg. *After that, patrols will be back at full strength. It has to be tonight.*

No problem, answered Jelt.

. . . . .

"You didn't ask," Hark said bitterly, as twilight settled on the island like a sour mood. "You never ask, Jelt."

"Wasn't time, was there? You got to grab these chances when they come. And we were only late because I spent hours finding you in that crowd!"

"You *did* have time to tell me!" Hark began, but already he knew it was pointless to argue. If Hark stuck to his guns, really stuck to them, that would lead nowhere good.

"Look," continued Jelt, "here's how we do this. We hide on the hillside till it's time, then I climb up near to the first lantern, and you take the ledge path to the second. You knock out your lantern as soon as you can, and I'll kill mine when yours goes dark."

"I still don't see why *I* have to do the climb along that ledge," muttered Hark.

"Are you joking?" Jelt halted in his tracks and stared at Hark with wide, angry eyes. "I'm trying to show Rigg what you can do, Hark! You think I couldn't have gotten somebody else for this? I brought you in because we're friends! You're a decent climber, and after tonight, Rigg's whole gang will know it."

In spite of his annoyance, Hark couldn't help feeling a little mollified by the compliment.

"Anyway," added Jelt, "that path's got an overhang. You're shorter than me, it won't slow you down as much. Also, the one hiding near that first beacon has to stay there, ready to break it, no matter what happens. What would you do if the governor's men showed up there? Give them a smile? Tell them a nice story?"

"What would *you* do, then?" Hark retorted. "Chuck 'em all off the cliff?"

Jelt gave a bit of a shrug and a dangerous little smirk. *I might,* said the smirk, *if I feel like it.* He was always like that in the face

16

of a potential fight. Bravado toothed with a hint of real threat. Joking but not joking. You couldn't prove anything either way.

"Why do they want the lights out, anyway?" muttered Hark.

The beacon lights had once been a signal to the gods— a plea. *Please let our ships sail through. Do not rise in your terrible majesty. We will appease you, we will feed you . . .* Many of the Myriad's islands had long since removed their beacon towers as symbols of a dead and regrettable era. The governor of Lady's Crave, however, was eternally practical. He had kept the towers, modifying them and adding lenses so that they cast a broad, dim beam on the coves the smugglers favored for their night runs.

"They're doing something they don't want anybody to see," Jelt said slowly and clearly, his tone patiently impatient. "Maybe we'll find out what if we show what we're worth."

Hark hesitated for too many seconds, and Jelt's short fuse burned out.

"Oh, grow a spine, Hark! Before I start wishing I'd left you out of this. This is a *promotion*. You got some other career plans, have you? You want to spend your whole life snatching scraps and wheedling pennies on the docks like a little kid, till you're too old and slow, and you starve?"

Hark chewed his cheek, hearing the truth in Jelt's words. Hark had a stubborn seed of hope in his soul that kept pushing up and up, however deeply it was buried, and building bright, strange futures for him. Although he felt a profound, blood-level love for Lady's Crave, many of his dreams involved leaving for Siren, or Malpease—some island that was bigger and brighter, with more hope. Every day he saw people who had probably once had dreams like his, but who had never left and never come to anything. Old men and women in damp rags, gathering clams or squabbling over tiny bribes, their eyes weary pools of disappointment. Seeing them, he could feel his dreams shudder.

Hark *had* moved up in the world, hadn't he? He wasn't hanging around the kids' Shelter anymore, begging for food or somewhere to sleep. He was sharing a shack behind the glue factory, above the flood line, and with warmth soaking through the wall from the glue furnaces beyond. His gaggle of housemates would probably kick him out sooner or later as their alliances shifted, but that was just what happened. Folks turned on you, so you looked for the next bunch of people to get you through. Nobody was permanent.

Nobody except Jelt.

Hark and Jelt had been orphaned by the same bitter winter, and this had somehow grafted them together. Sometimes Hark felt they were more than friends—or less than friends—their destinies conjoined against their wills. Unwanted children were not unusual, and Lady's Crave had shown them a certain rough charity in their earliest years. They had been given a home at the Shelter and one meal a day. Sailors had thrown them occasional scraps or turned a blind eye when they slept in their rowing boats. Even the territorial shore scavengers let the youngest children delve into their rock pools now and then for sea urchins and shellfish. But when you turned seven or eight, your time was up. You were old enough to fend for yourself without help and were chased off if you tried foraging in a territory claimed by a scavenger gang. In Hark's case, this did not happen until he was nine: an early lesson in the advantages of looking young and harmless.

But appearing that way was dangerous, too. It marked you as a victim, a soft target. Hark had survived because word got around about his crazy friend, the one who stood his ground against full-grown men and tried to smash their teeth in with rocks.

Jelt had kept Hark alive. Jelt could drop his fear and self-control in a second. Jelt thought big, could even think *himself* bigger.

"We got to move up," said Jelt, "or we're going nowhere. You take the world by the throat or you die."

A few hours later, the pair of them were hiding on the hillside watching the dusk draw in. Jelt didn't get nerves when he was about night business. Hark did, though he knew better than to admit it.

He dealt with it by telling himself a story. He watched himself as if he'd already done it, already survived, and was telling the tale of his adventure to an agog and adoring audience in a tavern afterward. It calmed him down and slowed his pulse a little. He was the hero, and everything was going to be all right. It already *was* all right. The things happening right now weren't real peril; they were just drama.

And we sat waiting under that overhang for two hours, he told his spellbound imaginary audience. *We heard the evening cannon sound, then watched the sky get darker, and the storm streaks deepen above Rue and Hullbrake . . .*

The yellow had spread across the sky like a bruise, and across the sea the pale streamers of distant downpours descended to the humped backs of other islands. Already he could hear the patter of rain outside the overhang and see the rock speckling and darkening.

Their hiding place was halfway up the headland. Jelt was looking out to sea, with that bland, ecstatic look of calm he always had before they did something stupid and dangerous. Only his blunt fingers were restless. He was tranquil but alive, utterly awake, open to every passing moment, weighing it for ripeness.

"Come on," he said suddenly. It was time. Jelt had an animal sense for these things.

Outside, Hark felt the icy sting of little raindrops on his face and hands—needle rain with a winter sting in it.

We had to climb up to the headland from further down the cliff, you see, Hark explained to his invisible future admirers, *so they wouldn't spot us. And it was tricky, with the rain coming down, right into our eyes, and the rocks getting slippery . . .*

The dark slope above was rugged with mottled gray-white rocks that bulged, jutted, and occasionally fell. Tiny trees twisted out between them like knuckly question marks, their needle-clusters quivering like fists in the wet wind. Gray sea-thistles starred the darkness: soft puffballs that looked like rocks but broke under your hand. Spindleweed held when you grabbed a fistful of it to pull yourself up but scored your palms and fingers.

Hark climbed, his fingers numb already. His teeth chattered.

And I was thinking, why was I doing this? But I couldn't leave Jelt in the lurch, could I? He'd be dead without me.

You didn't grow up on Lady's Crave without knowing how to climb. You needed it to reach the nests of seabirds on the eastern cliffs. The headlands and slick rocks of the coves were where you proved yourself and carved out your place in the pecking order. You jumped from Wailer's Rock and fell for a full second before the sea slapped the breath out of you. And you could stay ahead of danger, and trouble, and people who wanted their possessions back, as long as you could climb.

Glancing to one side, Hark could see Jelt was pulling ahead, scowling with concentration. Hark was the nimbler and lighter of the two, but Jelt was stronger and more reckless. So somehow Hark had spent his whole life trying to keep pace with Jelt.

. . . and of course it's getting dark, and we can hardly see where we're putting our hands . . .

They had chosen a route up a zigzag crevice, since it had more footholds and was deep enough for them to avoid being caught in the light of the beacon. Other nearby crags were illuminated, though. The oil of the beacons burned with a muddy violet light, and the shadows seemed to be a very dark, soupy orange.

As the crevice grew too narrow for them to climb side by side, Jelt pulled ahead. They had not counted on the rain when they picked their route. The crevice was a water channel, and already Hark could feel an insistent trickle of water running over his cold knuckles and could hear the *click* and *schlack* of small pebbles loosening their hold in dampening soil.

Then Jelt shifted a little to one side, to brace himself in the crack, and purple light flooded down into Hark's eyes. They were near the top, he realized with a shock. He shielded his eyes to protect his night sight. The flash of light left swirls on his retinas, swimming like orange fish through a dark sea.

This was where Jelt would hide. Jelt nudged Hark and pointed along the side of the hill. Peering through the rain, Hark could see his route—the great overhang and, below it, the little ledge. Jelt gave Hark a quick clap on the shoulder, a silent gesture of camaraderie.

Now Hark was continuing alone along the rain-slicked path, with ruined night sight, to reach the other tower. From a distance, he hadn't realized quite how low the overhang was, or how narrow the ledge, but there was no turning back now.

. . . so imagine me, flat against this wet rock, edging along this ledge the breadth of three fingers. And sometimes I'm bent over double because the overhang dips down in places. And there's a sheer drop on my left . . .

"Stupid scabbing plan," he whispered, his eyes full of muddy rainwater, feeling the moist ledge shift and squish under his feet.

After what seemed like an age, he passed a bold white streak in the rock and realized he was only a third of the way along the ledge. He was going too slowly, he knew with queasy horror. The longer he took, the greater the chance that Jelt would be spotted. Fighting every instinct, Hark started to move faster, no longer pausing to check every foothold. He could do this, he *would* do this. He—

He could not tell what betrayed him. A loose rock, a wet sole. Suddenly he lost his footing. The ledge scraped up the side of his leg and hip and bruised his hands as he vainly snatched at it. And then his wet fingers found a grip on a twist of young tree, and his other hand in a little crevice, while his feet flailed and slid against sheer, wet rock.

The tree was too weak to hold him. He could see it buckling, its bark splitting, its white fibers stretching.

It would give, and drop him. He was seconds away from a different story, one that he would never get to tell.

You know that kid Hark?

No. Which one is he?

Skinny. Runty. Lies a lot. Well, he fell off a cliff last night. Smashed his head in. They only found him after the fish had had him for a day.

And someone would tut, or grunt, or give a short snort of mirth. And that would be it. End of story.

No! he thought, something stubborn and desperate rising in him. *No! I'm the hero! I'm the scabbing hero!*

He took his hand away from its feeble grip on the crevice and fumbled for the sling at his belt. All his weight was on the other hand now. He could hear the crackle of the tree tearing and could feel his grip slipping.

With a desperate lunge, he threw out the length of the sling so that it tangled in a sturdier tree a little farther up. Chancing everything, he let go of the tree and snatched at the trailing end of the sling. He caught it—held it—pulled himself up until he could get one arm over the trunk of the tree, then slowly, painfully hauled himself back onto the ledge.

He lost valuable seconds sitting with his grazed cheek against the wet rock, shuddering and trying not to be sick.

"Hero," he whispered defiantly, his eyes stinging. It was only when he gingerly stood up again that he realized his sling was nowhere to be found. He had no time to search for it, and it had almost certainly fallen down to the rocks far below. Hark scrambled onward hastily, with bruised hands and knees that now shook.

When at last the overhang yielded to stars, he scarcely dared to believe it. He clambered up the little chute and found himself blinking on a dimly lit headland, purple as a dead man's vein. There was the beacon tower itself, a stone column with a cage-like metal structure raised above it. At its crest was fixed the metal housing of the lantern, with its great round lens. To his relief, there was nobody in sight.

Hark sprinted over, feet slithering on the wet undergrowth. He snatched up a rock and threw it up toward the top of the tower. It arced in the right direction but fell short and clattered down the tower. His second attempt was no better. Without his sling, he couldn't hit the lantern.

He glanced across to the other headland. If Hark didn't extinguish this light, Jelt would stay in his hiding place near the other tower. Sooner or later, a patrol would come by, and something would happen . . . to Jelt, or to somebody else.

So, he told his imaginary audience, *I realized there was only one thing I could do . . .*

Exhausted and shaky, Hark ran over to the tower and started to climb.

The stone part was easy enough. The mortar was weathered and cracked, so there were toeholds between the stones. But when he reached the metal, everything got harder. He had to twist his arms and legs around the wet metal poles, and shimmy up slowly, using the rusty places for grip. The governor's men used ladders to light the lanterns, then took them away with them to stop anybody else climbing the tower.

When Hark reached the very top, he scrabbled open the metal housing, yanked out the lantern, and let it fall. It plummeted, smashing thirty feet below. The liquid within splashed over the stone base, little mauve ghost-flames dancing over them before going out. Ten seconds later, the beacon on the other headland flared and then went dark. Jelt's sling had done its work.

So he must still be alive. Now he can run away, and so can I . . .

Hark was scrambling back down the tower when he saw a cluster of orange lights jogging their way toward him.

The governor's men reached the base of the tower and surrounded it while he was still on the metal frame, arms and legs wrapped around a crossbar. He hung there, catching his breath, feeling the cold in every cut and bruise.

He would be telling a story after all, it seemed. Not in a tavern among friends, but right here and now, in the rain, with lantern light in his eyes.

It would have to be a really good story. And above all, it would need to be one in which Jelt did not appear.

Chapter 2

IT WAS A POPULAR NIGHT FOR GETTING ARRESTED, as it turned out. When Hark was hauled back into town, it turned out that the governor's dungeon was already full. Instead, Hark was dropped into one of the "overflow" cells, a square-edged pit with heavy wooden bars crisscrossing above. Half of it was covered by a canvas, which kept out some of the rain, but the earth floor had already dissolved into slick mud.

Hark spent a cold and miserable night in this hole, wondering whether Jelt had been caught or killed. An hour after dawn, the bars were lifted away and he was hauled out of the hole. A lot of governor's men were around, looking armed and bored, so Hark didn't develop any fanciful notions about running for it and trying to scale the courtyard wall.

Instead, he tried to put a brave face on it as he was washed down with bucketfuls of cold water and handed some drab, dry clothes to put on.

"Why the luxury treatment?" he asked through chattering teeth. "Am I getting adopted by nobility?"

"Better than that," said a guard wryly. "You got your big moment at the Appraisal this morning."

Hark felt his heart flip over. Of course there would be an Appraisal this morning. Rigg had guessed as much. The remains of the Lady would be auctioned off quickly, before there were more attempts to steal them. But godware was not the only thing sold at the Appraisal. Things were moving much faster than Hark had expected, and he was not ready for it.

He had known that he wouldn't have a trial, of course. On Lady's Crave, a criminal case was handed to one of the governor's Justices, who listened to the guards and decided on the spot whether they'd been right to arrest you. You got a trial only if the Justice thought the guards had messed up, or if a powerful person was willing to vouch for you.

However, he had thought that he might be interrogated. When you were face-to-face with your questioner, you could get a sense of what made them tick, tell them the story they wanted to hear, maybe cut some sort of deal . . .

. . . but apparently that wasn't going to happen. The cells were full, so the governor had decided to clear them out and earn what he could from them. The prisoners would be Appraised and sold.

Hark was hurried through the marketplace and up the hill with a dozen other prisoners. At least none of them were Jelt, nor did he recognize any of Rigg's people, so they had probably all escaped. He wasn't dead yet, either. He had to keep his brain sharp. Despair was a numbing poison. The moment you decided the worst was inevitable, it was.

A casually thrown stone hit him in the ear. He flinched but didn't look around—no point in letting the next hit him straight in the eye socket. He swore, but didn't take it personally. He had thrown stones at captured criminals now and then, not through malice, but just because he could.

It had never really occurred to him not to just because someday the person in chains might be him. In fact, he had always known deep down that someday it *would* be him and that stones *would* be thrown at him, so it had seemed natural to make the most of it while he could be the thrower instead of the thrown-at.

It hurt, though. He was glad he didn't know who had thrown it. If it had been someone he knew, that would have hurt more.

Hark's mouth grew dry as the parade of prisoners drew nearer to the Auction House at the top of the hill. It had loomed on the skyline over Hark's entire life, but he had been inside only a few times.

The large, old building was deliberately misshapen, its roofline bulging and deformed, its windows ragged crevices like rips in the stonework. This was as it should be, because it had been sacred in its time. In its great hall, the island's priests had lived, passed their decrees, and chosen their sacrifices. How else should it look? Even so long after the death of the gods, everyone still knew that the sacred was twisted. There was a beauty that belonged only to the gods, and it was a twist in your eye, your gut, your mind . . .

When the governor had taken over the island, by the simple, honest method of having lots of armed men and declaring that he'd done so, he'd been too canny to take the great building at the top of the steps for his residence. Instead, he'd had a clean, white house of brick built not far from the docks, with a protective surrounding wall. He'd understood that the old priests' hall was a link to a sick past. It was beneath him.

Instead, he had converted it into an auction house. There were petty auctions every week, selling off salvage, ordinary cargoes, and confiscated goods. An Appraisal day was a grand auction, a chance to buy ships and submarines, the finest luxuries, prime godware . . . and criminals. Lady's Cravers were fiercely adaptable. Nowadays, the only thing they could boast more of than other islands was crime, but they had found a way to make money even out of that.

Today Hark would be put up for sale. That was bad enough. But if there were no decent bidders, he was doomed.

In theory, slavery was forbidden within the Myriad. However, if you were judged guilty of a crime, as Hark had been judged, you could be sold as an "indentured servant." All the islands of the Myriad respected the indentures. If they did not, how could they buy criminals for the jobs nobody wanted? The worse your crime, the longer the time you had to serve. If you tried to run away, you could be caught and dragged back to your "owner," who might punish you or sell you to someone worse.

There was always someone worse.

The great hall was designed to make people feel like ants. You knew it as soon as you walked in. It was too open, too vast, its vaulted ceiling too high, the windows too narrow and lofty, the shafts of light from them too meager. Even the two dozen rows of benches put out for auction buyers filled only half the hall. Human crowds were lost in it. Voices rebounded oddly, the echoes sounding higher and more startled than the original voice. Hark imagined them floating, aghast, up into shadows.

The governor had done what he could. The walls of the hall were now covered in white plaster, but here and there the damp had caused some to fall away, showing glimpses of the old red and black frescoes underneath. A dozen looming iron candelabras now cast light at the human level but could do little about the cavernous murk above.

The room bore too many scars of its past. In the middle of the floor there had once been a large, oval hole full of seawater, in which priests and sacrifices had been ritually cleansed. The governor had arranged for it to be filled with cement, but you still knew it was there, the new russet tiles obvious against the surrounding gray flagstone. Just as obvious were the series of slight, worn depressions that led up to it from the door and then passed on beyond it to a distant arch. Centuries of sacrifices had been made to follow in the exact footsteps of their predecessors, until the pressure of all those bare feet had worn away stone.

Hark felt as doomed as any sacrifice, but of course he was not led along those fateful indentations. Instead he and the rest of the chain gang were taken around the side of the hall, so as not to interrupt the auction of some boat called the *Kindwind*. They were made to stand in a gaggle, not far from the auctioneer's pulpit and the great abacus used to show the current bid.

As the auctioneer droned on, Hark tried to get a feel for the audience. His spirits sank even further.

It was a sluggish, early morning crowd. Most people there were napping, chatting, or reading. The first few rows of benches were crammed, but he guessed that many sitting on them had probably just come early so that they'd have a good seat for the *Abysmal Child* sales later in the day. They wanted a piece of the Hidden Lady, or at least a glimpse of her.

He caught himself looking for familiar or friendly faces among the crowd, even though he knew that there probably wouldn't be any. There was no sign of Jelt, of course. He was probably lying low somewhere with Rigg's gang. Hark didn't blame his friend, although Jelt's absence did make him feel lonelier.

As Hark watched, bidding for the *Kindwind* came to an end. One last reluctant raise of the hand from the audience. One last bead rattled along the abacus to show the new bid. The auctioneer made a lackluster appeal for more interest, then declared the boat sold.

"Next, an auction of indentured criminals," called the auctioneer, from his perch in the old pulpit. It was carved so as to look eerily molten, stone dribbles seeming to creep upward, as if obeying an inverted gravity.

The chained gaggle were brought forward. For a mad moment, Hark wondered what would happen if all the criminals bolted for the door as one. He felt sure he knew the answer, though. Up in the lofty gallery he could see some of the governor's men, the round, copper bottles of compressed air gleaming on their wind-guns. They were lounging and yawning, but they would probably become a lot more alert if the goods on sale decided to make a break for it.

He scanned the audience with desperate eyes. Most of them didn't even look up. Some glanced at him, but then their gaze slid toward the older, stronger-looking criminals instead. To their eyes, Hark probably looked like a scrawny scrap that could be of no use to them—nothing but a waste of food and lodgings, and perhaps an untrustworthy one at that.

Most people in the front row were watching the criminals and the auctioneer with careful attention, but that was to be expected. By unspoken consent, the front bench was left for the sea-kissed so that they could lip-read more easily, and see the under-clerk responsible for announcing lots in sign language. Continenters who obliviously flouted this hidden rule could never work out why everyone then made a point of treading heavily on their foot as they passed or leaning forward to breathe cheroot smoke into their faces. At the moment, no foot-stamping seemed to be happening, so presumably everyone at the front was sea-kissed.

After a moment, Hark noticed that one of them was staring straight at him.

It was a girl of about Hark's own age, or perhaps a little younger. She was short, dark-haired, and skinny, with large eyes and an uncomfortably intense gaze. What caught Hark's attention, however, was the dappling of freckles that covered her face, arms, and neck. Only one family was that freckled.

That must be one of Rigg's daughters. What's she doing here? Why is she staring at me?

For a wildly optimistic moment, Hark wondered if she was there to bid for him on behalf of Rigg's gang. It was an empty hope, however. The governor had been known to arrest people he suspected of buying the indentures of their accomplices, so nobody did that anymore.

No, she's here so that I know that Rigg's people are watching me. If I squeal on them now, they'll know. This girl is a warning.

With a sinking heart, Hark recognized a couple of scarred faces a few rows farther back, observing him with a speculative eye. They were dealers in the auction dregs, waiting to pick up the unwanted criminals for a song and sell them on as galley minions. Anyone they bought would spend the whole of their indenture in the murky belly of some boat or submarine, chained to their oar. Many did not survive, and those who did came out with crooked limbs, weak eyes, and broken minds.

Next to them was a tall man with a fashionably square beard and a good coat. One of the other criminals recognized him and muttered that he was the owner of a mine on Malpease who sometimes bought young criminals who could fit through perilously narrow gaps. This didn't sound much better than the galleys.

"First lot!" called the auctioneer. "Hark, no other name. The crime, breaking two of the beacon lanterns last night. Three years."

"Three years?" exploded Hark, involuntarily. The shrill echo of his voice spiraled up and up until the shadows ate it. He had feared that it might be one year, but *three* . . .

I'll be broken by then, he thought desperately. *I won't survive in the galleys that long.* He was to be made an example of. The governor must have taken the vandalism as a personal slight.

ive up, he told himself sharply, amid the rise of panic. *t dead yet*. As he was detached from the chain gang d forward, he tried to keep his breathing under control. *ot to be someone else!*

"Does anybody have any questions for the prisoner before the bidding?" asked the auctioneer, with the blunt air of someone with a busy schedule ahead. Most of the buyers had already turned their attention back at their catalogs. "No? Then—"

"Can I give my defense first?" Hark interrupted desperately.

"You're not on trial, boy!" called the auctioneer, and there was a ripple of laughter.

"But they don't really know what I did!" Hark's heart was banging. "They don't know why I did it! They don't know how!"

Oh please, come on! Somebody take the bait! Hark's gaze darted over the assembly, looking for hints of interest.

A husband and wife at the back, frowning in his direction and whispering. Were they interested or just disapproving?

A middle-aged woman in a good-quality jacket of brown wool, fiddling with what looked like a monocle on a chain. She was watching the proceedings with half-closed eyes, like a theatergoer waiting for the play to start. Or was she just half asleep?

Two men in sealskin coats from the Northern Myriad, laughing together quietly and glancing his way. Even if Hark was a joke to them, could he use that to win them over?

If I play to the whole crowd, I won't hook any of them. I need to pick a target and play to them. And I need to pick right.

Hark made his choice. Made eye contact. Held it. Raised his eyebrows in appeal.

Yes. You. Please.

The woman with the brown coat and monocle stared back for a moment, then smiled.

"All right," she called back. "I'll bite. Tell us, boy."

Chapter 3

HARK FELT HIS HEART BANGING. POSSIBLE STORIES crowded into his head.

It wasn't me! It was somebody else's idea! I was scared and it wasn't my fault! I was tricked into it!

Those were the stories you told if you wanted to convince people you were mostly innocent, or at least harmless. If some guard or merchant had you by the scruff of the neck, you could make them feel a little bit sorry for you, and they might just let you go with a kick in the rear.

But he was far beyond that now. This wasn't a trial. Right now, it didn't matter whether he was innocent; it mattered whether he was *interesting*. If he bored his audience, he was dead. And if he babbled, pleaded, and made big eyes, he *would* bore them. Worse, he would look weak and stupid. Maybe some of them would feel sorry for him, but they wouldn't buy him. Nobody wanted a weak, stupid servant.

He had to seem like an asset. Clever, but not too glib. Good-hearted but not too unworldly.

"I'm not going to pretend I didn't do it," he said, with quiet bravado. "But it wasn't for money or for fun. It was something I *had* to do."

Tease their curiosity. Keep their attention.

"Are you saying somebody forced you to do this?" asked the woman who had taken Hark's bait. It was hard for him to get a read on her. She wasn't a Lady's Craver—he could tell that from her accent—and yet she still sounded fairly local. Another island nearby, perhaps? Her expression seemed dispassionately amused, her voice sardonic and incredulous. With luck she would keep asking questions. As long as she did that, his fate still hung by a thread.

"No," he said. "It was my idea. It was a stupid thing to do—I know that. I knew it back then. But it was the only way."

Back up. Leave the explanation until later. Keep them guessing.

"I wouldn't have done it for laughs," he added quickly. "Have you seen that cliff? It's not something *anyone* would do if they had a choice. Would you?"

He was directing most of his attention to the woman now. *But don't put all your eggs in one basket. Keep talking loud enough for them at the back to hear. Look out at the others now and then.*

"See, I had to climb all the way up the cliff face under Soul-Eye Point. In the dark, while it was raining.

"At the top I . . . I broke the first beacon light with my sling." He let his eyes drop for a moment and gave a small, self-conscious shrug. "After that I knew sentries would be coming, so I couldn't run along the headland to the next one."

Since Hark was on trial for breaking *both* lanterns, hopefully the auctioneer didn't know that they had been smashed within moments of each other. He could tell a tale of a crime without accomplices and leave out Jelt and Rigg's people completely.

He glanced briefly at the freckled girl in the front row. Her large eyes were still fixed upon him, as if they could pierce through to his very thoughts.

"There's a ledge that runs under the lip—just a palm's width in places." Hark held out two hands a little apart, to show the perilous breadth. "Slippery. Crumbling away. But it was the only choice. Three hundred feet of drop just an inch away, with the rain in my eyes and the wind trying to scrape me off, like an oyster out of its shell . . ."

The mine owner shifted impatiently in his seat. *Too much description*, Hark told himself sharply. *Too flowery.*

"I nearly fell to my death three times," Hark went on quickly, "and I lost my sling to the drop. So I had to climb up the metal tower, all slippery with rain, and kick out the second lantern." He paused, hoping that his audience were remembering the height of the tower and starting to understand the doggedness and skill that the climb would have required.

"You're supposed to be answering the lady's question!" snapped the auctioneer. "Not wasting our time with some rambling, blow-by-blow confession."

"I know, I know!" Hark agreed hastily. "What I'm saying is, I wouldn't have done all that—risked all that—unless I'd had a really good reason."

Hark took a deep breath and committed to his tale.

"No," he said. "Nobody forced me. Nobody even asked me. But somebody *needed* me to do it."

A few raised eyebrows. A hint of interest.

"I grew up in the Shelter—" Hark began.

"There's a surprise!" called out the mine owner, and there was a muted rumble of grim mirth throughout the crowd. Most of the stray and orphaned kids of Lady's Crave found refuge in the Shelter, and more than a few of them emerged later as promising young crooks.

"Lovely place, isn't it?" Hark responded quickly with a wry grimace.

Don't get thrown off-balance, keep hold of the reins.

"Maybe some of you have memories of it, too.

"Now . . . I'm very grateful for the governor's mighty benevolence, of course. Goes without saying. But you end up owing other people, too. The ones who give you a bit of food or work."

He didn't mention that the food at the Shelter wasn't enough to keep you alive. He didn't have to.

"There was a woman who sometimes pitched a tent in Slike's Cove, selling pickled sea wrack. Sometimes she screamed at us and threw stones. She was a bit mad and had a nasty temper. But other times she'd leave food out for us on the rocks."

There really had been an old woman like that when Hark was little. He didn't know what had happened to her, but he silently thanked her now for fleshing out his story.

Some of his audience were hooked now, others impatiently fiddling with their catalogs. *Not too much heart-string-tugging*, Hark reminded himself. *Keep it brief.*

"Over the years . . . she went madder, I suppose. She started camping in the darkest caves she could find. She couldn't bear the beacon lights at night. You know how it is sometimes."

Again, he didn't need to say more. The beacon lamps used Undersea water, mixed with the right blend of fish oils and sparked with the tiniest filament of godware as a wick. These burned far longer and brighter than whale oil, but such lights were nicknamed "scare-lamps" for a reason. Something about their light tickled your instincts unpleasantly and made your heart beat faster. Hark's generation had grown up with them and were used to the effects, but older people often hated them and complained that the light gave them nightmares.

Old folk who had witnessed gods rising were the ones who hated the beacons most of all. They had seen that queasy, dancing purple light before, glimmering in the deep or murkily flickering across vast, shadowy hulks.

"What was her name?" called out the woman with the monocle.

"Katya," Hark answered promptly, giving the name of the old woman he remembered. It was a safely common name. "She camps all over the island. Other folks must know her. You can ask around!"

The woman raised an eyebrow. *Yes,* said her expression, *but I can't do that right now, can I? I can't check your story before I bid.*

It was the one potential advantage of the situation Hark found himself in. With luck, the auctioneer didn't know anything about his case except what had already been read out. Bidders would have to decide for themselves whether they believed Hark's story. If someone bought him, then found out he'd misled them, they would be angry, but at least he might have a chance to talk them around again.

"So Katya asked you nicely to put the beacon lights out?" the woman asked, her voice still cool and skeptical.

"Katya never did anything nicely, ma'am," Hark called back. He was pleased to see a slight smile flicker over a few faces. They were getting a feel for "Katya." So was he. "She even riled up some of the local scavengers, yelling at them and telling them to get off 'her' beach. They would have chased her off, or worse, if I hadn't asked them not to. And . . . if they hadn't seen she was so sick."

He let his face fall a little, and shrugged.

"I could tell she was ebbing out," he continued, his tone bleak. *Keep it plain, and blunt, and real.* "Her mind was gone. She didn't know me. She didn't know anyone. All she did was hide in caves, because she thought those beacons on the cliff tops were the flickering purple lights of a god. Back from the

dead, up from the deep, and clambering about the island looking for her in particular." He shook his head and gave a sad,
annoyed little tut.

Hark half believed his own story now. It was a lie, but like
all the best lies, it had fragments of truth in it. He had seen old
people sicken and madden in such ways, their childhood fears
of the gods bobbing to the surface like drowned corpses.

"Yesterday evening she turned up in Slike's Cove, and I could
almost see the bones under her skin. I knew she wouldn't last
till morning. She was hiding in a cave, almost too weak and
hungry to stand . . . but whenever she came out, that purple
beacon light would set her off again. Screaming and scrabbling
about on the beach, and running back into her cave. I tried to
take food and water to her, but she pulled a knife on me. Stupid
old mare!" He shook his head.

"So I told her that everything was fine. The god was going
away. If she waited, soon she'd see that the beach was dark and
safe. Then I climbed up that cliff and I saw to it."

"You left an unhinged and dying woman all by herself?" the
monocle-woman asked sharply.

"Yes," said Hark. *No defensiveness, no hesitation.* "I did.
And I don't even know if breaking those lamps worked. Maybe
she just stayed there in that cave. Or maybe she came out and
was able to die in her own tent on her little bit of rug, in peace
and darkness. I don't know, but I had to try. It was all I could
give her."

Hark took a deep breath and scanned his audience. He had
painted himself in the best colors he could manage—a lad who
had grown up wild, but who was brave, ingenious, and, above
all, loyal. The sort of bright, good-hearted lad who would go
out on a limb for you once you had his gratitude. He felt this

would appeal more than "sneaky small-time crook with expanding underworld connections."

The woman held his eye for a few seconds, then raised her eyebrows and looked away. She suddenly seemed disaffected and bored. Hark bit his lip hard, wondering if he had misjudged his play.

The auctioneer, who had been staring at his notes, cleared his throat sharply and made Hark jump.

"Any more questions?" the auctioneer asked tartly, his tone reeking of impatience. "No? Then we shall move to the bid."

Hark's blood banged furiously in his ears. He had managed to maintain a certain calm while he held the stage, but now he suddenly found it hard to breathe.

"Any starting bids?" called the auctioneer.

Hark reflexively glanced at the woman who had been asking him questions.

She appeared to be studying her catalog. Had she lost interest, now that Hark had sated her curiosity? He glanced around at the other bidders but realized that he had been quietly piling his hopes on her. He had directed most of his story toward her.

One of the scarred men put up his hand and named a tiny sum. In spite of himself, Hark's pride was stung. *But if they're bidding low, then I'm still a bargain*, he reminded himself. *There's still a chance that someone else will bid.* He tried not to think of being trapped in a stinking hold, manacles chafing the skin from his wrists and ankles.

The mine owner had been studying him through pocket binoculars and now put up his hand and named a sum only slightly less feeble. Hark imagined himself squeezing through narrow underground crevices, or being crushed by rockslides, and dug his nails into his hands.

Someone else bid on me! Please! Hark looked desperately around at the other bidders and in particular at the woman with the monocle. He even gave the freckled, sea-kissed girl a pleading look.

Nothing from any of them. Not a flicker.

The scarred man bid again, barely more than the price of a live goat, and the mine owner shrugged and let it go. Silence followed.

"No more bids?" asked the auctioneer? "Then . . ."

He reached across to dip his pen into the inkpot so that he could write down the details of the sale in his great book.

Hark's vision blurred. His story had been his last chance, and it had not been enough. His chest was tight, and it took him a moment to realize that the auctioneer had paused, his pen hovering above the inkpot.

"Ma'am?" asked the auctioneer. "Is this a bid?"

Hark turned to stare at the woman in brown, who had her hand raised.

"Yes," she said. "It is."

The sum she named was still trivial, but it was twice the previous bid. Hark could see the scarred men evaluating him again, his flimsy frame and weak arms so unsuited for pulling oars. They didn't mind picking him up for a song, but only if the song didn't have too many choruses. They shook their heads.

The auctioneer nodded to the woman and recorded the details of the sale, then Hark was hurried out of the hall into a little side chamber. He was saggy with relief. They let him sit down by the wall, and he slumped there, too numb and tired to pay attention to his surroundings, even as other purchased convicts were brought in, one by one.

He had survived. He would survive.

He could think of little else, even when a clerk in a dun

waistcoat came through to inspect him and question him. Did he have tattoos? Missing teeth? Distinguishing injuries?

Hark answered the questions numbly and let the clerk measure his limbs and catalog his scars, even though he knew the reason for it all. If he ever tried to run away from his new owner, all these details could be used to find him again. Next, a bored-looking artist drew his portrait. Hark watched the narrow-cheeked, unflattering sketch of him forming on the page and imagined it on a Wanted poster plastered up in dockyards all through the Myriad.

It was late afternoon before Hark's new owner finally arrived to collect him.

"If you could press your personal seal into the wax *here*, Dr. Vyne?" said the clerk who accompanied her, with careful politeness. "We will have the paperwork drawn up for you within the hour."

Now that the woman was closer, Hark noticed a few oddities. Tiny flecks of dark mauve in her brown eyes. A little patch of dead-white pallor near her right temple, almost hidden by her dark hair. These were Marks—subtle ones, but still signs that she had spent a lot of time handling godware or Undersea water. Given enough time, both these things subtly remolded the human body in unpredictable ways, and nobody knew why. Minor Marks like this were not uncommon, particularly among deep-sea submariners and workers in the god-glue factory.

"Do you want his ear clipped?" asked the clerk.

Hark gave his owner a desperate look of appeal. A notch was often cut into the ear of serious criminals. Once you had three notches in your ear, your next arrest meant a quick trip to the gallows. So far Hark had managed to avoid a clipping.

"No need for that," said the doctor.

Hark meekly held his tongue until the clerk had left. It was time for a change of tone, he decided—a little timidity to soften up his new owner. He risked giving her a small, rueful smile.

"I'm really glad you bought me," he said, with a deliberate break in his voice. "Thank you. I . . . I thought I was going to the galleys."

"Yes, you did, didn't you?" The doctor pushed her hands into the pockets of her long brown coat. "Well, I thought I'd let you sweat a bit, you slippery little snake." She laughed aloud at Hark's expression. "Oh, don't give me that seal-pup look. That story of yours was a reeking heap of tripe, wasn't it?"

Hark could have protested, but his instincts stopped him. Instead, he met the doctor's eye.

"Yes," he said. "Right down to the last scrap."

"That's what I thought," she said. "That's why I bought you. You're a good liar, and I have need of one."

The freckled girl waited outside the Auction House and watched.

At last she felt a shift in the crowd. Heads turned. Necks craned. Faces dipped closer to each other, mouths fluttering in whispers. Bodies pressed forward toward the side door of the Auction House, obscuring her view. She quickly clambered up onto the sloping roof of a bellows house, earning only a glance from those lining up to fill their air-bottles.

A gang of porters had emerged from the side door carrying heavy crates, while armed men kept gawkers and chancers at bay. These had attracted the greedy curiosity of the throng. Only the freckled girl's sharp eyes noticed the two figures who slipped out a few seconds later. There was Hark, the bought boy, trailing behind his new owner with a hangdog look.

The girl followed the little procession at a distance and watched the boy, the woman, and the crates depart on a small, gray-sailed sloop. After the crowd had thinned, she slipped down to the quay and approached a sea-kissed dockhand she knew. He respectfully greeted her by the name she now preferred, a hybrid of two different signs: *Big eyes. Sudden storm.*

When he had answered her questions about the boat and its destination, she went back to her mother to report.

Did the boy give us away? asked Rigg.

He didn't mention us, signed the freckled girl, *but he really likes to talk*. His rambling tale had annoyed her. Even with her level of skill, reading lips at that distance was tiring, particularly when the boy twitched his head this way or that to answer people's questions. Filling in those gaps in the conversation through deduction, over and over again, had become draining and irritating after a while.

What did you make of him? signed Rigg, narrowing her eyes.

Slippery, answered her daughter, after a moment's thought, using a sign like that for "eel." The Myriad sign language had grown from the signs divers used to communicate underwater, and this showed sometimes.

If he tries to sell us out, we know where to find him, signed Rigg, and shrugged.

I don't like his friend, either, the girl added suddenly.

You don't like anyone, her mother replied dismissively, and only a little unfairly. *We'll see how he shapes up. He did well enough last night, didn't he? We got what we wanted.*

The smuggler ran her fingers over the large, dark sphere that lay on the floor of the cellar, the scare-light glimmering on its seaworn, godware surface.

Chapter 4

THREE MONTHS LATER, ON THE HIGHEST POINT in Sanctuary, Hark sat watching the newly risen sun spilling its silver onto the sea.

A dip in a crenellated wall offered the perfect seat. Around and below him clustered gables, bow-backed ridges, blunt towers, and skeletal belfries, their weathered slate slick with the morning dew. The early morning mists were lifting, revealing low, scrubby hills on all sides. Nest was always a wild, lonely island, but at dawn it seemed almost ghostly.

"Planning your escape?"

Hark jumped, even though the voice and the joke were familiar. Sure enough, when he turned, he saw Kly, the Sanctuary foreman, grinning up at him from the hatch.

It was a routine joke, but as it happened, Hark *had* been hungrily watching the bright sails of distant ships. They were sailing south, toward his beloved Lady's Crave. In a few hours, they would see its double-humped outline, the great chimney of the glue factory almost as high as its hills. Then they would pull into the harbor, *his* harbor, where the gulls and black kites circled over a forest of masts, the docks full of market shouts, excitement, and the smell of tar and spices . . .

"Always," he answered with a grin.

Kly looked pointedly at Hark's comfortable perch. The stocky, middle-aged foreman wasn't exactly a bully, but he liked to feel in the ascendant. He would smile at a bit of cheekiness, but rein it in unexpectedly now and then to show who was boss.

Hark took Kly's hint and climbed down from the wall. He dusted down his yellow robes and picked up his abandoned broom and pan.

"Don't take too long up here," Kly added, as he turned to leave. "We need you to help serve breakfast."

Hark got back to cleaning out the gutters but couldn't resist a few glances at the panorama.

The mists had now lifted entirely. Sanctuary's roof offered the best view on the island. The ominous, old building squatted on the top of Nest's highest hill, in majestic isolation. Hark could look out in all directions and see exactly how much nothing the island had to offer. No towns, not even a village, just occasional small buildings dotting the gray-green scrubland. On any other island in the Myriad, the hillside would have been cut into terrace farms so as to put every inch of it to use. You never wasted land. Here, however, the slopes were virtually untouched, with just a few footpaths running like creases.

Even though Hark could see the faint shapes of other islands on the horizon, Nest felt solitary and remote. The busy sea-lanes carried the steady stream of shipping past it without stopping. Nobody fished in its waters. No scavenger gangs fought over its beaches. Nest had once been too holy for common feet, and now it was shunned as a sour reminder of the past.

Nest was so named because it had been the place where young acolytes had undergone their training and initiation, where they had "hatched" into full-blown priests. There were no acolytes desperate to train at Sanctuary now. The "nest" would never hold fledglings again.

Instead, Sanctuary had been put to a different purpose. Once the gutters were clear, Hark hurried down to his other duties.

Has it really been three months? he thought as he hustled along the dark and narrow corridors. He had grown so used to Sanctuary now. He no longer got lost in its rabbit warren of passages. These days he barely noticed the smells—the damp odor of the old building, the acrid, fatty smell of soap, and the nerve-tingling reek near the baths. At first, he had felt like the airlessness and quiet would choke him. Now they no longer bothered him.

Well . . . perhaps the quiet did still get to him sometimes. Its clammy hopelessness soaked into his skin if he wasn't careful.

In the kitchen, busy cooks boiled eggs and fried great pots of sliced sea wrack, the rubbery brown ribbons of weed turning a succulent emerald green as the hot fat touched them. Hark joined the other yellow-robed attendants in ferrying platters of hot food to the great dining hall with its high-vaulted ceiling.

In ones and twos, all over the hall, Sanctuary's residents sat waiting for their breakfast. Quietly, patiently, passively. Many of them still wore the brown, ceremonial robes that no longer had any meaning.

The priests.

Hark had heard of Sanctuary when he was growing up on Lady's Crave, so he had been horrified when Dr. Vyne told him where he would be working out his indenture.

That's where they keep the priests! The old, crazy ones whose minds broke when the gods died!

Not all priests had fallen apart after the Cataclysm. Some had managed to build themselves new lives. Others, however, had been devastated at losing the reason for their existence. Sanctuary had been turned into a haven for those priests who could no longer look after themselves, a retreat from the cruel, incomprehensible, godless world.

Hark had pictured a madhouse, full of gibbering, capering figures with wild, white hair. The reality proved to be quieter and stranger. Not all the Sanctuary priests were old, as it turned out. The youngest of them had been acolytes when the gods died and weren't much older than Kly. Some of the older ones *were* confused, but you could still talk to them most of the time. Nobody ran around naked or set fire to anything.

Nonetheless, during his first week working in Sanctuary, Hark had hated his new life.

The deluge of new duties from dawn to dusk had been a nightmare. The other staff had quickly realized that he was the newest, smallest, and lowest in the pecking order and that he could be sent to sweep floors, clean privies, fetch water, and scour grates. He was out of step with the rhythms and rituals of the place and had to keep getting people to explain things to him. He'd never been a servant before, so he kept making mistakes and breaking things.

Some of the priests had lost their hearing through age or from descending into the depths, but they were nothing like the sea-kissed Hark had met before. Some had ear trumpets of a sort he had never seen. They didn't wear ear-studs, and none of them seemed to understand sign language, even when he tried a few signs from other islands. Most of them had retreated from the world right after the Cataclysm, he realized. They hadn't seen the Myriad turn to deep-sea salvage, or the sea-kissed become common, or sign language spread through the archipelago. When they couldn't understand Hark, these priests tried to get him to write things down for them. When he stared at the paper and pencil with helpless misery, they usually got frustrated and called for the Sanctuary scribe instead. Hark had been useless, exhausted, out of his depth, and in trouble with everyone.

It felt strange and claustrophobic to be indoors so much of the time. He was used to being able to run, yell, and climb at will, bracing for the buffets of the wind, with the wild gray sky above him. Now his world had a vaulted lid on it, and he had to keep his steps slow and quiet.

The priests themselves made him uneasy, too. They were secretive, as if they had folded in on themselves, like the wings of dead insects.

Some of them had Marks, because of their many trips down into the Undersea to talk to the gods. A few of the mutations were particularly startling—a cloudy left eye twice the size of the right, or a fleshless little finger that still flexed and bent to its owner's will. However, that wasn't what bothered Hark. He had seen Marks just as strange among the sub salvage crews on Lady's Crave.

What really gnawed at him was the feeling of hopelessness in Sanctuary and the sense that everything around him was *old*. Even the priests who were only middle-aged *seemed* older than they should be. They had lost something that would never be given back. They were ghosts of themselves, clinging to a memory of a past life.

It was Hark's nature to snatch at hopes and look for chances. Sanctuary whispered that chances could run out. Sometimes you didn't achieve your dreams, you just got old or shattered and that was it. You were washed up on life's brutal shingle, a soft, broken, helpless thing.

So run away, said the imaginary Jelt-voice in Hark's head. Hark couldn't imagine Jelt sticking out such drudgery for more than a day. Where *was* Jelt now? Jelt hadn't been one of the convicts at the Appraisal, so presumably he hadn't been caught. Hark had nightmare visions of Jelt showing up at Sanctuary and trying to "rescue" him. Jelt wouldn't do something that reckless, would he? No, apparently not. Days passed with no sign of Jelt. Hark wasn't sure whether to feel relieved or hurt.

Hark knew that if he *did* run away, he would be caught. Dr. Vyne would be angry and would sell him on, and he would find himself in the galleys or the mines after all. In spite of that, by the end of the first week he had almost felt ready to take the risk.

Almost. All that stopped him were his conversations with Dr. Vyne. They reminded him that he hadn't been bought just as a drudge. She had another mission for him.

"You're a clever little weasel," she told him. "You'll find your feet soon enough. And once people take you for granted and aren't paying attention, you can get on with your *real* job."

She had plans for him, too.

"Some schooling would make you more useful to me. Well, we have three years to work on that. I'll have somebody start teaching you your letters." She had smirked to see Hark's eyes shining.

Reading makes your brain soft, Jelt had always said. *You live in the world, or you live in a book. You can't do both. And what's in those books anyway? Just a load of rot written by fat saps who never learned anything the hard way. What's the point of them?*

In Jelt's mind, illiteracy was a badge of honor. Whenever Hark remembered that, his excitement felt disloyal.

But he *was* excited. None of his friends on Lady's Crave could read. Reading made you useful and respectable. Reading made you look smart. It gave you toeholds in your upward climb, and Hark had always known it.

So Hark hadn't run away. He had held on, day after day. He had found his feet and kept his wits about him. He had learned and adapted.

There is always hope. There are always chances.

"Pale Soul?" Hark swooped in with a smile and a big platter of sea wrack. "Your breakfast."

Like all his fellows, Pale Soul had taken a new name on joining the priesthood. His suited him better each day. He was gray-haired and gray-skinned, and all color seemed to have drained out of his gaze.

"Is it time?" he asked Hark, in a tone of timorous urgency. "Is it time?"

Hark had never yet found out what Pale Soul meant when he asked this, and he wasn't sure that Pale Soul knew, either, but he had learned by trial and many errors the best way to soothe his worries.

"Not yet," Hark told him calmly. "Just be patient a bit longer, eh? It'll be all right."

These words had the usual consoling effect, and Pale Soul consented to eat.

"It's not time yet, Flint," he agreed conversationally. As far as Hark could tell, "Flint" was an acolyte Pale Soul had once known. Like the rest of the Sanctuary staff, Hark wore old yellow acolytes' robes, which were supposed to make the priests feel more at ease.

"No, that's right," answered Hark. "But we'll be glad we waited, won't we?"

The old man gave him a peaceful, fragile smile, and Hark felt a small glow of satisfaction. He continued passing out the platters of food to the other priests. He knew who liked an extra sprinkling of wild mallow, who was too proud to ask for assistance in eating, and who would grab his sleeve so that they could list their latest grievances or theories.

"Hark, *you'd* better serve Moonmaid," muttered one of his colleagues.

Hark was still at the bottom of the staff pecking order, but the others had grudgingly acknowledged his gift for dealing with the "difficult" priests. Moonmaid, an icily withdrawn old female priest, sometimes stole sharp things and had once tried to stab Kly in the eye. She didn't like or trust Hark, but at least she tolerated his presence.

He patiently dissected her food before her keen gray gaze, telling her what each ingredient was. At last she pointed to a particular chunk, and he ate it to show that it wasn't poisoned. This was their usual ritual, and it satisfied her.

"I know what you people want from us," she remarked in her clear, deep voice and picked up her spoon to eat. No answer was expected or required.

Hark had always been good at winning trust, but he'd never had to keep it before. Back in Lady's Crave, he'd usually found a mark, talked his way into their purse, and then made himself scarce before he could face any consequences. Occasionally there had been a longer con, where you spent days or even weeks working on someone, as if they were a chicken you were fattening for the pot.

This was different. He'd never spent so long learning about a group of people, hearing of their lives, and teasing out their secrets until he knew exactly what to say to them.

In a sense, this was a long con, too, the longest con he had ever played. But the strange thing was, sometimes he caught himself *enjoying* his daily work. He liked being good at it. In fact, he had even allowed himself to like some of the priests. Just a little.

There's no need to feel guilty, after all. They don't have to know why I'm so keen to listen to them. It's not like I'm hurting them, is it?

"Where's Quest?" Hark asked, noting that one padded chair by the window was empty.

"He's weak again today," muttered another staff member. "He's still in his room."

"I'll take his breakfast to him," Hark volunteered quickly, grabbing another platter and cup.

"Change the bandage on his leg while you're there!" one of the other attendants called after him.

The room Quest shared with two other priests was decked with rugs and wall hangings to keep in the warmth. The old man had been tucked under several layers of blanket for good measure and propped up with a small hill of cushions.

Quest was lean and long-limbed. His face had a gouged look, deep and bitter lines cutting curves into his cheekbones and brows. His expression brightened when he saw Hark, becoming slightly more watchful and amused. Hark found his own spirits lightening, too.

Unlike the other priests in Sanctuary, Quest had not suffered a collapse in the face of a godless world. He had apparently made a life for himself on Siren for twenty years after the Cataclysm, only joining his fellows in Sanctuary after his health declined.

"Do you need some help today?" asked Hark, glancing at Quest's hands, which shook slightly on the coverlet.

"The spoon holds no fear for me," Quest remarked dryly, "but I would appreciate another cushion behind my back, so my chin is above the plate. One tries to minimize indignities like dropping food on oneself."

Hark obliged. Quest watched him all the while with a slight frown.

"What is it?" the old priest asked suddenly.

"What's what?" Hark was startled out of his thoughts.

"You grind your teeth when something is bothering you," said Quest. "You are good at hiding things, but you have a few habits that give you away."

You are good at hiding things.

He had dropped remarks like that before, gentle hints that he had noticed Hark's devious streak. Quest's shrewdness and lucidity was a breath of fresh air, but occasionally it threw Hark off-balance. There was always a danger that the old man might work out why Hark was really in Sanctuary.

Hark tried to avoid lying outright to Quest, in case the perceptive old man sensed it. He didn't want to shatter their fragile rapport. In any case, sometimes it was a relief to be a little honest.

"I've been here three months, and I don't know how I feel about that," he admitted. "I should be happy. It's time served. But right now it feels like time I've *lost*. Three months of my life. And when I think of losing another two and three-quarter years the same way, I feel . . . like a rat in a trap."

"You're used to being outside," said Quest sympathetically. "And here you are, in this dark old crypt with us moldering husks."

"You're not a . . . That's not what I meant!"

"No offense taken." When Quest smiled, the bitter lines around the corners of his mouth spiderwebbed, but his eyes became brighter and bluer. "You're young, that's all. Of course you don't want to be trapped in this crumbling relic of the past. Nobody your own age to talk to, stuck listening to my rambling tales of dead gods . . ."

"I like hearing about the gods!" Hark protested.

"So you have said before," Quest remarked. "Why *is* a boy

your age so interested in them?" His tone was mild, but his gaze was coolly interrogative.

In spite of all his wits and wiles, Hark had trouble getting most of the priests to talk about the gods. Apparently they still considered their vows of secrecy binding and became suspicious unless questions were very cunningly phrased. Quest was a little more willing to talk of them directly, but the trend of Hark's questions was clearly not lost on him.

"Of course I want to know!" Hark tried to sort out his thoughts as he adjusted the pillows behind Quest's back. "I've lived my whole life on Lady's Crave, and I know it like my own bones, but at the same time I feel like I don't know it at all! It's . . . as if I've turned up to a story halfway through. Somebody's telling an old tale by the fire in the tavern, and I got there late. I'm picking it up as well as I can, but I don't really know who all the characters are or why the jokes are funny. When things happen in the story, I can't understand what they mean, because I don't know how the story *started*."

Every word was true. It wasn't the only reason for Hark's questions, but at least he could say it to Quest's face without lying.

"Hmm." Quest smiled wryly. "I hope your generation's chapter of the great story has more hope and joy than ours." He sighed. "I had promised to tell you about the Hidden Lady, had I not? Do we have time now?"

"They won't look for me for a while," said Hark. "They know I'm changing the bandage on your leg." He tried not to fidget with impatience.

"You go first, then," said Quest, picking up his spoon. "Tell your tale while I eat. I will tell mine afterward as you attend to the bandage."

It always had to be a trade. A story for a story. Hark *liked* telling stories but not the sort that revealed too much about himself or his own life. However, it turned out that these were exactly the kind of anecdotes Quest wanted to hear. Hark had the feeling that the old priest regarded him as a puzzle to be solved and was gradually piecing him together.

They had reached a wary bargain with each other and now exchanged stories like hostages. Hark had secrets he needed to keep, and he suspected Quest had his own, as well. Sometimes it felt like a game, in which you tried to find out as much as you could while revealing enough, but not too much, about yourself.

"What do you want to hear?" asked Hark.

Quest narrowed his eyes in thought.

"My first encounter with the Hidden Lady was almost the end of me," he said. "Tell me of a time that you nearly died, and I will tell you how I met the Lady."

Chapter 5

"I TOLD YOU ABOUT THE SHELTER WHERE I grew up, didn't I?" Hark began, after a few moments' thought.

Quest nodded and gave him a quick, sympathetic glance.

"It's all right," Hark said quickly, realizing that he didn't want Quest to pity him. "I was about three when my parents died and I don't remember them. Not really. I think there was a gull that used to come in through the window. A big gull that scared me. And our rug was red, really red. Sometimes I remember that rug and feel sad. But my parents are just names. I tried mourning for them when I was younger, but I just . . . kept . . . thinking about something else."

He gave Quest a lopsided grin, and shrugged.

"The Shelter wasn't too bad. Somebody in the governor's pay always came each evening to count us, check us for sores, and give us each a bowl of soup. Some of 'em even taught us a few things—rope-making, reed-weaving, sailor's knots, and shell-cutting for jewelry. But you never knew who you'd get."

"The governor arranged that?" Quest sounded amused. "He must have softened since I knew him. Or perhaps he thought you'd steal less that way."

"The Shelter isn't all one happy family," Hark went on. "You get some vipers. Real vipers. But that just means that when you do make friends, you stick tight as barnacles. You look out for each other all your lives.

"There was a girl I knew who left the Shelter and joined a beach-scavenger gang. One day someone saw her by the harbor with her face covered in bruises. Some traders from the western continent had cornered her on the cliff path while she was bringing the gang's goods to market and had forced her to "sell" everything for a quarter of its worth. So the gang thought she'd been ripping them off and had knocked her about as a warning, because you can't have that sort of thing going on.

"Well, she'd always stuck by us. And it's no good if folks start thinking Shelter kids make easy targets. So a friend of mine said we had to do something about it. We found out where the continenters were anchored, then three of us rowed out there by starlight.

"From a distance we could see the traders' big old boat, with all of them sitting around a yellow whale-oil lantern at the prow, getting drunk. We couldn't risk rowing too close, though, in case they heard the oars.

"So I swam over to their boat and climbed up on the stern, phantom-like. They didn't hear a thing. Sitting on the deck was a box, just the right size to be our friend's goods. I grabbed it and took an old barrel lid to use as a raft. While those traders were laughing and drinking, I was swimming back to our boat, pushing the box on that lid ahead of me.

"I thought I'd made it without being spotted. But then I heard yelling behind me. Next moment, something hit me in the back of the head."

"What was it?"

"I still don't know. One of the traders must have thrown something heavy. Whatever it was knocked me out cold."

"What happened?"

"I sank." Hark swallowed. "That's what my friends told me. I was just . . . gone. Nothing but black water and that box bobbing around on the barrel lid. Then those drunk idiot traders knocked over their own lantern, so *everything* was dark.

"My friend jumped into the water. He couldn't see me. He didn't know where I was. But he swam down, hard as he could, clawing through the water till he found me. He grabbed me by the collar and didn't let go. He dragged me back up the surface."

Hark could still remember waking to an agonizing pain in his head, doubled over the side of the little boat so that he could vomit. Jelt had sat next to him all the way back to Lady's Crave, gripping him so he couldn't fall overboard, the pair of them icy, drenched, and shivering.

"A brave friend," said Quest.

"He was always like that," said Hark. It had turned into a story about Jelt, but that couldn't be helped. All of Hark's near-death experiences were stories about Jelt. "I told you. At the Shelter you make friends like nowhere else."

"Did your friends also manage to retrieve the box from the barrel lid?" asked Quest after a moment.

"Of course!" Hark grinned. "The next morning, our friend had goods to return to her gang. All square."

"Were they the *right* goods?"

"Close enough. The gang didn't complain." Hark shrugged under Quest's quizzical glance. "It's not stealing if you're just taking back what's already stolen."

"I wonder if the traders would have seen it that way."

"They must have done." Hark smirked. "They didn't report a theft."

Quest laughed under his breath.

"Good enough?" asked Hark.

"Yes, I think so." Quest pushed away his platter, and sighed. "Very well. I shall tell you of my first meeting with the Hidden Lady.

"It happened shortly after I became a full priest. Back then, I was still not used to my brown robes or being regarded with awe and fear. The oldest priests still saw me as an upstart, of course. I would never *quite* be one of *them*. I had only become an acolyte in adulthood, you see. I hadn't been raised in a priestly family and prepared for the vocation since birth.

"I should not have been sent down that day. Diplomacy with those below was not a task for a novice. However, most of our senior priests were away on the island of Chaosim for a great conference. Thus none of them were available when the trouble began.

"Does the Entreaty Barrier still exist? Back in my day, there was a vast net of metal chains, trailing deep into the water, strung between a line of towers that jutted from the sea. It was supposed to protect Nest from any gods coming from the Under-sea to the west—"

"The net's still there!" interjected Hark. He had begun quietly peeling the old bandage from Quest's leg and dabbing ointment onto the graze beneath.

"It hasn't fallen down or been cleared away?"

"Nobody wants it gone." Hark shrugged. "The shellfish gather on those big chains like a dream. You can fill your bucket with barnacles on a calm day." He had done so himself from time to time.

"The great net turned barnacle farm," murmured Quest. The corners of his mouth puckered, but his expression was hard to read. After a moment, he continued his story.

"One day, that great net started to shake, snake, and whip-crack, almost pulling loose from its tethers. Fishermen reported seeing sick yellow clouds of something under the water, too lurid to be sand. On the west shores of Lady's Crave, fish leaped out of the surf onto the beach and lay there, twitching, rotten stumps where their heads should have been.

"A god was close, then. And they were unhappy. Or perhaps curious. Or grateful. Or feeling playful. It was hard to be sure. What was clear was that somebody needed to go down to the Undersea and talk to them before anything worse happened. I volunteered, so they took me out in a boat, onto the Embrace.

"Back then, nobody but priests would have dared cross the Embrace. Those were sacred waters, terrible waters. On that day, it was worse than I have ever seen it. The sun was pale as a poached egg, and the swirls in the surface were greedily deep. Our great, heavy ship was tugged and turned until we were all sick.

"I stepped into the bathysphere and strapped myself in. It was tiny, so I had to tuck my knees to my chest. The hatch closed, and I could hear the metal screws screaming as they were wound tight. The rock crystal of the windows was inches thick and foggy with scratches. I heard the creak of the crane. The bathysphere jerked and swayed, then started to descend in sickening jolts. The sound of the sea grew louder and louder, until I hit the water with a splash. Suddenly all I could see through the windows was dim water, glistening with bubbles. To tell you the truth . . . at that moment I felt sure that I would never see the sky again."

Hark swallowed. His imagination was too vivid, and he could feel his stomach tightening at the thought of being trapped in a little metal ball, at the mercy of the waves.

"I recited the prayers of descent to keep myself calm," continued Quest, "so I wouldn't use up too much air. The water outside grew darker and darker. And then, through the lower windows, I could see the surface of the Undersea approaching.

"It is like the surface of a second sea. A rippling sea of living ink, with dull purple lights in it. Thankfully, its surface was calm that day. It is not always so.

"As I dipped down below it, I found the water was *clear*. I could see much farther than before, despite the darkness. That is the nature of the Undersea, but it was the first time I had experienced it. There is a light that is not light. That is the only way I can describe it.

"And what I saw before me was a world full of weeds—or so I thought at first. Weeds tall as trees, glowing a green amber, snaking around each other in an endless dance. They seemed to go down, down, ever down into the darkness.

"They were not weeds. The rippling ribbons brushed against the bathysphere, flinched, and then responded. They clustered around the sphere, grasping it like an anemone entangling its prey.

"I tried calling out the ritual greetings, as I had been taught, but there was no response. After a while I heard a straining creak and knew that the boat above was trying to haul up the bathysphere but in vain. The tentacles held the sphere down with a terrible strength.

"If I waited to be rescued, I would run out of air. So I tried desperate measures. I had been told that the Undersea water was different from seawater. It might creep into your pores and change your very nature . . . but it would not crush you, the way other deep water would. And you could breathe it.

"So I cranked the hatch loose, and opened it."

Quest took a few slow breaths, as if his lungs needed reassurance that they were surrounded by normal air.

"I struggled to keep my nerve as the water found its way into my lungs. Undersea water may be breathable, but it is full of fear."

"Fear?"

"Yes, quite literally. Why do you think the fumes from scare-lamps leave us feeling haunted? Fear is an essence, as real as oil or blood. The gods breathed it—had you never heard that?"

Hark had often heard the saying but had assumed it was just a poetic turn of phrase.

"I am *not* a god," Quest continued, "so breathing fear was . . . a shock to the system. When at last I recovered my wits, I unstrapped myself and clambered out, letting the tendrils run themselves over me and examine me.

"She let me climb down into the depths, using those long tentacle-weeds to pull myself to her, hand over hand. It was her hair, her more-than-hair, floating in a living forest about her. I found her at the heart of it, the Hidden Lady. Above the waist she was a woman, or something like a woman, her skin blue-white like a bird's egg. Below the waist she had the body and spindled, ridged legs of an enormous spider crab, so long that I could not see their ends.

"The Lady pulled me close, swaddled me to the neck in her writhing hair, and whispered in my ear. She did not need me to say anything, not that day. She wanted someone to listen to her."

"What did she say?" Hark asked, rapt.

"Not all of it was in words," Quest replied. "She wanted to tell me of a battle fought in the deeps, one that she had started to forget." He smiled uneasily. "I suppose it is natural. We do not want our memories to disappear. So while we still have them, we drop them into the ears of the young—willing or unwilling. Perhaps we hope that will stop our lives fading without a trace."

"Then maybe you should tell me her story too?" suggested Hark hopefully.

Quest blinked, and his eyes came back into focus. He looked approvingly at the new bandage on his leg.

"If we start another story, we will be interrupted," he said. "Perhaps another time."

Chapter 6

A LITTLE BEFORE SUNSET, HARK LEFT SANCTUARY. Most of the time he worked under Kly at Sanctuary, but for two evenings a week he had to report to Dr. Vyne and work as her assistant.

"Have fun rock-weighing!" one of the other Sanctuary attendants called from the door. Hark waved back at him and made a wry face. When asked, he always tried to make his time with Dr. Vyne sound as boring as possible.

She has me gluing broken seashells back together. And weighing her rock collection . . .

Seen from the outside, Sanctuary was still vast and ominous, but one could see that it was also old and wounded. The snaking, abstract carvings around its windows were dingy and green-stained. The great double doors of the main entrance were boarded shut.

The road downhill to the harbor had been paved once, but now grass and gray thistles pushed their way up between the stones. Hark's steps were the only sounds except for the dry rasp of crickets. On either side, the earthen humps of squirrel burrows jutted between the shaggy shrubs.

Nest's harbor was little more than a bare bay, curving like an empty melon rind. It had one long wooden quay for moorings, a bellows house, and a weathered warehouse.

On a rocky outcrop above the harbor, however, squatted a large, square fortress of black and gray stone, its parapets weather-darkened. Its windows were old-fashioned arrow-slits. A few tarnished cannons peeped out between the crenellations.

Hark clattered the knocker at the door and heard echoing steps within. A key chain rattled, the lock clicked throatily, and the heavy door opened. Dr. Vyne stared at him, holding a tuning fork in one hand. Her leather apron was stained with ichor and varnish.

"You're early," she said, but then frowned out through the door, clearly surprised to see that the sun was setting. She hated anyone else to be late but sometimes lost track of time herself while working. "Never mind, come in." She took pains to lock and bolt the door again once he was inside.

The building had once been a keep. *It keeps things in and people out*, Dr. Vyne often said. Before the Cataclysm, it had been a base for armed troops protecting the priests. Now, however, it was a museum. Hark followed the doctor into the main hall, a long, colonnaded room, dimly illuminated by the light from the slitted windows. He stopped to stare, as he always did.

Seven gods stared back.

Their eyes were empty holes, filled with darkness and dust. Each great head was the size of a carriage and rested unsupported on the red mosaic floor. Some had two eyeholes, some had three, others a scattering of sockets that punctured ridged cheeks and bulging brows. Long jaws, short jaws, mandibles, bladed sphincter-mouths. One was a filigree tangle of chitinous plates and tube-casings that still managed to look like a face.

They were hollow, of course. Nothing but carapaces, huge shell-masks. Nonetheless, their majesty caught him off guard every time. Hark felt a butterfly flutter in his knees and stomach but tried to hide it.

"That one's new!" he exclaimed quickly, pointing at the nearest hulking head. It had a flattened face like that of a crab but with a wicked-looking grille where its mouth should be, filled with blade-thin vertical slats.

"Do you want to have a look?" asked Dr. Vyne, sounding almost gentle. She was always strangely tolerant whenever he showed signs of sharing her curiosity. "The shell's coated in thick resin so you can touch it safely. Stay away from those blades, though. They're razor sharp."

The shell was a dull, greenish off-white, like pus or tarnished silver. As Hark ran his fingertips over the resin's smooth surface, he could see beneath it scratches and gouge marks and imagined salvage merchants scraping away every shred of saleable god-flesh, then boiling the great shells for glue, until there was no ichor left in them.

Hark put his hand into one of the smaller eyeholes and ran his fingers around the rough inside of the socket. The touch made him feel queasy, like a cliff-top drop, and he could feel this moment squirming and burrowing into his imagination, ready to appear in a later nightmare. But that just made it all the more impossible *not* to do it.

"Who is it?" he asked.

"Kalmaddoth of the Pit," the doctor answered, in a brisker tone. "Otherwise known as the Gray Gentleman. I suspect it ate by drawing water in through its mouth with incredible suction. Any creatures drawn in would have been shredded by those blades. I'm still trying to understand how it digested them . . ." She sighed, and clapped Hark on the back. "Come on now, work to do. Let's go up to my study."

Vyne led him down the hall, past tapestries, display cases, and big, cloudy tanks full of things covered in glutinous frills. Hark followed, but as he passed one tank, he discreetly ran a finger along its glass. He always did this, as a form of silent greeting.

Hello, Lady. Within the lemon-yellow fluid floated a shapeless gray lump of matter, two feet wide. A deep, black crease weaved across its surface like a sigil. It was apparently a part of the Hidden Lady. He didn't know which part, and it seemed rude to wonder too hard.

Vyne led the way up a flight of wooden stairs to another door, which she unlocked. Hark followed her into the study.

The room was half the size of the hall downstairs and far more chaotic. Hark had helped tidy it only three days before, but already it was back to its usual anarchy. By the rosy light from the round window in the ceiling, he could see every trestle table groaning under sprawled heaps of papers, vials, flasks, varnish bottles, and translucent eyes in jars. It always seemed funny that the shrewd, self-possessed doctor should be so incurably messy.

On the wall hung a rectangle of embossed leather with important-looking ribbons and seals attached to it. Hark still couldn't read its lettering properly, but he knew it was Vyne's university diploma. She wasn't a medical doctor. Her doctorate was in "practical theophysics." In practice, this meant she was a recognized expert in the study of godware and its uses.

That was why she had attended the Appraisal on Lady's Crave three months before. She had been there to bid for pieces of the Hidden Lady and had bought Hark on impulse. Hark felt a lurking, irrational gratitude to the Lady for this, as if she had personally set out to save him.

"So." Vyne moved a few books off her chair so that she could sit down and dipped her pen, ready to make notes. "What has my pet weasel found out this time?"

Hark dropped down onto a stool and gave his report. He

repeated rumors and overheard conversations, and finally Quest's story of the Hidden Lady, as faithfully as he could. She seemed gratified when he mentioned gods breathing the fear in the Undersea but unsurprised.

"Ha, I knew that was not just a metaphor!" The doctor looked over her notes, fiddling with her pen. "Anything else you remember at all? Any impressions you got, while he was talking?"

The Lady was beautiful, Hark answered, but only in his own head. Quest had not said that she was, nor had he spoken of her with any softness, only a trancelike quietness. In his heart, however, Hark was sure that she had been. She would not have been *pretty*, in the way that girls or women could be. She would not even have had the beauty of moonlight on water, or the steely blue leap of winged fish, or the red berries on the cliff thorns. These things were fair. They filled your heart and made you glow. They were honey and spice.

There was another kind of beauty, however, and everyone on the Myriad knew it. A twisted beauty that turned your stomach even while it turned your head. *Frecht* was the old word, a harsh word ragged with superstitious awe. It was an ugliness and otherness that could only be holy, a breach of the rules that echoed those that no rules could bind. The ancient, sacred buildings aspired to that sublime distortion. *Frecht* transcended beauty and carried you into a realm of awe and terror. It demanded your slavish devotion. Nobody used the word anymore, for it dripped with the memory of the gods. However, sometimes people said *beautiful* and meant *frecht*.

"I don't remember anything else," Hark said, knowing that the Hidden Lady would be appearing in his dreams for nights to come, sometimes with empty eye sockets, sometimes with fingers that snaked like her hair.

"The priest who told you this . . . Quest . . ." Vyne frowned, and checked her records in a blue leather book. "He's been getting weaker, hasn't he?"

"He's still sick at the moment," said Hark, feeling uncomfortable. Vyne had made the old man's illness sound like an unstoppable decline. Hark didn't want to think of it that way.

"Damn!" muttered Vyne. "Why is it always the useful ones that fade away? Speaking of which, have you made any progress with Pale Soul?"

"There hasn't been a chance!" Hark protested, though he had known the question was coming.

"You're supposed to *make* chances!" insisted Vyne. "Why else would I need a slippery, baby-faced little crook like you? You're supposed to win those priests' trust and get their secrets out of them!"

"I found out that the Sanctuary archive survived!" Hark pointed out defensively.

For a long time, it had been believed that the great archive at Sanctuary, containing centuries of priestly records, had been destroyed after the Cataclysm. However, Hark had overheard Moonmaid interrogating Pale Soul one evening, demanding to know where the archive had been hidden so that she could destroy it and keep its secrets safe. Hark had of course reported this Vyne and had been in her good graces ever since. However, he could milk this triumph for only so long.

"That was a month ago." Vyne stood up and raked her fingers through her hair. "There's no use in knowing about the archive if we never actually find it. You need to wheedle the truth out of Pale Soul!"

"It's not that easy! He's always frightened . . . confused . . . If you say the wrong thing, he gets in a state . . ." Hark didn't quite want to admit that he felt uncomfortable pressing Pale Soul for information. The wan old man sometimes seemed as frail as a soap bubble.

"Well, *I* can't ask him, can I?" Vyne countered bitterly.

In theory, the governor of Lady's Crave had put Dr. Vyne in charge of both the museum and Sanctuary. In practice, she mostly left the day-to-day running of Sanctuary to Kly.

"It's the most frustrating situation!" This was an old refrain. "Here I am, told to look after thirty fascinating living relics but forbidden from asking them questions! The priests' knowledge is irreplaceable. They are *still* holding secrets, which might change our entire understanding of godware and the gods! But no, we have to 'respect their privacy,' and 'leave them in peace in their twilight years' . . ." She let out a long, annoyed breath.

Technically, Vyne wasn't supposed to send in anybody else to interrogate the priests, either, hence the need for secrecy. Hark had been bought as a spy.

"The governor's an idiot," he told her supportively. He found the doctor easier to handle when she was out of sorts. At least he could read her then. When she was calm and self-possessed, he often felt as though she were laying verbal traps for him and watching with amused detachment to see whether he fell into them.

"And the priests keep irresponsibly dying!" muttered Vyne. "A couple more every year—usually the old ones with the most valuable knowledge! You can't tell which will keel over next, either. Even the healthy-looking ones suddenly have a bad fall, or a cold that turns into a fever, or go to bed as usual but don't wake up. That's why every day matters, Hark. You *must* find out where that archive is before Pale Soul dies just to spite me!"

"I will!" Hark promised. "I'm working on him! You need to trust me!"

Vyne snorted.

"I'm certainly not desperate enough to do *that*," she remarked. Her gaze was amused and dispassionate again. "What have you been up to, anyway?"

"What do you mean?" Hark squirmed as he tried to work out whether Vyne's words were a veiled accusation.

"It's a simple question. I want to know whether my pet weasel is keeping his nose clean."

"It's clean," Hark said quickly.

Vyne sat very still and continued looking at Hark, not quite smiling. When she was like this, Hark couldn't read her at all.

"Do you remember the golden rule?" she asked him.

"I can lie to anybody else as much as I like, as long as I don't get caught . . . but I can't ever lie to you." Of course Hark remembered the rule. It burned in his mind whenever he was in danger of getting too comfortable with the doctor. "If I do . . . you'll sell me to the galleys to rot."

"That's right," she said. Only her mouth moved. She barely blinked. She was waiting. Hark caved.

"I *do* keep my nose clean," he reiterated, "but . . . other folks don't, and I turn a blind eye sometimes."

"Go on." Vyne raised her eyebrows. Hark winced, feeling like a rat.

"There's a Sanctuary attendant who's supposed to throw out the priests' bathwater," he admitted. "Some of it's Undersea water—good quality—so he bottles it up on the quiet and sells it as lamp oil. I don't help him, but I . . . don't tell anyone."

There were other rackets going on in Sanctuary, of course. One attendant was smuggling out medicine, another was chipping away carvings from the corridors and selling them to tourists. Hark was a silent accessory in those endeavors, too.

"It's useful, knowing people's secrets," he said defensively. "It means they have to look out for me."

"So you turn a blind eye to other people's dirty noses," said Vyne. "That's all? You're not making use of your old contacts?"

"No!" Hark insisted quickly. Vyne's second golden rule was that he shouldn't resume contact with his friends back on Lady's Crave.

During his first month in Sanctuary, Hark had been fiercely homesick and desperate to see familiar faces. He had found excuses to hang around the harbor, just in case anyone he knew came looking for him. Nobody ever had, and eventually he had realized that this was probably for the best.

If he had met his friends, there would have been gibes and inquisitive tugs at the sleeves of his yellow robes, as they tried to assess how far he'd sold out. He would have wanted to per-suade them that he was unchanged, a secret rebel disguised as an obedient repentant. Then he'd have been asked to prove it, by downing a drink, "borrowing" something from the museum, or revealing how to get into Sanctuary . . .

"No," he repeated. "I'm not stupid."

"Everyone's stupid," said Vyne. "Everyone's weak."

"Are you going to tell Kly about the bathwater?" Hark asked.

"No." Vyne idly picked up her notes and began scanning them again. "Why would I do that?" All the tension in the room had vanished as if it had never been there. "Just keep me informed, and don't get caught."

Hark suspected that he had skirted around another pitfall. What would have happened if he had pretended total inno-cence? Would the doctor have believed him?

Dr. Vyne liked him, he was fairly sure of that. She liked his cheek, his curiosity, and even his dishonesty. She approved of the progress he was making with his reading lessons, and sometimes she explained godware theories to him, on a whim. He wasn't just her latest tool; he was a project that she found interesting. Would she really toss him away if he disappointed her?

Yes, said his instincts. *She might.*

Hark didn't think Dr. Vyne was somebody who gave more than one warning. She had told him as much when she explained her rules to him on the day they met.

No exceptions. No excuses. No second chances.

Yes, she liked him. But if he ever disappointed her or broke her rules, even once, he suspected she would sell him to his doom without a moment's hesitation.

Chapter 7

EARLY THE NEXT MORNING, HARK WAS SENT OUT to forage for the Sanctuary kitchen. This meant getting up even earlier than usual and scouring the cliffs and beaches, but he rather enjoyed these errands. It got him out of Sanctuary and made him feel less trapped.

He scalded his tongue gobbling his soup, tucked his little braided loaf into his pocket, and before the sun could rise, he was outside in the wind, under the pale gold sky. It was good to leave behind his yellow robes and to stride rather than shuffle. He heaved cold salt air into his lungs, and his ever-buoyant spirits climbed skyward.

It still felt strange to wander the beaches unhindered. As he plundered the barnacles from the rock pools and the lush, flaccid green sea lettuce at the waterline, he half expected to hear yells and feel the sting of slingshots. On Lady's Crave, every decent beach was claimed by a scavenger gang, and most of them took a very dim view of "intruders" trying to forage or scavenge there. Repeat offenders sometimes left with fewer fingers.

On Nest, nearly all the beaches were unclaimed. Only one beach had a permanent guardian. Hark scrambled down to it anyway, not to forage but to chat. When Hark's feet crunched on the shingle, a shabbily dressed, middle-aged man burst out of his shack, then relaxed and lowered his boat hook.

"Oh, it's you." Old Dunlin was fiercely protective of "his"

beach, but Hark had long since won him over. The scavenger usually appreciated the chance to talk to someone.

The pair sat outside Dunlin's shack and shared Hark's breakfast loaf. Perched on a stack of whetstones, Hark looked around and noticed big pails of live crabs in water and heaps of salted fish drying on stone slabs.

"How did you catch all those?" he exclaimed admiringly.

"Didn't you see the storm two nights ago?" Dunlin grinned. "The Embrace was dark and frisky, so the sea went mad, and all the crabs and flying fish just *flung* themselves on the beach to get away from it. Like they were all rushing to get into my cooking pot." The scavenger chuckled. "The sea was wild enough, I thought I might even get some decent salvage washed up here, but . . ." He gave a wry grimace and shook his head.

"No luck?" asked Hark sympathetically.

"It's the usual story." Dunlin nodded toward a series of dark points marring the sea in the distance. "The Entreaty Barrier catches most of the good stuff."

Looking out to sea, Hark could see an irregular row of dark specks nestling near the horizon. He knew this was the Entreaty Barrier's zigzag line of dark towers jutting out of the water. They perched on rocks and underwater pinnacles, some barely a hundred feet apart, some as much as a quarter of a mile from the next. The great net of chains strung between them was invisible beneath the waves.

"Ah, well," Dunlin said philosophically, "if it didn't, I reckon there would be more gangs wanting to claim these shores. As it is . . . I got my own beach."

"Peace and quiet," said Hark.

"Yes—except when the doctor lady visits." Dunlin nodded toward the top of the beach, where a weathered, padlocked door was set into the cliff face. It was apparently the entrance to

an old mine that Vyne occasionally used for unspecified experi-
ments. "Wish she wouldn't—it scares the fish away for miles."

"Any news from the other islands?"

"Sorry." Dunlin shook his head. "You're the first person I've
talked to in three days."

Hark felt a sting of disappointment and was suddenly, bitterly
homesick. Living on Lady's Crave, he had always felt that he
were part of a *flow*. Boats, goods, people, news—they flowed
in and through and out of the island all the time. That was the
way the Myriad was. Everywhere was on the way to everywhere
else. Living without news made him feel marooned.

"Look at those clouds blowing in." Dunlin frowned. "More
rain coming."

Hark barely heard, his eyes once again fixed on the sails of
distant ships. Clippers, cutters, sloops, luggers. White sails, yellow, crimson.

Within sight, across the shining water, life was going on without him.

Hark scrambled inland again through the thick, bristling undergrowth. His steps startled crickets and blue-gray moths.

A striped squirrel darted right across Hark's path, and he
laughed aloud. Once there had been no squirrels in the Myriad,
but the cocky little vermin had managed to stow away in foreign
ships, gnawing through their supplies. These days you found
them on most islands in the Myriad, breeding as fast as rats. The
Myriddens forgave their presence because they were impudent,
acrobatic, and delicious in stew.

Hark always felt a sense of solidarity with the squirrels as
fellow vermin. The sight of one cheered him up immediately.

"Yeah, I shouldn't be here, either," he told it. "But they let us
on a boat, and here we are."

Here I am. Alive and well, in spite of everything. I've talked myself into something good here. Why am I moping?

An army of clouds had boiled in from the north while he walked. Now the sky was a jaded, stormy gray, and the air had a damp, cold glisten that promised rain. Hark knew he should seek shelter soon, too, but for the moment, striding north into the wind made him feel free and full of life.

He would walk as far as the old cairn. Last time, he had noticed a little knot of samphire sprouting between its stones. By now the plant might have grown enough to pluck sprigs from it without killing it. The cairn was so close now, its gray rocks embroidered with livid white lichen.

"Hark!"

Hark froze, his foot on one of the lower stones of the cairn. Suddenly he could feel the chill.

A face emerged from the cairn's shallow inner cavity. A familiar face, bluish with cold.

"Jelt!"

Jelt always came back. Even when you thought he'd died, or been arrested, or forgotten you, he always, always came back. When he did, that changed everything. Whatever you had been doing while he was away came to an end. Hark had missed his friend bitterly, but now he realized that he wasn't ready for Jelt's return after all. Hark was suddenly gripped by a strange sense of loss.

"Jelt," he blurted out. "What are you doing here?"

"Good to see you, too, Hark," said Jelt with a sour smile. " 'Hey, Jelt, you're alive! How have you been?' "

"It *is* good to see you!" Hark insisted hurriedly. He glanced nervously around, but there didn't seem to be anybody within sight. "I knew you must have gotten away! I couldn't find out what happened that night, but you weren't for sale at the Appraisal, so—"

"I wanted to talk to you," interrupted Jelt. "I've been waiting around on this island for two days." He made it sound as though Hark had failed an appointment.

"I'm stuck in Sanctuary most of the time! I only come out when they send me on errands . . ." Hark stopped himself and took a breath. Jelt did this—he pushed you onto the back foot. You ended up apologizing, explaining and defending yourself instead of pushing back.

"All right, I'm here now," Hark said instead. "And I'm glad you came. I . . . can't stay long, though. If anyone sees me talking to you, I'm in deep trouble." All at once, the prospect of three years in Sanctuary didn't seem like a trap. It was a future full of chances, precious and fragile.

"Is that all you've got to say after three months?" A dangerous scowl was creasing Jelt's brow.

"No!" Hark could feel his face getting hot, despite the chill of the wind. "I said we can talk! But I've got to be careful! I'm the one who ended up paying the piper, remember?" He realized as soon as the words were out that they sounded like an accusation.

"Yeah?" said Jelt. "And whose fault was that?" Hark could sense his insinuation, held back and ready, like a fist.

"What do you mean?" Hark felt an angry flush spread across his skin.

"You took forever killing that light, and then you got caught!" said Jelt. "You should have been halfway down the hillside before a patrol could get there! What did you do, stop for a picnic? Rigg was raging at me afterward because I'd vouched for you!"

"Oh, you don't get to blame this on me!" Hark hissed. "That stupid plan was *your* idea!"

"And I thought you were up to it. Blood in the water, Hark!

77

If you knew you weren't good enough, why didn't you just tell everyone so?"

"You made sure I couldn't!" Hark snapped. "You set things up so the smugglers were losing it before I even showed up! By the time I got there, it was either say yes or get chucked over the cliff! You always do this!"

"And you always let me down when it matters!" snarled Jelt.

It was untrue, so untrue, and the words stung. Hark could feel himself wanting to run headlong into a list of all the times when he'd backed Jelt up or saved the situation and been there for him. Jelt wanted him to do that so he could stand there smirking, or snorting dismissively, and then cut Hark off mid-flow, leaving him feeling dizzy and unmoored. Then Hark would be at the mercy of Jelt's current again, and right now he could not allow that.

"If that was true," he said sharply, "I'd have squealed on you when they caught me, wouldn't I? But I didn't. I left you and Rigg's gang out of my story. And thanks to that, I'm indentured for three years. Three years, Jelt!"

"Looks like you landed on your feet," said Jelt, with the same odd weight to his voice. "Landed in some pretty good shoes, as well."

"I could have been sent to the galleys!" Hark protested. "I only just managed to talk my way out of it! I could still end up there, Jelt!"

There was an icy downdraft, and the thorns hissed. Then the dark rain fell, so hard that the drops seemed to graze Hark's skin.

"C'mon, get in the shelter," said Jelt, grabbing Hark's arm and tugging him toward the cairn's hollow.

"I can't." Hark's words squeaked out. His breath caught in his chest as he realized what he was going to say. What choice did he have? He was walking a tightrope. If Jelt stayed in his life, he would find a way to cut it and send Hark tumbling to his doom.

"Jelt, I've covered for you." Blinded by rain, Hark was glad he couldn't see Jelt's face. "I'll keep covering for you—don't you worry about that. But you've got to stay away from me. If you came here to make sure I'm all right . . . well, you can see I'm still breathing. But if you're here because you want something else from me, I can't help you. Ask me again in three years."

He tried to pull his arm free from Jelt's grasp. Jelt held fast.

"Don't you walk away from me, Hark."

Hark could hear the hurt in Jelt's tone, lurking behind the anger. But there was a lot of anger, and Hark suddenly felt small, slight, and fragile. Jelt pulled him into the cairn's hollow, grabbed him by the shoulders, and stared into his face.

"What happened to you?" Jelt demanded. "Did your new owners rip your spine out? Are you going to let them tell you who your friends are? They only own you if you let them, Hark."

There was some truth in his words. There always was. That was one of the reasons Jelt was so hard to argue with.

"Jelt," Hark tried to sound firm, but a hint of pleading crept into his voice. "You've got to let me go."

"You're going to forget ten years of friendship, are you? Just like that? Just because you're scared, and somebody's decided to keep you as a pet? When they feed you, do they balance a biscuit on your nose and make you beg?"

Jelt's gaze was a cruel wind, stripping Hark of his little victories like so many dead leaves. Despite himself, Hark suddenly felt ashamed of his doglike determination to prove himself at his new tasks and of the pride he felt bringing Dr. Vyne information, like a stick in his jaws. His patient, obedient copying of letters . . . He could not mention that to Jelt. Ever.

"You know it's not going to last, don't you?" said Jelt. "They'll see through you. They'll find out something from your past that doesn't fit with whatever story you told them. What'll happen then?"

Were Jelt's words meant as a threat? Jelt knew Hark inside out. He knew about all the worst things Hark had ever done, because he had been right there doing them, too. It had never been a problem, because the two of them had been in the same dingy, stinking boat, and neither of them could think of ratting out the other. Jelt had protected Hark, fought for him, and shared his scant stock of food with him in the bleakest winters. Jelt would never betray him.

Would he?

Jelt sometimes shattered your idea of him, by doing unexpected things that you were sure he couldn't or wouldn't do. He was never sorry afterward, even when he had acted in anger or impulse. If he betrayed Hark, it would somehow turn out to be Hark's fault.

Hark was cold, so cold. The wind blew into the cairn, and the rain slid down his back.

"They've got no loyalty to you," said Jelt, "and you shouldn't have any to them. Loyalty's all that matters, isn't it? It's all we've got. Don't let them take that away from us."

Jelt's eyes were hard, angry, and earnest. Perhaps he really hadn't intended to threaten Hark. But Hark could still feel a nervous tingle in his throat, as if a blade were hovering near it.

"You *do* want something from me, don't you?" said Hark.

"I want to give you another chance," said Jelt. "A chance to make things right."

"Right with who, Jelt?" asked Hark. "With Rigg and her gang?"

"Forget Rigg," said Jelt. "I calmed her down. I even worked with her for a bit . . . though that's over now." He grimaced dismissively. Apparently Rigg's gang was no longer the unmissable promotion opportunity it had been three months before.

"Then—"

"You can make things right with *me*. Right with us. Get ourselves straight again."

"So you're saying things aren't right with us?" Hark asked, feeling a tingle of fear. "Is that what you think?"

Jelt shrugged slowly, his eyes still on Hark's face.

"If you're still my friend, you'll prove it, and then I'll know," he said. "Listen—you're the only person I can trust. I've gotten hold of something special. Really special. This is a *golden* chance, Hark!"

"What is it?" asked Hark reflexively, then realized that knowing too much meant getting involved. "Never mind, I don't want to know." It was too late, though, and he knew it.

"It's a bathysphere," said Jelt.

Despite himself, Hark pursed his lips and silently whistled. Deep-sea salvage missions always needed good diving bells and bathyspheres, and buyers would pay through the nose for them.

"Where did you get that?"

"I found it," said Jelt. "It's intact. The windows aren't even scratched. The hatch opens and it's dry inside, even after all this time. And that's not even the best part." Jelt gave Hark a wicked, confidential glitter of a grin. "It's one of the *old* ones. Priest-made. With godware in it."

Hark gaped at him.

"You're joking!"

An old priestly bathysphere could fetch twenty times as much as a modern one. They weren't as safe and comfortable as the newer models, but their godware shells still coped better with the really deep descents that reached the Undersea. There were only a few left in working condition.

"That would be worth a fortune!" Hark's excitement flared, then fizzled. These were riches he couldn't share. "That's . . . amazing, Jelt. But you don't need my help. You can sell it without me."

"No, I can't!" said Jelt. "If I tell too many people I've got it, the governor will find out, and then he'll confiscate it, won't he?"

Jelt had a point. After the Cataclysm, the governor had declared himself the new "custodian" of everything that the local priesthood had once owned. If he heard rumors of a priestly bathysphere for sale on the black market, he would almost certainly send someone to seize it.

"So find one good buyer, and sell it on the quiet!" said Hark, his teeth starting to chatter.

"Then they get to pick the price!" Jelt objected. "I get paid spit for it, and whoever buys it gets rich using it to dive for salvage! No, thanks. I'm keeping it. *We're* getting rich, Hark. Just you and me. We're going to dive with it."

"What?" Hark felt weak and heavy, as if a current were pulling him under the surface. "That's mad! We're not a salvage crew! We don't know what to do with a bathysphere!"

"No, but I bet *you* could find out," said Jelt. "You're talking to priests all day, aren't you? I'm going down in it anyway, Hark. Are you going to help me or not?"

Hark sighed, feeling trapped, and not just by the rain's onslaught.

"I'll try to find out more about bathyspheres," he said, "but that's all I'm doing."

Jelt reached out and gave Hark a brief cuff that might have been affectionate.

"I've got faith in you," he said.

Chapter 8

BACK AT SANCTUARY, HARK WAS SCOLDED FOR getting his clothes wet, but that was all. Nobody had seen him talking to Jelt. He hurriedly changed into his dry robes. At least Jelt hadn't seen him in those. Hark could imagine Jelt's look of incredulous contempt if he had spotted his best friend in yolk-colored fancy dress.

For three months, Hark had worried about his best friend and longed to hear from him. Now that Jelt had reappeared, Hark would have paid in blood to send him back to Lady's Crave. How had Hark forgotten what it was like when Jelt was around?

Jelt's plan was crazy. Lowering a bathysphere with just two people was clearly suicide. If Hark refused to help, then surely Jelt would give up on the plan and just sell the sphere instead. Or would he? Jelt had threatened to go down in the sphere even if Hark didn't help, and he could be unbelievably stubborn.

If Hark didn't meet with Jelt again, he couldn't be sure that Jelt wouldn't do something stupid. Hark imagined a long, cold silence with no word from Jelt, not knowing whether he was alive or dead. The idea horrified and hypnotized him.

I'll find out more about bathyspheres, he decided. *Then I can explain to him that it won't work.*

"Quest, how dangerous are bathyspheres?" The old priest looked up from his meal, and some of the wrinkles in his brow rearranged themselves.

"They're safer than other diving bells in a lot of ways. They're enclosed, so they can't tip over and let the air out. The round shape is a good defense against the crush of water. The Undersea does not crush in that way, but the true sea above it does, if one goes deep enough. If the outer shell of a vessel is insufficiently strong, the depths will squash it like this." He plucked a small bobble of egg-wrack seaweed out of his stew and squeezed it between thumb and forefinger until it popped.

Hark didn't much like the idea of being inside something that could be popped like a seaweed pod.

"How can you tell if it's strong enough?" he asked.

"You can only find *that* out by lowering them deep." Quest smiled wryly. "But I believe most of the modern spheres use a metal shell half a foot thick and windows of rock crystal covered in god-glass."

"Those must weigh a ton!" Hark tried to make his interest sound casual. "What about the old sort, the ones you used?"

"Oh, those were much lighter," Quest replied. "They were usually made of relics—what people now call 'godware.' Matter far stranger and more durable than metal. It was possible to make the walls much thinner without them caving in."

"But . . . even with that sort of sphere, you must have needed a big boat to take it out onto the water?" asked Hark hopefully. "And lots of people to lower it and haul it back up?"

"Oh yes," agreed Quest. "Only a large boat could carry the crane, the sphere, and the counterweight. We needed sailors to keep the boat steady and stop it drifting, strong fellows to turn the wheel that hauled in the chain, mechanics to watch and oil the mechanism, somebody hanging over the side in a helmet to watch the sphere go down . . . at least a dozen people."

It was better than Hark had hoped. Jelt's plan wasn't just stupid, it was impossible. He could tell him so.

"At least, that was the case in a boat," Quest added as an afterthought. "The fixed cranes required far fewer people."

Hark's heart sank.

In the Myriad, land tended to be steep, both above and beneath the water. There were many places where the seafloor dropped treacherously and precipitously, where you might step off the edge of land and plummet for a very long time. In such places, the priests had built towers or platforms, with great cranes for lowering diving bells and bathyspheres into the depths.

Many of these cranes had been destroyed in the Cataclysm or had collapsed through neglect. A few still remained, however, bleeding their rust down the rocks on which they stood.

"How many people were needed to use a fixed crane?" he asked, not at all sure he wanted to hear the answer.

"The more hands to the wheel, the easier and safer it was," agreed Quest. "I heard a tale of one man managing to lower and raise a sphere by himself, but few would take on a task like that. Even he had to come back another day with friends to help him raise the counterweight again."

Hark heard this with a tumult of feelings. Jelt's plan was stupid, dangerous, and almost certainly suicidal, but apparently not quite impossible.

"What's a counterweight?" he asked.

Quest's eyes brightened as he explained. His was a mind that was happier when it was active. While the old man talked of the crane's counterweight, cross-shaft, reels, and winch, Hark listened and committed every detail to memory.

"Then it's possible," said Jelt, when Hark met him two days later in the shadow of the cairn.

"Jelt—he said he'd heard *tales* of one man working a crane alone. That doesn't mean it happened! And even if it did, that doesn't mean *I* can do it. You'd need to be strong, wouldn't you?"

"Then why don't I lower you?" said Jelt. "I'm stronger. You're smaller and lighter."

"Not a chance, Jelt!" Hark could hear a squeak of panic in his own voice. "I mean it!"

"It's funny seeing your face so clean," said Jelt, changing tack in his jarring fashion. "I hardly recognize you. A couple of people asked after you—I didn't know what to tell them." There was an unmistakeable edge in his tone. "So what's the food like, then?"

Hark stayed sullenly silent, feeling clean, prissy, and well-fed. A pampered animal. A pet. He thought of his old acquaintances hearing Jelt's description and felt a searing shame.

"I bet the food's good," Jelt continued. "Is that what it takes to buy you, then?" He scrutinized Hark with a wide, unblinking stare that seemed to blast straight through him. "Are you *happy* there?" He made the word "happy" sound contemptible and treacherous.

"I'm making the best of it," Hark said sharply. "What do you want me to do—cry all the time?"

"Just never thought you were so easily trained. Well, if it's *that* good there, maybe I should drop by for dinner." Jelt grinned. "I can turn up as a pilgrim or something to pay my respects to the old priests. You can smooth things over, tell your owners a story to get me in, can't you?"

"Do you *want* me sent to the galleys?" hissed Hark. This playful threat made him feel sick.

"Better that than tame!" Jelt snapped back with sudden bitterness. "Trotting around with an invisible collar around your neck!"

He doesn't mean it, Hark told himself quickly. But he had a niggling fear that Jelt did mean it. Better that Hark should be doomed and shackled to an oar than happy somewhere out of Jelt's reach . . .

No. He can't mean that. He's angry, that's all.

There was a twisted nausea in the pit of Hark's stomach, and he knew that it was a knot of angry words he would never say and a threat he would never make. He still had the power to rat out Jelt, but even hinting such a thing felt impossible and unforgivable. Perhaps that was the difference between the strong and the weak—those who dared make threats and follow them through, and those who didn't.

"Relax," said Jelt, subsiding into nonchalance again. "I'm joking. You used to have a sense of humor."

"Ho ho," said Hark flatly, feeling chilled despite the sunlight.

"Listen," insisted Jelt, "it's going to be fine. There are some old cranes on the Entreaty Barrier, aren't there? We'll use one of those. They're close, so we can get you there and back quickly."

"People would see us!" pointed out Hark. "There's always folks moored by the towers!"

Aside from the bountiful shellfish, the Entreaty Barrier offered other opportunities. Intrepid or reckless individuals tried to dive for the debris that accumulated on the Embrace side of the great net of chains. You could find valuable salvage amid the rubbish and wreck fragments, providing the net didn't swing across and knock your brains out.

"There are places people don't go. I'll find something. Trust me." Jelt was talking as though they had already reached an agreement.

"No!" Hark took a deep breath and tried to find his feet again. "Jelt . . . I need to go now. I found out about lowering the bathysphere, just like you asked, but I can't do anything else. I just can't."

"I'll look for you here the day after tomorrow," said Jelt, and pushed on when Hark tried to protest. "You need to get that morning free. I'll have picked a crane by then, one that we can use. You can at least come and look at the machinery for me, can't you? Check it over and make sure it's got all the wheels and reels."

"You don't need me for that," said Hark, but he knew that he was losing ground. "I've told you everything I know!"

"But you've got a better head than me for things like this." Jelt rarely admitted to an inferior understanding of anything. Whenever he did, it was to give himself an advantage in an argument. "I'm not asking much, am I? A couple of hours. Just row out there, have a look."

"And if I tell you it's a death trap, you won't go down?" As soon as the words were out, Hark could have kicked himself. They would be taken as agreement.

"You're the expert." Jelt grinned. "See you next time."

"I can't make promises—" Hark said quickly, but it was too late.

"You need to do this for me." Jelt's smile faded, as if Hark had already made and broken a promise. "For yourself, too. I'm keeping you wild, Hark. You should be thanking me."

Chapter 9

THERE ARE TWO GOLDEN RULES, DR. VYNE HAD told Hark the day she bought him. *You can lie to anybody else, as long as you never, ever lie to me. And you must stay away from your old contacts. If one of them turns up in your life, tell me right away.*

The next day, Hark knocked on the door of the keep, his arm feeling heavy as lead. For three months, he had managed not to break Vyne's rules. When Jelt was around, everything broke sooner or later.

"Ah, there you are!" Dr. Vyne opened the door looking excited but harassed. "Come in! We have a lot to do this evening." She did not appear to notice anything odd in his manner.

The chaos in her study was even more dramatic than usual. The stacks of papers she kept on her second-best chair had been dumped on the floor, and table space had been hastily cleared for a great, wooden crate.

"Where did that come from?" asked Hark.

"Our friend from the League just dropped it off," said Dr. Vyne.

"Captain Grim-Breeches?" asked Hark.

"The very same."

The so-called Vigilance League was a sprawling movement with members on dozens of islands that claimed to be defending the Myriad from outside attack. It wasn't an official armed force, or an official anything for that matter, but it liked to act as though it were. On Lady's Crave, Hark had seen Leaguers ranting on street corners in their blue hats and sashes, and they had always seemed like a bit of a joke.

The League had built a little outpost on the very northern tip of Nest. Although Vyne technically worked for the governor, she had long since reached an arrangement with the local Leaguers, as well.

"They're tedious fanatics," she sighed. "But they keep giving me money and godware, which is an *immensely* redeeming quality." The doctor moved aside the lid of the crate, to reveal hundreds of small, smooth, translucent nuggets.

"Are those all god-glass?" Hark gasped, forgetting his own worries. Good quality god-glass was harder than diamond and extremely valuable.

"All of them? No." Dr. Vyne snorted. "The League seem to have bought everything on the black market that people *claimed* was god-glass. I'll warrant nine-tenths of it is just glass. They want the good sorted from the dross by tomorrow morning."

"That's what you get for being a genius," Hark said deftly. Dr. Vyne had made her name as the foremost expert in god-glass and was understandably proud of it. She had designed the famous crystal bells of Hullbrake and had invented a mirror that clouded before a storm. Even the round skylight above her study was glazed with exquisitely molded god-glass.

Dr. Vyne laughed.

"No, this is what *you* get for being an indentured servant." She threw him a pair of gloves. "Do you have your tuning fork? Good! Start sorting."

Hark donned the gloves, sat down beside the crate, and began numbly picking the nuggets out of the box one at a time.

"Why do they need so much god-glass?" he muttered.

"Oh, they're probably making another experimental submarine

to 'defend all our liberties,'" Vyne answered vaguely. God-glass was perfect for windows in submersibles. "They should ask me to design it for them, but they're so painfully *secretive*."

God-glass softened when the right musical note was struck, ordinary glass did not. Hark chimed his tuning fork over and over, squeezing each glassy blob in turn, and sorting them into two piles.

"Dr. Vyne," he said suddenly.

"Mmm? What is it?" Vyne looked up from her book.

Someone turned up from my past. I told him to leave me alone, but I don't think he will.

If Hark wanted to tell her, it had to be now. Telling the truth was dangerous, though. You could never un-tell it, any more than you could un-break an egg. It was better to let things be. If Hark could persuade Jelt to leave, Vyne would never need to know anything.

"I . . . was wondering how you discovered how to do this!" He held up the tuning fork and a lump of god-glass. It seemed the easiest way to change the subject. Everyone liked talking about their greatest triumph.

"Were you now?" Dr. Vyne regarded him with her usual feline skepticism. It did not stop her answering the question, though.

"You like stories, don't you?" she asked. "Everyone says that the gods used to breathe fear, but I think *you* breathe stories. Unless you're telling them, or hearing them, you wither up and die. So I'll tell you a story. You've heard of the Glass Cardinal, of course?"

Hark nodded. He knew the tales and had seen paintings of the great god, like a jellyfish of monstrous size, with barbed hooks at the end of its translucent tentacles.

"They say his dome rippled like silk, shot with a thousand colors," continued Vyne. "They say he had a scream so beautiful it broke people's minds. Though that doesn't make much sense, if you think about it. Who was unbroken enough to report it?

"A whaler ship once fired a harpoon at a whale on a foggy day, missed, and accidentally hit the Cardinal's dome instead. He surfaced, and those on the ship saw a great ragged tear left by the metal barb. They fled, and the Cardinal pursued, screaming. When they looked back, they saw that the gash had healed completely."

"Did they get away?" asked Hark, already knowing the answer. Most of the stories about the Cardinal seemed to involve the slaughter of entire ship crews.

"Of course not. A great hook ripped the belly out of the boat. As it sank, tentacles writhed up out of the water. One fellow stupidly tried to stab one using a whale-killing lance, but it bounced off with a chiming sound. The tentacles stung everyone to death except the fellow in the crow's nest. He was able to swim to shore after the Glass Cardinal left. What lesson do you take from that story, Hark?"

"Don't shoot harpoons at gods?" Hark hazarded.

Vyne shook her head slowly. Hark sensed that she did not mind him getting the answer wrong. It allowed her to make a particular point.

"That," she said, "is the problem with *everybody*. People listen to these stories, but all they hear is a legend of the terror of the gods. They're still thinking of these creatures as beings we can't ever understand and could only ever hope to survive. What does that story tell us about the Cardinal? It tells us that he could soften or harden his flesh at will. How did he do that? For a long time I had no idea. Then I listened to the stories again and noticed how many of the translucent gods screamed like the Cardinal or sang like the Gathergeist. They used sound— vibrations—to change their own bodies."

It crossed Hark's mind that people could be softened the same way. You said the right thing and struck the right chord, and then they were easier to manipulate. Bringing up Vyne's great success seemed to have sounded the right note.

"That is the trick of it," remarked Vyne. "Listening to someone's story and hearing what lies behind it. People always tell you more than they realize."

Hark looked up and found the doctor watching him again, in her unnervingly acute way. No, she was not softened at all. Her gaze was hard and bright.

"For example," she continued, "when I listened to your story at the Appraisal, what I *heard* you say was: 'I am a liar. I believe I am cleverer than everyone else in the room. But I am not quite as clever as I think.' This evening, you seem very keen to flatter silly old Dr. Vyne and put her in a good mood. Is there something you want, Hark?"

Hark had blindly wandered back into another game of cat and mouse. There was nowhere to retreat.

"Can I have the morning off tomorrow?" he blurted out.

"Must it be tomorrow?" asked Vyne.

"It . . . looks like it will be fair weather," Hark said quickly, "and I was hoping to go swimming. Kly says I need your permission—"

"Who are you meeting?" interrupted the doctor.

Hark gaped at her, thrown entirely off-balance. She knew. She had known all along. Now she had left an open trap before him so that he could damn himself with a word.

"Oh, for goodness' sake!" Vyne's steely look collapsed, and she erupted into unexpected laughter. "Are you being *gentlemanly* about this?"

"I . . . I don't . . ." Hark now had no idea what she was talking about or why she found it so funny.

"Hark, if you want to hide the existence of your girlfriend, tell her not to follow you along the road." The doctor smirked. "I could see her from my window, watching you walk down to the harbor. It was very romantic."

These words gave Hark a shaky grasp on the situation. Dr. Vyne had seen someone on the hillside behind Hark and had jumped to conclusions. Had it been a visiting scavenger, a lost Leaguer, or a trick of the light? Hark didn't care. All that mattered was that his unpredictable owner was amused rather than angry.

"I don't know whether to be scandalized or impressed," said Vyne. "How did you manage to conjure a girlfriend on *Nest* of all places? Did you make yourself one out of seaweed and . . . squirrels?" She narrowed her eyes. "This girl's not one of your friends from Lady's Crave, is she?"

"It's not like that!" Hark protested, then allowed himself a morose shrug. "I . . . probably won't see her after tomorrow, anyway." As far as he knew, both of these statements were true.

"Star-crossed, are you? Alas." The doctor still seemed entertained rather than sympathetic. "All right, if you sort everything in that box tonight, I'll give my permission. Be thorough, though, and don't even *think* of stealing any god-glass."

Sorting the jumbled glass took hours, and before long Hark's hands were aching and tingling despite the protective gloves. Vyne was busy with her books, but occasionally she glanced at him and snickered again.

Spying for Vyne had been fun sometimes. Hark liked reporting to her and showing a clever person how clever he could be. He liked the way they shared barbed jokes about the people they knew, mocking the world like two crows on a gallows.

Now he had broken both her golden rules. There was an invisible crack in the ground between them, gaping further every second, threatening to become a perilous ravine.

Chapter 10

ON HARK'S "MORNING OFF," A SEARING WHITE sun fought the film of white cloud. The wind was restless, and from the cliff top Hark could see a fine frill of pale crests lining each wave on the dark silver sea.

When he reached the cairn, Jelt was waiting.

"You look sick," was his greeting. "Tell me you got the morning off!"

"Three hours, that's all."

Jelt grinned and ruffled Hark's hair.

"Knew you'd do it," he said. Hark's heart leaped a little, even though he wasn't sure if Jelt was congratulating Hark on his cleverness or himself on being right.

"It wasn't easy," said Hark sharply, "and I can't do it again." Even as he said the words, Hark knew that he *would* be asked to do it again. And again. And again. He had said that he couldn't get the time free, and he'd been wrong, hadn't he? Jelt would point that out. Not for the first time, Hark had made the mistake of achieving the impossible on demand.

"We need to hurry," said Jelt. "The wind will be stronger later. We want to get out there and back before it does."

"You found a crane where we won't be spotted?" asked Hark. "You're sure there won't be anybody else there?"

"Yeah," said Jelt. "I wouldn't have left the bathysphere there if I wasn't sure. Come on, I'll take you to the boat."

Jelt led him down to a little wedge-shaped inlet. On the narrow pebble beach rested Jelt's old skiff, a lean, red streak of wickedness.

They shoved the skiff out into the shallows, splashing barefoot, and scrambled aboard as the waves caught her. In spite of everything, Hark could not help feeling a little pang of joy at the icy, fizzing touch of the water, the suck of sand under his feet. He had missed this, the harsh glisten of the barnacle-covered rocks and trusting himself to the dizzying tip and swell of the sea.

Both of them grabbed paddles at once, matching their strokes with the ease of long practice, to fight against the shoreward push of the breaking waves. It was second nature, so easy and right. Hark's muscles knew the motion so well. He knew the worn dip in the seat where he always sat and the best places to brace his feet without getting splinters. He blinked in the sun and salt-laden wind, and he realized that he was smiling.

A little way out from the cove, Jelt gestured to Hark to stop paddling and let the current carry them for a while. The waves were not rough yet, but they continued to wear their ominous frill of white.

"The Lady is lace-making," Hark said aloud, then gave a short, startled laugh under his breath. It was an old Lady's Crave saying, for those times when the waves were crested with foam. Sometimes old people still said it, reflexively echoing what they had heard as children, then halted in confusion when they remembered that there was no Hidden Lady anymore.

The phrase had been little more than a pattern of words to him, an old-person-saying, like "tight as a merchant's purse-knot" or "the sly bird borrows the wind." Now he imagined blue-white fingers wielding pins or teasing out long loops of floating, snow-white thread . . .

"Are you reciting nursery rhymes now?" asked Jelt, looking over his shoulder.

"Do you think people ever believed it when they said that?" asked Hark on impulse. "I know they believed in *her* . . . but the lace-making?" His mind flitted to other islands' orphaned sayings. "What about 'Gathergeist's Washboard'? It's just a scummy old sand flat, with oystercatchers paddling about on it. Did the Siren folks really think Gathergeist crept up onto it at night, with its laundry—"

"Why do you care?" asked Jelt, in a tone that suggested that he didn't and that Hark shouldn't, either. This was a cue for Hark to stop talking. Yet there was a contrary part of him that always wanted to share his thoughts with Jelt.

"I don't think they did believe it. Gods making lace? Washing socks?" Hark narrowed his eyes. "I think . . . it was like a game of make-believe. They could pretend for a moment that the gods were just big, scary neighbors, with their own chores. Something they could understand. Something that might understand them."

Of course the gods hadn't been doing anything homely or domestic. But then, what *had* they been doing, all those centuries in the lightless cold of the Undersea? How *had* they passed their days? Had they even noticed the days at all, or had they lived in an eternal night? Had they thought, planned, dreamed, or talked? Or had they lived like sharks, swift and sinuous nightmares swimming in eternal search for food? It was a dark, cold thought, and as Hark stared down into it he could see no bottom.

An icy scoop of water splashed him in the face, shocking him out of his thoughts. Jelt watched Hark with a grin, the paddle used for the splash still in his hands.

"Back to reality, are you?" he asked. "I saw you drifting away." He shook his head. "I knew I'd been gone too long. Whenever

I leave you to yourself, you get like this. All these weird ideas push up in your head like weeds. Takes ages to pull 'em up so that you start making sense again."

For some reason, his words chilled Hark more than the shock of the water. The day no longer seemed so bright.

They're not weeds, Jelt. They're thoughts. And they're mine.

Was it always this way? Did Hark start to get ideas of his own when Jelt was away, ideas that Jelt took pains to kill as soon as he got back?

As they took up their paddles again, Hark tried to smother an uneasy nagging resentment of Jelt. *You're not allowed to go places he can't go*, said a small voice in his head. *You're not allowed to have things he can't have. You're not even allowed to think things he can't think.*

Ahead, Hark could see the long line of the Entreaty Barrier's towers of brick and metal jutting out of the water. From this angle, you could see how irregularly they were spaced and how unequal their heights were, some raised up on little islands, some emerging from the water itself. There would be others that were now completely underwater, waiting to rake the bellies out of passing boats or submarines. Between them ran a faint ribbon of white foam, where the waves broke on the great, submerged chain from which the net was suspended.

On the far side of the net was the Embrace.

To the untrained eye, it simply looked like open sea. A Myridden like Hark, however, could recognize the danger signs—the dark, dull color of the water and the strange, coiling wisps of high cloud that spiraled instead of obeying the wind. In the distance, a glittering shoal of flying fish cleared the surface for a quick skim. They might be avoiding a predator, but they were more likely escaping some treacherous whim of the sea itself. These waters were not merely deep. The Undersea was unusually high here, and so the ordinary sea above it could not be trusted.

"Head for those!" called out Jelt, and nodded toward two of the Entreaty Barrier towers that rose close to each other on nearby islands, as if conspiring. They were separated from their other neighbors by a sizeable gap on either side.

"We're going to the Strides?" Hark asked, surprised. "Nobody dives there!"

There were good reasons for this. A great iron bridge had once crossed the gap between the Strides, and its wreckage now lurked perilously underwater. Metal railings and broken spires poked viciously out of the submerged rubble, waiting to rend flesh or puncture diving bells. The currents and eddies around the Strides were notoriously unpredictable, too.

"That's why it's perfect," Jelt answered with maddening calm. "Nobody will see the bathysphere, and you won't be spotted running around without your leash." His argument had a twisted logic.

"But there's no crane!" protested Hark. The larger island's crane had been torn from its roots during the Cataclysm and left sprawled across its island.

"You'll see," was all Jelt would say.

After some vigorous paddling, they brought the skiff up against the larger of the two islands, a helmet-shaped pinnacle of red rock about fifty feet across. Jelt scrambled out of the boat and up the uneven, rocky slope. Hark followed, his wet feet slithering on the smooth rock. When they reached the top, Hark stared around, seeing no sign of the island's mangled crane.

"This way!" said Jelt. He strode toward the end of the island that was closest to its neighbor. Hark joined him and peered down what looked like a sheer cliff face. The sea sluiced hungrily between the islands, chewing at the red rock. As each fierce wave receded, little plumes of red silt flourished in the water.

Fixed in the rock above the ledge was a rusted iron ring, with a weather-bleached rope attached.

"Trust me, you'll like this." Jelt took the rope in both hands, then started to climb down the cliff face, finding toeholds in the slippery rock. He edged down until he was almost out of Hark's view. Then he kicked away hard, let the rope slide a few feet through his hands, swung back and . . . vanished into the cliff.

There was a muffled but echoing *slap!* below, like wet feet hitting rock. There had to be a hidden hollow in the cliff down below.

"Your turn!" Jelt's voice was faint and echoing.

The old rope was frayed and bristling, but Hark's palms were tough, and he lost no skin as he let himself down. His toes were deft, his feet and ankles strong from climbing. He edged his way down the cliff, with the old feeling that if Jelt trusted him, he could trust himself.

I'm bigger when I'm around Jelt, sang the little voice in Hark's head. *I'm better. I do things I'd never even try if I was by myself.*

He kicked off, let the rope slide a little, tightened his grip again and swooped into the darkness of an overhang, releasing the rope as he landed in a crouch.

Jelt barely gave him a glance.

"Took your time. Come and look at this!"

Hark blinked, his eyes adjusting to the darkness. He realized that the overhang was actually a large cavern, its size hard to guess from the outside. Behind Jelt, taking up half the space, was an ungainly metal structure, as if a giant iron spider had tucked itself into a crevice.

Hark's eyes were drawn at once to the large, dark orb that

rested on the rocky floor next to the contraption. The reflected sea light undulated slightly on its tarnished, green-brown surface.

He walked slowly forward and laid his hand on the side of the bathysphere.

It was smaller than he had expected, narrower than he was tall. The round door-hatch in the front was barely a foot and a half wide, the little windows only six inches across. It was blotted and blackened by the elements and studded with limpets.

Its surface felt strange under his hand. It wasn't exactly warm, but it wasn't as deathly cold as metal would have been. There was a strange, waxy smoothness that caused the hairs to rise on his neck. He had felt the same tingle touching the great carapaces in the museum.

Hark pushed very gently, wobbling the sphere with unexpected ease. Quest was right. The bathysphere was surprisingly light.

"There's so much godware in this," he whispered, and smiled in spite of himself.

"Beautiful, isn't it?" Jelt grinned. "And look at that!" He pointed out at the surging water between the two islands. "Perfect for a trial run. The water's deep, but not as deep as on that side." He nodded toward the Embrace. "There's a gap in the net here, too, so we won't have that banging into us, either."

"Where did the crane come from?" asked Hark. Obviously Jelt hadn't thrown it together in the last two days.

"Some salvage divers grabbed what was left of the old crane and put it together down here a couple of years ago, so they could drop diving bells. I went drinking with one of them once. He said there were some real treasures down there—lots of things washed up from the deeps and the Undersea."

"So why aren't they here, then?" asked Hark.

"They gave up. The swell was too strong, too many spikes . . .

the bells couldn't cope. But we'll be fine in this." Jelt knocked on the sphere's surface, and it gonged huskily under his knuckles.

"Let's have a look at the machine," Hark said, trying to cover his confusion. He had intended to show Jelt how dangerous and unworkable his plan was, but now he was looking at a shallower descent than expected and a crane that had apparently been used within the last two years. The prospect still filled him with dread, but the ground for his argument had suddenly been hacked from under him.

He stared at the mechanism. It took a little while for him to disentangle it in his mind and understand what he was seeing. There was the thick crane mast, of the sort Quest had talked about, fixed to the cave's floor and ceiling with big daubs of cement. From it stuck two sturdy metal arms, one dangling the sphere, the other suspending a tough, metal-mesh net filled with rocks. A counterweight, Hark realized. And to lower the sphere, you had to wind *that* chain around *that* reel, which you could do by turning *that* wheel . . .

"Well?" demanded Jelt.

"I can't see any parts missing or broken," said Hark reluctantly at last. "But I don't know for sure how it's meant to look. It's all really old, Jelt."

"It's fine," snapped Jelt. "You can see it's fine! Look, we're in a hurry, remember? We need to get you down there and up again before the wind rises, don't we?"

Hark's heart sank. Since their last conversation, Jelt's suggestion that Hark be the one to descend had solidified into an assumption.

"Jelt—"

"We agreed, didn't we? You're lighter than me. I'm stronger. You just talk me through these wheels and everything, and it'll be fine."

Cornered by Jelt's logic, Hark tried to explain the mechanism for slowing the chain's passage through the crane, so the sphere wouldn't descend too fast. Jelt nodded impatiently, then repeated it wrongly. He got more annoyed every time Hark tried to set him straight. At last he seemed to comprehend what Hark was trying to say and immediately acted as though he had understood it all along.

"I got it a long time ago! You're just stalling now. Look, you're the one who needs to be home before the morning's over, aren't you? The sooner we do this, the sooner you get back to your precious Sanctuary." Jelt tapped a crank handle on the inside of the door hatch. "See this? If there's trouble, you can uncrank this, get out and swim up."

Hark leaned over and peered into the little doorway. The interior was almost entirely empty, with only a little seat inside and some leather straps presumably to keep the occupant in place. The leather had not rotted, and there was no smell of damp or the sea, only a faint, strange scent of incense and something animal.

"Calm down!" Jelt was holding up an old copper diving helmet, with its air-hose and float bladder. "Once I've lowered you, I'll use these to look down and make sure the sphere's all right. If there's trouble, I'll haul you up again."

Hark let out enough of the crane's chain to attach its hook to the bathysphere. Then, with a deep sense of dread, he pulled himself head first through the narrow door and wriggled his way in. The space inside was small, high enough to kneel but not to stand. The wooden seat was dry and showed no sign of rot. The leather straps were rough under his fingers as he looped his arms through them.

"Are you in?" Jelt's darkened face appeared for a moment in the hatch, then the little round door swung closed and the light dimmed in the enclosed space. Outside, metal squealed as Jelt turned the external door crank. The old dry smells seemed to become more intense, almost choking. There was a clang, and the sphere wobbled slightly, leaving Hark feeling vulnerable and sick.

Hark imagined the sphere descending into darkness and leaving the daylight behind. He remembered Quest's fears that he had seen the sky for the last time, and suddenly Hark was filled with the same terrifying conviction.

He needed to know that he could loosen the door if he had to. He reached forward, and gripped the crank handle with both hands. It did not budge. He wrenched harder, yanking with all his might. It remained fast.

Panic took over. Hark gave a yell and banged on the door, then kicked out with his feet. He pummeled the strange false metal in desperation, with a dread certainty that at any moment he would be raised aloft and swung out over the unforgiving sea. He kept kicking and thumping even when the squeal of the external crank resumed.

The hatch opened. Hark hastily struggled out through it, pouring himself out on the wet rocky floor of the cave. Even now there didn't seem to be enough air, and his heart was racing.

"What the billow's shriek is wrong with you?" demanded Jelt.

"I . . . I couldn't turn the . . . the crank . . ." Hark managed between gasps.

"Is that all?"

Hark glared at Jelt.

"Yes," he muttered, recovering his breath. "I wouldn't be able to get out if I got stuck or started to drown. Yes, that's 'all.'"

"That's not going to happen! Get a grip! I can't believe you freaked out like that!"

"It's not going to happen, because I'm not going down there!" Hark picked himself up, his embarrassment making him angry at last. "This is stupid, Jelt, and I can't do it! Not this time!"

"I bet you could undo the crank if you had to," said Jelt remorselessly.

"You always think like that! 'Oh, Hark'll do it if he has to!' So you always arrange things so I *do* have to. Like when you made me agree to Rigg's plan! Every time I find I've got no choice, and it's life and death, so I just have to make it work somehow."

"Yeah, and I'm always right, aren't I?" said Jelt. "You always *can* do it. You just need a bit of a kick sometimes to get your nerve up."

"No!" shouted Hark. "You're not always right! I couldn't manage the beacon-smashing as fast as you promised, could I? My neck *was* on the line, and I still couldn't do it!"

"You could have done it," said Jelt, without hesitation, his eyes hard and dark. "If you'd really gone all out. But I guess you panicked, the way you did just then. You slowed down so you wouldn't fall. Maybe you thought you'd rather be arrested than that."

Hark stared at him, mouth open, his heart quivering in his chest.

"Go kiss a shark, Jelt!" he blurted out. He had just enough time to see Jelt's eyes go bright and empty with rage, and then a savage punch hit him in the temple, knocking him over. A sharp kick bruised his ribs, and Hark reflexively curled up, arms shielding his face.

"Don't you talk to me like that!" Jelt stood over him. "You *never* talk to me like that! I'm the only reason you're alive!" Another hard kick in the small of Hark's back.

Hark's anger gave way to pain and surprise. Jelt had only

turned his fists on Hark a dozen times in all the years they'd known each other. Hark was usually good at avoiding it, but this time he had missed the warning signs. Perhaps this anger had been burning away in Jelt ever since Hark's indenture, looking for an excuse to lash out.

"You don't get to walk away!" Jelt was yelling, increasingly incoherent, as he rained kicks on Hark. "You don't get to do that, Hark! They're . . . they're *training* you, Hark! You don't get to talk like . . ." A particularly hard kick, in the meat of Hark's calf. "We're *brothers*, Hark! You little . . ."

Hark stayed curled, teeth gritted, face shielded. If he tried to get up, he knew from experience that Jelt would pin him to the rock and put him in a choke hold.

Weather the storm, he told himself. *At least he's kicking you in places where the bruises won't show.* His own anger had put out its head for a moment, like an eel, but had pulled back into the crevice the way it always had to. There were sharks in the water. Jelt's rage was always more dangerous.

When at last the kicks stopped, Hark stayed curled for a while, and then very carefully pulled his arms away from his face.

Jelt was standing with his back to Hark, staring over at the bright red cliff of the opposite island.

"I really want to smash your head in right now, Hark," he muttered under his breath.

He turned his head and cast a withering look at Hark.

"So it looks like you're going to wet yourself if you go back in that sphere," he said. "I'll go down this time to show you it's safe. But next time it's you." Without another word, he walked over the sphere, and wriggled in through its narrow door.

Hark had come there to talk Jelt out of going down, but now all the will to do so had been kicked out of him. What good would it do anyway? He reached out, hesitated, then pushed the door closed and cranked it tight.

It was a struggle to turn the great handle that swiveled the mast, but at last he had the bathysphere swung out over the water. Then he began slowly, slowly turning the wheel to lower the sphere, using the toothed support to stop the wheels turning too fast.

The bathysphere dipped, jolted, then descended while waves patted playfully at it. It dropped lower until only its very dome was visible, foam lathering over its greenish surface.

There was a sudden crack. Hark spun around, and stared in confusion at the mechanism. A faint creak drew his eye to the counterweight.

The net was giving under the weight of the rocks. As he watched, a second metal chain holding it to the hook snapped. With ponderous inevitability, the great rocks tipped and tumbled out of the net in a deafening cascade.

The whole winch jerked violently, and suddenly the chain was rattling and racing around the reel at terrifying speed. The toothed strut to slow the turning lay sheared and useless at his feet.

Hark stared at all of this, his mind blank with panic. What could he do? Grab the great chain? It would take the skin off his hands and drag him into the water for good measure.

Then the racing chain abruptly halted, no longer being dragged into the water. Several loops were still on the reel. Down below, the plummeting sphere had suddenly stopped its descent.

It must have hit something, thought Hark.

Chapter 11

HARK STARED, FEELING ODDLY EMPTY AND LIGHT.

The water that had swallowed the sphere was dark in the shadow of the cliff. Waves gently jostled, then parted, spreading glossy water between them. Foam tracery spelled out letters in the language of the sea, letters that Hark might read if he stared long enough.

The breeze in the underhang was very cool. Soothing. The cool puddles in which he stood tickled pleasantly against the skin of his feet. The lightness and emptiness spread through him, right to his fingertips. His head was quiet.

What am I doing?

Hark shook himself hard. How long had he been standing there like that? He didn't know. He had to act now, or Jelt . . .

Perhaps it's too late already, whispered the quiet in his head. He could fall into that quiet, and then it *would* be too late, nothing more he could do . . .

Jelt's down there, Hark told himself. *Think!* Precious seconds were speeding beyond his control, like the chain-links rushing off the reel.

He ran back to the great wheel and heaved at the nearest spoke until his arms ached. By straining with all his might, he managed to haul the chain up half an inch, only to see it slip back down as soon as his grip weakened. Without the counter-weight, the sphere was too heavy for Hark to haul up by himself.

Hark grabbed handfuls of his hair and yanked it to make himself concentrate. Could he swim down to Jelt? No, the winch must have let out seven fathoms of chain. He might reach him, but he would run out of air before he could do anything useful.

On the floor of the cave, he spotted the dented coppery dome of Jelt's diving helmet. The oiled-leather air-hose wouldn't be long enough, but it was better than nothing.

He tore off his shirt and filled his trouser pockets with rocks. Grabbing the helmet, he knotted the air-hose twice near the bladder float so that no air could escape upward from it. He hurried to the edge of the rocky platform, taking deep, rapid breaths.

Hark crammed the helmet on his head, and the world shrank to the view through two dim glass eyeholes. He fastened the pitch-covered leather gorget snugly around his neck. Then he sprang forward and dropped toward the water.

The icy surface rammed him and swallowed him. His vision filled with red-tinged murk, tiny bubbles scooting upward past the eyeholes. The stones in his pockets dragged him downward, and the swell pulled him this way, that way. He kicked out reflexively, one heel grazing the submerged cliff behind him.

The surface was two yards above him, now three, now four, a flexing silver cloth, pearled with foam. Looking up was a mistake. A few bubbles escaped his gorget, and an icy trickle of water leaked in through the neck. Hark windmilled his arms and legs to keep himself upright.

The great chain connecting the crane to the bathysphere was a vertical bar of black, surprisingly far away and receding. Fighting the current, he swam over to the chain and grabbed it with both hands.

Hand under hand he let himself rapidly down the chain, surrendering to the downward pull of gravity and loyalty. As he sank, Hark let the breath out of his lungs slowly, so very slowly.

Colors dulled and cooled. More water leaked into his helmet, tickling icily at the nape of his neck and the front of his chin. The air in the helmet was being squashed by the insistent pressure of the deeper water. There was a pain inside Hark's ears, which eased only when he swallowed hard.

A few bubbles hurried past Hark from down below, filling him with dread.

Staring down the length of the chain, he could just make out the indistinct shape of the bathysphere. It lay among jagged fragments of broken cliff and black twists of mangled metal, their outlines woolly from the sediment clouding the water.

Down, down. His lungs were empty, and he took a breath that smelled of pitch. Out of the silt haze a long spear of metal suddenly loomed, the swell carrying him toward it. He wrapped his legs around the chain just in time to stop himself being impaled. Something scratched a line across his bare back.

Down, and Hark's bare feet came to rest on the sphere. He peered through one of the windows, but it was too dark inside to see anything.

What was that shadow in the sphere's upper flank? A dent. A deep dent. At its center was a ragged, dark puncture.

Hark swam down and grabbed the door crank.

I bet you could undo the crank if you had to, goaded Jelt's remembered voice.

Hark braced his feet against the rock. Gripping the crank handle with both hands, he yanked at it with all his might. The handle was immovable as stone. He clenched his teeth and closed his eyes tight and yanked again, putting all his will into his muscles.

He gasped another panicky breath and strained again. A tiny shift, yes! He heaved again, galvanized by panic and hope. The crank was turning, very stiffly. The effort forced him to take breath after breath. The air in his helmet was growing stale. At last the crank turned freely, and the hatch came loose.

Hark yanked open the door. Within, he could see a murky person-shape drifting, arms spread-eagled. Its back had settled in the base of the sphere, its limbs afloat.

Sinking means drowned, thought Hark, feeling sick. *Lungs full of water.*

And then, just as despair closed on Hark's heart, something happened.

A pulse. A physical tug that he felt in every nerve. A ripple of strange light.

During that pulse, the drifting body of Jelt suddenly flailed. His legs kicked, and his hands clawed the water, as if he were trying to swim to the hatch. The pulse passed, and Jelt spasmed, twitched, and fell still.

Hope reared its pitiless head. Hark stared around desperately, looking for the source of the ripple. It had come from farther down the long slope, amid the bewildering tumble of broken things. Hark swam down past a half-buried diving bell, the prow of a sagging skimmer sub, a peeling wooden figurehead . . .

There! The pulse came again, hitting Hark in the chest like a fist. This time he saw the water shimmer and distort above a crack between two rocks. He swam over and peered in.

Beyond the black spines of sea urchins lurked something bone-pale and round, about the size of a grapefruit. As he watched, it clenched for a moment, then released, sending out another shock wave.

Hark squeezed his hand into the gap, trying to avoid the spines, and gripped the yellow-white object. He pulled it out, scraping his knuckles, then swam back to the bathysphere.

If you can make Jelt un-drowned, you're coming with me.

He reached in through the hatch, caught at a trailing hand

and pulled hard. With difficulty, he dragged Jelt's lanky frame out through the tiny hatch, then wrapped one arm tightly around Jelt, holding the strange orb against his friend's side. He was chilled by Jelt's vacant expression, his open mouth.

The air in Hark's helmet was turning to poison, but Hark took one last deep breath of it, anyway. Then he shook the rocks out of his pockets. Tore loose the gorget. Pulled off his helmet. Kicked off from the ravine floor. Fought his way up, up, dragging the deadweight of his friend.

Help me, Jelt.

Hark felt the strange orb shift like an animal in his hand. Jelt's body jerked, kicking out as well so that they rose faster.

The surface was too far, almost too far, tantalizingly close, arm's length, *there*—Hark's head broke it, and he took a deep breath. Then a small wave hit him in the face and made him choke. Hark changed his hold on Jelt to keep his friend's head above water and flailed his way toward the rocky ledge of the overhang cave.

By the time Hark had laboriously dragged his friend up onto the ledge, he was exhausted, his arms weak and aching. Hark rolled Jelt over so that he was face down, but with his head turned to one side, mouth and nose away from the puddles. Jelt was so heavy. Drowned-heavy. Cold, too, like clay.

What else did you do when someone was near drowned? Press them hard in the back—that was it. Squeeze them like a bellows, so the water came out and they drew air in.

Hark nestled the mysterious orb against Jelt's neck, in the blind hope that it might help. Then he pressed both hands hard against Jelt's back, and shoved downward with all his weight. Again. Again. Again. A little water dribbled out of Jelt's mouth, but he still wasn't breathing. His skin looked blue.

Perhaps it was too late after all. Maybe Hark had only imagined Jelt's strange, lifelike frenzies of motion. His body could have been swaying in the water's swell.

In daylight, the ball's yellow-whiteness gleamed. There were hundreds of tiny holes in its surface, each perfectly round. The inside of each hole seemed ragged, perhaps toothed.

It was godware. It had to be.

"Wake up, Jelt!" Hark whispered, his throat feeling choked. "You were right—there *was* godware down there! But you can't gloat at me if you don't wake up!"

Jelt did not wake up.

Hark shoved and shoved at Jelt's cold back, but he could feel tears of anguish and self-hatred stinging at his eyes. His bruised temple and kicked ribs didn't matter anymore. All he could think of was Jelt taking punches for him; Jelt "finding" their first bottle of rum and sharing it with Hark one long summer night on the beach; Jelt outpacing him as they ran from a theft, then stopping to wait for him and help him over a fence.

Brothers. That was what Jelt had called the two of them while he was lashing out in bitterness and hurt. Brothers. If Jelt wasn't family, then who was? What did anyone else matter?

Why hadn't Hark jumped straight into the water as soon as the bathysphere plummeted? Why had he stood there like a daydreamer, letting those precious seconds slip away, while his best friend was drowning below?

"Come on!" he whispered. "Come on!"

The orb shifted.

For a moment it flexed and contracted, imperceptible seams sliding over each other. The tiny holes briefly closed like mouths, and there was a faint grinding, like shells against rock.

The pulse came again. Not as forcefully as it had underwater, but Hark could still feel it. A knock in the breastbone. A throb in the blood.

Jelt jerked violently. His mouth and eyes opened wide, and then he shook with violent, choking coughs. He retched, gasped, spat. His wet hair slathered his cheeks, dangled and dripped.

Hark backed away a little, nauseous with relief. Jelt was still in the world after all, bluish but alive. Hark felt his dread and grief start to ebb. Soon he would be embarrassed about them.

"I told you we shouldn't use that thing." Hark couldn't stop his voice wobbling.

Jelt would probably have a defiant answer to that later. Yes, there *would* be a "later," it seemed. For now, however, his only response was a long, retching vomit of seawater.

Chapter 12

THE JOURNEY BACK FROM THE STRIDES WAS LONG and slow. The skiff was more difficult to handle now that Hark was the only one paddling. Jelt lay wrapped in a blanket, mute and gray-faced, one hand curled around the bone-colored orb.

Hark talked and talked, even though he couldn't spare the breath. Silence was a dark, cold place that stole your breath and where everything floated. Hark knew he was being annoying. He wanted Jelt to snap and tell him to shut up. He wanted to force Jelt to be his usual moody self.

Jelt said nothing. Now and then, Hark felt the orb pulse. It was less frequent and intense now, but it still made him feel like a string being twanged.

At last, Hark guided the skiff into the narrow inlet where Jelt had left it before. Jelt didn't make any move to get out. Instead he plucked at the damp folds of his shirt.

"There's something . . ." Jelt murmured hoarsely. "I can feel . . . something . . ."

With clumsy fingers, Jelt peeled up his shirt, revealing his right flank. There was a deep, dull gray groove in his side. A wound, Hark realized, his skin crawling. A long gash, as bloodless as a slice in a slab of raw pastry.

The rip in the side of the bathysphere, thought Hark. *There must have been a sharp edge inside, and Jelt was thrown against it . . .*

But then where's the blood? It looked like the wound you might find on a drowned corpse, washed out and colorless.

"It . . . itches," said Jelt. He reached out and prodded at the pale, swollen skin near the wound. A single bead of clear water bulged in the gash and leaked out to run down his stomach.

"Don't," said Hark reflexively, trying not to wonder why Jelt was bleeding seawater. "You need to wrap something clean around it." He swallowed hard, trying to convince himself that such measures would help. "You better keep hold of *that*," he added, tapping the orb in Jelt's grip. "It'll sort you out. And then when you're better, you can sell it." He gave a grin that hurt his mouth. "Don't forget to save half the money for me."

Jelt blinked slowly and painfully, as if finding the daylight too bright.

"Jelt." Hark had to say his friend's name a few times before Jelt looked at him. "Are you going to be all right here?"

"Do I look all right?" growled Jelt. He did not.

"Listen, Jelt . . ."

"You're going," said Jelt, with leaden incredulity. He stared emptily at Hark. There were dogs that stared at you that way sometimes, sodden with heat and half mad with hunger. They didn't hate you, but they had sharp teeth and a great numbness inside them, and there you were.

Hark glanced up at the sun, gnawing his lip. He had watched it edging higher as he was paddling back to Nest. He had already been out far longer than the permitted three hours.

"I don't have any choice!" Hark said desperately. "If I don't get back, they'll send somebody to find me. They mustn't see us together!"

The look in Jelt's eye made Hark feel sick. He felt like a coward and a traitor, for wanting to leave his friend at death's door so that he could scamper home and grovel to his new masters . . .

He hadn't saved Jelt. Jelt wasn't saved yet. He was sick and too weak to stand. He might lie there in the boat till he died. But if Hark stayed, how could he make anything better? He wasn't a doctor. He wasn't anything.

"There's a scavenger living in a shack on the next beach," Hark suggested, clutching at straws. "I could run to him and ask him for help."

"A scavenger?" Jelt glared at him. "So he can knife me and steal the godware?"

Dunlin had never struck Hark as the robbery-and-murder type. Then again, you never knew how people would react when a fortune in godware was within reach.

"What do you want me to *do*, Jelt?" Hark blurted out.

"Just get me to that cave up there," said Jelt. He said it with a slight shake of his head, a tone of weary disgust. It left Hark feeling that this was the least Jelt could expect from a friend, the very least. Hark smothered his panicky sense of urgency and helped Jelt out of the boat. They struggled up the beach, Jelt's feet heavy and sloppy on the rough stones.

Inside the tiny cave, Hark lowered Jelt down to sit on a broad slab. At least Jelt would be out of the sun and above the tide line. He brought Jelt's water bottle and damp clothes from the skiff and draped the latter over stone ledges. All the while he was watched by Jelt's hard, expressionless gaze.

What if Jelt really couldn't move? What if he just lay here, with no food and hardly any water, unable to get help?

"Look . . . I can get you some bandages from Sanctuary. Some medicine, too, maybe. I'll probably be able to get out again in a day or two—"

"What use is that?" Jelt's voice had no force, but it was full of husky venom. "A day or two? Don't even bother, all right? That's what you want me to say, isn't it?"

Hark suddenly imagined picking his way down to the cove in a couple of days' time and finding Jelt's gray-faced corpse in the cave. He blew out his cheeks, furious at himself, his life, and Jelt.

"I'll try to sneak out tonight and come back here," he said, sickened by his own words. "I can't make promises. But I'll try."

Hark stumbled back into Sanctuary sodden and exhausted. He knew that his best bet was to sneak into the building and busy himself with chores in an obscure corner. That way he could pretend innocence when confronted. *I've been here for ages! I didn't know I had to report in when I got back!*

As he drew near to Sanctuary, however, he saw Kly standing outside the only unboarded entrance. Worse still, he was not alone.

"Oh, *great*," muttered Hark, recognizing the blue uniform of the tall man standing beside the foreman.

Members of the Vigilance League were always easy to spot. Even their street ranters wore dark blue coats, a sash scattered with dots, and a silver braid or ribbon sewn to their hats. Recently, the richer members had taken to wearing sharper versions of this outfit, modeled after the uniforms that some continental military officers wore. Although the League wasn't an official force, a few of them had even started giving themselves military-sounding titles.

The "captain" currently arguing with Kly was the one that Vyne and Hark had privately nicknamed "Captain Grim-Breeches." He was stationed at the Leaguer outpost on the northern tip of Nest. Usually he came south only to see Dr. Vyne at the keep, but occasionally he turned up at Sanctuary, and his visits were guaranteed to put the foreman in the worst possible mood.

"All I am asking for is a chance to look around!" the captain was saying. "If the priests are being treated as well as you say, then you have no reason to stop me!" He had thick, black brows. His cheeks twitched and puckered when he was annoyed, which he usually was. Hark wondered whether anger was something he put on with his uniform or if he'd bought the outfit to give his anger shape.

"This isn't a zoo!" growled Kly. "We don't let people wander in to gawk!"

"I have gifts for them," insisted the captain, "and I want to make sure that they receive them." A leather-bound box lay by his feet.

"Nobody wants your books and pamphlets! It's my job to see that folks here are left in peace!"

The Leaguers had visited with similar demands before and had always been rebuffed by Kly. According to Sanctuary gossip, the League had been putting pressure on Vyne to fire him. So far, she had apparently defended her foreman, insisting that he was just following her orders. Now the Leaguer captain had turned up in person, presumably to throw more oil on the fire.

Hark could easily guess the Leaguers' real reason for objecting to Kly.

Most islands on the Myriad were a riotous jumble of accents, skin colors, and dress styles. You couldn't always tell where somebody was from straightaway, but sooner or later you usually worked out who was a Myridden and who was from one of the continents. Continenters had funny beliefs, made weird mistakes, didn't know sign language, and got seasick. As far as Hark was concerned, it didn't really matter. It was just something to laugh about. People like the League, however, didn't find the presence of continenters funny at all.

When Hark reluctantly approached, Kly seized upon the distraction and dragged Hark aside by the collar.

"Where the reeking sun have *you* been?" The foreman's face was thunderous. "And why are your trousers soaking wet?"

"I was coming back on time!" Hark protested. "Then . . . I slipped and fell in a rock pool. Knocked myself silly for a bit." He knew he must look bruised and battered and could only hope a story of a fall might cover it.

"Fell in a rock pool?" Kly glared at him. "Do you think I'm stupid?"

Hark swallowed dryly. No, Kly wasn't stupid. He braced himself for the next question. *Have you been in a fight?*

"Is this what happens when I put trust in you?" said Kly fiercely, shaking Hark by the collar. "You decided you could push your luck, didn't you?" He gave Hark a hard cuff about the head.

"Hey!" shouted the captain. "Leave that boy alone! He gave you an explanation!"

Hark bit his lip hard to stop himself swearing. The last thing he needed was the Leaguer captain taking his side.

"This is none of your business!" bristled Kly.

"That's the indentured boy, isn't it?" said the captain. "I am sure Dr. Vyne would not appreciate you battering her property."

Hark flushed and gave Kly a small, anguished grimace. *It's not my fault, I didn't ask him to get involved!* This look wasn't wasted on Kly, who slowly released Hark's collar.

"That's better," said the captain, who clearly thought that he had won a small victory.

"Go and change into some dry clothes," Kly told Hark more quietly, "then help this . . . gentleman . . . carry his 'gifts' back to his boat. Make sure he doesn't accidentally leave them behind."

Hark hastily sprinted into Sanctuary, now unsure whether getting caught in the crossfire had helped or hurt him. At least

Kly didn't seem to have noticed Hark's injuries yet. Maybe they weren't too obvious after all?

As Hark changed his clothes, he quickly examined himself for bruises and was surprised to find no sign of any as yet. The places where Jelt had kicked and hit him didn't feel as tender as he had expected. Remembering the cruel metal prong that had scraped along his back underwater, Hark ran his hand over the place that had stung. His fingertips found only smooth skin, with no trace of a scratch.

He stole a glance at his reflection in a pail of water. He looked pale and shaky, but there was no bruising or swelling on his temple where Jelt had punched him. Apparently he had been lucky. The day's disasters seemed to have left him with no visible injuries to explain.

As Hark had expected, the Leaguer captain's box of books and pamphlets were still outside the Sanctuary entrance when he returned. He was rather more surprised to see that the captain had waited there, too. Hark had thought he might need to chase the captain with the box and physically hurl it onto the man's boat before it left. Instead, the Leaguer offered no objection as Hark picked it up.

"Be careful with that," was all the captain said, before turning and striding off toward the harbor. Hark followed, a pace behind. The Leaguer kept silent until they were a reasonable distance from Sanctuary, then slowed a little so that they were walking side by side.

"Thanks for putting in a word for me," said Hark, trying to sound meek. No doubt the captain was waiting for some show of gratitude.

"He has no right to strike you," said the captain. "He should not be given power over *any* of you."

Ah, there it is . . . As usual, the captain hadn't said what he meant explicitly, but his meaning hung in the air like a smell.

"You are shaking," observed the captain. "Are you afraid of that man? Does he beat you a lot?"

"No," Hark said truthfully. "Not much."

"You do not need to defend him," said the captain. "Loyalty is not a virtue in its own right. Its worth depends on where it is spent."

The captain was a crank, but he seemed to be rich and well-connected. He had influence with Dr. Vyne, too. He was probably a useful man to keep happy and a dangerous man to annoy. If Hark kept defending Kly, he was likely to annoy him fairly quickly.

"Do you love the Myriad?" the captain asked suddenly, with quiet intensity.

Hark had visited only about twenty of the Myriad's thousands of islands. He loved Lady's Crave, though, and the feel of living on the sea road, where the tide brought you songs, spices, and stories from the farthest islands . . .

"Of course I do," he said.

They had begun the last, steep descent toward the harbor. The captain halted, staring out across the water.

"Look at them," he said flatly. "Dozens of them."

"Do you mean the ships?" Hark guessed that the Leaguer wouldn't be staring so grimly at the gulls.

"What do you see out there?" asked the captain.

Hark shielded his eyes from the sun.

"Lots of fishing boats." Grimy and dogged, most of them from Lady's Crave. "Three-masted clippers, the sort that carry tea or orchids or dispatches." Sleek and fleet despite their size, tipping until it seemed they might kiss the waves. "Some big merchant ships." All of them big-bellied with opportunities, excitement, mysteries, luxuries. "That big galleon's from the east continent. It's got a cannon deck, so it's probably bringing timber from the Scathian forests. They always have cannons to protect them against river pirates."

The captain made a muffled sound. It might have sounded like mirth if it had come from somebody else.

"Every year the foreign merchant ships are bigger and carry more cannons," the Leaguer said. "Have you noticed that? Have you ever wondered what would happen if those cannons were aimed at our ports—at us?"

"Why would they do that?" Hark stared aghast at the distant galleon.

"Because whoever controls the Myriad, controls the sea trade routes. At the moment, our ports are getting rich because of that, charging a fortune in taxes and mooring fees from every ship that docks. What happens when one of the continental nations decides that *they* want to control the Myriad instead? We do not even have a navy to defend ourselves! Do you really think peaceful trading vessels are the only boats other nations are building?"

Just for a moment, Hark saw the view as the captain did. He remembered all the great ships jostling in the harbor at his beloved Lady's Crave and imagined cannonballs biting holes out of wooden warehouses and stone facades . . .

"You can say what you like about the gods," the captain said, "but while they were alive, we ruled the waves. Nobody else dared sail these routes. We are acting as though we *still* have that protection, and we do not."

"Well . . . there's nothing we can do about that, is there?" asked Hark, struggling with the idea of the gods as "protective."

"We can be vigilant," said the captain. "Even the lowliest of us can all help to defend the Myriad. We can keep watch over continenters who are welcomed in too easily or who sneak into positions of authority . . ."

Oh. So that's *why he wants to talk to me.*

As soon as he returned to Sanctuary, Hark sought out Kly.

"That Leaguer captain wanted me to spy on you," he told him.

"Hmm." Kly didn't look very surprised. "What did you say?"

"I told him I'd do it," Hark replied promptly. "I just needed to get Dr. Vyne's permission first."

"Did he take that well?" Kly smirked.

"About as well as a cat knocked into a rain barrel. He told me not to trouble her and stormed off."

Kly snickered and ruffled Hark's hair. Evidently Hark was no longer in trouble.

Hark knew he should have tried to keep the captain happy, but the Leaguer's proposal had needled him. He was surprised to find that he *did* feel some loyalty to Kly. Solidarity crept up on you sometimes, when you spent months battling the same chores and challenges side by side. Kly trusted Hark, or at least wanted to trust him.

Hark liked winning Kly's praise and respect. Did that mean he was being tamed and trained, just as Jelt had said?

Loyalty's all that matters, isn't it? Jelt had said. It's all we've got. Don't let them take that away from us.

Jelt was Hark's best friend, more of a brother than any brother. Of course he had the biggest claim on Hark's loyalty, now and always.

If Kly trusts me, he's a fool, Hark told himself firmly, as he stole bandages and medicines from the Sanctuary store.

Chapter 13

THAT NIGHT, HARK SLIPPED SILENTLY OUT OF THE dormitory he shared with the other junior attendants. The Sanctuary doors were locked all night, and the windows were narrow and squinting, but one second-floor window was just wide enough for Hark to wriggle through. He scrambled across the uneven, contorted roof, and then down the wall, finding purchase on the carvings of the facade.

Hark arrived back at the cave while the faint sliver of moon was still hovering above the horizon. He had expected to find Jelt still sprawled on the slab. It was a shock to see his friend's indistinct shape standing in the shadows at the very back of the cave.

"Jelt! Is that you?" For a moment some fuzzy instinct told Hark that it couldn't be Jelt. It was a stain on the wall, one of those tricks of the light that looks like a person but gives itself away by staying too still . . .

"Of course it is!" hissed a familiar voice. "Who were you expecting, the Hidden Lady?"

The dark stain stirred and came forward into the faint starlight, and of course it *was* Jelt. Hark felt a pang of embarrassment. His nocturnal escape had clearly taken its toll on his nerves. Jelt grabbed Hark by the sleeve, his face eager. In fact, he looked almost happy for once.

"Come on!" he hissed. "I've got something to show you!"

Hark let himself be dragged along, boggling at Jelt's miraculous recovery. Jelt led him around the nearest headland, and Hark realized that they were heading to Dunlin's beach.

"Not that way, Jelt!" he whispered. "The beach is claimed!" The last thing he wanted was to have to explain a midnight trespass to an enraged scavenger.

"It's fine, you'll see!" insisted Jelt.

He continued ahead across the beach, heading for the far end, where the squat, gray shape of the scavenger's shack perched up on the black rocks. Hark followed, with increasing unease. As Jelt reached the shack, Hark expected him to call out a greeting or at least knock. Instead, Jelt walked straight up to the wooden door and opened it.

Inside on a little table a lantern gleamed purple, dulling Hark's night sight. The little hut was arranged with the meticulousness of someone with orderly habits and limited room. Nails and hooks had been hammered into every spare inch of the walls, and from them hung tools, tin cups and cooking pots. A worn, rolled-up bed-rug lay in a corner.

There was no sign of Dunlin.

"Where's the man who lives here?" asked Hark.

"He's letting me use this place for a bit," said Jelt, as if this were quite unremarkable. "He had to go away, so I'm keeping an eye on everything for him."

"When's he coming back?" asked Hark, too quickly, too nervously.

Jelt paused and stared at him for a few seconds, his mouth curling into an annoyed smirk.

"Relax," he said. "He won't be strolling in through that door for weeks. Or . . . are you scared that I bashed his head in, or something? Is that what you think?"

"No need to get touchy!" retorted Hark. "I was just asking!"

Defensiveness made his voice a little squeaky. Of course he did not *really* believe that Jelt would murder someone in cold blood, let alone for the use of a hut. However, the thought had slithered across his mind, leaving dank and greasy tracks behind it.

At the same time, the sight of Jelt looking so alert and matter-of-fact was starting to steady his nerves. Hark had risked everything sneaking out for no good reason. He was overwhelmed with annoyance and relief.

"You need to see this," said Jelt. He stood close to the lantern and pulled up his shirt to show his abdomen.

Hark's blood ran cold. The long gash in Jelt's side had closed. There was a grayish ridge where the slit had been. Peering closer, Hark could see that it was made up of tiny, conical bumps, clustering together.

"Limpets," said Jelt. "Hundreds of them." He looked at Hark with hard, bright eyes. "Your godware-ball must have done it."

Hark flinched, not knowing if Jelt was angry or excited. There was a fine line between the two sometimes.

"Better than a hole in your side," he said quickly. "It might be temporary, anyway. Like a scab."

"I can feel it in my lungs as well," Jelt continued. "At first it hurt when I breathed, but now that's stopped. Something is happening. There's a tingle in my chest sometimes. A . . . lot of little pops, like bubbles bulging and bursting." He looked at Hark as if expecting a comment or explanation.

"I don't know what it is," Hark answered. "When I dived down to get you, you looked . . . dead. But then there was a pulse in the water, and you seemed to come alive for a moment. So I scrabbled around and found the thing that was pulsing, and brought it up with you in case it could keep you alive . . ." He trailed off.

"Good thinking," said Jelt, and continued peering at his strange injury.

Hark suppressed a sigh of relief and felt a swell of pride. Jelt was stingy with outright praise, so it meant a lot to actually receive some. It left him unprepared for the backswing.

"So what the scourge happened up at the winch, anyway?" demanded Jelt, fixing Hark with a hard gaze. "How come you dropped me?"

"How come *I* dropped you?" exclaimed Hark, outraged. "Your counterweight fell apart! The safety prop broke, and the chain ran off the reel till you crashed! I told you the winch was old!"

"You didn't say anything about the counterweight," said Jelt steadily.

"I told you the whole thing was a stupid idea! I told you again and again! Everything was old, and there were only two of us, but you wouldn't listen! I didn't 'drop' you, Jelt! I was the one who dived down and pulled you out of that sphere—"

"Yeah, you already told me," Jelt cut in. "You don't have to keep rubbing my nose in it."

Hark's anger ebbed into something more purposeful, almost serene. Jelt's unreasonableness made everything much simpler.

"I'm going," he said. "I'm glad you're fine, Jelt. But I'm going back to Sanctuary now, and I'm not meeting up with you again. I'm finished with this."

"Hey!" Jelt said sharply. "Don't just walk out! You think I'd drag you here if I didn't need your help? Calm down, all right? You're like a snake on a hot rock."

That little word *need* halted Hark, but he stayed by the door to show that he was still leaving.

"What, you think I'm not grateful?" Jelt said. "You want me to grovel a bit, then?"

"I don't know what you are, Jelt," said Hark.

"I've saved your neck a hundred times," said Jelt. "Did I ever go on about it? Did I make you thank me on your knees?"

"No," Hark said reluctantly. Jelt liked to know that you hadn't forgotten such things, but he didn't hammer them home.

"No. Because looking out for each other is what friends do." Jelt seemed to be relaxing again. "Scud o' the winds, Hark, I only asked you what went wrong with the winch. You don't need to freak out and run away, like I'd just accused you of something." A small malicious glint appeared in his eyes. "So you *did* manage to get the hatch open, then? Told you you could if you really wanted to."

Looking out for each other is what friends do.

Guiltily, Hark remembered his strange languor immediately after the bathysphere crashed. For a little while he had simply stood there, letting his friend drown. A true friend would have leaped straight for the helmet and dived into the water. A friend like that might have reached the sphere before Jelt's lungs filled with water, before the godware pulse was necessary, before Jelt was left with strange changes that might affect him for the rest of his life.

A faint pulse surged through the air. Jelt gave a small gasp and grinned slightly. He thumped his chest.

"There it goes again," he said. "Pop-pop-pop-pop."

Hark looked at him, feeling sick. Perhaps Jelt would be ill forever now, one of those wheezing, old-before-their-time men who ended up begging on the quays.

"What did you want, anyway?" Hark asked.

Instead of answering, Jelt levered up a floorboard, reached down into the dark cavity, and hauled out a cloth bag. He peeled back the fabric to reveal the pale godware ball, which looked a bit cleaner than before.

"Look at this thing," Jelt said, almost tenderly. "Crazy, isn't it?

Those holes are sharp, too. You can cut your fingers on them—particularly when everything moves."

As if in response, the ball stirred in Jelt's hand. The whole thing seemed to contract very slightly, before expanding to its usual dimensions again. Hark still couldn't see how it worked. There had to be invisible, overlapping edges, which slid over one another like scales.

"It clenches," said Jelt. He abruptly closed his free hand into a fist, then loosened it again, to illustrate. "Like that. Over and over. Did you ever hear of a bit of godware that *moves by itself*?"

"No." Hark had been wondering about that himself. "It must be some kind of machine. Maybe somebody carved it out of god-bone, and then a submarine crew took it with them out to sea . . ."

It was a sensible conclusion, but even as he voiced it he felt uneasy. The orb's flexing had reminded him of something very different, but he would have felt foolish saying it aloud.

"We need to find out what it is, and how it works." Jelt wrapped it up again and lowered it back through the hole under the floorboard. "That god-ball is healing me, isn't it? Maybe we can heal other people. If we play things right, it could be a nice little earner . . ."

"This is the bathysphere all over again!" erupted Hark, then took a deep breath and braced his will. "If you want to do that, go ahead," he added more calmly. "You can have the god-ball. Do what you like with it."

"I can't do much by myself right now, can I?" retorted Jelt. "I'm still sick some of the time. If I'm away from that god-ball for a while, it . . . gets bad. I can't carry it around with me, either, or people would notice it pulsing. So I have to hide here with it till it's finished healing me.

"Besides, you're the one who can find out about godware, aren't you? You can ask your friends up on the hill! Never mind the money, I'd like to know what that thing's doing to *me*! Is that too much to ask?"

Hark took a deep breath. Until the words came out, he wasn't sure what they would be.

"Yes, Jelt," he heard himself say, firmly and clearly. "Yes. It's too much to ask." Even as Jelt leaped to his feet, Hark yanked open the door and stepped out into the night.

He froze in the doorway and felt Jelt collide with his back.

There were three shadowy figures down on the beach at the base of the rocks, barely ten yards way. Their faces were upturned and staring at the shack. Each held something long and dark at the ready. Light from the hut's lantern glinted on metal blades.

Chapter 14

"RUN!" JELT HISSED, THEN CHARGED PAST HARK into the darkness.

"Grab 'em!" yelled a hoarse female voice from farther down the beach.

Two of the dark figures below moved to intercept Jelt. He barreled right through them, knocking one down, and sprinted off down the beach to the right. The third stranger scrambled up the incline toward Hark, a long knife in one hand.

Hark spun around, ran past the side of the shack and started clambering up the rocky incline behind it. This was the way Hark and Jelt had often dealt with trouble. *Flee and scatter. Run in different directions. Meet up later.*

Hark's night sight was still blotchy. Rocks slid and rolled under his feet. However, he was light and fast and had both his hands free for climbing. Behind him he could hear his pursuer panting and swearing, amid the rattle of dislodged rocks. Hark was outpacing him.

"Don't bother with the runt!" the female voice shouted again. "We've got our thief!"

Hark dared a glance behind him. Sure enough, the man behind him had given up the chase and was slithering back down the rocky slope instead.

Hark's night sight was returning now. He could see the blaze of the stars overhead and the foam of the waves raking the beach, like a chain of white smiles. Down on the beach, he could see three dark figures pinning down a single person, who struggled and swore in a very familiar voice.

They've got him. They've got Jelt.

"Get that knife away from him!" shouted the woman. Her voice was familiar, too, Hark realized. A moment later she strode into view, and the lanternlight from the shack revealed her boxer's build and the freckles that covered her face and shaven head. It was Dotta Rigg, the smuggler from Lady's Crave.

"Now, you little plague-sore!" bellowed Rigg, aiming a kick at Jelt's sprawled shape. "Where the abyss is *my bathysphere?*"

Oh, Jelt. What have you done?

"Rigg!" yelled a panicky voice from near the shack. "Coram's bleeding everywhere! That scum-leech must have slashed his belly open! I can't stop the blood!"

The smuggler leader looked up toward the shack, her face blank with surprise. It looked naked without her usual scowl. She hurried toward the source of the yell, and Hark could see her kneeling beside a prone shape.

"Take this—press it against the wound!" she growled, then turned her head to yell at Jelt again. "You little *slug*! If my boy dies, I'll *flay* you! I'll cut your eyes out! Do you hear me? You'll be fishbait!" Beneath the guttural rage was a hint of panic.

They've all forgotten me, Hark realized. *Nobody cares about me. I could climb this cliff now and go back to Sanctuary. I could leave them all to stew in their own juice.*

Hark clenched his eyes tightly shut and recited several of his favorite swear words. Then he took a deep breath.

"Rigg!" he yelled down to the beach. "We can stop your man dying!"

"What?" The smuggler stared up toward his voice, blinking in the lanternlight. "Is that the runt?"

"I'm coming down!" called Hark. "Just . . . don't cut my head off!" He scrambled and slithered back down the slope. "You need to get him into the hut, so he's near the light! Then me and Jelt can heal him—"

"Shut up, Hark!" yelled Jelt, from under the pile of attackers.

"What the scourge are you talking about?" snarled Rigg.

"I'm telling the truth!" Hark came forward, hands raised to show they were empty. "I'll explain later, but . . . but we have to do this now! Before he dies!" Hark imagined lifeblood gushing out of severed veins with each passing second.

Rigg scowled at the darkening cloth she was clamping to the wounded man's side, then swore.

"All right!" she snapped. "Boys, help me carry Coram into the hut!"

The wounded man was helped into the hut. Hark let himself be grabbed and manhandled in after him. A few moments later, Jelt was dragged in with his hands tied behind his back and dropped onto the boards with a thud.

Coram was youngish and unshaven, with a scrawling of gray scars over his forearms. Even in the muted purple light of the lantern, Hark could see that the whole of the man's belly was dark and glossy with blood. His gaze mirrored Hark's own panic. A familiar mottling of freckles covered Coram's ashen face. *My boy*, Rigg had called him.

Oh, billows' shriek! thought Hark, horrified. *Jelt's gutted one of Rigg's sons.*

"Go on then!" thundered Rigg. "Help him!"

Hark passed her the clean bandages that he had brought for Jelt, then rested his trembling hands on Coram's shoulders. Beneath the boards on which he knelt, the strange god-ball was waiting unseen in its little hammock of net.

Pulse, he begged it in his head, *please pulse! If you play dead now, we'll be playing dead forever!*

"What are you doing?" demanded Rigg. "What's this playacting?"

"We need to concentrate!" insisted Hark. "This . . . this isn't easy!" He couldn't tell her about the healing relic. If he did, she would no longer have any reason to keep Hark and Jelt alive.

Other smugglers were crowding into the doorway, brows furrowed, blinking in the light. He recognized the girl from the Appraisal among them, her large, dark eyes fixed on Coram, as if she thought *she* could heal him by concentrating.

The injured man's breathing was shallow, his face pallid and shiny like wet sand. Hark was afraid that at any moment his breath would hiccup and halt, his eyes fix, and the tide of his life go out, never to return. For a long minute, Hark continued his masquerade of concentration, hearing the floorboards creak as the smugglers fidgeted and grew impatient.

Then the pulse came, sending its invisible shock through the air. Hark felt it shudder in his core. Coram twitched and gasped, his eyes opening wide for a moment. The other smugglers flinched and reached for weapons.

"What the purple deep was *that*?" demanded Rigg.

"It came from us!" squeaked Hark, his throat tight with relief. "That . . . was a flood of healing. We had an accident, and . . . now we're not the same as we used to be." Hark had been forging a story in his head. Now he just needed to sell it.

"What kind of accident causes *that*?" asked Rigg.

"We tried to use your bathysphere—" began Hark.

"Hark, *shut up*! Right now!" growled Jelt.

"She knows we had it, Jelt!" Hark interrupted. "She's not stupid!" He exhaled bitterly. "We borrowed an old winch-boat and took the sphere out over the Embrace. We had some smart idea about using it to spot wrecks and selling the information to salvage crews.

"Jelt went down in the sphere. I watched the chain lower it . . . but then something happened. The weight on the end got heavier all of a sudden, and I couldn't haul it back up, and I realized it must have filled with water."

This was a plausible bundle of half-truths. Now for the big lie.

"I dived down to pull Jelt out—"

"I was already pulling myself out," growled Jelt.

"Yes—I know you were." Hark felt a throb of relief and gratitude for Jelt's interjection. His belligerent tone gave the tale a convincing roughness. "But then there was this . . . wave. We saw it coming out of the murk, a great, black, glossy wave of Undersea, rearing up into the normal sea like a tidal wave. It must have been twice as high as the cliffs here—more maybe. And it came at us, fast as a clipper in full sail."

"I never heard of an Undersea wave that near the surface," said Rigg, surly and unconvinced.

"Undersea eats rules like shark eats fish," recited Jelt grimly. It was the old saying. The gods and the Undersea were bound by no rules. All you could do was hope to survive them.

In truth, Hark doubted that *anybody* had heard of such an occurrence. The surface of the Undersea rose and fell in strange and unpredictable ways, and there were tales of great waves, but none mountainous enough to hit someone who had swum down from the surface.

"I never saw anything like it, either," he went on quickly, "and I hope I never do again. Huge. Slick like oil. All the fish were fleeing it, fast as darts, rushing past us on either side! But there was nothing we could do to escape. It caught us."

Hark tried to remember Quest's descriptions of the Undersea. Weird details made a story seem more real.

"It hit us, and we plunged into it. It was . . . dark inside, a purplish darkness, but light at the same time. It made my eyes hurt. And it was cold, in a way that made your soul shiver. There was other stuff whirling about in that wave—loose weed, bits of timber, crab shells, all tumbling and spinning in the darkness.

"Then it passed on, and we were back in good, salt water. Just drowning in the normal way, instead of whirling forever inside that wave. So we swam back up. But we weren't the same anymore. We were . . . Marked."

"Marked?" Rigg stared at him, her eyebrows rising in superstitious unease. "So quickly?"

"I don't understand it either!" Hark looked wide-eyed. "It feels like there's a tide in our blood now. If we concentrate on it, we can change how it flows. And if we get the flow just right . . . we can heal people."

As if on cue, another pulse shivered the air of the hut. Two minutes later, the hidden relic pulsed again. Hark had no way of knowing if it was really helping, but at least Coram was still breathing, his eyes turning glossily to stare this way and that.

Ten pulses later, the smuggler staunching the wound cleared his throat uncertainly.

"The bleeding's stopped."

"You're sure?" asked Rigg suspiciously.

"Yeah. Whatever they did, it closed the wound."

There was a long silence. Coram's expression of alarm dimmed into a look of exhaustion and pain. The other smugglers all looked at Rigg.

"You two," she said, "are the luckiest little weevils that ever lived. You should be rolling around the deep, feeding fish, and instead look at you . . ." She tailed off, shook her head, and then frowned. "So, where *is* my bathysphere, then?"

"Ah. It . . . got swept away by that great wave." Hark swallowed, feeling the atmosphere become arctic again.

"We can pay you back for it," Jelt said suddenly. "I've got a business proposition. Sit me up, will you? It's hard to talk with a mouthful of someone's knee."

Rigg gave a nod, and Jelt was heaved up into a sitting position. He was looking more like his confident, brash self now.

"Better," he said. "I was thinking . . . people will pay for healing, won't they? Wounds sealed up tight, no stitches, no questions asked. Hark and me, we could use a partner. Someone to bring us customers. You'd get your share of the fees. And we'd heal your people for free."

Rigg frowned and nodded to herself very slightly. Hark couldn't tell if she was agreeing or just taking in his words. However, she wasn't decapitating anyone, which he took as a good sign.

"We could just keep 'em both in a cave," suggested a smuggler.

"We can't keep the runt," answered Rigg. "He's indentured to Sanctuary, remember? If he goes missing, there will be a search. The governor might even start poking around. No, the little whelp needs to go home before he's missed."

For a moment, Hark was surprised that Rigg knew he was indentured to Sanctuary. Then he remembered the presence of the freckled girl during his Appraisal. She would have been able to tell the gang who had bought him. An uncomfortable suspicion started to form in his mind. Perhaps the gang had been keeping an eye on Hark, in the hope that he would lead them to Jelt. Perhaps tonight he had done exactly that.

"All right, bright boy." Rigg stared down at Jelt. "Come with

us, so we can talk about this proposition of yours. As for you"—
she turned to Hark—"you can run home for now, but don't
get any funny ideas. You're fond of your friend, right? You'd
probably like him to keep his face. So you'll keep your mouth
shut, and you'll come back here when we tell you."

"Yes, ma'am," Hark said quickly, trying to ignore the numb
ache in his mind. His past was spilling into his future, his hopes
and dreams quietly dying.

After the Sanctuary boy had gone, Rigg's gang argued late into
the night. The freckled girl was the most forceful opponent to
her mother's new plan, but others objected, too. Most of the
crew had been looking forward to going home to Lady's Crave
and didn't like the idea of a temporary base near Nest.

Why were they going into business with somebody who had
betrayed them? And why did they need a base, anyway? It would
make them easier to find!

When tiny, glutinous tendrils were found embedded in
Coram's long, sealed wound, protests became more determined, and the freckled girl thought she had carried her point.
Then someone noticed that Coram's clipped ears had also been
healed. The crew's mutters became approving and speculative.
Some in the gang already had two notches cut out of their ears
by the governor's men, and a couple were triple-clipped and in
continual danger of the gallows. Healing these notches could
remove the threat hanging over them.

I don't like this healing! Rigg's daughter argued, over and
over. *There's something wrong with it!*

"It just came with Marks, Selphin," said Coram, reaching up
weakly to ruffle his half-sister's hair. "Anyway, I *like* my scar.
It's . . . special. Those two boys, with their healing—they're
special, too. The way they were Marked, that great Undersea

wave . . . I think it's a sign. A blessing." Something about his entranced, lethargic smile made her blood run cold.

Since Selphin's birth, her half-brother had been there, bear-like, protective, and big enough to pick her up. When she let him hug her, it felt like being enveloped by a mountain.

He was six years older than her, but sometimes she was very aware that she was cleverer than him.

Chapter 15

"WHAT IS EATING AT YOU?" QUEST ASKED THE next morning. The question caught Hark by surprise.

"I slept badly last night." This was true enough. After sneaking back into Sanctuary, Hark had managed only three hours' sleep. He had compensated by being relentlessly chipper. This had apparently fooled everyone but Quest.

"You have not been yourself for several days," the old priest said quietly, as Hark emptied the replenishing bucket of hot water into his bath.

The old ritual baths were rocky, rough-hewn pools, all in the same high-vaulted hall. Once, these had been used by the priests to cleanse themselves after a descent into the Undersea, so as to avoid Marks. Now most of them, including the one in which Quest sat, were used for medicinal purposes.

One solitary pool at the far end held darker water, which slipped and slopped in an oily fashion. This was an Undersea water bath, for those priests who now wanted to keep their Marks, not cleanse them away. *They lost their gods*, Kly had explained, *so the Marks are all they've got left.*

Quest had been suffering pains in his chest, so he was reclining in a one-person pool of warm, chalky, fresh water that looked a bit like frothed milk. His head and angular neck jutted out of the bath, looking unusually ruddy, his hair damp and disheveled. It made Hark realize how dignified Quest usually appeared. Hark felt uncomfortable seeing him so vulnerable.

"Are you still feeling trapped here?" asked Quest, looking genuinely concerned. "I hope you are not thinking of running away?"

"There's nowhere to run." Hark felt his smile wobble. He needed to seem normal, but he was unexpectedly grateful to Quest for seeing through his act. It made him feel slightly less alone. "I'm . . . on a tightrope all the time. I can't put a foot wrong, I can't see my old friends, or Dr. Vyne will sell me to the galleys." He was sailing as close to the truth as he dared. It was a relief to say even this much.

"You miss your friends," said Quest gently.

"I'm worried about one friend of mine," admitted Hark. "He might be in trouble without me." He had been trying not to think about what Rigg would do to Jelt if Coram died after all. Worse still, the healing relic was still hidden under Dunlin's hut. If the smugglers dragged Jelt away, could he survive without its healing pulses?

"He needs your guidance?" asked Quest, and Hark could not help laughing out loud.

"He never listens to it," he muttered.

"Then you probably could not help him anyway," suggested Quest. "Has this friend tried to contact you recently?"

Too close, too close to the wind. Hark could have kicked himself for saying so much.

"Nest is the end of the world." Hark dodged the question. "Who would come here?"

"It is the relic of a world that has ended," Quest agreed wryly. "That much is true."

The word "relic" brought Hark's mind full circle, back to the pale god-ball under Dunlin's shack.

"Quest," Hark asked slowly, "did you ever hear of a relic that . . . moved?"

"Moved?" Quest's brow furrowed deeply.

"Someone once told me they'd seen something like that," Hark added, trying to sound unconcerned. "He said it clenched and sent out an . . . invisible ripple."

"When and where did your friend see this?" asked Quest, his frown now quite alarming.

"It was years ago!" Hark improvised. "I don't remember!"

"A shame," Quest said grimly. "I would like to know who has the object now. Should you ever find out, I do hope you will tell me, Hark."

Hark was taken aback by the intensity of Quest's interest. Perhaps the priest *had* heard of such a relic before. Although Hark didn't like to think about it, he knew that Quest's health was failing. It would be natural for a sick man to want to track down healing godware.

"Do you know what it might be?" Hark asked, trying not to sound too eager.

"I have a suspicion," said Quest.

Hark waited for him to explain and then realized that the old man had no intention of doing so. Quest often retreated into maddening reticence when the conversation strayed into sensitive territory. Hark vented his frustration in a sigh.

"Sometimes I think you're playing games with me," he said, letting his tone sound sulky. "Throwing out hints like bait to get me curious, then laughing at me when I bite."

"Perhaps I do." Quest rubbed at the tiny flecks of gray stubble on his reddened cheeks. "At my age, there are few greater fears than discovering that one has become dull."

Hark got up and took down one of the cloths that hung from a hook. The walls were always clammy with condensation and grew moldy if left unattended. But for now, scrubbing the wall was an excuse to look away and let the pause lengthen. Yes, he could let himself seem bratty and offended and leave it up to Quest whether to break the silence.

I am young and easily bored. Perhaps I will get tired of talking to you altogether.

After a while, he heard Quest sigh sadly.

"I can give you your answer and a story," said Quest, "but I think it is your turn first."

Hark racked his brains in search of a good story, but they were swamped with his worries. All the memories that rose to mind were full of Jelt. Growing up with Jelt, Jelt's fist in his cheek, Jelt unbreathing on the wet rock, Jelt with a smuggler's knife to his throat . . .

"I can't think of any," he said helplessly.

"What is the worst thing you have ever done?"

It was a brutal question, an unfair question, but the sheer weight of it made Hark realize that he was asking Quest for no ordinary secret. *This* was what Quest felt was an equal trade. If Hark made something up, he suspected that Quest would notice. Their conversations would end forever, and Hark would have lost something important.

What's the worst thing I ever did?

Hark's mind flashed back to the bright air over the water at the Strides, the chain hissing off the wooden reel of the winch, then the infinite peace afterward, the cool of the puddles against his feet as he stood there, and stood there . . .

"Nothing," he said.

A moment later, he cursed himself for blurting it out. Did Quest think that he meant he had never done anything wrong? How childish that would have sounded!

Quest did not mock or protest, however. He waited silently for Hark to continue.

"Something happened," Hark said numbly. "Somebody needed my help, and I did nothing. I don't know why. They got hurt. Badly hurt. I go back to that moment, over and over. I don't know what was wrong with me."

"Did they survive?" asked Quest quietly.

Hark's cloth had paused on the wall. He didn't trust himself to face Quest.

"Yes," he muttered.

"If nobody died, then most other things can be mended in time. Sometimes they are not quite the same as they were before they were broken, but nothing and nobody stays unchanged, anyway."

Hark knew that the words were meant to be comforting.

If nobody died . . .

Now Hark could not help thinking of another time when he had done nothing. It was the night he tried not to remember and could never ask Jelt about.

On a pitch-black night a year before, Hark and Jelt had crept down the mudflats on Rattleguise. The flats had dips in them, like valleys, and after a wild storm these became pools, jumping with cod and eels. The friends knew the local scavenger gang would be hauling out the fish with nets and leaving them in big barrels before moving to the next pool. Jelt's plan was to sneak down with buckets and scoop fish out of unattended barrels.

Hark had stood lookout, ready to whistle if he saw the scavenger gang's lanterns return. Then Hark had heard a cry echoing from farther down the mudflat. A solitary sound like a seabird.

Hark had stood there where he had been told to wait, feeling a fine, cold mist of rain on his face. He stood there knowing that the cry had been human and that it had been cut short. Hark had done . . . nothing. He had waited until Jelt ran up out of breath with no buckets and a glare like fury.

"Sometimes," Hark said, wiping his cloth in vague, slow circles, "sometimes you tell yourself there's nothing you can do. Maybe there's nothing anybody can do. And maybe there's nothing wrong, anyway. But if you asked—if you ever asked—then you'd know. So you never, ever ask."

One of the other islanders had gone missing that night. Not a scavenger gang enforcer, or a smuggler, or one of the governor's men. Just a fisherman walking home from the tavern across the flats.

Perhaps the sea took him, perhaps a scavenger gang killed him, perhaps he took a job on a merchantship . . .

And Hark would never know, because he could never, ever ask Jelt.

"Sorry," muttered Hark. He stopped pretending to wipe the wall. "'Nothing' doesn't make much of a story, does it? I'll come back when I've got a better one." He turned to leave, wanting to get away from the conversation so that he could push those memories down, down, out of the way where they belonged.

"Wait," said Quest, and Hark halted in his tracks. "Better a poor story than a false one. Bring that stool over—you don't want to sit on the wet rock." He waited while Hark brought over the small wooden stool and settled himself next to the pool.

Quest frowned into the cloudy water, as though his words needed to be marshaled through intimidation.

"The gods were not as we are," he said at last. "They did not have brains or lungs. Many did not even have bones. But all of them had a core, somewhere within them, that held their life. It sent out a tremor through the waters, one that could be felt even before the god was seen."

"Their life . . ." Hark felt his shadowy suspicions coalesce into solid form. From the very start, the god-ball had reminded him of something, but until now he had pushed away the idea as wild and fanciful.

"I will tell you the story the Hidden Lady murmured to me in the deeps," Quest continued. "It was told in confidence, but perhaps she would understand.

"Did you ever hear of a god named the Swallower?" Quest seemed unsurprised when Hark shook his head. "No, I had not heard of him either until the Lady told me of him. He had other names—Devour-all, Father Gullet, Custodian of the Great Purse. But Swallower was his best-known name, and in his day, Swallowsbay was named after him.

"The Swallower was, the Lady said, a thing of unending hunger and infinite bitterness. His body was like a black knife but longer than a galleon. His fins were ragged black leather. His narrow tail was forked, each tapering tip adorned by a gleaming green-blue light.

"Half of his body was jaw. His great belly was supple as black silk. When he had not fed for a long time, his belly would be wrinkled and folded under him, like a bound-up sail. When he stretched his mouth and swallowed with that vast jaw, the stomach stretched and stretched to a colossal size and hung beneath the lean, knife-like body. As the Swallower zigzagged through the sea, its great, stretched belly swung and swayed under it. Through the translucent skin one could see the crushed shapes of swallowed galleons and frigates and even the faces of perishing sailors pressed against the terrible membrane.

"Around Swallowsbay, the ships came and went above him. He saw the eyes painted on their underside, the same pleading eyes that the soft, skin-clad drowners wore when they came down to him with their lungs full of water. He knew those painted eyes meant fear, submission, worship. It meant that the flimsy things in their wooden vessel were his and knew it. For the most part, he would not swallow them if they kept to the routes he permitted them. Of course, he changed the allowed routes now and then and dragged ships to the bottom when they broke the new rules.

"One day, a boat was driven off course by a storm and broke the rules. Instead of trying to turn back, the sailors panicked and fled toward the open ocean. The Swallower pursued them to devour them, leaving his usual territories behind.

"The ship soon found itself in turbulent waters. A great whirlpool dragged the ship down, as though the very depths were drawing breath.

"As the ship plummeted, leaving a trail of drowning sailors behind it, the Swallower pursued, because it was his. The light went out of the water as he dived. If it had not been for the Swallower's great eyes of black glass and the radiance of his taillight, he would have been swimming blind. As it was, he could just see the glimmer of the ship's pale sails.

"Then, in the darkness and the deeps, the Swallower came upon the Gathergeist."

Quest hesitated and gave Hark a quick, wry glance.

"You know *that* name at least," he said, and Hark nodded.

"It had no name in those days. No human eyes had ever seen it, nor godly eyes, either, perhaps. It drifted unsuspected for many years, in the depths beneath those fretful waters. Shipwrecks floated down to it, so it had not needed to hunt. It had simply hung there in the water. Waiting. Growing."

Hark knew of the Gathergeist from paintings and stories. It had been a tangle of long, translucent chains that slowly swayed and swirled and glimmered. Its luminous tendrils had trailed for miles, and its song had been sweet and terrible.

"Is it true it had no head?" he asked. It was the thing that bothered him the most about it. You could watch something's head to see what it was thinking, even if it had a *weird* head. That was the part that watched you back, and might listen if you were lucky.

"Yes," said Quest. "No head. No body. Only the chains. Once the Swallower and the Gathergeist had discovered each other, it was too late. Their fight was inevitable. You see, they had sensed the throb of each other's life."

Hark remembered how strong the god-ball's pulse had been underwater. He imagined the two vast monsters circling each other in the abyss, feeling each jolting tremor sent out by the other.

"From that moment," said the priest, "they could not bear each other's existence. They were gripped by a madness and could think only of the other's destruction.

"Of the two, the fastest was the Swallower. While the Gathergeist swirled and drifted, slowly pulling in its coils to deal with the threat, the Swallower darted forward, trailing his bulbous stomach. He bit through the nearest chain as easily as if it were jelly. The viscous ooze covering it tasted of poison but did not affect him.

"The Gathergeist convulsed slowly, and the Swallower attacked again, thinking that he would take his enemy apart, one tendril at a time. This time, however, the Gathergeist changed its song, and its glassy tendrils became cold and hard. The Swallower's jaw was mighty, though, and the chain splintered under the force of his bite.

"Still the thing of many chains lived. Growing impatient, the Swallower plunged forward toward the center of the writhing, glowing mass that was his enemy. All his ancient instincts told him that if he delved into the middle, he would find the Gathergeist's core. But he could not see it. There was no trunk or body, only the long snaking chains, forking and arcing and entangling, and nothing, nothing else. Where did this strange creature keep its life?

"As he hesitated, all of the Gathergeist's lights suddenly went out, leaving the Swallower alone in the deep blue-black. Somewhere in that blackness, the Gathergeist's coils still floated, but now softly and silently, and the Swallower did not know where they were. He tried to flick his twin tails to bring his own lights to bear, but something clammy entangled them. Only the faintest glassy glint now and then showed him his foe's sinuous, trailing form.

"The Swallower lunged again, and once more his jaw closed upon his enemy's tendrils. This time, however, a bundle of thick coils had been offered to his bite. Though he felt them crack and buckle, he could not fully snap his jaw shut. As he struggled to bite down, more and more of the chains forced their way into his mouth, wrenching it further open. He beat his fins of ragged leather, but more soft, clinging tendrils draped over him, gluing themselves to his black scales.

"There are no days in the deep, nor nights, either, so nobody can say how long the Swallower struggled while the Gathergeist surged farther and farther into his maw. Up in the land of light, the sun may have skipped on its giddy orbit many times before the Swallower's jaw joints finally cracked.

"The Gathergeist then oozed into the Swallower at its leisure and began hollowing him. From inside his vast, translucent stomach, it patiently burrowed upward into his flesh. It had felt the tremor of his core, so it dug until it found it and broke it. Then there was no Swallower, only the Gathergeist.

"After it had slowly consumed him, it changed. It no longer wanted to stay in its cautiously chosen feeding territory. Instead, it thought only of the islands and the flimsy, skin-clad things with hopeless eyes waiting to look on it with fear and love. So it changed the direction of its drift and moved slowly, relentlessly, from the black, to the blue-black, to the blue-gray, to the green. For the first time, men saw it and heard its song, and it took its place in the gallery of human nightmares . . ."

The old man stirred his hand through the water. Beneath the milky surface, it looked misshapen, blurry. Only after a long silence did Hark realize that the story was over.

"Where *did* the Gathergeist keep its life?" Hark asked.

"In one of its tendrils. Given time, the Swallower would probably have found it, so the Gathergeist did not give him time."

Hark was struck by another puzzle.

"How did the Hidden Lady know all this? She wasn't there, was she?"

"No, she was not," Quest said, sounding unusually tired. "But I hope you do not expect me to unravel *all* the sea's mysteries in one afternoon."

"Sorry," Hark said, and meant it. He had been so caught up in the tale that he had not noticed how drained and pale the old man was looking. "Thank you for the story."

Hark went back to scrubbing the wall, barely able to digest what he had just learned. His wildest suspicions were true. He knew now what the relic was, and why it pulsed.

It was the heart of a god, and it was beating.

Chapter 16

THE NEXT MORNING, HARK SET OFF FOR HIS "foraging" errand even earlier than usual. Rigg's people would be waiting for him on the beach at dawn, but he wanted to get there before they did.

When Hark reached Dunlin's beach, there was no sign of anyone around. He clambered quickly up the rocks to the shack and pushed open the door.

Even in the predawn dimness, he could see that the scavenger's possessions and tools were still there. In Lady's Crave, most of them would have gone missing as soon as people heard that the shack was unattended. The absence of the scavenger still bothered Hark, but perhaps Jelt had just bullied him into leaving and claiming another beach instead. Hark could imagine that happening.

Hark closed the door, pried up the loose floorboard, and reached down through the gap. To his relief, his fingers closed around a familiar, rounded shape, still hammocked in its netting. He pulled it out, staring with new fascination at its perforated surface.

The heart of a god . . .

A sudden sound made Hark jump, but it was only the rattle of a tumbling rock, somewhere behind the hut. The door did not open. He exhaled, then tucked the ball into a cloth bag he had brought with him and covered it with some rolls of bandages.

Hark opened the door of the shack and stopped dead. Down on the beach stood the freckled girl from Rigg's gang, staring right back at him. She watched him as he clambered down the rocks to the beach.

By daylight, and at close proximity, the resemblance to Rigg was even clearer. Apart from the wind-browned freckles that covered her face and arms, her strongly defined brows and angular fierceness reminded him of the smuggler captain. The girl was, however, a good four inches shorter than Hark was.

Have you come to collect me? he signed. He had seen her using sign language the night before. Remembering the way she had watched him during the Appraisal, he was fairly sure that she could lip-read, too, but signs seemed better given the dim light.

The sub will be here soon, she answered. *But I wanted to talk to you first.* She continued staring at him with her large dark eyes, making him feel self-conscious.

Hark noticed some oddities. The girl's brown hair was long enough to tie back in a knot, a style more often worn by those whose diving days were done. Folks who spent time underwater usually had their hair hacked short or shaven. Stray hairs sometimes got caught in the edges of masks and helmets, breaking the seal and letting water leak in. If you free-dived, long hair would swirl around your face and get in your eyes.

Hark was self-conscious about his own hair's three months of growth, since it made him feel fleeced and landlocked, like a continenter. This girl, however, had made the length of her hair obvious. Her oddly mature hairstyle made her look young-old and a bit otherworldly.

What did you do to Coram? she demanded.

He's alive, isn't he? asked Hark.

He's got jellyfish bits coming out of his scar, the girl commented darkly.

That won't harm him, Hark insisted, hoping it was true.

It better not, she replied. *Nobody hurts my crew. Remember that.*

That appeared to be the end of the conversation.

At dawn, Hark saw the pitch-varnished back of a submarine emerged from the water. It was a timber-and-leather ten-footer lightly built for shallow depths, its four oars drooping slack in their leather collars. A small stealth "skimmer" like this was no good for deep dives, but handy enough if you wanted to cruise just below the surface and dodge the eyes of the customs men.

The hatch of the stubby turret opened, and Coram put out his head. He looked flushed and sweaty, but a lot less deathly than the night before.

"Climb over the rocks and get in!" he shouted. "Leave the basket on the beach. Selphin there will do your foraging for you. We'll have you back here in two hours."

There was little room in the dark, confined belly of the sub, and only two seats for the rowers, so Hark had to squeeze himself under the map table. He tried not to bump against the nearby rack of round copper bottles. These contained compressed air, and nudging their tops loose prematurely could result in them flying around with bruising force. Such bottles had also been known to explode when punctured.

Coram pulled down the hatch, cutting out the daylight from above. Now there was only light from the portholes and the two murky, purple scare-lanterns hanging from the ceiling. The air smelled of pitch, sweat, hot breath, and the low-grade god-glue used to waterproof the leather.

"Where are we going?" asked Hark.

"Wildman's Hammer," answered Coram. "Not far." His square, stolid face was hard to read. He seemed neither friendly nor unfriendly.

Well, did I expect him to be grateful? We healed him, but we stabbed him first.

"Ready?" asked Coram's crewmate. He was already seated at one set of oars, his face red with perspiration, his hair limp. The oar-handles extended out through the walls of the cabin, via leather collars dripping with pitch.

Coram creaked his way across the wooden flooring and turned a handle to revolve a long timber that stretched across the sub. The long pigskin bladders fastened to it bulged as sea-water from outside the sub flooded into them. The skimmer began to descend.

The crash of the waves grew more indistinct. The leather walls bulged gently inward and became taut as the water pressure increased.

Coram took his seat at the oars, and both smugglers began rowing hard. They had been doing so for several minutes when the relic hidden in Hark's bag sent a pulse through the sub. The two smugglers flinched and swore.

"What was *that*?" Coram stared at Hark.

"It's only a blast of healing power!" Hark yelled from under the table. "It won't do any harm! I can't control it, though, unless my friend's helping."

After some muttering, the two smugglers continued rowing. They watched the great compass above the map table and kept up a whispered song to keep track of strokes. However, sometimes Hark noticed Coram looking at him, as though trying to bring him into focus.

They had been traveling for only a quarter of an hour when Coram manned the scope and began calling directions to his crewmate. Then the long timber was revolved again to empty the pig bladders and raise the sub. The turret hatch was opened, letting in daylight and sweet air.

When Hark put his head up through the hatch, he found that the sub had settled in a very small, sheltered inlet, next to a couple of rowing boats and a larger submersible. A cloud of gannets wheeled about the low red cliffs and quiet red beach.

Beyond a narrow corridor of sea, he recognized the eastern shoreline of Nest. He realized he must be on a little isle he had seen from the hilltops, crescent-shaped and barely a hundred feet across. Apparently this was Wildman's Hammer.

On the shore, Rigg and Jelt stood waiting. Jelt looked ill and gray-faced, but at least he was alive. To Hark's surprise, Jelt was also rather better dressed than before, in decent boots and a coat without patches.

Hark was hauled out of the sub, and after a slithery scramble down a gangplank, he found himself hobbling up the slick rocks.

"Come on, brats, your patients are waiting!" said Rigg, nodding toward a huddle of figures at the far end of the beach. She seemed to be in rather a good mood. "There's only four of them today, but we'll see more when word gets out about *this*." She reached out and tweaked at Coram's right ear. "Mind you, next time don't do any extra healing without our say-so. I'll let it go this time, but no more surprises."

The upper curl of Coram's ear was flawless, apart from two very faint, pale streaks. Hark began to understand. Coram's ear had been clipped in two places, and now it wasn't.

"Who are the patients?" Hark peered at the distant figures.

"The one with the bandaged arm is one of Skeeler's boys—they're spice-runners based on Drymouth. We're doing some jobs with Skeeler, so we said we'd stop his man dying."

"What's wrong with him?" asked Hark, alarmed.

"Nasty accident," Rigg said, deadpan, "involving somebody else's sword. Now the wound's poisoning his blood. The fever's already taken hold."

Once again, Hark and Jelt had to save a dying patient. Hark didn't fancy their prospects if they failed.

"The one with the walking stick is a fixer who got his leg crushed years ago in a rockslide," Rigg continued. "He's willing to pay well to get his knee untwisted. The other two are crew of mine. They're not injured, but their ears are triple-clipped. If either of them get seen in the wrong place, they'll be hanged. Get rid of those notches, and you take that noose from around their necks."

"Healing those four clears the debt, does it?" Hark asked, but without much hope.

"You're a very funny lad," said Rigg, without a hint of mirth. "You two stole a *godware bathysphere* from us. It was worth a fortune. When you boys have earned us a fortune in return, then you'll start getting your cut of the fees."

"Don't worry, Hark," said Jelt. "It's all sorted out. Rigg and me shook on it. We'll clear the debt in a year, you'll see."

A year. Jelt wanted Hark to keep sneaking away to heal strangers for a year. How could he manage that without Vyne finding out? He was clever, but he wasn't invisible.

"You boys ready?" asked Rigg.

"We need some time alone in our healing cave first," said Jelt, with his usual blunt confidence.

"Yeah—to let our spirits flow together," Hark agreed quickly.

"You can have five minutes."

Jelt led Hark away down a gap between two huge crags. It formed a natural corridor, with high rocky walls on either side and the sky above. At the end, Jelt tugged aside a sackcloth curtain and beckoned Hark into a small cave.

"Tell me you brought it!" whispered Jelt, once they were concealed by the curtain. Hark nodded, and Jelt's face went slack with relief. "Give it to me!"

Hark took the relic out of his cloth bag and passed it to Jelt. As it changed hands, a throb went through the air, and Jelt physically twitched and let out a long breath, as though he were lowering himself into water on a hot day.

"Jelt," whispered Hark, "I think I know what this is." He peeped quickly through the curtain to make sure nobody was nearby. "It's the heart of a god. And . . . it's alive."

Jelt gaped at him for a few seconds, then snorted with laughter.

"I'm serious!"

"I know! That's why it's so funny. It's not a god's heart, Hark! Look at it! It's too small!"

"Maybe it was a little god!" Hark felt stupid, but even Jelt's mockery couldn't shatter his certainty.

"It's ali-i-ive!" Jelt waggled the relic in Hark's face. "Hark, it's a godware machine, that's all." He tapped a fingernail against its surface. "Dead bone."

Nonetheless, Jelt continued staring at the relic and turning it over in his hands. He had always been hardheaded when it came to godware, teasing Hark for his dreamy-eyed love of the gods' legends. It was unusual to see him hypnotized by anything but the promise of wealth.

"It does make a better story if it's the heart of a god, though, doesn't it?" Jelt murmured. "Wouldn't that be something?"

Chapter 17

THE FIRST PATIENT TO PULL ASIDE THE CURTAIN was the man with the bandaged arm. He gave a little yelp of shock at discovering Hark standing stock-still two feet from him, sallowly illuminated by the solitary whale-oil lamp. The man's jowly face wobbled nervously as he stared at Hark's ominous mask of gray rags.

Despite himself, Hark felt a rush of excitement. He wasn't some runty little chancer right now; he was a mysterious being with arcane powers. Hark was only wearing the mask to avoid being recognized, since he couldn't risk rumors reaching Dr. Vyne. Now he saw the visitor hypnotized by the gray, shapeless shell of a face, barely noticing the human eyes behind it.

Everybody in the Myriad knew in their gut that true power could only come from something twisted. If Hark and Jelt were soothing or friendly, nobody would believe in their healing for a moment. The two of them needed to be frightening. Uncanny. Frecht, like the old gods.

Hark carefully pulled back the stranger's bandages, trying not to wince at the sight of the dark, oozing mess underneath.

"Was this hurt taken in the darkness or the light?" he asked, in a soft, sibilant whisper. He suspected his ordinary voice would sound too young to impress.

"What does that matter?" asked the patient in confusion.

"Night air is more poisonous." Hark was sure he'd heard that somewhere.

"Draw closer," Jelt demanded coldly, from the shadows at the back of the cave. Arrogance and menace came naturally to him.

As the patient approached unwillingly, a pulse issued from the god-heart hidden under Jelt's tunic. The patient flinched and cried out.

"We're making your bones talk to us," Hark whispered, the rags of his mask tickling the man's ear.

"And your blood," said Jelt.

"There's too much night in your blood," said Hark. "If we don't work fast, you'll die. Stay as still as you can. We need to put moon into you, to flush you out."

"If it hurts, don't scream," said Jelt.

In the stranger's frightened eyes, hope slowly dawned. The promises of peril reassured him.

Now and then, the hidden god-heart beat. Hark watched each change with nauseated fascination. The edges of the wound bulged with pearly blisters. The blisters spread like pale, molten wax, which then inched inward over the raw flesh. By the time the wound finally closed, the patient was looking less feverish.

The man turned over his arm, looking uncertainly at the faint, pearly sheen of the new skin. Then he frowned, opened his hand and stared at it.

"What . . . ?" he asked, holding out his hand toward Hark. Scattered across the palm and fingers were five small, yellow-ish discs, looking at first glance like calluses. As the translucent ovals flexed slightly, Hark realized that they were suckers, like those found on octopus tentacles.

Oh, scud o' the winds, he thought.

"You'll find out in the future why you have been given these," he hissed, trying to hide his disquiet.

"For now," said Jelt, "it'll be a reminder of the day your life was saved."

"Storms!" Hark muttered, once the patient had tottered away. He had wondered what the god-heart considered a problem to be fixed. Apparently "Not enough squid-suckers" was on the list.

"What are you upset about?" asked Jelt. "That went fine, didn't it? The rest will be even easier."

To Hark's frustrated relief, Jelt was right.

The straightening of the maimed leg went well but was painful to watch. Each pulse from the relic caused unnerving bulges and shifts under the skin of the knee. By the end the leg was straight, and the fixer could walk without his cane. Whatever subtle engine of bone now lay beneath the flesh looked and behaved a lot like a knee.

The clipped ears healed smoothly, with only faint traces of scar tissue. Hark could only hope that no exciting side effects would be discovered later.

"That was a good morning's work," said Rigg, as she walked Hark back to the sub. "Very good." Despite her words, she sounded preoccupied. Hark and Jelt waited while she chewed at the inside of her cheek, as if the words she wanted to spit out were sour-tasting. "Tell me, do you only patch up bodies?"

"We can't fix holes in a sub, or mend clothing, if that's what you're asking," said Hark. As far as he knew, this was true.

"I'm not talking about *things*!" Rigg said impatiently. "I mean what's inside people's heads. Sometimes people's heads go a bit wrong. Not a *lot* wrong, just a bit. Can you fix that?"

"So it's a crazy person?" Jelt asked with his usual bluntness. "One of yours, is it?"

"I didn't say crazy!" Rigg glared at him. "And don't you say it either!" She let out her breath through her teeth. "It's my daughter Selphin. She's a good girl, good crew apart from this—one of my best lookouts. I just want to sort her out!"

Hark recognized the name at once. Coram had called the freckled girl on the beach Selphin.

"She never had a problem when she was little," Rigg continued. "Bold as anyone, swam like a fish. She and the other kids used to take turns diving with a suit and hose, the others working the pumps. I let 'em borrow the equipment, get 'em used to it. She was the youngest of them but always the bravest. One day when she was down in the suit—three fathoms—there was a run-in with the local scavengers. They cut her hose."

Hark winced and swore under his breath. He could imagine it all too clearly—being nearly twenty feet down in the dim greenness, in a diving suit too heavy for a quick ascent, then feeling the terrible hiss of air leaving the helmet. The valve would stop water running into the helmet from the hose, but the next intake of breath would strain the lungs, heaving in only thin, stale air. Any hole in a hose was bad, but "surface sucks" pulled out the air much faster. The change was too brutal, too sudden, and he'd seen the way divers' bodies could suffer as a result.

"What happened?" Hark asked.

"They had a rope on her, so they pulled her up fast. She had the helmet-squeeze pretty badly. Bleeding from the ears, eyes red as berries, wheezing for a while. Most of that sorted itself out. Her eyes are fine, her lungs got better. The holes in her eardrums won't heal, but *that's* not the problem. Some of my best crew got their ears sea-kissed when they were kids, and they're all the better for it." Sea-kissed deafness was like a dueling scar or ship tattoo, proof of boldness and belonging.

"Then what do you want us to heal?"

"She's not a coward," insisted Rigg. "And she's not crazy. But since that day . . . she's been afraid of the sea."

Hark stared at the smuggler. It was like being told that some-body was afraid of the sky, or thoughts, or the color brown. How could you live like that?

"What?" Jelt looked incredulously. "What do you mean, *afraid of the sea?*"

"Won't go underwater," explained Rigg. "Won't even go out in a boat unless she has to. She'll wade but won't swim. I thought she'd grow out of it, but she's fourteen now. Fourteen! She should be real crew now, maybe learning a bit of leadership! How can she do that if I can't get her in a sub? I can't have a daughter of mine afraid of the sea. Something went wrong in her head that day. Maybe that hose sucked out some of her sense. I need you to fix it. Fix her. Sort her out."

Hark hesitated, choosing his words carefully.

"We haven't been healers for long," he said, "and we're still learning how it works. We haven't done any brain-wound heal-ing before—"

"But we can try," Jelt interrupted, keenly watching Rigg's face. "What's it worth to you?"

"You fix Selphin," said Rigg slowly, "and you'll have paid back your debt for the bathysphere. You can start getting your cut from our partnership."

"Then we'll do it," said Jelt, and held out his hand to shake Rigg's.

No! screamed Hark silently. *Jelt, don't make another promise we can't keep!*

But he saw the mischievous triumph in Jelt's eye and real-ized that Jelt had been expecting his response. *Stop making a fuss,* said the look. *You'll manage it if you have to. And now you have to.*

Chapter 18

BACK IN THE DARK LITTLE SUB, HARK WATCHED ghostly outlines of jellyfish billow past the portholes and tried to think. Rigg would never release him from healer duties until she considered his debt paid. If he played along, however, it was only a matter of time until Dr. Vyne found out.

We do need to cure this Selphin girl's fear. Jelt's right, whether I like it or not. It's the only way out. I don't know if the god-heart works on minds, but maybe there's some other way to fix her. She just got scared, didn't she? It's not like she thinks she's a lobster. Perhaps I can talk some sense into her.

As promised, the little skimmer sub dropped Hark off at Dunlin's beach. Selphin was waiting for him there but in an unexpected place.

She was standing barefoot at the water's edge. After hearing Rigg's description of Selphin's fear, Hark had not expected to see her near the sea. Yet there she was, letting the foam of the little waves rush over her feet and ankles. She seemed utterly absorbed in watching the ballet of the gulls and terns over the water, the skitter of red crabs at the water's edge, the gleaming rattle of pebbles drawn back by the waves' withdrawal.

As soon as he entered her peripheral vision, her head snapped around to look at him. Selphin jerked her head toward his basket, which was resting on the pebbles farther up the beach. As arranged, it was full of samphire, mallow flowers, sea beet, wild fennel, and flabby sea wrack. She had been thorough.

You're Rigg's daughter, aren't you? he signed. He didn't know Selphin's sign name, but the sign for Rigg was well-known all over Lady's Crave.

She nodded.

I thought you were afraid of the sea? Hark gestured at the wavelets surging over her toes.

Selphin put her head on one side and gave him a look of weary, withering contempt. She glanced pointedly at the inch-deep water around her feet, then met his eye again.

"Terrifying," she said aloud. "I expect I'll drown immediately." Her voice was measured and level, with no weakness in consonants, not even the 's' sound. Either she could still hear her own voice a little or she had a good recollection of how to use it. "So Rigg has talked to you about me, then?"

Not "Mother," just "Rigg." Hark wondered how well they got on and what it was like having Rigg as a mother.

He nodded. There didn't seem to be any point in lying.

I heard what happened to you. Hark kept his signs small and confidential.

Selphin rolled her eyes.

Everybody has heard about it, she signed bitterly, her "everyone" a great circular gesture that seemed to suggest the whole of the Myriad and beyond. *She tells everyone I'm broken.*

I wanted to talk to you about that, Hark signed carefully.

Why? signed Selphin suspiciously, then her face darkened in horror. *Rigg asked you to fix me, didn't she?*

She wants to help you! Hark signed. *She wants you to be great!*

I know what Rigg wants, Selphin answered sullenly.

"But . . . think of all the things you could do if you stopped being afraid of the sea!" Hark blurted out loud. Hark wasn't as fluent in sign as Selphin was. He could get his meaning across but without the same vividness or verve. With words, he was a storyteller, but with signs, he lacked the skill to make the images sparkle. "Do you never want to swim down and chase fish? With the sand grains sparkling in the water? Do you remember what it's like? It's . . . flying!"

Again Hark was getting a contemptuous, incredulous glare, as if he were missing some obvious point.

"Well, what are you going to do, then?" Hark's time and patience were both running out. "You can't avoid the sea forever!" He was used to making difficult cases. He didn't know how to argue the obvious.

Yes, I can, signed Selphin. *Watch me.*

"But it's . . . like being afraid of the sky!"

No it isn't! Selphin signed furiously. *Nobody asks me to go up in the sky! I can't fall into it by mistake! And if I was in the sky, I wouldn't drown, or freeze, or change shape, or get eaten by fish!*

Her signs continued, in angry stabs of motion.

People I know who have drowned. Eight fingers held up. *People I know who have hurt their lungs.* Nine fingers. *People I know who lost limbs scavenging underwater.* Three fingers. *People I know who vanished.* Ten fingers, then two more.

"But that . . . just . . . happens!" said Hark. "That's normal!"

Selphin threw up her hands, then hit the heels of her palms against her forehead in frustration. *You're stupid*, she signed. *Rigg is stupid. Everyone around me is stupid.*

I'm not broken! she continued, her brow creased with frustration. *I'm not crazy! I'm just not* stupid *like everyone else! I stopped going into the sea so it couldn't kill me!*

When I was twelve, after that hose got cut, I realized . . . that nearly killed me. If I keep going in the water, it will *kill me. It will kill or cripple everyone I know, sooner or later. All of them. Everyone kept telling me I'd be fine, I'd be back in the water in no time, like that was a good thing. It wasn't a good thing, and nobody else could see it. I don't mind danger. But this was . . .* stupid *danger. I don't want a* stupid *death! I tried to explain this to everyone . . .* She gave the sign for "explain" over and over, with increasingly exaggerated weariness.

I don't need to be made better! Selphin continued. *I just made a decision Rigg didn't like! So what are you going to do? Change my thoughts? Make me want something I don't want? If you do that—if you even try—I'll kill you. And it'll be self-defense.*

Hark took a deep breath and let it out slowly. The conversation was not going well, and he was starting to regret beginning it. He didn't much like Selphin's description of "healing" as altering somebody's mind against their will. Could it really work like that? He could certainly see why she was upset about it, but what could he do?

"Look," he said, "I'm sorry, but I don't have any choice. Your mother wants me and my friend to try to 'heal' you, and she's got us by the throat. If we don't look like we're trying, then *she'll* kill us. No offense, but she's scarier than you are."

That's what you think, signed Selphin.

"I don't even know if we *can* affect minds," Hark added quickly. "Maybe it'll just get rid of some blisters or something." He hesitated, sizing up a gamble, then took it. "What about this? We say you only need a quick healing session at first. After that, if you show signs of recovery, maybe Rigg won't think you need any more fixing . . ."

That means I'd have to go underwater, to convince her! signed Selphin, with a glare. *No!*

"Just for a bit! Just for . . ." *Just for long enough that you realize that you're being silly*, he thought privately. *You'd be back to normal, and our debt to Rigg would be paid off.*

He couldn't stand around talking forever. He needed to get back to Sanctuary.

"Think about it," he said. "Do you have a better plan?"

Selphin raised her thick brows slightly and pouted in a pretense at deep thought.

I could tell my mother you're lying about your healing powers, she suggested.

Hark felt the skin of his face grow hot. She was bluffing, she had to be bluffing!

"What do you mean?"

You told her that it's you and your friend who do the healing. Selphin's eye glittered. *But I saw you in that shack, taking something out of the floor.*

Hark reflexively glanced around, making sure there was nobody else who might have read Selphin's signs. She grinned, and he knew that he had betrayed himself. He had shown her that he *was* afraid of discovery.

Somehow she had been spying on him when he had recovered the relic. Too late he remembered the rattle of stones behind the wooden wall of the hut. Perhaps she had been peering in through a knothole.

You don't *heal anything*, she signed, triumphantly. *You* don't *cause the throb in the air. This morning I felt a vibration near the hut before you even arrived! That round thing is godware, isn't it? That's what heals. What do you think Rigg would do if I told her?*

Hark chewed his lip hard, feeling angry and frightened. Suddenly he was tired of people giving him ultimatums and forcing him up against precipice edges.

"I think she'd kill me and my friend," he said bluntly. "Then she'd search until she found that relic. After that, she'd lock you in a room with it until you were 'fixed.' Do you still want to tell her?"

Selphin gnawed her knuckle, scowling bitterly. He seemed to have made his point, but he felt bad about it. She looked anguished and cornered, and he knew how that felt.

"I never wanted any of this," he said. "I never thought we'd have to heal anybody who didn't want it. But you and me— there's nothing we can do about this, is there? Maybe it'll be fine. Maybe the relic won't do anything to you."

Selphin's only answer was one swift, fluid sign. It was the expressive sign for a jellyfish, pulsing its way forward, fingers trailing as tentacles. Of course, above water it generally had a different meaning.

Spineless.

"I've got a spine!" Hark felt his temper fraying. "But spines are meant to bend so they don't get snapped! You can't just . . ."

He trailed off. Selphin had coldly and deliberately looked away from him. He had been silenced, he suddenly realized. If she wasn't looking at his signs or mouth movements she couldn't "hear" him. His voice, his treasured power to persuade, had been taken from him in an instant.

"You make sure that *thing* never comes near me," she said aloud, her voice quiet but hard. "I won't let someone change me and control my brain. I mean it. Find a way out of this, or you and your friend will regret it. It's not Rigg you should be worrying about. It's me."

Chapter 19

CREW WERE FAMILY, FAMILY WERE CREW.

Selphin had been brought up with Rigg's entire gang as a cantankerous, protective coterie of honorary uncles, aunts, and siblings. Her love for them all was so fierce that she sometimes felt she should be able to see it, stretching from her to them like ribbons of red flame.

By the age of twelve, Selphin had become a little queen of Lady's Crave. Around the harbors, she led her own gang of children the same age. The rest of the time, she performed daring acts of mischief with her half-siblings. They all had different fathers, some unidentified, but that never really mattered. They were Rigg's children, Rigg's crew. Selphin was the youngest but one of the boldest.

Then one day Selphin went down in a diving suit and came up choking on seawater, her eyes and ears full of blood.

After a fortnight, her eyes were no longer bloodshot, but she could still hear almost nothing but a droning, buzzing hiss. It went on and on, sometimes changing its pitch like an insect's whine.

The bees, Sage called it and looked at Selphin thoughtfully. Sage was Rigg's sea-kissed second-in-command, and Selphin had always found her a bit intimidating.

The sound was maddening, and it wouldn't go away. Everything was really hot as well, which made her feel more out of sorts. It took her family a while to realize that she was running a fever. Her ears hurt more than before, and when the fever passed, even the faint sound of other voices had disappeared. She could hear nothing but the "bees."

After a few months, it became clear that this would not change. Selphin was sea-kissed. Rigg was ferociously proud. Everyone was.

Selphin also had her pride, in a different sense. She was too proud to admit that she felt lost, or that she experienced a deep ache in her soul whenever she woke from a dream of sounds to a world of buzzing silence. In those early days, learning to lip-read made her want to cry with frustration, and when other sea-kissed chatted among themselves, their signing was often too fast for her to follow. Suddenly there seemed to be no conversations where she belonged.

Most of all, she was too proud to tell anybody in her mother's crew about Venna.

Venna was one of the stronger characters in Selphin's own little gang. She wasn't a match for Selphin's streetwise daring, but she had one thing Selphin lacked—subtlety. Venna didn't risk treating Selphin with outright rudeness, which would have angered everyone since sea-kissed were universally respected. Instead, she did a hundred little things that were hard to prove.

She must have known that Selphin was new to her deafness and still learning to lip-read, so Venna made things as hard as possible. Suddenly Venna was always suggesting that the group of them go somewhere dark, where she knew Selphin would struggle to follow the conversation. Sometimes Venna would lead the conversation off at an excited gabble, too fast to follow, or managed to speak when Selphin was looking away for a moment. Selphin would stoop to pick something up, and when she looked up again she found everyone was laughing. Was the joke about her? What had happened?

Every time Selphin lost the thread of the conversation, she knew that Venna was waiting, gloatingly, for her to ask what everyone was talking about. She hated asking. It stung her pride and made her feel stupid. But if she didn't, sooner or later Venna would ask:

"What do *you* think, Selphin?"

Then Selphin would have to guess what was being discussed and give a reply she hoped would pass. Sometimes Venna would nod slowly with an expression of carefully blank politeness, then flicker a look to one of the others. Other times she would stare at Selphin with an exaggerated look of confusion.

"I don't understand. What do you mean, Selphin?" And Selphin would feel her face burn, knowing that she had guessed wrong.

If Selphin *did* ask what everyone was talking about, Venna would "helpfully" explain it to her in exaggerated mouth shapes that she *must* have known Selphin couldn't read. Or—worse— she would say:

"Don't worry about it. It would take too long to explain."

And just like that, Selphin was cut loose from the conversation and set adrift. She was made to feel like an outsider, an idiot child who had to be humored and helped.

The rest of their friends were clearly unhappy with seeing a sea-kissed treated this way. However, the balance of power in the group was shifting. They had always been in awe of Selphin, but time after time they saw her tongue-tied, confused, and on the back foot.

If Selphin had told her mother's gang or other sea-kissed what was going on, Venna would have had hell to pay. Selphin could not bring herself to tell tales, however. She also knew she could beat Venna in a straight fight, despite their size difference. But would she look crazy if she punched the bigger girl's teeth down her throat?

One day, when Selphin had mulishly refused to be drawn into Venna's games, Venna rolled her eyes impatiently and said:

"Selphin, you need to *tell* us if what we're saying is too complicated for you."

It was as though she were lecturing a small and silly child. Selphin couldn't take it anymore.

"No," she said. "It wasn't complicated; it was boring. When you start talking I can't concentrate, Venna, because you're always *so boring*." She got up, knowing that if she stayed there any longer she would cry or break somebody's jaw. "I'm tired of hanging around with children."

And she turned and walked quickly away from the whole pack of them, so they wouldn't see her shaking with rage and misery. Did they call to her to come back? Did they burst out laughing? Did they whisper wonderingly and make faces at each other? She would never, ever know.

Selphin had saved face, she supposed, but she had yielded the battlefield to Venna. She hated herself for that, but she knew that her pride would never let her go back to that group of friends. She spent the next few days morosely hanging around her mother's gang, without explaining why or wanting to talk to anybody. Everyone was proud of her, but she felt like somebody had died.

One evening, Sage and the other adult sea-kissed got up from the gang's campfire to walk off together. They did that sometimes, and the other members of the gang accepted it. This time Sage turned and beckoned Selphin to join them. The gesture was utterly matter-of-fact, the same one that Sage had used for her fellow adults.

Selphin never forgot what it was like to walk with Sage and the others through the busy harborside that first night. Wherever they went, crowds parted for them. They were sea-kissed, warriors of the deep. They had a calm, quiet swagger, a cool and dangerous panache. On the streets of Lady's Crave, they were bandit kings and queens.

As Sage was handing Selphin her first ever cup of honeymead, Selphin happened to see Venna staring out of a casement opposite, gaping with envy and astonishment.

Selphin pretended not to see her and walked on with her sea-kissed crewmates, loving them all so fiercely that she thought she might explode.

Two years later, Coram's healing seemed to have changed everything. Selphin could see her ferocious, beloved crew-family altering before her eyes. There was a new craven eagerness and reverence that made her skin crawl. Her friends were starting to think, feel, talk differently, and nobody else seemed to have noticed.

Straight after the argument with the Sanctuary boy, Selphin went to confront Rigg. The resulting row was typically spectacular. Rigg didn't deny planning to "fix" Selphin and refused to yield an inch.

"First you won't go near the sea, and now you're afraid of the healers too? I'm sick to death of your obsessions, Selphin!"

I'm not broken! Selphin told her, losing her temper as she always did. *You're the one whose head needs fixing!*

Rigg always forgot that when she yelled she was harder to lip-read. When her mother's mouth movements became too contorted, Selphin stopped trying to understand them. Instead she looked away, cutting the conversation dead, which she knew Rigg hated.

Selphin often felt that her mother didn't really understand her anymore. Rigg was proud of her daughter and loved her in her own aggressive, domineering way, but she was not sea-kissed. She did not inhabit Selphin's world. At first Selphin had missed her mother's harsh, crow-like voice, with its tireless throb of energy. She tried to imagine it sometimes, but these days the remembered voice was faint and mechanical.

They were drifting apart. Rigg thought that their conversations went badly because Selphin didn't catch everything she said. However, the biggest problem was Rigg's refusal to believe that she no longer fully understood her daughter. There was so much that Selphin found hard to explain to her mother. She couldn't make Rigg see how the last two years had changed her, and tempered her patience and tenacity like steel. She couldn't share the heightened alertness that had become habit to her, so that everything she saw danced with detail. The world spoke to her now in breaths and vibrations—movements of air against her skin, the sweetness of music felt as a tremor in her bones, and door slams sensed as shudders in the floor. Sometimes Selphin felt like she and her mother were meeting as ambassadors from different lands.

Nowadays Selphin never confided in Rigg when she was upset. Sometimes she went to Rigg's second-in-command, Sage, whose harsh features and cold voice had seemed so alarming when Selphin was younger. Now that Selphin's signing was fast and fluent for them to chat naturally, she had come to know a different Sage. The older woman's sharp face came to life when she signed, and her wit tumbled out, brash and cutthroat. She didn't often tell you everything would be fine, so when she did, you believed her. Most sea-kissed in the gang still had some hearing in one ear or both, but Sage was like Selphin and knew how it was to hear nothing but the "bees."

Rigg must have noticed that Sage was replacing her as Selphin's confidante, but she never said anything. She never admitted to her own wounds, fatigue, or illnesses. If she felt sadness at the estrangement, she hid that, too.

. . . . .

Selphin kept volunteering to forage for the Sanctuary boy while he was on healing duty. It allowed her to steer clear of the healing sessions.

I know my way around Nest better than anyone else, she had pointed out. *I was following the Sanctuary boy around for days, wasn't I? I know his best foraging spots.* She was the one who had tailed Hark until he met up with Jelt, allowing the gang to surround them in the shack. She now wished she hadn't managed it quite so successfully.

Selphin heard all about the healing sessions from gang gossip. Each time, there were more patients, arriving with agues, cuts, scurvy, and age-stiffened joints. Word had spread fast. Soon the patients had to visit the healers in batches. By the end of the second week, there were visitors from islands a day's travel away.

Not all of the patients were ill or injured, Sage told Selphin one evening by the campfire.

What do you mean? demanded Selphin.

A group of four turned up and said they wanted to be made "better", answered Sage. *They didn't explain what "better" meant, though.*

What happened? asked Selphin.

They spent ten minutes with the healers, Sage explained wryly. *When they came out, a woman was crying with happiness, because her nostrils had closed up. Smooth as an egg, not a hole in sight. All the others were congratulating her. A sign, they called it. Apparently she was "chosen." Chosen to have no sense of smell, anyway.*

Sage was one of the few gang members who showed some skepticism about the healers. She seemed to find the whole racket amusing rather than worrying, though.

However, this was not the last visit of the strange group seeking to be made "better." They were back two days later with five friends, all equally keen on self-improvement. The group emerged from their healing session apparently unaltered, but one of them claimed that his eyes had been changed in ways he couldn't describe, so that he saw the world anew.

A few days later, they returned again in greater numbers. This time they brought tents and blankets and refused to leave. All they wanted was to attend upon the healers, they explained, and be close to them. They were willing to pay for the privilege, so Rigg shrugged and took their money. Most of Rigg's gang treated them like a joke at first and nicknamed them the "grovelers."

They're creepy, Selphin commented, peering across at the huddle of figures seated between their tents. *What do they want? Do they even know?*

"They're not so bad when you talk to them," insisted Coram.

Coram talked to them a lot. Afterward he usually sat alone, staring raptly at his scar as if it were unfathomably beautiful. Ever since his healing, he had seemed heavy, like he was drugged. Selphin had seen him like this before, and it was always a bad sign. When he was lumpish and distracted, it meant a big thought was forming in his head. It usually took much longer to get the thought out of his head again.

After a while, other members of the gang began chatting with the grovelers, as well. Selphin's friends came back from these conversations looking dazzled and talking of signs, omens, and changing times.

"I'm not saying I agree with them," they said, "but it makes you think . . ."

"I've never been one for goddish stuff," they said, "but it's like the Leaguers say . . ."

"I don't say those healer boys *are* a message from the Under-sea," they said, "but . . ."

The older members of the gang were the most easily infected

by these ideas. Those were the people who remembered the time of the gods. Now they walked around with a look of fearful eagerness on their faces.

The "healing cave" looked different now. There was a dark brown canvas tent around it, over which long, frayed mooring ropes dangled like ornamental tassels. Faint frills of crusted salt had been left at the edges of dried-out damp patches, but this just made it seem more mysterious, as if the sea had hand-embroidered the weather-beaten canvas.

The presence of the tent affected people. Within a week of its arrival, the ground around it was littered with shells, pieces of agate, painted bird eggs, and gray coral beads. Nobody had asked the patients to bring them, but they all intuitively understood that when visiting such a shrine, money was not enough. An offering was needed.

Selphin always kept a distrustful distance from the tent, so it was a while before she realized that some of her crewmates were secretly leaving offerings, too. They also stopped talking and signing when they were close to the tent and walked past reverently.

Why are you all being so respectful? Selphin wanted to slap them. *We're Rigg's gang! We don't crawl to anyone!*

But this no longer appeared to be true.

Deep down, Selphin had hoped that the base on Wildman's Hammer couldn't last. The gang would get restless, as they always did. They would miss Lady's Crave and grumble about the lack of taverns. Besides, the gang had deals to attend to, goods to supply, ships to meet. Day by day, Selphin expected Rigg to change course in her blunt, unapologetic way and declare that they were all going back home . . .

Instead, Selphin visited Wildman's Hammer one day to discover two changes. Most of Rigg's gang were absent, and the grovelers were now armed.

What's going on? she asked her mother. *Why are you letting them bring weapons here?* The grovelers were equipped with knives, blackjacks, and axes and now defended the narrow rock-walled path that led to the healing tent.

"We can't keep our people here all the time," said Rigg. "The *Pelican* is due in a few days, isn't she?" Foreign ships like the *Pelican* sometimes dodged the heavy taxes, customs duties, and mooring charges by trading offshore with smugglers' skimmers instead of docking at an island. This was completely illegal but was profitable if you could get away with it. "So we'll be getting those grovelers to guard the healers and the base while our people are on Lady's Crave. Why not make use of them, if they're here anyway?"

Selphin had a nightmare feeling that the world was slowly somersaulting to stand on its head.

What are you talking about? she demanded. *We have guards here to stop the healers running away, not to keep them safe! The grovelers aren't our people! They're loyal to the healers!*

"It won't be a problem," said Rigg. "Coram's vouched for them—they're friends of his."

And who tells Coram what to say? signed Selphin furiously. *He goes into that healing tent to talk, and he comes out with new opinions that don't sound like him! He's taking orders, and not from you! And he's not the only one!*

"You're talking nonsense!" said Rigg.

This isn't your base anymore! Selphin told her. *And if you don't watch out, this won't even be your gang!*

Rigg obviously didn't believe her. She was too sure of her gang and her leadership of it. Crew were family, family were crew. How could somebody who was neither steal her family and crew away from her? It was unthinkable.

Instead she glared at Selphin with a blank, angry, pained look. She clearly thought that Selphin was broken-headed and delusional. She wanted to fight it and make Selphin better again.

Selphin turned to Sage to back her up, but for once the older woman was not on her side.

I know you don't like the healers, Sage told her, *but they're doing us a lot of good. We've got spare money to repair the subs properly for the first time in a year. And even creepy healing is a lot better than a noose.* She fingered the two newly mended notches in her ear. *Anyway, your mother's word is law. Sorry, but my first loyalty is to her.*

I'm loyal to her too! signed Selphin, outraged. *But that doesn't mean I do what she says when she's wrong!*

The only other person who seemed to be miserable about the entire healing racket was the Sanctuary boy. Talking to him was like trying to grip an eel, though. Selphin always ended up threatening him and wanting to hit him with rocks.

She didn't even try talking to the older healer boy.

There wasn't much chance. She didn't go near his healing tent, and he rarely ventured out of it now. Besides, an instinct told her that talking to him would be useless. She might as well try to persuade a shark to live off kelp.

Even from a distance, Selphin could sense the vibrations from the unknown relic in the healer tent. She could imagine it pumping its dark energies through air, rock, and flesh, rippling them as it did so. She visualized veins slowly blackening, minds twisting, bodies subtly melting and morphing. It was a poison none of her friends could taste or see, and it was changing them all, inch by inch.

I'll stop you, she promised it in her head. *I'll make them listen to me.*

But none of them did.

Chapter 20

"*THERE* YOU ARE!"

Hark jumped out of his skin. He had just returned from one of his "foraging expeditions" and had barely slipped in through the Sanctuary entrance, his basket over his arm and his head still full of patients.

Dr. Vyne was standing there just inside the entrance, hands on hips. Gone was her air of amused, lackadaisical menace. Today her eyes were white-rimmed, her voice a whiplash. Behind her stood Kly, looking uncomfortable and anxious.

"In here!" Vyne said curtly, hustling Hark and Kly into a small meditation room. For some reason she appeared to be really angry. Hark's mind fizzed with panic. What had she found out? "Kly, talk him through our notes, and get him into that room as soon as you can. I don't know how much time we have."

"What's happened?" asked Hark.

"Pale Soul's sick," answered Kly quietly. "We think he's waning."

"I told you he was a priority, Hark!" Dr. Vyne erupted. "I told you to find out where he'd hidden that archive as soon as you could! I made that clear a month ago!"

Hark felt as though he were falling. Dr. Vyne's good humor had given way beneath him like a trapdoor. Of course he had known that Vyne wanted him to find out about the library, but it hadn't seemed urgent. There had been so many other things to worry about. Over the last month, his healing duties had left him distracted, exhausted, and barely able to keep up with his chores.

"If there *is* still a secret library," said Vyne, "this is our last chance to find out where it is! If you care about your future, Hark, find out *everything* you can! And do it fast!"

Hark nodded, mouth dry.

"I need to go," Vyne declared, her expression still stormy. She raked both her hands through her hair, gave a snort of annoyance, and marched out. Kly slowly exhaled.

"Pale Soul wasn't ill yesterday!" exclaimed Hark. "Was he?" He wondered whether he should have noticed that the gentle old priest was ailing.

"Sometimes there's a slow twilight," said Kly, dropping into a chair. "Sit down. The doctor wants you to know more about Pale Soul before you talk to him."

Hark listened to Kly's hasty account of the old priest's history. Before joining the priesthood and taking the name Pale Soul, he had been Karriter Thistle. His father had been a nightwatchman, his mother a seamstress, his stepfather a priest. Six siblings, a childhood on Siren. Acolyte at age ten, priest by sixteen. Ten years as a priest on Siren, occasionally speaking to the Gathergeist, then archivist on Nest.

Hark had known very little of this, despite all his conversations with the old man, and this gave him a pang of self-reproach. Then again, these were dead facts, both personal and impersonal, like dry bones in a box.

"Pale Soul's calmer around you than he is with anyone else." Kly rested his elbows on his knees, and stared down at his clasped hands. "I think your neck may be riding on this," he added softly. "Be as kind as you can, but find the information the doctor wants, for goodness' sake."

Pale Soul had been put in a room of his own, to avoid infecting others. It was lit only by the hearth and the dim, purple flame of a little lantern hanging from a hook on the wall. The old priest deserved his name more than ever before, his skin so pale it was deathly, like gray clay. Even in his exhaustion, though, Pale Soul seemed agitated and nervous. He twitched slightly as Hark sat down beside him.

"It's all right," said Hark. "It's me." Nothing was all right, and he felt a sting of guilt as Pale Soul's expression softened with recognition and trust.

"It's too quiet," Pale Soul confided with quiet wretchedness. "I try to listen, but . . . the quiet gets in the way. There!" He raised a finger and looked entreatingly at Hark. "Can you hear? Music . . ."

Behind the relentless murmur of the wind outside and the muffled sounds of distant footsteps and door-slams, Hark heard a faint jumble of metallic notes, indistinct and haunting.

"It's just the wind chimes," he said, recognizing the sound.

"Yes," said Pale Soul, deflating. "Of course. It will never come back. What was the point of it all?" His eyes forlornly begged Hark for an answer or perhaps a rope to cling to. "Did *you* ever hear the Gathergeist sing?"

Hark shook his head, finding it hard to follow.

"I did," said Pale Soul, very faintly. "It made me think of birds. It didn't sound like them, but it reminded me of the way that birds don't care about us. They don't. They don't care whether they're beautiful, they just are. I heard it once up on the cliffs when I was small, back on Siren. I knew the Undersea was ris- ing because of the clouds. Sudden black clouds by themselves, like thumbprints above the horizon. Then the wind changed . . . and I heard the song."

"What was it like?" asked Hark. If Pale Soul wanted to talk about the gods, perhaps the conversation could be guided toward the archive.

"It was not a tune you could sing." Pale Soul cleared his throat, then tried a small eerie undulating mewl of sound. "No, it was not *music* . . . and yet it was. It . . . broke me, that sound.

"I ran home and told my older sister, and she said I never needed to go up on the cliffs alone again. She would go with me. Anila. Only nine, but the eldest—she brought up the rest of us. I was her favorite."

Hark's heart sank. These were childhood memories, then—too old to be useful. Somehow he needed to haul Pale Soul's mind forward several decades.

"We went up on the cliffs at sunset sometimes," Pale Soul continued, his face looking more serene. "Sea so big—Anila called it a patchwork, because there were blotches . . . silver shimmers, cloud shadows, purple sometimes. Ships—they looked so huge back then. Sails pink in the sunset and puffed like peaches. We had lucky rhymes to stop them sinking, and when they reached the horizon safely, I thought *we* had done that. It felt . . . I felt useful . . . powerful . . ."

Hark didn't ask where Anila was now. If she was older than Pale Soul, she might well be dead.

"Is that why you decided to be a priest?" he asked instead. "To protect people?"

Pale Soul's face slowly lost its pensive brightness, like a moon submerged in cloud.

"We did protect people," he said, and started to tremble. "They were so proud of us once. Now they're ashamed of us. They do not want to remember how frightened they were and how much they needed us. But they *did*." He stared at Hark in dazed fear, as though this boy in yellow robes were his judge and executioner. "Everyone did. We did everything we could . . . everything . . . everything . . . and now . . . and now *they* come and . . ."

Fear and confusion shook the old man, until it seemed they might tear him to pieces. Apparently Hark had succeeded in dragging Pale Soul back to the bitter present. The old man looked up at Hark with sudden surprise, as if the latter had appeared unexpectedly.

"You!" Pale Soul looked aghast. "*They* sent you, didn't they? They want you to squeeze information out of me!" One frail hand made a weak clenching motion, as if crushing the juice from an even frailer fruit.

"No, no!" Hark told him soothingly, even as his conscience stung. Pale Soul was right. That was exactly why Hark was there. What choice did he have, though? "You remember me! I live here—we've talked lots of times. I'm Flint, one of the acolytes. They're going to rename me Will of the Waves. Remember?" Pale Soul had often mistaken him for an acolyte long gone, and Hark hoped this would serve him well now.

The old man blinked at him uncertainly, eyeing Hark's yellow acolyte robes.

Hark followed up his advantage. "I never heard the Gathergeist sing," he said calmly, "but I saw the Glass Cardinal once, when I was young. My family was out in a little boat, and it passed us in the water." He closed his eyes for a moment, remembering the story Vyne had told him. "It moved like it was water itself. There was a cloudy rainbow on its skin that rippled. Its scream sounded the way moonlight looks."

Hark leaned forward, holding Pale Soul's gaze.

"That's why I became an acolyte," he went on, in hushed, confidential tones. "So that I could protect people . . . and so

that I could see beings like that again. *They* would never understand that, would they?"

"You are right!" The suspicion had melted from Pale Soul's
eyes. "The beauty and the terror—they could never understand.
I . . . am sorry, Flint. My eyes are not so good today." The priest
put out a hand and gently laid it on Hark's arm. "Tell me, are
they still in Sanctuary, asking questions?"

"No," said Hark. "They've gone. They gave up." He didn't
know who "they" were, but he had no intention of arguing with
Pale Soul about it.

"They'll be back," said Pale Soul in an urgent whisper. "They
want what we know, for their warships and bridges and medicines to change their bodies. They want to trick us. Nothing is
sacred to them—they sell *everything*, they cut apart *everything*,
they want to know *everything*. They do not understand that
some secrets are dangerous! Why do they think we hid such
things from the world?"

There was enough truth in the old priest's words to make
Hark feel uneasy, but there was no turning back.

"We hid everything well, though, didn't we?" asked Hark. "I
don't think *they* found anything."

"You are sure?" Pale Soul's brow frowned uncertainly.
"They . . . didn't find it?"

"I don't think so," answered Hark, his heart banging with
excitement. Could "it" be the secret library? "Do you want me to
check? You'll . . . need to tell me where to look."

"Yes . . . yes . . . ." Pale Soul beckoned Hark to lean closer,
until Hark's ear was close to his mouth. "Everything is under the
lighthouse on the tip of Gimlet Point."

Hark's spirits plunged again. He had walked past Gimlet
Point many times and had seen the pile of rubble that had long
ago been a lighthouse. Even the foundations had fallen in. If

there had ever been a hidden cellar, by now its contents would probably be crushed by rockslide or destroyed by the weather.

"You should take the crab dance," whispered Pale Soul clearly and carefully into his ear. "One bottle will see you there and back."

Hark bit his lip hard and tried not to panic. Apparently the old man had slid into nonsense. He waited, but apparently there was no more coming. He sat back in his seat.

"The crab . . ." he began, but Pale Soul furrowed his brow and put a hasty finger to his own lips.

Hark tried to keep his face serene, even as he boiled over with frustration and alarm. If he asked more questions, he would probably make Pale Soul suspicious again. Evidently the old man thought he had been perfectly clear.

"I'll go and look later," he said, and saw the priest's face relax a little. "How will I know if it's all there?"

"The archives . . . for four hundred years. Thirty-nine scrolls, in cases of ivory. Twenty books in a great chest of black oak. The great Volvelle calculating the Festivals of the Year. The four Knives Whetless . . ." The list went on, in a meticulous, careful drone, while Hark tried to remember everything he was told.

The more he heard, the lower his spirits became. It sounded like most of it was paper. If these precious documents were buried in the lighthouse rubble, rain and time would have rotted them years ago.

Kly had told Hark that his neck was on the line. Hark needed more information, something that would satisfy Vyne and save him from her sudden, icy anger. Probing Pale Soul for information was starting to turn his stomach, though. He felt like he really was squeezing the juice out of the weak old man.

I don't have a choice, Hark told himself fiercely. *He's dying anyway. It won't make any difference to him in the long run . . .*

"This . . . is as it should be, is it not?" The nervous wariness and distress was creeping back into Pale Soul's gaze. "I can tell you this now? Is it . . . is it . . . is it time?"

It was the old question that he always asked and that Hark had always answered in the same calming way. *No, not yet.* This time, for some reason, Hark could not force out the usual words. If it was not "time" now, it never would be. Pale Soul would have waited meekly for something that never came, on Hark's assurance that it would. It would feel like breaking a promise.

"Yes," he said, on impulse, then regretted it as he saw pan-icky urgency blossom in his companion's eyes. "I mean, you don't have to do anything! It was 'time' a while ago and . . . you were ready for it. You did everything you needed to do."

"I did?" Pale Soul asked faintly.

"Yes," faltered Hark. "It's all done now. It's over. You . . . can be very proud."

Pale Soul let out a breath, and it was as though some weight had been lifted from him.

"Anila was proud of me," he said quietly, as his trembling slowly faded. "She always was. She said so."

Hark watched Pale Soul recede from him again, through scores of years, beyond his reach. A kind sisterly hand was wait-ing, and a patchwork sea. This was Hark's last chance to force Pale Soul to recall his priestly days.

"What was she like?" he heard himself ask instead.

"Anila?" Pale Soul smiled. "She was fair, but not white-haired like me. She had a scar on her hand from cutting open nuts." He laughed. "She used to bring some with us when we went up to the cliffs. Most of them were too hard. We had to smash them with rocks . . ."

The old priest's eyes lowered and closed. His breathing became more rhythmic, and there was a slack peace in his face. Perhaps he had slid into a dream of that happy time, before tragedy, disillusionment, and despair.

"Sir?" Hark put out a hesitant hand and prodded him a bit. There was a hiccup and a small moan, then more gentle snores.

What do I do? Wake him up again?

Hark could shake the dying man's frail shoulder and force him back into his adult memories. He could yank him out of his last sleep, away from the warmth of the cliff top, the bright sky and the pink sails . . .

Well, I can't. I can't do that, I guess.

It was stupid, but there it was. He couldn't. As soon as he knew that, everything was simpler, which was a bit of a relief somehow.

Hark would just have to hope that the description of the archive was enough to appease Dr. Vyne. She would probably have little interest in the story the old priest had most wanted to tell. As it turned out, his most treasured possession had been a vision of two children on a sunset cliff top, wishing oblivious ships on their way.

Chapter 21

HARK HAD TO BANG ON THE MUSEUM DOOR several times before Vyne answered it. She looked less than pleased to see him.

"Why aren't you with Pale Soul?" Her brow slowly cleared. "Oh, no. Already? Tell me you got him to talk!"

"I did!" Hark said quickly. "But there wasn't long—"

"Did he say anything about the archive?"

"Yes . . ."

"Well, come in, don't stand there like you're selling spoons."

The doctor led Hark up to her study. By the time she dropped into her chair and grabbed a pen, Hark's insides were playing leapfrog. He quickly rattled through as much of the archive's inventory as he could remember, while the doctor made notes.

"There's a catch, isn't there?" Vyne said abruptly. "I can see it from your expression." Her eyes widened accusingly. "He never told you where it was, did he?"

"Yes, he did . . ." Hark trailed off, looking for a way to soften the news.

"But?"

"He said it was under the lighthouse on Gimlet Point."

Vyne stared at him for a few seconds, then threw her pen across the room.

"The lighthouse on Gimlet Point? The one that was smashed into chunks during the Cataclysm? That lighthouse? Then this"—she brandished the paper with the archive inventory—"is useless, isn't it? All the books on this list are waterlogged or padding gannet nests by now!"

It wasn't Hark's fault, but he had too much sense to point this out. People weren't fair when they were angry. Vyne couldn't punish the weather, or the fallen rubble, or her own bad luck, but she could lash out at him. If he annoyed her, she would lash out even harder.

"Did you get *anything* useful out of him? Think!" She listened with furrowed brow as Hark recounted all that he could remember. "'Take the crab dance' . . . ? 'One bottle will see you there and back' . . . ? You can't have heard that right. I wish you'd asked him to repeat it!" She pressed her fingers against her temples.

I should have done, thought Hark, his stomach hollow with dread. *I should have pressed him. But I didn't, and it's too late.*

"Crab dance," Vyne was muttering. "What did he really say? It *can't* have been 'crab dance.' Crabs scuttle and run. They don't dance!"

Crab dance. When did I ever see a crab dance? Delicate as a moth, a thought settled on Hark's mind.

"Wait," he said slowly. "I've never seen a 'crab dance,' but I've seen a *Sharkdance*. And a *Marlinwaltz*. And a *Herringleap*."

"What?" Vyne looked up at him with confusion and irritation.

"They're *boats*," said Hark, with growing excitement. "They're the names of boats!"

The doctor's scowl was replaced by a look of hungry animation as she stared at her notes again.

"He told you to 'take the *Crabdance*' to check on the archive. He was asking you to travel by a particular boat?"

"Maybe! No, wait, he told me one bottle would see me there and back—"

"Air!" exclaimed Vyne. "One bottle of compressed air!"

"Not a boat, a sub!" Hark eagerly finished the thought. "The *Crabdance* must have been a sub! So maybe there's a hidden cave, and you need to be underwater to get to it!"

Dr. Vyne's eyes shone. She leaped to her feet.

"We need to find that cave right now," she said. "Come with me."

"Do you have a sub?" asked Hark, surprised.

"Yes," said Vyne, with one of her less reassuring smiles. "After a fashion."

Once they were outside the fort, she led him around the headland to Dunlin's beach. She ignored the lone shack and instead walked up to the mysterious door in the cliff and unlocked it.

Hark followed her through the door into the dark and down a set of stone steps to the left. Soon he could hear the lapping of water. The steps led to a passage, which widened out into a cave. A few feet ahead of him, the stone floor ended abruptly, and he could see the sinuous motion of dark water beyond. Vyne picked up a lantern and lit it. Hark felt the familiar tickle of chemical unease as the purple scare-light licked over the cavern.

On the surface of the water lay something fifteen feet long, tethered with chains and suspended in a hammock of rope strands. As Vyne had promised, it was a sub "after a fashion," but not after a particularly reassuring fashion.

It appeared to be made of clouded glass, its glossy surface gleaming with a pearly iridescence. It was shaped like no other submersible he'd ever seen, with a sleek sphere in the middle, tapering winglike flaps on either side, and a long tail ending in a propeller. The elegant, fluid outline resembled that of a gelatinous sea creature. It looked like it might slither under the touch.

Inside the central glassy sphere, Hark could just make out a rounded metallic cage containing seats and a tangle of machinery. A long metal shaft ran like a spine inside the translucent tail, all the way to the rear propeller.

"Is that made of god-glass?" he asked, already knowing the answer.

"My own invention," explained Dr. Vyne with surprising warmth, turning a large wheel to lower the sub into the water. "I call her the *Screaming Sea Butterfly*. She's a prototype."

"What does that mean?" asked Hark.

"It means that every voyage is a safety test, and it'll be scientifically fascinating if we die in her," Vyne answered cheerfully.

The *Screaming Sea Butterfly* wasn't as slimy as it looked, but its glassy surface was still treacherously smooth. Vyne draped a knobbly waxed mat along one of the "wings" so that they could crawl to the open hatch.

Hark was used to subs and diving bells with windows, but it was different sitting in a vessel that was *all* window. On every side, he could see the undulating waterline licking against the side of the sub. Above it was dim, mauve-lit cavern, below it was dark water. The god-glass distorted everything, adding rainbow halos to outlines. Only the racks of air-bottles and breather boxes behind the seats were reassuringly familiar.

In front of Vyne's seat was an intriguing mechanical tangle, with three wooden wheels, great square bellows, assorted levers, and jutting metal pipes like those in a musical organ. Each seat had a flimsy-looking safety belt that buckled across the waist and a set of bicycle-style pedals in front of it.

Vyne pulled the hatch closed, its underside a mere inch above her head. Hark was impressed that the doctor had managed to create a craft that could make you feel exposed and claustrophobic at the same time.

"Don't worry!" she said, as if reading his mind. "This won't be more dangerous than any other sub you've been in. Skimmers, turtles, barracudas—they're all death traps, most of them. Ten-year-old hand-me-down parts, stuck together with hope and watered-down god-glue. At least this one's new, and I know what most of the dangers are!"

She lit a little lantern in the front of the cockpit, and the murk under the water became cloudily visible. Grains of disturbed silt glittered as they swirled.

Vyne pulled a handle, and something behind Hark gave a long mechanical squeal. The surface of the water climbed up the side of the *Butterfly*, until they were completely submerged.

"We'll have to pedal at first, until we're out and clear," she said. "I'll steer."

Hark fastened his belt, then slipped his feet into the little metal pedals, with their leather stirrups. He followed Vyne's cue and pedaled hard, while she wrestled a great wooden wheel. The sub turned itself around, by jerky, sullen degrees, to face away from the ledge. Soon Hark was out of breath, and his leg muscles were burning. He started to understand why Dr. Vyne hadn't wanted to pilot the sub alone.

"Here we go!" exclaimed the doctor.

The sub eased itself forward, the surrounding water gradually growing lighter. The darkness above yielded suddenly as the sub emerged into the sea, the shimmering, sun-jeweled surface ten feet or so above their heads. Below them extended a green-gold underwater rockscape, sloping gently away toward the greater deeps.

"Stop pedaling—I'll take over now." Vyne dropped a rounded, leather helmet with straps into Hark's lap. "Put this on and fasten it as tight as you can. Quickly!" She was donning a similar helmet but leaving the straps loose.

Confused, Hark pulled on his helmet. It turned out to be heavily padded with cloth inside and came all the way down to his eyebrows, covering his ears completely. It fit with uncomfortable snugness, and he was pulling it off again to ask about this when the *Butterfly* screamed.

The sound was deafening and agonizing. It sounded as though somebody had tortured a hundred seagulls for a small eternity, then forced their screams through a huge glass whistle. The undulating cacophony carved through his brain, ear-splitting, mind-splitting.

Eyes clenched shut, Hark forced the helmet back onto his head again. When he had drawn the straps as tight as he could, the padding at last blunted the edge of the terrible sound. He could still feel the seat, the pedals, even his own teeth vibrating.

A moment later, when he opened his eyes again, a second shock awaited him.

The first thing he saw was Vyne, her face locked in a grimace as she adjusted one of the wheels while squeezing the bellows under one arm. Then a motion beyond her caught his attention, and he realized what the *Butterfly* was doing.

The sub's great, tapering fins were no longer rigid. They were moving up and down with supple ease, and rippling slightly as they did so. The motion reminded Hark a little of the gray-speckled eagle rays he had sometimes seen swimming with silent grace through the dappled shallows. The wings' rise and fall matched the oscillations of the eerie, screeching note produced by Vyne's machine.

Reflexively Hark reached out to touch the side of the cockpit bubble. To his relief, it was still cold and hard, not jelly-soft or quivering with life.

Vyne flashed him a grin, then shouted something that got lost in the screams of her machine. He hoped it wasn't important.

The *Butterfly* moved out of the silt clouds into clearer water and skimmed over the underwater rock pinnacles. A shoal of silvery mackerel parted before them and flowed past on either side. The sub slid over a stretch of rippled sand above its shadow, then ascended without effort, soaring above weed-furred crags like an underwater bird.

Hark's breath caught in his throat. He had been in many subs before, but none that moved with this speed, none that rippled as though they loved the water, and knew it, and were part of it. He could look all around him, as if he *were* the *Butterfly*, this supple, gleaming beast of the deep.

For a single, mad moment, Hark was glad of everything. He was glad of his arrest, and his Sanctuary chores, and even the god-heart. He was glad of all that had resulted in him being there, right then, in that strange and beautiful craft. Just for one blissful, forgetful instant, he was in love.

Then the craft tilted wildly to turn a corner, and Hark came perilously close to redecorating the cockpit with his breakfast. He realized that he was laughing helplessly.

Ahead, Hark could see a place where the seafloor rose abruptly, the incline only a little shallower than the cliff. He knew that they must be close to Gimlet Point, because the broken bricks of the wrecked lighthouse lay scattered down the steep slope before him. Vyne turned the sub to glide parallel to the slope, with the rise on the right.

"There!" Hark tugged Vyne's sleeve to get her attention.

Some distance below was a long, ragged slit of darkness amid the rocks. As the *Butterfly* descended toward it, the opening seemed to gape wider. It was no mere slit or hollow; it was a cavern some twenty-five feet across and fifteen feet high. Its upper lip dripped with weed that swayed in and out as though the cave were breathing.

Aided by the lantern at the front of the cockpit, Vyne steered into the widening cavern until a wall loomed ahead and then slowly brought the *Butterfly* into an ascent. At last she turned off the siren. The ensuing silence was almost shocking.

Vyne pulled her helmet off her head. When Hark followed suit, he could make out a faint *plip, plap, plip* of tiny wavelets stirring against the side of the sub.

"We've surfaced," said Vyne. By the reflected light from the lantern, Hark could see that she was grinning.

"What . . ." Hark put out a hand to stroke the glassy inside of the *Butterfly*, all his questions shoving to be allowed out first. "How did you make this sub *do* that?"

Vyne's explanation was quite brief, but it involved words like "tempered," "extruded," "composition," and "differential," so it didn't really help. She soon seemed to realize that Hark was floundering.

"I found a way to tune different parts of the god-glass differently," she elaborated. "At different notes, some parts soften, some remain hard, some expand, some contract. If you place and combine them correctly, you can orchestrate movement through sound manipulation. It's a very great deal more complicated than it sounds. Even after I mastered the tempering process, the *Butterfly* took me six years to design and make."

"It's amazing!" exclaimed Hark. "Why isn't it famous?"

Vyne looked slightly furtive.

"A lot of this god-glass was given to me by the governor," she explained, "and he *may* be under the impression that I am using it to research better optical lenses. Years ago he told me that there was no place for a submarine that screamed all the time and that I should stop trying to develop one. I think he was worried that it might melt the portholes off other subs in the vicinity, even though I told him that was *extremely* unlikely."

Hark could see why the governor might be worried. He could also see why Vyne kept the *Butterfly* a secret, if she had diverted a fortune's worth of god-glass into a forbidden project.

"What if you made the wrong note and the bubble with us inside it went soft?" asked Hark.

"That won't happen," Vyne assured him. "My instruments can't create notes of a high-enough pitch."

"But what if something else made exactly that note?"

"Then the cockpit would collapse, the water would punch its way in, and we'd both die," the doctor answered promptly. "Try not to whistle while on board," she added as an afterthought. "And if you have to scream, keep it low-pitched."

"Can I . . ." It was a stupid question, but Hark knew he would hate himself forever if he didn't ask. "Can I drive it a little bit on the way back?"

"Not the slightest, flimsiest chance in a world of hells," Vyne told him brightly. "It's taken me two years to learn to use the controls this well, and they're sensitive as baby skin. Even now it's all too easy to get a key change slightly wrong and flip the *Butterfly* onto her back."

By the light of the lantern, they could make out a series of metal rungs set into the cave wall opposite. These disappeared into an upward shaft. As soon as Vyne opened the hatch, Hark noticed a staleness in the air.

"Dr. Vyne? I don't think we should stay here too long."

Hark clambered out first, with a lantern slung around his neck, and crawled along the mat-covered wing, the doctor following close behind. He took a breath and jumped to the lower rungs. Rust crunched under his fingers as he climbed the "ladder."

He emerged into a square-cornered room that had clearly been hand-carved. Threadlike, caramel-colored stalactites dangled from the ceiling and dripped sporadically. Damp blotches marred the serpentine mosaic that tiled the floor.

On the far side of the room was a cluster of heavy wooden boxes, some filled with sallow, grimy scroll cases. One huge chest of black oak towered over the rest.

"Oh," said Vyne softly, as she climbed out of the shaft into the room. She approached the chest and knelt before it, her fingers running tenderly over its carvings. She loosened the cracked leather buckles that held it shut, then lifted the lid. Within lay a stack of great books bound in black leather. "Oh, there you are."

It took three trips in the *Butterfly* to transfer the whole archive from Gimlet Point back to Dunlin's beach, and then another hour for Hark and the doctor to carry it all to the keep. When at last the new finds were safely installed in the fortified museum, Vyne carefully pried the great chest open once more. She pulled out one of the leather-bound books, opened it, and peered at the first densely written page.

"Priest script again," she muttered. "How I hate priest script! These will take months to translate." Nonetheless her eyes were bright, as if she were rather looking forward to the challenge. "Now, let's look at *you* beauties."

Very carefully, she pulled away the wax seal from the first scroll case and opened it. Her expression was almost painfully eager. Tipping the case, she let the curled parchment slide out into her hand. She laid it on the floor, then delicately unfurled it a little at a time.

It was a beautifully illuminated parchment, bordered with ornate black and green curlicues. In the center was a flawlessly detailed painting of something that might have been mistaken for a jellyfish, were it not swimming immediately below a galleon half its size.

"The Cardinal!" exclaimed Hark. The scroll contained other pictures of the gelatinous god, one showing it from above, and another revealing a tentacle-fringed darkness that Hark thought might be a mouth. The next scroll showed Kalmaddoth of the Pit. The next depicted the Swallower. The following three were devoted to the White Sentinel, Dolor, and the Fourfaced.

When Vyne unrolled the seventh, Hark saw a pale shape surrounded by a twisting forest of hair and realized that he was looking at the Hidden Lady.

He felt a jolt in his chest and for a moment wondered if somehow he had the god-heart with him. No, it was his own heart that had lurched at the sight. The painted figure's skin was pallid, almost ugly, and the face was half masked by the water's dappling. The eyes were gilded clots of dark and light, burning from within the dark hollows of the eye sockets. It was only paint, cunningly and carefully applied, but every stroke hinted at a dark majesty.

The scroll unwound further, and he saw an image of her back and shoulders, almost girlish until the skin yielded to the crab-like armor-plating of her lower half. A sinuous black line snaked around the base of her spine like a tattoo.

"They're beautiful," Hark said, his throat tight. He meant "frecht," and they both knew it.

"They're *labeled*," breathed Dr. Vyne, looking at the scrolls the way most people looked at babies. "Look at these!" She pointed to lines of green and silver squiggles that fizzed around the figure of the Lady like inquisitive fish. "These are for priests about to meet the gods! So they have notes, telling them which parts of the god you should look at to make eye contact, which parts listen, which are poisonous, which bite, which sometimes move with a life of their own . . ."

"Dr. Vyne." Hark was still staring at the image of the Lady's back, with its strange black marking. "Isn't there something like this in the display case over there?"

Vyne looked stunned. Both of them scrambled to their feet, and hurried over to the glass case in which a slab of the Hidden Lady floated in pale yellow fluid. It was the case that Hark always touched in greeting. He knew it like a familiar face.

"You're right," whispered Vyne. Her fingertip resting on the glass, she traced the shape of the curling, sigil-like black slit that marred the gray flesh. "It's the same!"

She ran back to the scroll, peering at the tiny, swirling text.

"It's her gills," she whispered. "I have the Hidden Lady's gills!" She sounded almost tearful with excitement. "She must have used them to extract the fear from the Undersea water!"

"Gills?" Hark stared into the oblong, golden world where the Lady-fragment floated. "Like . . . like a *fish*?" Gills didn't fit his idea of the Lady. They were so mechanical, so ordinary.

"Oh, Hark!" said Vyne, almost kindly. "Don't look so distraught! You *should* think of the gods as fish. That's what the continenters always say they were, isn't it? Sea monsters. Gigantic, savage fish that we were determined to worship. We *can't* keep thinking of them as gods, or we'll always be groveling to them in our heads, even as we carve them up! We'll never truly understand these . . . huge, preposterous animals!"

The doctor had never expressed this view so clearly and starkly before. Even though Hark had guessed her opinions, her words were still a shock.

As Vyne returned to her scroll, Hark remained with his forehead pressed against the glass of the case.

I don't believe what the doctor said, he mentally told the floating fragment. *She probably doesn't believe it, either, Lady.*

Chapter 22

A FEW DAYS AFTER THE RETRIEVAL OF THE ARCHIVE, Hark arrived on Wildman's Hammer and sensed that something was different. He had been coming there for a month and had never before seen such flickering, apprehensive tension among Rigg's people. Nobody would tell him what was going on, however.

As usual, Hark's heart sank as he passed the seven so-called grovelers who now guarded the natural rocky alley that led to the healing tent. They knelt as he passed, pressing their foreheads to the bare stone. At first he had felt a guilty thrill at the power his healer act gave him, but these people made him deeply uneasy. In Sanctuary, he had seen too many friezes showing faceless humans kneeling in just this way before the terrible glory of the gods.

Whatever these people wanted, he probably couldn't give it to them. Even if he could, his gut told him that he probably shouldn't.

"Those guards of yours are pretty creepy, Jelt," Hark said quietly, once he was inside the tent. "You know, sometimes a con goes too well? You get a mark who's in *too* much of a hurry to believe you, like the world will fall apart if you're not who you say you are? That sort really can't handle disappointment."

"We're not going to disappoint them, stupid," said Jelt,

obviously enjoying the way his shrine echoed his gravelly tones. "We're giving them what they want."

Hark could hardly make out his friend in the smoky darkness of the tent. Only a few holes and tears in the canvas let in needle-shafts of light. He could just about make out the old cargo sacks strewn on the floor and the tall, shadowy outline that was Jelt. There was also an unpleasant reek in the tent that reminded Hark of a rotten seal carcass he had once found on a beach, gouged by gull beaks. It grew worse all the time, but Jelt always told Hark that he was getting soft and just couldn't remember how the sea smelled.

"What they want is frecht," Hark whispered, using the old word that he usually avoided. "They want something godlike. Something to fear."

"And that's what we'll give them," said Jelt calmly.

Jelt had his own mask now, carved from three different pieces of wood and glued together. One of his eyes glimmered through a hole cut in rugged bark while the other was lost in darkness. Over his decent new clothes he now wore a trailing cape of black ropes and frayed ribbons with rattles attached to the ends. Fine fishing net hung gauzily from his sleeves, like translucent fins.

He had a sense of theater. During the healings he was mostly silent, but on one occasion he had suddenly ordered everyone out in a deafening bellow. Even Hark had been shaken. It had not sounded like Jelt—within the voice there had been a low, buzzing hiss that tingled in the teeth. But echoes did that sometimes. Fissures in the rock maimed sound, winds blew through crevices like whistles.

The visitors loved it. Over time, Hark had realized that he was gradually and insidiously being demoted. During the healings, he talked and gestured more than Jelt, but he was only the master of ceremonies. The tall and sinister figure behind him was clearly the true source of power, the real master of the shrine. Hark had never really wanted to be the focus of creepy adulation, but even so there was something bittersweet in his feeling of relief. Even as a creature of supernatural power, he seemed to have become a sidekick.

"Relax," snickered Jelt. "It's going to be a good day. You'll see." Clearly he knew something that Hark didn't but had no intention of warning him.

The two friends had just healed their last batch of patients for the day, and Hark was restlessly waiting for somebody to call him to the sub, when he heard the sound of raised voices.

One of the voices belonged to Rigg. She was yelling something with hoarse impatience, a couple of other voices calling answers. Most of the words were unintelligible, but he could hear a higher, younger voice shouting the same word over and over again. The word was "no."

"What's that?" whispered Hark. The voices were drawing closer.

"Sounds like they've found her," was Jelt's laconic reply.

"Found who?" asked Hark, but he already had an uncomfortable suspicion.

"About scabbing time!" Rigg was bellowing. "Where was she?"

"Hid herself in Ladismile Cave, Captain!" answered a male voice. "Then she led us a merry chase along the cliffs. Took us an hour to catch her."

"One more patient for you!" Rigg called to Hark, as he emerged from the tent. Behind her, one of the larger smugglers appeared, carrying a struggling, flailing figure, arms pinned to her sides. Small and skinny, with an angular face and defiantly long hair. It was Selphin. "It's that matter I told you about."

Selphin had stopped screaming. There was no point in noise—nobody would be coming to her aid. Instead she fought with a silent, ferocious determination, digging her nails into the arms of her captor, kicking her heels hard into his kneecaps, trying to slam the back of her head into his nose.

"She's got some crazy ideas into her head about this, that's all." Rigg gave her daughter an angry, weary frown. "Stop this cat scratching, Selph! You're embarrassing yourself, and all of us. You're too old for this nonsense!"

"Put up a good fight, though," remarked the male smuggler respectfully, and Hark wondered whether he was trying to compliment Selphin or Rigg's parenting.

"Can you fix her while we're holding her?" Rigg asked, glancing at Hark and then Jelt.

Selphin glared straight at Hark, and there was no mistaking her meaning: *Don't you dare. Don't you* dare.

"I . . ." Hark swallowed. "Look, it works better if she's willing—"

"We'll manage," Jelt interrupted sharply behind him. There was an edge of annoyance in Jelt's voice, like a dig in the ribs. Hark could almost imagine his friend saying, *What's wrong with you? This is what we need to do, this is how we solve everything . . .*

"Oh, pull yourself together, Selph!" barked Rigg. Perhaps it was a blow to her own pride to see her daughter fearful, let alone feeling a fear that Rigg herself could not understand. "Hey!" She waved to draw Selphin's attention. Mother and daughter locked gazes, with a force like frigates colliding. "It's not going to hurt you!"

"It'll *kill* me!" hissed Selphin, her face red with effort and fury.

"Don't be foolish!" snapped Rigg. "Lots of people have been healed by those two, and it didn't do them any harm! Does Coram look dead to you? What about Maelick and Stone?"

Selphin kept staring straight into her mother's face, her eyes so wide the whites could be seen around the irises.

"I won't let you kill me," she said through her teeth.

"I've had enough of this," Rigg muttered. "You two! Come on! Get this over with!"

Hark edged forward, his face feeling hot under his mask. *Rigg's right*, he told himself firmly. *Using the heart isn't going to hurt Selphin. Once she sees that, she'll calm down.*

Even as he was thinking this, the god-heart decided to stir into life. A pulse surged through the air, shimmering the shadows and sending a throb through Hark's bones.

Selphin gave a scream of terror and rage. One of her hands snaked down and plucked her captor's dagger from its belt-sheath. Before he could react, she slashed at the underside of his forearm. He swore violently and shifted his grip. The moment's loosening was enough. Selphin clawed her way free and sprinted away, the dagger still in her hand.

"She used a knife on me!" The smuggler had clamped one hand to his wound and was staring at it in disbelief. "A *knife*."

Hark was just as appalled. You didn't use a blade on family, crewmates, or close friends—you didn't use it on *your own*. You might use your fists or your feet, but not a blade, unless it was a duel everyone had agreed upon. Selphin had cut through more than skin.

"Not a word about that to anyone," Rigg said in a cold and dangerous undertone. "Not yet, anyway. I'll think about it and decide how Selphin pays for that." She glanced at Hark and Jelt. "You two—heal my man's wound. Keep it light on the limpets if you can. And you didn't see anybody cut anyone, right?"

"Too busy being holy to see anything," said Jelt, and Hark nodded.

"She's not herself," Rigg said quietly. "Just needs fixing, that's all. We'll bring her back."

"Captain!" Hark couldn't hold his tongue any longer. "Why don't we leave it for another day? I need to be getting back, anyway." He could buy Selphin a little more time to make her case.

"No." Rigg scowled. "We get this done today. It's been going on too long." She marched off and could be heard shouting orders to coordinate the search.

The knife cut was shallow and closed quickly, leaving only a faint scar. The smuggler gave Hark a grateful clap on the shoulder, then ran off to join the chase.

Hark chewed his fingers. He had always hated waiting. This time he was waiting to see Selphin dragged into the alcove again, fierce and frantic with desperation . . .

Jelt gave a faint snicker.

"What?" Jelt asked, when Hark stared at him. "Why are you looking at me like that? It's funny, isn't it? Whole family's crazy."

Jelt had settled into the darkness at the back of the cave again and was just a shadowy outline once more. He was enjoying playing at being uncanny and frecht, Hark could tell.

Suddenly Hark didn't want to be in the tent anymore, with the darkness, Jelt's snickering, and the rotten, dead-seal smell. He got up.

"Where are you going?" demanded Jelt.

"I'm going to see if I can help find that girl." Hark pulled off his mask and left the tent.

Hark clambered up to the little island's highest point, in the hope of getting a decent view. He could see some of the smugglers below, running, clambering, or using a spyglass, but no sign of Selphin.

How was she hoping to escape, anyway? Wildman's Hammer was tiny, so she would be found before very long, unless she left its shores . . .

Hark's eye fell on the expanse of wild water between Wildman's Hammer and the shore of Nest. It was not a great distance, but the waves jarred and crashed, maddened by the rocky ridges beneath. Foam streaked the waves and floated upward in soft clots like fat snowflakes. It was swimmable, but nobody would choose to swim it . . . unless they were desperate.

"Oh, gullet of night!" he muttered, hoping to be wrong. He scrambled back down the slope, watching little rocks slide ahead of him.

On one side of Wildman's Hammer there was a stubby promontory. Someone planning to swim to Nest might jump from that point. The water was still wild there, but there was less chance of landing on rocks.

That's stupid, Hark told himself. *She's afraid of the sea. She won't be there.*

She was.

He almost missed her. She was crouched behind a boulder at the end of the promontory. He wouldn't have spotted her at all, if he had not already guessed where she might be. As it was, he noticed the trailing end of her windblown cloth belt and then the side of her face as she peered around the boulder.

It was a good hiding place. Nobody would expect someone afraid of the sea to tuck themselves there. But he had seen her, and she must surely know it.

There was a small pause, and then Selphin slowly stood up. She still had the dagger in her hand, held out menacingly. There was barely ten yards between them.

What are you going to do? signed Hark. *Stab everyone until you get your own way?*

Selphin's expression suggested that she considered this a valid option.

Fine, said Hark, feeling exhausted. *I'll call your friends, and you can stab them. Sorry, I don't feel like getting knifed today.*

As he backed away toward the base of the slope, he saw Selphin lower her knife and then cast a wary glance up at the headlands. She tucked her weapon into her belt, then edged toward the frothing sea, keeping her eye on Hark.

Stop! Hark signed. *Let's talk!* He didn't know how to handle the situation, but for now he clearly had to keep her talking and not jumping. *It's not how you think it's going to be,* he told her. *Your mother's right. The healing won't kill you.*

If I'm not me, I'm dead. Selphin's signs were bold and clear. *Still my body, but someone else. Nobody knows I'm gone, but I am.*

It's not like that! Hark recoiled from the picture she had painted. *You won't be a different person just because you're not afraid of the sea! People change their minds all the time! What if I talked you into not being afraid anymore? I wouldn't be killing you and replacing you with somebody else, would I?*

That's different, signed Selphin, *and you know it.*

The healing just fixes what's broken. Hark changed direction again. *If you're not broken, then it won't change anything.*

Do you think I'm stupid? demanded Selphin angrily. *Your lump of evil is* always *adding new things to people without asking! It's* always *changing people so they're how it wants them. I've watched it changing my friends—people I've known all my life!*

What about me? Hark had a moment of inspiration. *I've been spending hours with it. Dozens of pulses going right through me. It hasn't changed me at all.*

There was withering pity in Selphin's glare.

How do you know? she signed.

Because nothing's changed! signed Hark, feeling his stomach drop. *I'd notice!*

Not if it changed your mind, answered Selphin. *If it made you remember things differently, you wouldn't know you'd died and been made into somebody new.*

"Yes, I would!" Hark protested, forgetting to sign. "I'd know!"

How?

There was no talking to Selphin. She came up with crazy, stupid ideas that were somehow impossible to answer or disprove.

Suddenly Selphin started and stared up at the top of the cliff. Hark followed her gaze and spotted Coram standing up against the sky, staring down at them. Selphin took another sideways step toward the water.

"Wait!" shouted Hark. He gestured to Coram, both hands raised, entreating him not to come down, not yet. But Coram didn't seem to understand and began crashing down the incline, kicking rocks and startling birds.

Selphin was at the edge now, staring hypnotized at the water, taking deep breaths, both fists clutched defensively against her chest. She seemed to be willing herself to face it, but her legs were shaking.

She is *afraid of the sea*, thought Hark. *It isn't just that she's decided to avoid it—she's afraid of it, too.* Then again, fear of such waves seemed pretty sane.

He risked a few steps toward her. She seemed almost paralyzed, and he could see her struggling to will herself to jump.

She can't do it, he thought with relief.

You're too close to the edge! Hark signed, as soon as she looked back at him. *You'll get blown over! You don't want a stupid death, do you? That's what you said.* Her unsteady stance on the brink made him nervous. *Come back! You're not really going to jump, are you?*

In Selphin's gaze Hark saw desperation, terror, rage, and a will as relentless as winter. He had just enough time to see how wrong he was before she turned and jumped.

Chapter 23

WHEN CORAM AND HARK GABBLED OUT THEIR report, Rigg was incandescent.

"She *jumped in the sea*?" Rigg hissed.

"Maybe she's cured?" suggested Hark. It was worth a try.

"Little *vixen*!" Rigg exploded. "Coram, get the boats out after her, find her, and drag her out of the surf! Tie her up if you need to!"

There was something reassuring about Rigg's anger. She at least seemed to have no doubt of Selphin's survival. Hark hoped she was right.

"You can't keep doing this," Kly said when Hark staggered in, half an hour late. "And I can't keep covering for you. What's wrong with you?"

Hark had a story to explain his lateness, of course. It was a good story, involving a run-in with a visiting scavenger gang. Today he couldn't make the tale dance, and he could see that Kly was barely listening.

"Every time you say you're sorry, it sounds like you mean it," Kly said at last. "Every time I tell you that you could lose everything, I think it's sunk in. But it hasn't, has it? Or maybe it just keeps on sinking and vanishes into some bottomless hole in your head."

Hark felt a weight in the pit of his stomach. You wore people out like shoes. You didn't mean to, but you did. This is what it felt like when the sole started getting thin.

He had promised himself that this time would be different. He wouldn't waste the chances offered by Vyne, Kly, and Sanctuary. It was happening again anyway, and this time he couldn't walk away or make plans for when he was kicked out. Exhausting everyone's patience would destroy him.

"You're covered in dust," said Kly wearily. "You can't go into the halls like that. Clean yourself up before you put your robes on."

In the dorm room, Hark dunked his face in a bucket of water to clear his head.

"It's not my fault," he told the drab, empty walls.

It wasn't his fault if Selphin was drowned. She probably wasn't, of course. Hadn't Rigg said she was a good swimmer? But even if she *had* drowned, he wasn't to blame. He'd tried to stop her jumping.

It's not my fault. And I'm not going to think about it anymore.

But of course he did. He kept thinking of her face at the promontory's edge. He remembered her utter terror, even as her will locked into place behind her eyes. Jelt could let go of his fear at will. Selphin clearly couldn't, but she'd jumped anyway, right into the sea that she thought was waiting to kill her. What kind of a freak could make themselves do that?

"She's not just crazy," Hark muttered under his breath. "She's . . . *frecht*."

He was suddenly incredibly angry with her, for having no bend or compromise in her. People like that died, usually sooner rather than later.

Hark slammed down the bucket and felt cold water slop over his feet. Somehow she had put thoughts and doubts in his head, and he couldn't get them out. He could still remember her telling him that the god-heart was turning her friends into freaks and that changing her into someone else meant killing her and that maybe it had already done that to him . . .

What if she's right?

"She isn't," muttered Hark.

But what if she is?

The very idea was silly. If he himself had changed, he *knew* he'd notice. Other people around him certainly would, wouldn't they? Vyne, or Kly, or the other staff at Sanctuary . . .

Or would they? None of them really knew him. He was play-acting for them, and maybe a new version of him could play-act just as well. Even shrewd Quest hadn't known him that long, and there were still so many walls between them.

Jelt would know, Hark thought with relief. *Jelt knows me inside and out*. Then again, Jelt was already claiming that Hark had become more soft and docile during his time at Sanctuary. Would he notice another change on top of that?

Hark splashed handfuls of water into his hair to wash the grit out of it. His fingers worked a tangle free, then faltered as they touched something jutting from his scalp. Something small, hard, and tapering, like a limpet . . .

To his relief, it came away and sat in his palm, looking tiny and ridiculous. It was only a fragment of seedpod that must have blown into his hair.

The scare had set Hark's heart banging. He could not bring himself to laugh about it yet. Instead, he began a hasty inventory of himself, by touch and by the pale light from the narrow windows.

His face still felt like his face. No new teeth seemed to be pushing through in his jaw. He searched his arms, legs, and everything else, craning over his shoulder to look at his own back. He could see nothing new, nothing weird. It was only gradually that he noticed what was missing.

Like most kids on Lady's Crave, Hark had earned his share of scars. A sea urchin's spine had left a puckered white scar on the sole of his left foot. He'd pulled a hot crab out of somebody else's pan and been left with a shiny burn on the pad of his left thumb. He'd once cut a squiggle into his upper arm on a hot, starry, drunken night because Jelt and a couple of other Shelter kids were doing the same, and since then the little white zig-zag scar had always filled him with slight embarrassment but a sense of belonging. Then there were all the nicks and cuts on his knuckles, each a reminder of a chance taken or missed . . .

They were gone. All of them. He had been too busy, harassed, and grubby to notice. He stood there staring at his unblemished knuckles and felt cold and empty. Scars weren't useful, and of course the god-heart might have seen them as "something to be fixed," but Hark felt as though a little record of his life had been taken from him.

He *had* been changed without noticing. It wasn't in the way Selphin had suggested, but Hark felt a sense of loss. Worse, he felt violated. He hadn't willed the god-heart to change him. It had simply decided in its mysterious, arcane way that he needed to be improved. His own wishes had not mattered at all.

That evening, when he reported in at the keep, Vyne let him in without a word and led him up to the study. She was so pale it startled him.

"Doctor? Are you all right?"

Vyne blinked, then seemed to remember who he was.

"Yes," she said. "Yes, sit down. Sorry." The last word was one that he had never heard her utter before, and it didn't sound right coming from her. "I'm having a very strange day."

"Something's gone wrong?" asked Hark. Of course there had been some disaster. It just wasn't clear how it would spoil his life yet.

"No," said Vyne. "Quite the reverse."

Her eyes came back into focus, and she looked at him in her usual, skewering way.

"I am telling you this in confidence, Hark. Don't disappoint me. You recall our wonderful archive? Well . . . I mentioned it to our Leaguer friends. They were quite rabid to see it, of course. So I sent them a little note explaining that trust could only be earned by trust. They could hardly expect me to hand over the greatest find of our generation, when they would not share any of their research with me. Sure enough, Captain Grim-Breeches came to see me this morning. I expected him to be pompous and outraged, as usual. Instead . . . he came to me with a proposal."

"You're *marrying* him?" Hark stared at her, battling with unwanted mental images.

"Not that kind of proposal!" Vyne snorted with laughter. "No, the proposal was from the Vigilance League. Not only were they willing to let me see their main project . . . they want me to take it over. They will put all their research and resources at my disposal. This afternoon I visited their base to see what they've been working on."

Her eyes were glassy again, hypnotized by memory.

"What is it?" Hark was now curious. "Is it a submarine, like you thought? A war machine? What does it look like?"

Vyne was shaking her head very slightly.

"It's crazy," she said. "It's beautiful. I can't believe how far they've got with it. Already I can see how to fix some of the problems they've been having. Oh, there are a hundred obstacles! Maybe some will prove to be insurmountable. But . . . I need to be part of this project! For one thing, I can stop them doing anything unhinged with it!"

"The League *are* unhinged, aren't they?" Hark remembered his conversation with the captain. "There aren't really any big continenter navies getting ready to invade us?"

"Oh, probably not right now." Vyne waved a dismissive hand. "In a few years, maybe, but only if we're stupid about things."

"What?" This was not the reassurance Hark had hoped for. "But . . . we can defend ourselves, can't we? We've got the best sailors and submarines in the world!"

"Our submersibles could probably *slow down* an attack," Vyne agreed thoughtfully. "But you need to understand the sheer size of the continents. Do you see that map over there?"

The chart on the wall was of a sort that Hark had seen a hundred times. It showed the world, or the part of the world that mattered. Across the central expanse sprawled the Myriad's great Y-shaped scattering of islands, each of the three "arms" hundreds of miles in length. The three continents barely peeped in at the edges, almost part of the frame. Why would you care about somewhere you couldn't sail?

"I've seen *their* maps," Vyne went on. "They still have the Myriad in the center, but we look . . . small. The continents are as big as the ocean we know. The Scathian forest alone is sixteen times the size of Malpease. Think about all that timber! Imagine how many warships they could build!"

Malpease was the largest island in the Myriad, four times the size of Lady's Crave. Hark tried to visualize trees after trees after trees, stretching to the horizon where the water should meet the sky. His mind faltered.

"The League are mostly idiots," Vyne said crisply, "more likely to start a war than end one, but they're not *completely* wrong. That's why they're becoming more powerful these days."

She gave herself a little shake.

"Anyway, what I need *you* to do," she continued, "is persuade the priests to tell you about Marks."

Hark jumped despite himself. It was a subject too close to the worries preying on his mind.

"Marks?" He tried to pass off his jolt as surprise. "I thought you were just interested in gods!"

"The subjects are related," declared Vyne. "The Sanctuary archives have some references to Marks, and I'm already transcribing those." She tapped a gray moleskin notebook affectionately. "But I'm sure the priests know more. They had a lot of Marks in the old days, and even managed to remove some, so they *must* have understood them . . . Marks are *fascinating*, Hark. I've been experimenting. Do you know what happens if you dunk squirrels neck-deep in Undersea water for three hours?"

"They get wet?" suggested Hark, wondering how many damp, miserable squirrels he should be pitying.

"Yes. And they get angry. And they get out, sooner or later, and start breaking things. But do you know what they don't do? They don't develop Marks. I'm starting to think that Marks affect only gods and humans."

"And that . . . helps with your project?" Hark asked, bewildered.

"Yes," said Vyne, firmly but cryptically. "Yes, it does. Anyway, I'll be away a great deal over the next few weeks. Most people don't need to know where I am. But if you get a breakthrough, or if you need to talk to me, come to the north point of the island. Find one of the sentries and give them this, so they know you're working for me." She scribbled on a piece of paper and signed it. "Then they'll fetch me from the warehouse."

Hark took the piece of paper and stashed it in his belt pouch. It all sounded very cloak-and-dagger.

"Are they worried about spies, then?" he ventured.

"You have no idea," murmured Vyne. "Whatever you do, don't go wandering into that village unannounced. They will almost certainly shoot you."

Chapter 24

THE NEXT DAY, HARK SET ABOUT HIS DUTIES with a brisk cheeriness that sounded hollow to him. Nobody saw through it. He caught himself wishing that somebody would.

Quest was asleep. This felt like a betrayal. Hark came back and checked on him repeatedly, but his thin, almost inaudible snores sawed on. Only after several hours did Hark drop in to find Quest finally awake, blinking slowly at the world as if surprised to find it still there.

"Everyone else has eaten," Hark said, as he brought over Quest's tray. "I put yours aside."

"You're too bright," said the old priest, narrowing his eyes as though his words were literally true. "Something is troubling you again. What is it today?"

Hark felt an unexpected wave of gratitude, and for an embarrassing moment his eyes stung. He sat down next to Quest.

"Do you think I've changed since I've been here?" he asked impulsively.

"Yes," said Quest, after a moment's thought. He raised his eyebrows as Hark's shoulders sagged. "That was not what you wanted to hear?"

"How am I different?" Hark asked, fidgeting.

"When you arrived here, you had smiles for everyone," answered Quest. "Nearly all those smiles were false coin. There was no malice in it; you simply did not want to spend real feelings on anyone here. Why should you? Why care about people when they might kick you in the teeth tomorrow?

"I do not think that is true anymore. You have been stuck with all of us for a while now, have you not? You cannot con us with a smile, then run away to charm someone else. Instead, you must deal with the same people day after day. You have started to care what we think and how we feel. You sat with Pale Soul when he was dying, and when he was gone, it upset you. I do not think it would have when you first arrived. You would have looked solemn for form's sake and said all the right things, but his passing would not have got under your skin."

Quest was right. Never demanding, mildly uncomplaining, the thought of Pale Soul had been following Hark from room to room while he was about his duties. He felt a pang every time he saw the pale priest's favorite chair or thought of the frail word-threads that had trailed between them without quite becoming conversations.

"But I'm not . . . That's just . . ." Hark didn't even know what he wanted to say. How could he explain what he meant without explaining what he meant?

"Why does that idea distress you?" Quest raised an eyebrow. "Why would you want to stay the same forever?"

"But . . . what if I change so much I turn into somebody else?" Hark blurted out. "Then I'm not me anymore, am I?"

"A very philosophical question for someone who has just woken up!" retorted Quest. There was an intrigued glint in his eye, however. "Perhaps you need to work out which parts of yourself are essential to your nature. Who are you? What aspects of yourself would you fight to protect, as if you were fighting for your life?"

Hark's mind went blank. What could he say about himself?

Hark is Shelter-bred. Hark tells stories. Hark lies. Hark can haggle in fifteen languages. Hark is Jelt's best friend, closer than blood. Hark holds the Shelter record for the longest time holding a racing crab with bare hands . . . None of these sounded right. They were true, but they didn't describe the heart of him.

"I don't know," he said. Suddenly he felt like the soft, glassy jellyfish that Selphin had accused him of being. There was nothing solid inside him.

"You are still young," Quest said phlegmatically. "You will find out who you are when your choices test you. In the end, we are what we do and what we allow to be done."

What we allow to be done. Hark thought about Selphin's desperate face as she was dragged in to be "healed." What did that make him, then?

"What if . . ." Hark took a deep breath and let it out again slowly. "What if something else is changing me?"

"What do you mean?" asked the old man, frowning slightly.

"I don't know!" Hark said sullenly, swerving in despair from the secrets he could not share. "This place, maybe . . . Sanctuary . . . all the goddery and worship and *oldness*, and the Undersea water in the baths." He was babbling now, but he pushed on. "What if . . . what if living near all of that could change you? Not just your body, but who you are inside?"

For a few seconds Quest watched him in silence. He no longer seemed to find Hark's comments merely diverting or intellectually stimulating.

"Yes," he said simply at last. "I have seen this place change people. One must change to live, but . . . not all changes are good. Some warp the spirit. I have seen friends so changed that I no longer knew them."

"What happened?" Hark felt the hair rising on the back of his neck.

"We joined the priesthood." Quest gave a grim smile. "We were told to think of it as a rebirth, of course. We were given fresh names and trained to treat the other neonates as our only family, but that was only the beginning of the change.

"In order to do what we did in those days, we needed to believe in our own holiness. However, if you believe that you are holier than other people, then I think after a while you lose something. Humility. Warmth. Humor. Many of us agonized over the sacrifices at first, but habit deadens you. The scars build up on your soul."

Hark stared at him. He did not want to think of Quest gazing on, dead-eyed, as sacrifices walked trembling to their doom.

"Oh, I could feel the calluses growing on my soul, too," insisted Quest with quiet ruthlessness. "If I altered less than most, it was because my situation was different. Most of my fellows joined the priesthood because of a sense of vocation or because their family had raised them from birth for that destiny. My reason, however, was entirely stupid. I was following a girl."

"A girl?" Hark stared at him, startled and embarrassed. It seemed too personal a confession, coming from someone as old and dignified as Quest.

"Her name was Ailodie," said Quest. "She was the daughter of a priest, from a long line of priests. Her elder brother became an acolyte when he was very young, in the usual way, but died not long after his initiation. She was the next child and agreed to take his place so that none of her younger siblings would have to do so. She was kind, you see, and honorable.

"Since there were no rules against priests having lovers, I saw no reason to stop courting her . . . but she told me that she intended to be celibate. She was afraid that if she fell in love it would lead to children. She had watched her father become distant and Marked over the years, and she did not want any child of hers to watch the same thing happen to her.

"I thought that if I became an acolyte alongside her, I could win her over. She would realize how important she was to me and would be overwhelmed by my romantic gesture. Instead, she thought I was an idiot. She was right.

"We became priests and took on new names. At first hers hung loose on her, and we kept forgetting to use it. Slowly she grew into it. She was changing and deadening inside, becoming somebody who she did not like and did not want to be. It was as though this new priest-self was killing Ailodie, inch by inch, and taking over her body."

"Did she notice that she was changing?" Hark could not help asking.

"I suspect so," Quest said, and sighed. "But she was not changed by visiting the gods, or the Undersea waters, or handling divine relics. We changed her, just as we changed each other and ourselves. We are all squeezed into new shapes by the people around us. If we are paying attention, though, we always have some say in how we are altered. The priesthood corroded Ailodie because she was resigned to it."

"And you weren't?" From the start, Hark had been puzzled by Quest and his curious detachment from the other priests.

"Oh, Sanctuary changed me in a completely different way," said Quest, smiling as though something were darkly funny.

Hark sensed that confidences were over.

"If you saw me becoming somebody else . . . the way Ailodie did . . . you'd tell me, wouldn't you?" Hark felt miserably pathetic asking the question. It was like a small child asking a parent to check the shadows of the eaves for monsters.

"If I see signs that your soul is drying out and deadening, then I will be sure to mention it," said Quest. "But at present I do not think you have anything to worry about."

Quest's words were interrupted by a heaving, gasping, coughing fit that shook him for nearly a minute. At last the coughs subsided, and the old priest breathed carefully for a little while, wiping tears from his eyes with one knuckle.

"Do you need some medicine or something?" asked Hark, but the old man shook his head.

"It will not help, I fear. I suffered a bad case of Riser's Bane during the Cataclysm, and my lungs have never quite forgiven me."

Riser's Bane was the sea's punishment for rising from the depths too fast or in the wrong way. It ravaged your soft and tender inner workings, such as your eardrums, the fine veins of your eyes, or the frail florets of your lungs.

"Change is a lot more frightening when you are older," Quest continued, conversationally. He did not look afraid. If anything, he seemed slightly wistful. "Gradually, gradually, your body lets you down. You reach a certain age . . . and almost every change is bad news. Bulletins from the front in a war you are losing. At *your* age, you are still asking yourself: *Who should I be?* I must ask myself: *Did I manage to be the person I wanted to be, in the end? And how many chances do I have left to be that person?*"

Of course, Hark *did* have urgent reasons to be afraid of dying, but he understood that there was a difference. Hark was facing danger; Quest was facing inevitability, and facing it with his usual ironic, analytical smile.

Chapter 25

THREE DAYS LATER, HARK MET CORAM ON THE beach again.

"Any news of Selphin?" Hark blurted out, before the tall man had even hailed him.

The news was not good. Selphin had not returned. If she had reached shore, she was avoiding her mother's gang and doing so more effectively than anybody had expected. Nobody voiced the other possibility in Rigg's presence, of course. Selphin's body had not been found, but the sea was hungry and mysterious and did not always give back its prey.

The gang had chased a few clues that came to nothing. A fisherman thought he had seen her aboard a lugger, but this turned out to have been a different girl. There were stray reports of her on the island of Rattleguise, forty miles away, but that proved to be a red herring, too.

Hark had hoped for news of her alive so that he could settle finally on anger—clean, uncomplicated anger—instead of his current mess of doubt, guilt, and dread.

"Rigg thinks somebody's hiding her," said Coram. "Otherwise we'd have found her by now."

Maybe she's run far away, thought Hark hopefully. *She's stubborn enough. If she worked passage to the far end of the Myriad, that would explain why we haven't heard from her.*

He was not sure whether he believed it, however. She had

been afraid of the god-heart's effect on herself but also fiercely concerned about the way it was affecting her crewmates and friends. Would she really abandon them?

They climbed into the submersible as usual, and Hark huddled under the table, absorbed in his own thoughts. It took him a while to notice that Coram kept darting glances at him as he rowed.

"What's wrong?" Hark asked, too tired to play guessing games.

"Nothing," said Coram. "I was just wondering something." He cleared his throat. "I was wondering about that Undersea wave—the one that Marked you and your friend. I never heard of one that close to the surface. Do you reckon a wave like that is a . . . sign of something?"

"What kind of something?" asked Hark.

Coram puffed out his cheeks, then rowed for another few strokes without answering.

"People are saying maybe the Undersea's angry, or . . . trying to tell us something."

He looked at Hark again. By the light of the dim, purple lamps, his expression looked perplexed but slightly hopeful, as if he thought Hark might have answers for him.

"Why would the Undersea be angry?" asked Hark in bewilderment.

"Well . . . my wife's uncle thinks it's my fault. Our fault. Everyone doing deals with the continentals, letting their ships sail the Myriad. He knows we're going out to trade with the *Pelican* tonight, and he doesn't like it. 'Opening the sluice gate,' he calls it. He says the continentals will all pour in and never stop until they've taken over everything."

Hark had heard plenty of mutters of that sort in the marketplace growing up, but that was just the sort of thing old people said, or Leaguers. He was learning that a lot of other people felt that way, too.

"Did you hear about what happened on Rattleguise?" Coram went on. "Some sailors from the east continent came ashore and started snooping around the docks, looking at the cannons on the parapet. So a crowd of lumpers and dockworkers strung the sailors up from a crane as spies, before the guards even got there. Then the ship trained its cannons on the harbor and wouldn't leave till the warehouse owners banded together and gave them a lot of money."

"Bet it didn't happen like that," Hark said with stubborn nonchalance. "It was probably just a fistfight that got out of hand. Makes a good story, though, doesn't it?" He didn't want to believe that his fellow Myriddens were so frightened of continentals that they would murder them for walking along an artillery parapet. He didn't want to believe that those vast merchant ships from the continent might start firing on harbor fronts and extorting money.

"This is just the start," said Coram, the purple light glinting in his earnest eyes. "That's what everyone's saying now. So maybe that's why the Undersea's angry. Maybe it sent that wave on purpose to Mark you. Maybe you and your friend are what the Myriad need right now."

Hark was starting to understand why Selphin had been worried about her half-brother. Coram was too young to remember the Cataclysm, but some young people still had an odd hole inside them, left by the deaths of the gods. He had always seemed rather levelheaded, but you couldn't always tell with the quiet ones. Sometimes they got hold of a crazy idea and sat there in secret turning it over and over and over, like a dead kitten.

At Wildman's Hammer, Hark numbly went through the

motions during the healing session. Jelt seemed to have forgotten about Selphin altogether, and Hark was rather happy about it, since he didn't think he could bear any jokes on the subject. As he was waiting to be taken back to Nest, however, Coram ran over to him.

"Hey! Just got word from the captain. You're to come out again tonight. Be at the usual place by midnight."

"What?" Hark stared at him. "Why?"

"Someone says they saw Selphin, down at the old docks at the Pales." Coram seemed brighter and more cheerful than he had for a while. The Pales were a set of old dockyards on Twice, an island on the far side of Lady's Crave. "She might have been living down there in one of the old warehouse cellars."

Of course she's alive. Of course she was alive all the time. She was probably laughing at us all for thinking she might be dead.

"The lucky thing is, the Pales is on a spit, so if we get half a dozen men down there, we can cut her off." Coram rubbed his neck. "I hope six is enough," he muttered.

"Why only six?" asked Hark.

"The *Pelican*'s hanging offshore tonight, so we're sending out a boat to trade with them. Rigg needs most of the gang for that."

"So . . . you want me to help catch Selphin?" Hark's spirits sank.

"No," said Coram. "We need you waiting here. If we set off for Twice now, we can catch Selphin and be back tonight. Rigg wants her healed as soon as we can get her to you. It ends tonight."

For the rest of the day, Hark stumbled through his chores, unable to think of anything but his conversation with Coram. Selphin was apparently alive, but that very night she would probably be caught. Then he would be expected to "fix" her, the very thing she had risked her life to avoid.

We are what we do and what we allow to be done, Quest had said.

Even if Selphin was wrong about the god-heart rewriting her personality, it still meant forcing something on her that terrified her. What could he do, though? If Hark refused, or failed his appointment, Rigg would skin him alive at the first opportunity.

Maybe I could help Selphin escape. The thought hit him while he was mopping the floors and brought him to a halt. His chest tightened. It was an insane idea, but for some reason it was also exhilarating, liberating.

What *could* he do?

Rigg had talked about having Selphin tied up. Hark could try to slip the smuggler girl something sharp so that she could cut through her bonds.

She would still need to get off the island, of course. Hark pondered this as he pounded laundry in its bucket and hung up robe after robe on a roof terrace. Maybe Selphin could steal whatever vessel brought her to Wildman's Hammer, or perhaps the boat belonging to Jelt's pet bodyguards. Darkness would help her a little.

Selphin would be heavily outnumbered. Jelt's creepy followers guarded him throughout the night these days, so they would be there, as well as whichever members of her own gang brought her. There was nothing Hark could do about that—or was there? He couldn't get rid of them, but perhaps he could make them less alert.

Some of the cordials in the Sanctuary storeroom were sedatives. Quantities were recorded to discourage staff from selling the medicines on the black market. However, Hark had an understanding with the attendant who was doing exactly that, so he was sure he could divert a dose.

"Have you seen Kly?" asked one of the other staff, as Hark returned to the dining hall. "I can't find him anywhere."

"No—but I can have a look for him!" Hark offered eagerly. Now if he was spotted going into the storeroom, he could just claim he was making a thorough search.

He slipped to the storeroom, opened the door, and stopped in his tracks. His "search" for the foreman had been unexpectedly successful.

Kly was standing very still, his face carefully calm, but Hark could see a nervous pulse in his temple. The old woman known as Moonmaid was holding a long shard of glass against his throat. Neither shifted an inch as the door opened, though the priest's eyes flicked instantly to Hark.

"It's all right, Hark," said Kly, very quietly. "We're . . . just having a conversation. Moonmaid thinks we're hiding Pale Soul and interrogating him."

"Tell your underling to return him to us," said Moonmaid, in her deep, resonant voice. "Or you will never see another morning, unbeliever!"

"You head off now, Hark," said Kly, in the same matter-of-fact tone. A bead of sweat ran down his cheek. "Moonmaid's just a bit . . . confused right now."

We are what we do and what we allow to be done.

Hark looked into Moonmaid's sharp face, with its cool eyes and stern, unrelenting mouth.

"You're not confused, are you?" he said. "You're just an ice-cold harridan who needs watching." He ignored Kly's attempts to panic signal using tiny frowns. "I'm not very nice, either. But Kly over there is a big, soft idiot. You tried to stab him before, and he still lets you run around loose. *I* wouldn't. And if you stab Kly, the next foreman definitely won't. Kly thunders well, but he wouldn't swat a wasp, Moonmaid. He wouldn't have let anyone hurt Pale Soul."

Hark remembered all the secretive whispering between Moonmaid and Pale Soul, comrades in their suspicion of the Sanctuary staff.

"I know you want to save your friend," he said more gently, "but you can't. He's gone. I'm the one who saw him pass on. I'm the only one who talked to him in his sickroom. If that makes me an interrogator, I guess you should be stabbing me."

Moonmaid's eyes silvered with a damp sheen, and then she lunged for Hark, far faster than he had expected. He barely caught her thin arm as the shard sped toward his face.

She gave a wail of anguished rage, and Hark almost let go, afraid that he had hurt her. He only just kept his head and his hold. Between them, Kly and Hark restrained Moonmaid until other attendants came to carry her away.

"Make sure she hasn't cut her hand!" Kly called after them, then sat down heavily on a crate. "Why me?" he muttered, rubbing the sweat from his face. "Why does she always try to stab *me*?"

"You're just the nearest unbeliever," said Hark.

"I'm not an unbeliever!" snapped Kly. He was reddening now with embarrassment and annoyance. "Just because I don't worship your . . . rotting, murderous fish-monsters! What's the point of a god you can pickle?"

"What's the point of a god that you can't see, that doesn't do anything?" Hark flashed back, unable to stop himself.

"You *can* see the sun. You *can* watch the seasons."

"I thought you folks from the west continent worshipped imaginary people in the clouds!"

"The continent," Kly said through his teeth, "has a name. It's called Revda. The country I come from is Alemgarr. The people who believe that their ancestors watch from the clouds live in Fefia, on the opposite side of the continent. You people really don't see anything outside the Myriad, do you?"

Hark couldn't understand how they had ended up in an argument. Belatedly he realized that being rescued from an old woman by a boy half his age might have been a blow to Kly's pride.

"You people," murmured Kly, staring at the shard on the floor. "It's like there's a bit of Undersea in all of you, waiting to rear up."

Chapter 26

WHEN HARK REACHED THE BEACH AT MIDNIGHT, there was no sign of the usual submersible. Instead he saw a small, single-masted sailing boat in the bay. In it sat a man and a woman, the latter holding a lit scare-lantern, their breath steam in the cold night air. As he drew closer, he noticed the woman's sealed nostrils and recognized the pair as members of Jelt's new bodyguard. Hark had known that Rigg's gang would be busy this night, but he hadn't stopped to wonder who might be picking him up.

The two of them bowed silently as he climbed into the boat, and the man handed Hark his gray mask. Hark put it on, sensing that this was expected, but the action made him uneasy. He was agreeing to be what they wanted. They didn't wish to see his nervous, human face.

They let out the boat's dull brown sails and took it out of the bay without a word. Hark sat hunched, watching the sea. He was glad that he did not need to say anything, and yet as the silence dragged on, it wore at his nerves.

By the time they moored in the little crescent harbor at Wildman's Hammer, Hark was shivering. The black crags looked higher in the dark. The crash of waves was louder, the eruptions of foam almost luminous. As Hark clambered ashore, he felt his knees trembling a little, and not just from the cold. The whole islet had become a sacred place, filled with icy, malignant mystery.

It made him feel small, transparent, and *judged*. This site of dark pilgrimage knew about the betrayal he was planning. It was watching him.

Hark adjusted his mask then walked slowly along the familiar path, down the rocky corridor toward the tent. His two companions walked wordlessly behind him, their footsteps crunching on loose rocks. The purple lamplight picked out boulders and rocks jutting from the cliff but bleached and flattened them.

On the way to the tent, he encountered three more of Jelt's bodyguards, standing like statues, their lamps dim and set on the ground at their feet. The purple radiance underlit their faces, making them look even more unnerving than usual. They saw him and instantly readied their weapons. Hark held his lamp aloft so that it fell on his mask, and they relaxed.

"Your resolve shows you worthy," he said, in what he hoped was an eerily commanding tone, "but you should have noticed me sooner."

The three armed figures all silently moved aside to let Hark past, then kneeled and touched their foreheads to the naked rock. They had no campfire, Hark noticed, though there was a little pile of firewood nearby and what looked like a pack of provisions. By lamplight it was hard to tell whether they were going blue with cold, but some of them seemed to be shivering.

He strode silently past them and into the tent. Inside he found to his surprise that only one lamp was lit, and it was turned right down so that its glow was faint as a fading ember.

"Jelt?" Hark whispered loudly. "Are you asleep?"

"No. Of course I'm not." The gravelly whisper came back immediately. "We've got work to do tonight, haven't we?"

"Then why is it so dark in here? I'm going to turn the lamp up."

"Leave it," Jelt hissed sharply.

Hark halted, his hand almost touching the lamp. There was menace and urgency in Jelt's voice.

"Why?" Hark demanded.

"Light kills your night sight, doesn't it?"

"So what?"

"I want to be able to see in the dark. Just in case I need to."

"Why would you need to? What do you think is going to come out of the dark? A gang of killer seals?" Hark kept his tone mocking, but it was unnerving being unable to see Jelt at all. Since the alcove echoed, he couldn't even be quite sure where the voice was coming from. "Is that why your bootlickers don't have a campfire?"

"It's not that cold," said Jelt.

"Yes it is!" Hark was getting frightened and annoyed now. "It's freezing, Jelt, and they're standing outside. They need a fire, Jelt. *I* need a fire, or something hot to eat, anyway. Don't try to tell me that's because I've gone soft."

"Sounds like I don't need to say it," said Jelt with quiet nastiness. "You can go and make a fire, if it'll stop you whining all night, but make sure it's not too close to the tent. Get them to make some soup while they're at it." It was almost a concession, but as usual Jelt had managed to stop it sounding like one.

Hark left the tent, and the faint starlight was welcome after the indigo murk of the tent.

Trying to keep his sinister mystique intact, Hark ordered the bodyguards to make a fire, which they did with alacrity. He ordered them to make a soup and they hurried to obey, hanging a little pot over the fire and digging out their water flask and provisions. Hark let himself slowly warm by the fire, as wisps of steam licked out of the top of the cooking pot, and the lid started to jump and jiggle. Hark was used to having to wheedle, trick, and bargain people into doing what he wanted. It was strange and wonderful to give orders and see them obeyed.

None of his elaborate plans for adding the cordial were needed. All he needed to do was give the weird followers permission to prostrate themselves while he "spoke words of power" over the soup. He quickly spooned out bowlfuls for himself and Jelt, then poured in the sedative and stirred. All the bodyguards remained motionless until he gave the word.

"Eat," he said, "so that you may serve us better."

Again they obeyed without question. It gave Hark a dangerous glimpse of how easy life would be if he let these people do everything he said. That power had a sour aftertaste, however.

"Soup," said Hark bluntly as he reentered the tent. Jelt's invisible hands took the bowl from his grasp. Hark sat down and wrapped blankets around himself. He would have to go out and warm up by the campfire now and then, he decided. He just hoped he could do that in an unnerving and mysterious way. "Some of those lackeys of yours are new, aren't they?"

"They guard me in shifts," said Jelt. Hark could almost imagine the self-congratulatory shrug.

"How many of them are there now?"

"The ones who come here? About twenty. Including the rest . . . nearly forty, probably."

"The rest?" Hark's instincts tingled with unease. "What 'rest'? What do they do?"

"Spread the word," Jelt rasped laconically. "Find things for me. Set things up."

Hark ate in silence for a few seconds. The soup burned his tongue but had fat shrimp and good crabmeat in it, with some spices. Nothing but the best for the healing monsters.

"What are you doing, Jelt?" he asked at last. "You're up to

something new that Rigg doesn't know about. You're waiting for me to ask what it is. So I'm asking."

"You always think too small, too low," said Jelt from the blackness. "Reaching as high as Rigg gave you a nosebleed. Now we're rising higher. We're not going to need her soon, and we'll be too strong for her to touch us. She hasn't worked out that Wildman's Hammer is *our* base now, not hers. She thinks she's smarter than us—that's why she can't see it."

"Great," said Hark, with false jocularity. "You're the king of Wildman's Hammer, all six square feet of it. Long may you reign."

"We're not going to stop at *this* flyspeck," said Jelt coldly. "Or Lady's Crave, either. We're what the Myriad's been waiting for."

It sounded a lot like Coram's words in the sub that morning. Hark felt an all-too-familiar sinking of the heart. This wasn't a Jelt plan just starting to rumble into motion. This was one with momentum behind it—and a downward slope.

"You really want this, don't you?" he said. "A religion of you, with people knocking their foreheads on the floor to please you. And you've got people 'spreading the word'? Jelt, we can't afford to be famous! You're wanted everywhere, and I'm *indentured*!"

"It's always the fears with you, isn't it?" rasped Jelt. "This is the chance of a lifetime!"

"What is wrong with you?" Hark could feel his frustration breaking loose. "I can't talk to you like this. I'm going to turn up the lamp."

"No!" hissed Jelt.

As Hark reached for the lamp, something cold batted his fingers away. Hark pulled back and rubbed his fingers against his chest.

His skin was stinging, and the thing that had touched him had not felt like a hand.

Chapter 27

SOMETHING HAD LASHED OUT AND STRUCK Hark's fingers in the dark. Something fast as a whip, but cold, slippery, and soft, that stung like an anemone's caress. There was something sticky clinging to Hark's hand, and he wanted to run out of the tent to the water's edge, to wash it off.

He didn't. Instead, he silently wiped his hand on his sleeve and tried to breathe normally. Instinct told him that he was balancing on a knife-edge. No sudden moves, then. No sudden screams.

Nothing wrong, just sitting here with my best friend, Jelt. With a posse of his crazy armed worshippers waiting outside. And nobody else on the entire island.

But if I can keep him talking, I get time to think. He gets time to calm down. And the folks outside have time to get groggy.

"No need to freak out," Hark said, and marveled at how natural his voice sounded. Petulant, defensive, but not terrified. "Fine, sit in the dark and be mysterious. I don't care." With luck, Jelt wouldn't guess that Hark had noticed anything. With luck, Jelt couldn't hear the banging of his friend's heart.

Hark had driven himself to distraction trying to work out if the god-heart had changed him in some horrific, invisible way. Somehow he had forgotten that Jelt had been in the presence of the relic day in and day out, for weeks. Every strange pulse, every contraction and surge had flooded through Jelt's body and mind.

When had Hark last seen Jelt by daylight? It had been nearly a month, he realized. Hark had assumed that while he was away, Jelt probably came out, relaxed, fished, swam, and ate with Rigg's people. Perhaps he didn't. Perhaps *nobody* had seen him in daylight for some time . . .

"Your hand is *really* cold," he said, managing to sound conversational but concerned. Scraping his spoon against the bottom of the bowl filled the silence with a comforting small sound. "Have you been sleeping without a fire every night? Are you crazy? You need to keep warm. You nearly died, remember?"

Jelt was silent. Had he noticed the slight tremble in Hark's voice? Could he see Hark's expression in the dark?

"All right, *don't* listen then." Hark took a last mouthful of soup and made himself swallow. "What I'm saying is, if you're going to be a cult leader, why not get your creepy slaves to find you somewhere warm? Maybe on the mainland? Your voice sounds . . . like there might be trouble with your lungs. Riser's Bane, maybe. We came up pretty fast that day." He remembered Jelt talking about the way his lungs kept "pop-pop-popping" in response to the god-heart's pulses. Perhaps they hadn't just been healing, after all.

"I'm not sick," said the voice from the darkness.

Maybe not. Maybe you're all better. Better than ever. Improved.

"If you say so," said Hark, and then dropped his voice to a whisper. "But if you're not . . . why are you still hugging that relic like you're drowning and it's a timber? If you're better, you don't need it with you all the time, do you?" He was in dangerous territory now; he could sense it.

"I know what you're doing," rasped the voice that was so like and unlike Jelt. "You want me to leave it with *you*, don't you? You think you can wheedle it away from me and then . . . what? Sell it? Throw it in the sea? So you can run away from the best chance we'll ever get?"

"Jelt." Hark slowly let out a breath. "You really want the truth? I *do* want you get rid of it. Yes, I'm scared for myself! But I'm *terrified* for you." That was as close as he dared to go to admitting what he had felt in the dark. "You haven't seen those priests I deal with every day. Too much goddery . . . it twists you up, Jelt. Let's just dump the freaky bone-lump and get away from this place! We can find other chances. Jelt, this is me. Hark. Your friend. Your best friend. Listen to me, just this once! I'm *begging* you!"

"You don't understand," said the darkness. "I'm not the one who has to give something up. You are."

"What?" Hark's mouth was dry. "What are you talking about?"

"You can't go on like this," said the other voice. "Toing and froing. Sneaking out to meet us, then running back to Sanctuary again. You said it yourself, didn't you? Sooner or later they'll get wise and send you to the galleys."

"So what are you saying? That's it, you don't need me anymore, goodbye?" Even though the thought hurt, Hark secretly hoped that this was what Jelt meant. He knew that it wasn't, though.

"You need to give up being the Sanctuary lapdog," came the inevitable answer. "You need to disappear and never go back. Make them think you're dead."

"It won't work!" Hark answered too quickly. "They always find the runaways! They'll have my picture up in every dockyard! I can't wear that mask for the rest of my life!"

"You won't have to," rasped the shadow, "if your face doesn't look like that anymore."

Hark was aware of the narrow slit of half-light that was the opening of the tent. He could leap for that if he had to. But whatever sat in the tent with him was fast, he knew that now.

"We can change your face," continued his companion. "Cut it up, move it around a bit, heal it. Nobody'll recognize you after that. We can change your voice. Slit your tongue, cut your throat, heal them up. They'll work just fine. They just won't be the same."

"I'd look Marked." Hark's voice sounded tight and panicky, and he couldn't help putting up one hand to protect his throat. "I wouldn't be able to walk about in daylight without people staring and noticing me. Think about it, Jelt. I couldn't buy stuff, or spy, or make deals, or run cons."

"You won't need to do all of that anymore," said the Jelt-shadow. "We got other people for the daylight stuff now."

"I don't want that, Jelt!" erupted Hark. "Why would I want you to fillet my face, so I have to hide in shadows forever? I *like* my face. I *like* my voice. They're *mine*. If you want to sit in a dark hole for the rest of your life, I can't stop you. But leave me out of it!"

But even as he spoke, realization was dawning, like a strengthening of his night sight. Jelt wouldn't let him go. Once again, Hark had committed the unforgivable sin of having something Jelt didn't. If Jelt could no longer walk down a street in daylight . . . then neither would Hark.

"You always say no," answered his friend. "But you'll thank me for it later."

Jelt wasn't asking permission. The realization hit Hark like a brick. He opened his mouth to protest, but there was no breath in his lungs.

In that moment of silence, there came a tumult of yells from outside, and the whistle of slingshots.

"What the scourge—" rasped the Jelt-shadow.

"I'll go!" gasped Hark, and scrambled out of the tent into the firelit night. For a moment, he felt grateful for the excuse to leave.

That moment ended quickly. The bodyguards were in disarray, crouching and shielding their faces as stones whistled down toward them. Beyond them he could hear rapid footsteps, then saw a torrent of dark figures running in with weapons raised—belaying pins, knuckledusters, blackjacks with thick rope.

The bodyguards who had seemed so intimidating jerked, reeled, and twisted as they took blow after blow. They moved too slowly and groggily to dodge. Their swings missed. Their clumsy blades struck sparks off the cliff. Hark's drug had been all too effective.

The campfire was kicked apart, the embers quickly dulling in the damp breeze and losing their light. Bodyguard after bodyguard was knocked to the ground, their weapons kicked from their grasp. Warning boots were placed against the backs of their necks to keep them down.

Hark darted behind a boulder. Nothing would persuade him to run back into the tent. There was no obvious escape route. The "shrine" had been placed somewhere with only one easy approach, so it could be defended. On either side rose steep walls of rock, difficult to climb quickly in the dark.

There seemed to be about a dozen attackers, their faces muffled with scarves. Well organized. Good boots. Good knives in their belts, too, though for some reason they hadn't drawn them. To judge by the sounds, the fight was now over. Hark held his breath and stayed in hiding.

"Hey!" shouted an unfamiliar male voice. "We know you're in there, boy. Be smart and come out. We're only here for the relic."

The relic? How do they know there's a relic?

Hark stayed still and silent. If they were calling for someone to come out of the tent, they probably hadn't spotted him ducking behind his rock.

"Just hand it over and we'll go. Then you can get on with your singsong."

Hark saw a glimmer of desperate hope. Perhaps these enemies were the answer to his problems. He couldn't force Jelt to part with the god-heart, but they probably could. They'd take it by force if necessary. Surely he could make Jelt see that fighting them was useless.

"We're willing to talk!" Hark called out quickly, standing up. "Just don't hurt any—"

That was as far as his negotiation went, because something exploded from the front of the tent, with a sound of ripping canvas.

The figure was of Jelt's height. It turned to him, and he was glad that the light of the dying fire was behind it so that he could not see its face—only two pools of paleness where its eyes should be. It grabbed his wrist in a cold, slick grip and slapped something round and hard into his hand. Hark recognized the god-heart from its weight and pitted surface.

"Don't lose it, or I'll kill you!" hissed the figure. Then it raced away toward the waiting attackers.

"Stop!" yelled Hark. "You can't! We need to talk to them!"

It turned out that Jelt didn't need to talk. He didn't need to do anything.

He didn't need to avoid the embers, his bare feet kicking showers of sparks as he sprinted. He didn't need light to guide his footing. He didn't need to run like a person. His legs didn't need to bend in just the usual ways.

He didn't need to draw a blade. Something long lashed out from the direction of his throat, like a pale cord two yards long. It struck a man in the face with a sickly spasm of pale yellow light, so that he reeled away, screaming. Then, as Jelt came within reach of the stranger, he flung out one arm in a sideways slashing motion, and . . .

. . . and something happened in the dark brawl like a black explosion, dark blood detonating almost silently. The man's torso was falling one way, his legs the other . . .

Now there was a lot of screaming and yelling, but Hark could only stand where he was and stare.

There's only one of him. They'll cut him down. Hark no longer knew if this was a fear or a hope.

Those strangers unlucky enough to be at the front hastily drew their knives. They flailed desperately at Jelt and blundered backward into their confused comrades. A moment ago they had all looked invincible. Now they were backing away in panic from something that leaped, and darted, and slashed. With each slash there came a scream, the sort of scream that nobody gives twice.

"Back to the boats!" someone yelled, and all of the strangers turned tail and ran. The Jelt-shape leaped on the rearmost enemy, and a moment later a lone head was bouncing soddenly down the path.

"Wait!" called Hark. "Let them go! You don't need to do that!"

Jelt didn't need to chase them. But he did. He chased them as a fox chases chickens in a coop, killing them with a swift, pure pleasure that had nothing to do with need.

The screams continued, but they grew more distant. The attackers were fleeing back toward their own boats, but they would probably never get there. Their pursuer was faster than them and could see in the dark.

Hark suddenly felt the god-heart flex in his tight grip. The perforations grated harshly against his fingers. The pulse was like a punch.

He wondered if it could smell blood or detect conflict. Perhaps it just sensed that some nearby human bodies were marred in ways it could fix. With nausea, he imagined it "mending" its battered cultists in new and interesting ways, or even gluing together the mangled bodies along the path and stirring them into misshapen life . . .

Hark clenched his teeth and glared down at it.

"Oh, *scab this!*" he swore under his breath.

He stuffed the relic in his bag and gritted his teeth. Then he ran past the sprawled, half-stunned cultists and into the limb-strewn darkness of the rocky corridor. His feet slithered, and there were splatters on the stone floor like dark flowers, and there was a smell, and he tried not to think about it, any of it. His foot caught on something, and he went down, one knee and one hand hitting the ground and feeling its slickness.

Get up. Keep running. Don't think about the wetness, or the shapes lying on the ground.

He had to be quick, because if Jelt came back, if *it* came back . . .

Hark ran out onto the craggy shore. The distant calls and screams were now coming from the other side of the island. He sprinted for the bodyguards' boat. He had imagined Selphin escaping on it. It had never occurred to him that he might need to do so.

There she was, her dull brown sails tethered and her oars resting neatly in her belly. She was too big for one person, really, but she would have to do. He yanked her moorings loose and leaped aboard, staggering as his feet hit the boards. Using a paddle, he pushed off as hard as he could, then grabbed two oars and started heaving on them.

Away. Get away. Row out until I'm in the wind, then loose the sails and go somewhere, anywhere, as long as it's not here.

He flinched as he heard a long, hoarse cry from the dark island.

"Hark!" it called, and then again, "Hark!"

Hark kept rowing, his hands shaking.

"Hark, where are you? It's safe now. You can come out." Another long pause, then the voice called again, more urgently. "Hark—come here! Bring it to me! I need it!"

Hark was cold. He didn't think he'd ever been so cold. The chill bit his fingers and caught in his throat, but he kept rowing, even though it was hard to breathe. There were so many stars tonight, like a powdered-sugar accident. What was the point of them?

"Ha-a-a-ark!" The cry was more desperate now. "Hurry up, will you? I need it! I'll die without it!"

The cry went through him like an arrow. Hark couldn't see straight. His fingers couldn't grip the oars properly. The strength had gone out of him, and he couldn't will himself to make the next pull.

Killing Jelt. I might be killing Jelt.

He looked over his shoulder at Wildman's Hammer, its black mass eating the charcoal sky and stars. With a sick sense of inevitability, he saw that it was slowly moving toward him, like a great predator approaching by stealth. The current was undoing all his efforts. It was carrying him back to Jelt.

All his life, there had been a current dragging Hark back to Jelt, over and over. He had never been able to fight it. When Jelt needed him, Hark had always, *always* come running.

Tightening his grip on the oars again was the hardest thing Hark had ever done. Dragging them through the water felt like murder. But he did it, and did it again, and again, and again, gritting his teeth as the spray chilled his face.

He rowed until he was far enough from the tiny islet to risk standing and letting out the sail, his fingers fumbling numbly against the lines. Even after Wildman's Hammer had melted into the night behind him, Hark kept listening for that voice in the wind's cry. He couldn't stop shaking, and every lurch of the boat felt like a blow.

The sea had never looked so black.

Chapter 28

THE GOD-HEART LAY IN HARK'S PACK, STILL AS a stone. Only when he ran the boat aground on one of Nest's shores and jumped into the knee-high water did he feel it give a small pulse. He had grazed his shin on a submerged rock, so perhaps the heart had sensed a chance to fix something.

Hark waded ashore, stumbling with exhaustion, then pulled the heart out of his pack. He drew his arm back, wanting to fling the heart into the waiting black mouth of the ocean. If he did, though, some visiting scavenger gang would find it, sure as winter. Even if he took the boat out again and hurled the thing overboard, it would wash up on a beach or be found by the divers searching for salvage.

Then it would be someone else's problem. But Hark didn't want to think about some unwitting person picking it up, then getting unexpectedly altered, or murdered by Jelt for having it.

"I can break you," Hark growled, staring down at the ivory-like surface. "I can smash you with rocks." It looked fragile. If he broke it, though, there was no going back.

I need it! I'll die without it! Jelt had shouted.

Maybe it was just an addiction. Addicts sometimes talked like they were dying. Hark had seen drunks tapping and pleading at the locked door of the tavern and Old Besh's customers desperately haggling for a twist of bilesmoke or arrowsnuff. *I need it, I need it!* they always said.

Then he remembered the way that Jelt had talked about getting sick every time he was away from the heart. He had said that even at the start, before he started hiding in shadows.

"I don't understand!" snarled Hark, overcome with frustration and tiredness. "Why does he still need you? I *saved* him! Why doesn't he *stay* saved, like Coram? And why is he . . ."

Hark closed his eyes tight, but he couldn't shut out the pictures in his head. The Jelt-shape leaping and slashing at a dark mass that screamed with human voices . . .

That *thing* was Jelt. Hark felt a miserable horror at the memory, but as always there was the tug of their connection. Hark couldn't destroy the heart if that might condemn Jelt to death. As Hark put it back into his pack, he felt thwarted and depressed, as though he had argued with the relic and lost.

Hark was nauseous and shaking by the time he reached Sanctuary. The sky was still very dark, with no hint of the coming dawn. Clambering up over the roofs took longer than usual because his knees kept trying to give way.

Hark was just closing the window behind him when he was caught in a purple light.

"Hey! What are you doing there?" Two of the night guards were standing at the end of the corridor. Hark hoped they hadn't seen him climb in.

"I work here!" he answered quickly. "I help look after the priests!"

"Wait, I *have* seen him around," said one of the guards. "What are you doing up here, then?"

Hark knew that he must look sweaty, shaky, and out of breath. Perhaps this could be turned to his advantage.

"I'm hot," he said, a little tremulously. "I . . . don't feel right. I was looking for somewhere cool."

"Hot?" The first guard drew closer, holding up his lantern. "You look like death. We'd better put you in a quarantine room. I'll let Kly know."

Hark was led to a dusty little chamber where the straw mattress was flattened and moldy. He collapsed on it and didn't care. Very soon he slid into an uneasy dream, in which a silent bell rang again and again, vibrating his bones. Eventually its thrum grew gentler, until it became the purr of a gigantic cat.

Hark was allowed to sleep late. When he awoke, he no longer felt weak or shaky. Perhaps the god-heart had given him a little burst of healing to win him over, like a stray dog groveling and whimpering to be allowed near a campfire.

It was midafternoon before Hark was allowed out of quarantine. There was a grueling interview with Kly, who didn't believe that Hark had suddenly come down with a convenient fever and then just as conveniently shaken it off in a single night.

"I thought I'd be calling you in today to praise you," said the foreman at last, sounding tired rather than angry. It was the nearest he had come to mentioning the Moonmaid incident. "Then this happens. Understand, I *can't* let you play fast and loose, or I'd be betraying the people who trust *me*. I don't know where you went last night or what you took that left you looking so sick and sweaty, but this can't happen again. I don't want to know how you paid for whatever it was. If you stole anything, find a way to put it back before I notice it's gone."

He held up a hand to silence Hark's protests and left.

Kly's patience and discretion had been eked out one more time, but Hark guessed that they were probably at their limits. "This is your last warning" was something people might say several times, but there was always a *last* last warning, and

Hark thought he might have reached it. It had a different sound, something you could feel in your bones.

Hark splashed water on his face and got ready for work. He wrapped the heart in a sling of cloth and tucked it under his robes so it hung down beneath one arm, hidden by the loose folds of cloth.

He still didn't know much about it. He didn't know whether it had its own thoughts, feelings, or schemes. He didn't know why it was still alive, thirty years after the death of the gods.

But Quest might.

Deep down, Hark had been wanting to bring the god-heart to Quest for a while. The old man was slowly dying, and Hark wasn't ready for Quest to die. He didn't know how it had happened, but their conversations had become necessary to him. The medicines at Sanctuary couldn't cure lungs mangled by Riser's Bane, but perhaps the god-heart could.

As he entered the halls of Sanctuary, the smells, dim light, and gentle hum of conversation was almost comforting. Stealthily, all these things had become, if not home, then at least homely. He had started to feel safe there.

"Where's Quest?" he asked.

"In the infirmary for lebineck oil and hot stones."

This was worrying news. Treatments like lebineck-oil rubs and pressure from hot stones were what you tried when the usual medicines weren't working. That was something to ask Quest about when he emerged from the treatment room.

Hark was picking up some empty bowls from the floor when he felt the god-heart stir against his side. It was the smallest throb, but one of the bowls slipped from his fingers and clattered on the floor. He picked it up and grinned ruefully at those who had been startled by the noise.

Most people returned their attention to whatever they had

been doing before. A tiny, half-blind female priest called Seamist, however, continued staring at him. When he carried the bowls to the kitchens, he realized that she was slowly hobbling after him, her misty eyes fixed on him.

She had been close enough to notice the throb. Hark kept walking and hoped that she would get distracted.

The second pulse came about a minute later, just as he was passing Moonmaid in the corridor. She halted in her tracks and slowly turned to look at him. In a nearby chamber he saw Wailwind struggling out of his chair, staring around him with a fearful alertness. Hark paced away from them as nonchalantly as he could and ducked into a cupboard, trying not to panic.

Why now? Hark wanted to ask the heart. *Why are you beating now?* He could already guess. He had brought it to a place of sickness, frail bones, failing eyes, and dimming memories.

It pulsed again, and Hark flinched. There were slow steps outside. The door of the cupboard rattled, first tentatively then furiously. Other steps were approaching now, some plodding, some dragging. Hark felt a rising bubble of panic. He was cornered and becoming more so by the moment.

Hark took a deep breath and burst out of the cupboard. He had to push past Moonmaid, dodging as she made a snatch at his arm, then ducked around Seamist and Wailwind a few yards behind her.

Halfstar was standing in a doorway as Hark sprinted past. As the heart pulsed again, Halfstar's gaze became glassy, and his mouth dropped open, letting out a thin, breathy noise. He reached out one hand and clutched loosely at the air.

"You came *back*," he whispered, his voice hollow with hope and a sort of despair. "Why did you go?" he called after Hark's retreating figure. "I have been waiting *so long* . . ."

Another pulse. Call-of-the-Air flung her door open, her long gray hair wild and a bandage unfurling from one leg. She stared at Hark, and past him, and all around, as if looking for something that she needed and feared to find.

"Where is it?" she screamed.

Hark did not stop to answer. He kept running down corridor after corridor, hearing wails and hoarse cries behind him. He had to find somewhere to hide, away from everyone else.

They're old, he told himself as he fled. *They're confused, they're harmless. I just can't afford to get caught up in a fuss, that's all. People might start asking questions, and then someone might notice the heart . . .*

That was not why he was running, however. It was the desperation on the old priests' faces that filled him with panic and pity. It was like finding yourself surrounded by starving faces and suddenly realizing that you were made of bread.

He ran past the baths chamber, hearing a splash like someone hastily struggling out of the water. He didn't look back, in case wet and naked figures were hobbling in his wake.

As he sprinted into a quieter corridor, he smelled woodsmoke and the bitter-sap smell of lebineck oil. Of course, Quest was being treated with oil and hot stones. Hark hadn't intended to interrupt the old man's treatment, but he was changing his mind quickly. After all, the treatment room could be secured for privacy.

Kly looked up in surprise as Hark barreled into the room. Quest was lying on a table nearby in only some loose white trousers. His bare back was glossy and golden with oil, a few polished black stones placed down his spine. Most of the light came from the little furnace set in the wall, its chimney disappearing into the ceiling.

"What's going on?" Kly asked quickly. "Where's all that yelling coming from?"

Hark was startled to find Kly there, but he recovered quickly.

"I don't know what started it," he lied. "But Moonmaid just lunged for me, and now a lot of the others are getting excitable. I thought I'd better find you."

"Don't tell me Moonmaid's found something sharp again!" Kly groaned.

"I didn't see her holding anything." Hark fidgeted, wondering if he was imagining the sound of slow footsteps approaching outside. "But I don't know."

Kly hesitated, glancing at his patient.

"I can take care of things here," Hark said quickly. "I've done the rocks before."

"Fine," muttered Kly, shaking his head. "I'll go and deal with Moonmaid."

As soon as Kly was out of the room, Hark bolted the door.

"What are you doing?" asked Quest, peering through a tangle of oil-beaded hair. "What's going on out there?" There was now no mistaking the sounds of steps and murmurs outside. The door briefly rattled, then footsteps receded a little. Hark could hear the sounds of other doors being opened, furniture scraping. The blind, blundering search had moved away, but not far.

"Don't worry," said Hark. "I just . . . I wanted to talk to you privately. You don't need to get up!"

It was too late. Quest had pushed himself up to a sitting position, letting the coin-sized stones slide off his back with a clatter.

"Never mind those," the old priest said wryly. "The stones aren't unpleasant, but they don't do any good. The staff just put them on me because they want me to feel better about things. And I let them so that *they* can feel better about things. A harmless lie on both sides."

"I've got something better than hot stones," Hark said. Here it was, the moment of trust, and he didn't feel ready for it. Quest might betray him. He might even start staggering toward the heart like the other priests, in a glazed and feverish trance. Apprehensively, Hark reached into the hidden sling and pulled out the heart.

Quest's gaze fell upon it, and his expression stilled. Hark was not even sure he was breathing.

"They don't know I have it," whispered Hark. "Don't tell anybody, please! If they find out, they'll take it away, and a friend of mine *needs* it."

"Where did you get it?" asked Quest, very quietly.

"It was in the sea, near the Entreaty Barrier." Hark swallowed. "It heals. I . . . I thought it might heal you. But I need to know if it—"

As he was speaking, the heart suddenly flexed and sent a pulse through the room. Quest jerked as though he had been stung.

"That's how it heals people," Hark whispered. "It looks for things to fix. Only . . . sometimes it has a funny idea of 'fixed.' " He was a little frightened by Quest's pallor.

"Can I have a look at it?" asked Quest.

Nervously, Hark handed it over. Quest took it carefully, letting it rest on his fingertips as if trying to minimize skin contact. He walked over to the furnace where the light was better, inspecting the relic minutely by the reddish glow.

Then, without warning, Quest flung the heart into the blazing embers of the furnace. He snatched up a poker and used it to aim stab after stab at the heart.

"Hey!" Hark rushed forward and wrestled the poker out of Quest's hands. "Stop it!" He pushed the old priest away, harder than intended, so that Quest fell back against the wall. The heart was nestling between embers. Golden flames licked its underside. Hark snatched at the relic and felt a searing pain as he knocked it back toward himself. It fell out of the furnace, hitting the floor with a crack.

As Hark snatched the heart up, Quest's poker cracked down on the floor where it had been, a split second too slow.

"What are you doing?" Hark backed away from Quest, the relic cradled in the crook of his arm. With his unsinged hand, he wiped the heart, looking for damage. It seemed uncracked, and the soot came off to show no charring underneath, but he didn't know whether its delicate inner workings were damaged.

"You need to give that to me," said Quest. He was still holding the poker, drawn back ready to swing. Hark felt angry despair at the sight. This always happened. You trusted people and they turned on you. "You don't know what it is."

"It's the heart of a god," Hark retorted. This did seem to give Quest pause.

"So you do know what it is," the old man conceded. "Do you know which god's heart?"

"Do *you*?" countered Hark, startled by Quest's question. Quest did not answer, and that was answer enough. "You know what this is! You've seen it before, haven't you?"

Hark wondered why he had ever thought Quest was frail. Seeing him now, Hark sensed a will like steel wire. The priest wasn't frenzied or enraged. He was frighteningly calm.

"You are holding the heart of the Hidden Lady," said Quest. "Now put it on the ground, please. We need to break it apart."

The Hidden Lady.

Hark's face grew hot. He had known that the relic was the heart of a god, but he really *hadn't* wondered which one. It was easier to think of it as a lump of godware if it didn't have a name. Now he would never be able to look at it the same way.

He had felt the Lady's heartbeat. The delicate perforations suddenly looked feminine, like a carved ivory fan. Guarding her heart now felt chivalrous, almost romantic.

"Why do you want to break it?" he blurted out. "You were

the Lady's . . ." He faltered, since "friend" was clearly not the right word. "She wound you in her hair and told you secrets! She trusted you!"

"I know what you are thinking," said Quest gently, as though he really did, "but there is no Lady now. She is gone." He took another careful step forward.

"Don't!" Hark said miserably. "I don't want to hurt you. But I *can't* let you break this. My best friend says he'll die without it!"

"And I don't want to threaten you, either," said Quest, in a quietly regretful tone. "I'm sorry about your friend. But if you don't give me the heart, I will have to call for help and tell them what you have." He nodded toward the bell rope provided for older patients to summon assistance when getting off the table.

Hark's blood surged with terror, then subsided bitterly.

"No, you won't," he said, feeling bruised and betrayed. "If you did, they'd take the heart away and give it to Dr. Vyne, wouldn't they? She definitely wouldn't smash it. She'd use it to power a submarine or something. Then she'd sell me to someone else, as punishment for lying to her. I'd die in the galleys, and you'd die slowly here with nobody to talk to."

"True." Quest slowly lowered his poker, acknowledging the impasse. "It was worth a try." If he felt hurt by Hark's words, he showed no sign of it. "Then I need to make you understand why the thing must be destroyed and why this matters even more than the life of your friend. Will you listen to me, if I tell you something that must never be repeated to another?"

Hark slowly nodded. He waited while the priest sat down on the treatment tables once again, golden trickles of oil running down his narrow arms.

"The gods," said Quest, "were not what you think. And they must never, ever return."

Chapter 29

"WHAT DO YOU MEAN?" ASKED HARK, KNOCKED off-balance by Quest's intensity. "Why would the gods return?"

"Every time that *thing* beats"—Quest nodded at the heart, his face still dangerously calm—"it changes the world around it just a little. Does it not?"

"It heals!" protested Hark, feeling all his doubts rising in his chest once more. "It saved my friend's life, and he needs it! He gets sick without it!"

"Is that all it does?" said Quest. The sympathy in his gaze made everything worse. "How is your friend? Does he seem . . . different at all?"

Hark gritted his teeth and said nothing, feeling angry, stupid, and transparent.

"You say the heart heals," Quest continued. "Yes, I am sure it does. I am sure it glues, reshapes, and makes things stronger. It is a thing of the Undersea. It transforms and warps, just as the Undersea transforms and warps. But the heart doesn't care about your friend. It is the beating core of a god. All it wants—all it has ever wanted—is to devour, absorb, and grow. With every pulse it is trying to build itself a new body, piece by piece. Humans are its favorite clay."

"A new body?" Hark stared. "You mean, a new *god*?"

"Yes," said Quest. "It has probably been adapting your friend, inside and out—making him into a vessel that it can use."

Hark remembered the Jelt-thing's bloody rampage. And yet it was still Jelt—Jelt! Uncanny and frecht as it was, it still had Jelt's surliness, Jelt's humor, and all their shared memories.

"I won't let it," Hark declared fiercely. "I won't let that heart take him over!"

"Then it will find something or someone else," said Quest earnestly. "You cannot hide that thing forever! Its pulse will be felt. Its effects will be noticed. When others know it exists, they will want it. We must destroy it now, before someone else takes it from you!"

Quest's animated speech was shaken by a burst of coughing. The old man was shivering now, in the after-ebb of the fight's adrenalin. Hark wanted to pass him one of the warm robes hanging on the wall. But they were almost-enemies for now, and Quest had already surprised him once. Instead Hark watched, conflicted, as the old priest recovered his breath.

"If that abomination falls into unwise hands," Quest went on, "it *will* find ways to build itself a body. Once it can move by itself, it will probably seek to return to its home in the Undersea."

"Well, suppose it did?" exclaimed Hark. He remembered his angry yearning to throw the heart into the sea. "You *want* it gone, don't you?"

"No! Listen to me, Hark! If the heart succeeds—if it gets back to the Undersea—then we have all lost our future.

"Once it is in the Undersea, it can become stronger. It can feed, build, and grow. It may be sluggish up here on land, but it will be another matter down there. All human fear runs down into the Undersea, just as streams and rivers run into the ocean. Human fear has a terrible power. It changes everything, distorts everything, maddens everything. Fear is the dark womb where monsters are born and thrive.

"The gods *breathe fear*. That is not a metaphor invented by the poets. They need it, just as we need air. The larger they are, the more of it they need. Without it, they weaken and fall into torpor. With enough of it, they can become colossal. The waters of the Undersea are dense with our fear. There a god could grow, and grow, and grow, in the silence of the deep, far beyond our reach.

"Ten or twenty years ago, I would not have worried. People were recovering from their centuries of terrified awe. They had become bold and curious, daring to seek their fortunes beneath the waves. A new, growing god would not have found enough fear in the Undersea to keep it alive. But now times are changing *too* fast, and people are learning to fear again. Have you noticed? There is a fear of foreigners and their big ships, a fear of change. Yes, a god *could* thrive in these times.

"So one day a vastness would surface offshore, like a glistening island. Harbor walls would crack, and great waves would crush our little houses like seedpods. The bays and beaches would stink with dead fish and dolphins, and the sky would be dark with flies, and another era of horror would be upon us. We would be slaves again."

Hark blinked. The image Quest had painted was vivid and horrible before his mind's eye.

"We wouldn't," Hark heard himself say. "We're different now. Everything's different now."

"Is it?" asked Quest. "I would love to believe that, but I do not. I had hoped that younger generations would grow up without our craven god-fever, but I still see traces of it everywhere—even in you. There is an eagerness, a poisonous nostalgia. No, throughout the Myriad people would fall onto their faces and give in to their ancient superstitious terror."

Hark's palms were sweating. The heart felt cold in his grip.

"Why are *you* talking like this?" he said accusingly. "You were a priest! You served the gods!"

"Yes, I did. That is how I know what horrors they really were." Quest leaned forward. "What do *you* think the gods were, Hark, in your heart of hearts? Do you secretly think that they were majestic? Terrible but just, in their own inscrutable way? Perhaps all their actions would make sense if our minds could only rise to a high enough state of being?"

Hark was shaking his head. No, no, that was the old, crazy way of thinking. He didn't think like that; only old people thought like that. Nonetheless, he could feel his neck flushing.

"Of course you do," said the old man, and shook his head bitterly. "Everyone does, deep down. That is *our* fault—the fault of the priests. It is a fantasy we sold to the people of the Myriad so that everyone's oppression would be more bearable. We let everyone tell themselves that they were watched over by gods, rather than terrorized by monsters. And we reassured everyone that the priesthood had everything under control. We had treaties with the gods and knew how to negotiate with them.

"All of that was a lie. The gods had no great or benevolent plan for us. There were no treaties. We never truly learned to reason with them, because *they were not reasonable*. Even those whom we could talk with were all crazy, to some degree. And the biggest gods—the mightiest among them—had no more power of reason than beasts."

Hark's breath caught in his throat. Quest seemed to have run out of breath as well and sat with his eyes half closed, breathing carefully.

Gigantic, savage fish, Vyne had said.

Hark had never worshipped the gods, or so he had thought. He couldn't explain why all of this made him feel ill and angry, as if something were being taken from him. He had always lived in a godless world, and yet . . . everyone he knew had grown up with a lurking pride in their island's "patron" god. Their remembered might was yours, somehow. Even their horrific nature had a majesty that you could borrow. You got into drunken arguments with folks from other islands about whose god could have beaten the other in a straight fight.

"I don't believe you!" said Hark. If he hadn't been afraid of the other priests roaming the corridors, he would have stamped out of the room before Quest could say anything else.

"I did not take that news well, either," said the old man, watching Hark sympathetically. "Acolytes and younger priests were not told the truth. Only when I was rising in the ranks did some elders take me aside to brief me in a small, dark room. They kept me in that room for four days afterward so that I had time to calm down.

"Then I was lowered into the deeps, and I saw the gods for myself. Those great, lightless eyes . . ."

"You're lying!" Hark erupted. "What about your conversations with the Hidden Lady! She wasn't just a . . . big fish!"

"No, she certainly was not," Quest agreed. "The Hidden Lady was always an anomaly. She was clever. Understand me, it was not a human cleverness. She had a complex mind and could be reasoned with better than the others, but even her reason worked . . . differently. Talking to her was like accepting an invitation to someone else's house, only to find that the walls are made of teeth and all the doors lead to the moon. You realize suddenly that you have not been talking about the same thing, and never could. It was the really large gods that became beastlike in their intellects. But even those were never just fish."

Quest narrowed his eyes and squinted down the telescope of time.

"Those vast gods *were* mysterious. Hypnotic. Their strangeness, their sheer size . . ." He shook his head. "They left you stunned with awe. But I would have seen more warmth and kinship looking into the black eyes of a shark, and almost as much intelligence.

"Something happened to the gods as they became larger and more powerful. Their minds dulled. They started to forget things and forget themselves. They became more unpredictable and less able to communicate. On some level they knew it was happening to them. They could feel the light of their thoughts guttering and threatening to go out. But they did not know what to do about it.

"So the priesthood had to go down into those dark waters and try to remind these terrifying, ravenous mountains why they should not kill us all. We kept the messages simple. If they crawled up onto the islands and slaughtered everyone, no more fear would spill into the Undersea. If they devoured our ships and towns, they would grow too big and their minds would wink out. We had big, colored boards for communicating with Dolor, and a string of lights for distracting the Cardinal in emergencies."

"Like talking to children," Hark said bitterly.

"No," said Quest. "Children do not crush cities. Children learn, if a lesson is repeated often enough. The greater gods forgot what we told them, again and again, and every time it was harder to make them understand.

"Sometimes we failed. The Dawn Sister occasionally slaughtered whole fishing fleets and left dozens of eyeless heads bobbing in the surf. The Silver Cataract caused a tidal wave that drowned half the population of Hullbrake. Graymantle would crawl ashore and murder people by the hundred every ten years or so. We always had to come up with excuses for these 'punishments.'

"We lived in dread of them growing so large that they could no longer understand us at all. If we could not reason with them, we had no way to stop them killing us. Their size had to be controlled by any means. Believe me, you have not experienced fear until you have descended forty fathoms to convince a shadowy colossus to let you prune it. It took all our persuasion to make the gods realize that it was for their own good. Even then, you could never predict what they would do—sometimes they forgot why we were carving pieces off them. Sometimes they simply changed their minds.

"Dolor occasionally let us pull off one of her legs, though that was unpleasant—the bones were hollow and filled with tiny, luminous beetle-like creatures that swam and bit. Kalmaddoth gave us spare eyes, like fat, pearly melons. The Armored Prince would shudder, until one of its pincers shrugged off the hard case of its shell and was left slick and pink—"

"I get the idea," Hark interrupted sharply. He did not want to think of the greater gods surrendering their relics with a terrible meekness, barely understanding why.

"Most of all," Quest continued. "The priesthood worked to keep the big gods away from each other. If two gods sensed each other's heartbeats, their instincts conquered their reason completely. They flung themselves at each other and fought until one was dead and in the other's gullet. The victor would then be twice its original size, a blind hulk of hungry instinct beyond our control. We had to train each of them into a sense of territory, give them an island that was 'theirs.'"

"You *gave* them islands?" Hark asked sharply.

"If a beast has a good feeding ground, it stays within it to defend it." Quest seemed to recede within himself a little, become more cold and distant. "We made sure that the waters around each island were particularly rich with fear so that the 'patron' god would not stray. That was why the priesthood decided there had to be sacrifices."

"The *priesthood* decided?" asked Hark, taken aback. "But . . . I thought the gods *demanded* the sacrifices! I thought they ate them!"

"I dare say some probably were eaten by passing gods," Quest remarked coolly. "But that was not the reason it was done. We killed a handful of people each year, chosen from all walks of life and without hope of appeal so that *everyone else* would be frightened all the time."

"You murdered people to keep everyone scared?" Hark didn't know why this was worse than feeding them to hungry gods, but somehow it was.

"We kept everyone scared to keep nearly everyone alive," Quest answered levelly.

"There must have been a better way to protect everyone!" protested Hark.

"The priesthood only knew what *had* worked for hundreds of years," said Quest. "Put yourself in their shoes. You could try a new strategy, and maybe it would save lives, or maybe a lamprey-faced leviathan the size of an armada would crawl up into the shallows and start taking bites out of harbor villages. Would you really want to take the risk? Do you understand what I am saying? I am telling you that we priests risked our lives and sanities for centuries, and we *never* had the situation under control. Everyone on the Myriad was always one divine whim away from annihilation."

Hark stared down at the heart. It felt heavier than before.

Could it really have a god furled up inside it, like an oak inside an acorn?

"There is one more thing that you must know," added Quest. "Something I learned from the Hidden Lady.

"As I say, she was . . . special. She had managed not to become too large, so her wits stayed sharp, but she paid a price for that. Can you imagine anything lonelier than being the only intelligent being in that abysmal darkness? By the time I knew her, the weight of her loneliness was crushing her. The craving to devour, grow, and become numb was gradually overwhelming her. That was why she was so willing to talk to me. I was not a god, but I was better than nothing, and it gave her a chance to pass on her stories so that they would not be lost even if she forgot them.

"She recounted even her very oldest memories. They were in pieces by that point, washed smooth and shapeless like pebbles. She couldn't even understand the emotions attached to them anymore.

"She remembered a pool beneath a waterfall, on a bright day. There was somebody else there. Perhaps he was her lover. Or perhaps she was drowning him. Or maybe she just saw him once and remembered him afterward. All she could really recall was brown skin and gleaming water and the sound of one of them laughing.

"She remembered a thorn that got lodged in her big toe for so long that the skin became swollen and yellow. She asked me whether it had ever hatched, but of course I had no answer. She remembered seeing an albatross smash into a cliff, or perhaps a cliff smash into an albatross. She wondered later which of them had been angry, and why."

"But that doesn't make sense!" exclaimed Hark, trying to

disentangle the garbled memories. When would the Hidden Lady have encountered freshwater pools or sunlight? How could thorns ever have pierced her armored, crab-like feet? "None of that could have happened! Those sound like . . . *human* memories!"

"Yes," said Quest. "That's exactly what they were."

"What?" Hark stared.

"She *was* human, Hark," said the old priest. "Once, a very long time ago. All the gods were. At the center of each of them was a twisted core that was once human and the groaning, mad-dened remains of a human soul."

No, no, that couldn't be right. The gods were the gods were the gods . . .

"The Lady could not remember clearly how she found herself in the Undersea," Quest continued. "She said she 'rained' into it alongside other sinking human bodies, so I suppose there might have been a shipwreck. When she sank down into the Under-sea she stopped drowning and started changing shape. Some of the other bodies warped and moved for a bit, but their hearts gave out one by one, strained beyond endurance by their new strangeness.

"She did not die, because her heart transformed faster than theirs. She felt it harden, shift, and contort. It was a time of anguish beyond pain, but the heart became strong enough to keep beating. As it did so, she tasted the fear in the water and drew it in, her gills gaping to suck life from the sea. Each throb strengthened her and healed her injuries. Each throb honed her, brought her closer to her god-shape, and allowed her to pull new matter into herself."

As if in response to the words, the heart in Hark's hand suddenly pulsed. Quest flinched but continued staring hard at Hark's face.

"Do you understand what I am telling you?" he demanded. "I am saying that in those fearful days gone by, any drowner who sank into the Undersea had a small chance of becoming a god. Do you know why it has not happened again in the thirty years since the Cataclysm? It can only be because people are less frightened, and the Undersea is less rich with fear. Even now, in these unstable times, drowners simply drown. They do not become gods.

"But if one god *were* to rise, and everyone collapsed back into their ancient, superstitious terror, then the Undersea would coruscate with fear as it did in the old days. Drowners swept down into the Undersea might start to transform. More gods would rise. And more. And ever more. The cycle would begin again, and we would never escape it. Is that what you want?"

Hark stared down at the heart in his hand. None of this was fair. Why was he stuck with this decision?

His limbs tingled as he imagined wrapping the heart back in its sling, dropping it on the floor, and stamping on it. He wouldn't have to see the fragile, ornate perforations break. He wouldn't have to think about exquisite ivory chambers shattering, the Hidden Lady's mysterious, lonely heart trampled to powder . . .

But it would not be her heart that he was really stamping on. It would be Jelt's. It would be Hark's own heart, too—his past, some vital thing knotted into the core of him too densely to be tugged out.

"No," said Hark quietly. "I don't want the gods to come back. I *will* destroy it, all right? But . . . not yet. I need to keep my friend alive a bit longer, so I can find some other way to save him, and change him back—"

"Every moment it exists, the future of the Myriad is in danger!" interrupted Quest.

"I'm sorry!" said Hark, feeling conflicted and ragged. "I can't let him die. I . . . just . . . can't."

"Not even if it means the ruin of everything?" asked Quest.

"He'd risk that for me," said Hark wearily. "Quest . . . you're clever, and you know about gods. Help me help my friend, so we can put him back the way he was! When he doesn't need the heart anymore, I'll destroy it. I promise!"

Quest said nothing, but he seemed to subside inward. He looked very old and very, very tired.

Chapter 30

QUEST KNEW OF SOME WAYS TO REMOVE MARKS, but none of them seemed promising. In the old days, he explained, the priests had sometimes rid themselves of mild Marks through several months of thrice-daily baths in clean water mixed with sulfur and plant oils. This would be useless in the case of somebody as Marked as Jelt.

"That would take too long, anyway," muttered Hark. "We need something much faster." Every moment the heart was in Hark's possession was a disaster waiting to happen. Even if nobody else discovered it, very soon Jelt would come looking for it. Hark had a nightmare image of Jelt breaking down the doors of Sanctuary and slashing his way through the guards, the unarmed attendants, the old priests, anything that stood between him and his goal . . .

"I fear I do not know enough about the mechanics of Marks themselves," admitted Quest.

Hark knew somebody who did.

"Quest . . . you can read, can't you? If I brought you some books or scrolls, you could read them to me, couldn't you?" After four months of reading lessons, Hark could recognize some words, but he knew this would not be enough.

"What do you have in mind?"

"Dr. Vyne has the Sanctuary archive," Hark said bluntly, and watched Quest's eyebrows climb up his forehead. "There are scrolls on the gods, with pictures and labels. There are documents on Marks, too. She's been making notes on them." He remembered her tapping a gray moleskin book as she talked about them. Perhaps that book held her research notes.

"And . . . you can gain access to these?" asked Quest.

The walls of the keep were impenetrable, and Vyne had the only keys to the two solid doors. But Hark had had four months to come up with ways of breaking into the museum, with its precious store of godware.

"I think so," he said.

Hark emerged from the treatment room with trepidation, but thankfully the corridor outside was empty. The little group of priests that had followed him had apparently moved on elsewhere. He sprinted away down the darkened passages, mentally begging the god-heart not to pulse, until he reached the dining room, where he found Kly giving hasty orders to a few of the other attendants.

"It's chaos," said Kly, looking wild-eyed and distracted. "Something sent half of them frantic—I've never seen them as bad as this! We've had to lock eight of them in their rooms, and Moonmaid tried to maim someone with a spoon."

"Do you want me to run down to the museum and tell Dr. Vyne?" asked Hark, trying not to sound too eager.

"I don't know if she's there at the moment," said Kly uncertainly, raking his fingers through his hair. "Go on, run down and see if you can find her. Come straight back afterward."

Hark was sprinting away before Kly had finished the last sentence.

Outside Sanctuary, Hark used a dry streambed to head downhill, instead of the open, grassy road. Jelt knew where he lived and might be looking out for him. Rigg was probably on the warpath, too. She would have returned to Wildman's Hammer to find Jelt and Hark missing, Jelt's bodyguards sprawled unconscious, and the islet littered with unfamiliar corpses.

Then there were the mysterious people who had demanded the heart and been slaughtered by the Jelt-thing. Who had they been? Were there more of them? And how *had* they known that he and Jelt were hiding a relic anyway?

That was a very good question, and Hark had not thought about it before. How could these strangers possibly have found out about the relic? Nobody knew about it, apart from Hark, Jelt, and . . .

Hark stopped dead in his tracks, his mouth falling open.

And Selphin. She was the only other person who knew of the heart's existence. The armed attackers could only have found out about it from her.

He remembered Selphin's grimly desperate warnings and threats. Nobody had listened to her. So perhaps she *had* tipped off some other group about a juicy piece of godware and told them where to find it. He remembered the bewildering care with which the mysterious attackers had disabled Jelt's bodyguards without drawing their blades. Perhaps they had promised to do so as part of their deal with her.

"She's *insane!*" muttered Hark under his breath, genuinely aghast. Whatever her reasons, this was a serious betrayal of her family and crew. It went far beyond drawing a blade on a crewmate.

It's not Rigg you should be worrying about, Selphin had told him. *It's me.*

He was starting to think that she might be right.

At the museum door, he knocked, just to make sure Vyne was out. There was no answer.

He looked around, feeling exposed in the broad daylight. There were a couple of boats tethered in the little harbor, but no sign of anyone about.

Dr. Vyne had said that keeps kept things in and people out. It had been a military base, designed to hold out against intruders. Most of the windows were too narrow to squeeze through.

There was just one window that might be wide enough.

Hark hastened around the building to the back and began to climb. The stone blocks were large, so he had to stretch to reach each new foothold, but thankfully the mortar between them had started to crumble, leaving narrow crevices.

At the top, he pulled himself up onto the roof, sending a disgruntled coterie of pigeons into the sky. He cast a nervous glance at the steep hill that rose behind the fort. He would be obvious to anyone on the higher slopes, but for the moment he could see nobody.

It was windier on the roof, though the blocky crenellations shielded Hark a little. The flagstones all around were streaked with bird droppings, and there were a few grimy puddles. In the very middle of the roof was a circular hole a foot wide, filled with a shallow dome of gleaming glass. It was Dr. Vyne's god-glass window. It wasn't large, but someone skinny might be able to wriggle through it, if they could get the glass out of the way.

Hark hurried over to it and laid a hand upon the cold, hard god-glass. It left his fingertips feeling slightly numb. He tried to rattle the dome in its metal rim, but it was snug in its seal.

With his free hand, he took out his tuning fork and rapped its tines hard against the stone floor. As its hum became a clear, pure note, he held the fork close to the domed glass.

The surface of the glass softened under his hand. Instead of the glass dome slipping out of its socket, however, his right hand sank into the glass. A moment later it had hardened around his fingers, imprisoning them in diamond-hard glass.

"Oh, great," he muttered.

The gulls' chorus changed, becoming shriller and more unsettled. Hark looked up to see what had disturbed them, and froze. In the far distance, near the top of the hill, something was zigzagging down the slope in leaps. It was man-size and too far away to see clearly, but it was drawing closer rapidly. It was a thing of nightmare, coming after Hark despite the daylight . . .

In panic, Hark tried to yank his hand free. The god-glass held it fast, and he only succeeded in cutting his knuckles.

Hark rapped the fork again and held it against the glass with a shaking hand. The dome abruptly fell away from its rim, releasing his fingers. There was a deafening clatter below. Without hesitation, Hark swung his feet in through the gap, and wriggled through. He dropped into the darkened study, landing in an awkward crouch.

There was a rustling thud on the roof overhead. Half winded, Hark looked up. Above him, he could see the round, bright hole of sky where the glass had been. Then a silhouette leaned into that bright hole and blocked out most of the light.

"Don't you come down here!" shouted Hark, struggling to his feet. "Stay away from me, Jelt!"

The thing put an arm down the hole, then gave a faint hiss of frustration. Perhaps it was too large to fit through.

"I'll break this!" Hark fumbled the heart out of its sling. "If you come any closer, I'll smash it!"

The buzzing and scrabbling above ceased, and there was a long, cold pause.

"If you do that, I'll kill you." It still sounded like Jelt, even with the grating rasp that made Hark's ears tingle.

"I know," said Hark, his mouth dry. "But I mean it. Stay away, or I'll do it!" Not an hour before, Hark had been desperately protecting the heart, but now fear was singing in his veins.

"You left me to *die*," came the voice from above, and Hark felt the cold bitterness of those words close around his heart like a vice.

I didn't, he wanted to say. *It wasn't like that. I always intended to save you. And I kept the heart safe for you, didn't I?* But trying to defend yourself to Jelt was always a pit trap. You fell, and fell, and there was no bottom to the shaft.

"I'm going to find a way to fix things, Jelt," Hark said instead, trying to stop his teeth chattering. "Then you won't need that heart."

"Just. Give it. To. Me."

"No."

There was a roar from above, a bruising gale of sound, with an angry, anguished human voice at its core. Hark gritted his teeth. He had said no to Jelt many times before, but somehow the "no" had never stuck. This was different. There was nowhere left to back down.

Hark took a deep breath, then held the heart up over his head.

"This is close enough!" he yelled over the roar. "You're in its range. Stay there and wait till it pulses. That'll keep you going for a bit."

Sure enough, after a few seconds, Hark felt the heart in his grip shift and clench. The pulse followed, like a jolt down his arm. It was as if the relic had sensed Jelt, his willingness, the clay of his flesh ready to mold and sculpt.

The Jelt-thing on the roof grew quieter as the heart sent out pulse after silent pulse. It leaned its head in through the window, reaching down toward the heart, but made no attempt to writhe through. It was still a dark outline against the light, and Hark was glad he could not see its face.

"You've damaged it," it whispered at last, in tones that made Hark's blood curdle. "You've *burned* it! I can smell it."

Again Hark had to bite his tongue for a few moments so that he wouldn't start defending himself.

"I'll see you again tomorrow," he said, his voice sounding thin and tremulous. "At the cairn. You can come near the heart again then. I'll fix this, Jelt. I promise. But you need to go now, and *stay away from me*. If I see you when I'm not expecting to, I'll smash the heart. I will, Jelt. I swear it."

"I kept you alive for *years*," hissed the voice, "and now you want me dead. You do, don't you? That's why you dropped me in that bathysphere, isn't it?"

"That's not true, and you know it!" exploded Hark, Jelt's words twisting his heart like a damp cloth. He stopped himself and took a deep breath. "You're not . . . yourself at the moment, Jelt. It's not your fault. It's the god-heart. It's changing you."

"You're the one who's changed," said the familiar-unfamiliar voice. "I don't know you anymore. You're not Hark. You're nobody I know."

The shadowy head disappeared from the opening above, leaving an unbroken circle of sky once more. There was a rustle and a scrabble and rattle of something scrambling back up the slope. Silence followed.

The god-heart gave out one last throb, then lost enthusiasm. It took longer for Hark's own heartbeat to come under control. He silently thanked the keep's designers for its thick stone walls and the solidity of its stone-flagged roof.

Remembering the urgency of his quest, he looked around the study. Immediately his stomach dropped away. There was no sign of the piled scrolls or books bound in black leather. The archive was gone. There was no sign of Dr. Vyne's gray mole-skin notebook, either.

Hark swore under his breath. He had known that the doctor was conducting her new research in the Leaguer base. It hadn't occurred to him that she might take the archive and all her notes with her.

Had she really taken everything? In desperation, he quickly flicked through the other notebooks and papers scattered on her desk. A few had pictures that jumped out at him. He grabbed them and tucked them into his hidden sling next to the god-heart.

Hark peered up at the window. There were no sounds of movement above.

I'll have to take my chances sooner or later.

Hark pushed Dr. Vyne's desk under the circular window, balanced her chair on it, then used the top of the headrest as a boost. As he caught hold of the window rim, he heard a clatter of falling furniture beneath him. He heaved himself up until he could get an arm out through the hole, then wriggled his way out onto the sunlit roof.

Jelt won't have gone far, thought Hark. *He's probably watching me right now. But for now he's keeping his distance, and that's better than nothing.* Hark didn't want to think about their appointment at the cairn the next day, with no stone walls between them. He had needed to promise something, however, so that Jelt stayed away from Sanctuary.

It was only after Hark had recovered his breath that he remembered the cut across the knuckles of his right hand. It had healed, leaving a slender crease-like scar. Gleaming beads of god-glass were embedded along its length.

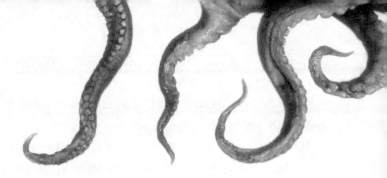

Chapter 31

HARK HURRIED BACK UP THE PATH TO SANCTUARY. With every step, the god-heart felt more like a curse. Hark had planned to hide it in some deep crevice in the rocks before going back to Sanctuary. That was no longer an option, now that he knew Jelt was probably watching him.

As he approached Sanctuary, Hark noticed that one of the first-floor shutters was slightly ajar. Staring up at it, he saw an indistinct face peering down at him. A pale hand emerged, palm out, gesturing to him to stop and stay where he was. The face pulled back, and the shutter closed.

Hark tucked himself against the wall, out of the wind. Bolts rattled, the Sanctuary door opened, and Quest emerged into the chill daylight.

"What are you doing here?" Hark exclaimed, his own concerns forgotten. "You shouldn't be out in this wind!"

Over his usual clothes, the old man had thrown some brown priestly robes, a blanket, and what looked like someone else's coat. Nonetheless, his figure seemed so frail that the cruel gusts might pull it apart like thistledown. Hark realized that he had never seen the old priest in full daylight before. All the little creases, veins, and freckles were suddenly startlingly clear against Quest's papery skin. The priest's face, however, wore a look of quiet determination.

"You cannot take that *thing* back into Sanctuary." Quest held up a warning hand. "The attendants have calmed the chaos and are asking my hysterical brethren why they were running through the halls. Your name has been mentioned a lot. Mr. Kly apparently wants a word with you."

Hark covered his mouth with his hand. The last thing he needed right now was a long interrogation. Sooner or later the heart would pulse. If he was searched, the heart would be found and taken away from him.

"But Kly said I had to hurry straight back!" he said in despair.

"You can tell them later that you had no choice but to divert course. You saw one of your frail old charges wandering loose on the heights and had to pursue him." Quest's eye twinkled. "I shall be sure to tell them that you pulled me back from a cliff edge."

"How did you get out, anyway?" Hark could not help asking.

"I have been notoriously docile for years," Quest remarked blandly. "It never occurred to anyone that I might try. Now, do you have documents for me to read?"

"I do . . . but let's do this quickly, and then you need to go back in."

The two of them found a hiding place around a corner, away from the main entrance. Hark stood between Quest and the wind, very aware of the priest's shaking hands and husky breathing.

"The archive isn't in the doctor's study anymore, but I found these!" Hark pulled his stash of notebooks and papers out of his sling. "Look!" He opened the first notebook, leafed through it and spread it, with a pencil drawing visible.

"I want to know what she says about Marks like *that*!" Hark said eagerly. "That long looping thing coming out from under the chin, with the light on the end . . . and the teeth . . . and all of the rest. What does she say?"

Quest stared at the picture in silence for a few moments.

"She is not writing about Marks here," he said quietly. "This is a notebook on creatures of the deep and lightless sea. This sketch is of a creature she calls a dragonfish, a breed that we priests nicknamed 'lantern wraiths' when they swam around our bathyspheres." He gave Hark a compassionate but piercing look. "Exactly how Marked is your friend?"

Hark flushed and swallowed. Instead of answering he reached for another notebook and fumbled it open.

"What about this one, then? This *must* be about Marks!" Hark pointed to a meticulous sketch of a hand with an extra finger and another of a leg with a strange seam running around it just below the knee.

Quest started reading, and slowly a frown began to deepen in his brow.

"It *is* about Marks," he agreed. "The doctor is trying to understand why they happen the way they do, and whether they can be turned to good use. 'When flesh is softened and biddable, it can be persuaded to return to old shapes or adopt new ones. It can even be taught to accept something alien as a part of itself.' Ah—that is very interesting!"

"Is it?" Hark was confused.

"The doctor believes that a human body has an inborn idea of what shape it *should* be. When it encounters Undersea water or godware, however, it becomes confused about what its 'true shape' is. It becomes convinced that its actual shape is wrong and broken, so it tries to heal itself by making itself more like what it now *thinks* is its true shape. That results in Marks. Dr. Vyne sees this as an opportunity. If the body can be persuaded to change its notion of its 'true shape,' then perhaps it can be persuaded to accept replacement body parts from other people, or mechanical limbs, or even pieces of godware—"

"I don't want to add anything new to Jelt!" Hark said impatiently. "I want to put him back how he was!" He struggled to understand what Quest had just told him. "So . . . if somebody's becoming Marked, it's just because their body thinks it should be a different shape? And if you can tell it to go back to being its old shape, it will?"

"That is her theory," Quest said carefully.

"Then how do we do it? How do we make him change back? Does the notebook say?"

Quest shook his head.

"I suspect this is just a portable notebook for jotting down ideas as they come to her. It looks as though her research into Marks is documented in full in a different book."

Hark's mind fizzed with frustration. The more he thought about it, the more convinced he became that the gray-covered volume must contain her complete research notes.

Maybe I could still talk to her and beg her to cure Jelt, Hark thought desperately. *She doesn't trust me, but she likes me.* His hopes rose, then sank again. She liked him, but she had made it clear from the first day that if he lied to her, broke her rules, or renewed contact with his old friends, there would be no forgiveness. He couldn't explain Jelt's plight without admitting his own crimes.

"I think I know where it might be," Hark admitted. "She's been working in the north of the island, at the Vigilance League base. Most people don't even know where she is."

"But you do," Quest said quietly. Hark could sense the line of questions waiting patiently behind those three words.

Even after their fight, Hark was afraid to lose his friendship with Quest. He didn't want to admit that all these months he had had an ulterior motive for talking to the priest. But what was the alternative? Another lie. Another evasion. He was so very tired of lies.

He took a deep breath and looked into Quest's face. He saw the bitter lines carved by experience, the feathering of laugh creases like the veins on autumn leaves, and the sharp, wise, watchful eyes.

"You already know, don't you?" Hark said. "You knew I was spying for Dr. Vyne. You've always known."

The old priest gave him a very slight, gentle smile, with a touch of sadness that Hark found hard to look at.

"I was never *quite* sure," Quest said, "but it seemed likely. That was one of the reasons that I encouraged you to talk to me rather than the others. Even gentle interrogation would have caused some of them terrible distress. I could spare them that. I owed them that much."

Hark's feelings were stung at the thought that the old man had just been talking to him to shield the other priests. Their friendship was such a fragile, papery thing, built upon deceit on both sides.

"It wasn't the way you think!" he blurted out on impulse. "It wasn't all lies! I know you won't believe me . . ."

"I know," said Quest, not unkindly. "Do you think I would leave my stories in the keeping of just anyone?"

Hark hastily rubbed his stinging eyes with his sleeve, not quite ready to look at his friend. Their odd, misshapen camaraderie had taken another knock, but somehow it was still not dead.

"If I get that book, will you read it for me?" asked Hark.

"Are you really planning to steal it from the League base?" asked the old priest, looking aghast.

"Vyne told me that if I had news that wouldn't wait, I should come and find her at the Leaguers' base." Hark rummaged in his belt pouch and brought out the paper Vyne had given him. "If they catch me, I'll give them this."

"*The bearer of this letter is Hark, my servant,*" Quest read out. "*He can be counted upon to be discreet, so please try not to shoot him. Let me know of his arrival.* Hark, I urge you not to do this. I will help you if I can, but I must tell you this now: with or without the doctor's book, I do not believe that you can save your friend."

"Maybe I can't!" blurted Hark, feeling exhausted. "Maybe I'm being stupid. But I have to try!"

"Then at least leave the heart behind with me," persisted Quest. "I give you my word of honor that it will remain unharmed."

Hark gave a hollow laugh. "As soon as I was out of sight, you'd decide the fate of the world mattered more than your word. Wouldn't you?"

Quest made no attempt to deny it. Instead, he gathered his warm clothes around himself a little more tightly.

"In that case," he said. "I will be coming with you."

"What?" Hark was horrified. "No! You need to go back inside!"

"If I step into Sanctuary," said Quest, "I will be apprehended and forcibly coddled. Worse, I will be watched. That will make it hard for me to help you. For now, I must remain at large."

Nothing Hark could say would persuade Quest to return to Sanctuary, and Hark had to admit that the priest had a point. However, Hark didn't like the idea of dragging a sick man to the far end of the island, over windswept hills.

"You'll get ill," said Hark with brutal honesty, "and you'll slow me down. I'm more likely to get caught that way."

This argument carried some weight with Quest, and at last

they struck a compromise. Quest would wait for Hark in Dun-lin's shack.

When they reached the beach, Hark ventured ahead to make sure the shack was empty before leading Quest to its shelter.

"I'll be back soon." Hark fidgeted uncomfortably. "And if I'm not . . . go back to Sanctuary and I'll see you there." He was unhappy about leaving Quest in the cold, damp shack. His daily routine at Sanctuary had trained him into new habits of mind. He could almost feel how the drafts would bite into Quest's flesh and make his joints ache . . .

"I will wait here until you return," said Quest with steely firm-ness. "Fear for yourself, not me."

Chapter 32

BY THE TIME HARK REACHED THE HILLTOP WITH
the cairn, the sun was dipping toward the horizon. Ahead of
him, the green-brown scrubland descended smoothly all the way
to the sea, broken only by occasional black crags and gorges
worn by streams. In the distance, clustered along the shoreline,
he could make out the gray roofs and dull red walls of the Vigilance League outpost.

The wind was blowing from the north, and it brought him the
faint clangs and clacks of metal striking metal. Somebody down
there was making or mending something. Beyond the village,
he could see a small boat moored in the bay, and alongside the
quay lurked a slender shadow that might have been an unusually long submersible.

If Hark walked down to the village openly and showed his
piece of paper to the first person he met, he was less likely to be
shot as a spy or a thief. However, he would have to explain his
presence to Vyne and probably wouldn't get a chance to steal
her notebook. If he really wanted to raid her research notes, he
had to creep down by stealth and steal them. It was a shaky,
dangerous plan, but he couldn't see another way.

Hark remembered Vyne's words when she had given him the
piece of paper.

Find one of the sentries and give them this, so they

know you're working for me. Then they'll fetch me from the warehouse.

The warehouse. With luck, that was where she was conducting her research. He scanned the village, looking for anything that might be a warehouse. One building on the left-hand side of the camp did seem to be larger than the others, its walls glimmering a yellowish white.

Hark slid into a deep, dry ditch and scrambled along its twisting route down the hill. The thistles and juniper bushes sprouting from its banks were man-high, offering decent cover. Sometimes he thought he heard a faint rustle farther up the gorge behind him. Whenever he looked back, he saw nothing. The back of his neck tingled, however, and he kept imagining Jelt quietly stalking him down the shallow ravine.

Above him, the sun set and the sky dulled to a dark copper. The sound of gulls, the sea, and the metallic clanging grew louder, until Hark was fairly sure that he must be close to the Leaguer village. As silently as he could, Hark clambered out of the gorge and crawled quickly between two mottled crags.

Peering through a crack, he had a narrow view of the outpost below him, much closer now.

About twenty yards farther down the slope was the big white building, just as he had hoped. He was close enough now to see its dropping-spattered metal roof and peeling paint. It was one story high but about fifty feet long.

To the right of the warehouse were a dozen other buildings, built of rough-baked bricks and roofed with scrub-thatch. They looked hasty and temporary, as did two wooden shacks down by the quay.

In the growing dusk, he could make out a couple of figures moving between the shacks. Now and then they laughed or called out to someone farther away. There were also signs of motion on the farthest side of the village, around the bare walls of a half-finished building. The cracks and clangs seemed to come from that direction.

A couple of men sat on the deck of the boat, but they looked like they were in conversation. Beyond them, Hark could see the long, dark, semi-submerged shape he had spotted from the hill. It *was* a submarine; he could see that now. Furthermore, there was something familiar about its dimensions, its three propellers, the line of its black withersteel fins . . .

It was the *Abysmal Child*, the sub that had brought the Hidden Lady back to Lady's Crave.

Her broken oars had been replaced by new ones, their wood paler and untarnished. The broken rear panels looked as though they had been mended, too. Could this be Vyne's secret project?

None of my business. It's her research into Marks I care about.

Hark was just about to creep forward toward the warehouse when he heard someone to his right clear their throat and spit. He froze, then peered in the direction of the sound. Thirty feet away, on a little rocky platform, a young man leaned against a small cannon, idly pushing a wad of tobacco into his mouth. His scruffy blue jacket and the lead buttons on his cap proclaimed his League allegiance. A musket lay across his knees.

Hark picked up a stone and tossed it hard and high, back the way he had come. It landed amid the vegetation with a soft *plap!* A startled egret burst from the hidden ditch in a blaze of white wings.

The young man leaped to his feet and stared through a spyglass in the direction of the hillside. Hark seized his chance and sprinted to the warehouse, flattening himself against its west wall out of sight of the sentry post.

Hark edged along the wall and peered around the corner. Nobody was close by, and the warehouse door was mere feet away. He darted through it before he could think twice.

He found himself in a little office. The walls were covered in bookshelves and maps, and the desks with logbooks and sketches. On one shelf he saw a row of jars in which pickled deep-sea fish floated in a cloudy yellow fluid. To the left was another door, presumably leading to the rest of the warehouse.

Hark almost missed the gray book because it was too obvious. After the acrobatic break-in at the museum and the long scramble down the hill, part of his mind expected it to be locked in a cabinet or hidden at the bottom of a traveling trunk. Instead, it lay open in the very middle of one of the desks, showing neat handwritten paragraphs and a detailed sketch of a foot with webbed toes.

He stared at it. Picked it up. Turned pages. Stared at drawings of an eye with two pupils, a stubby fin on an elbow . . .

There was no mistake. This was the right book.

I've found it. I can take it back to Quest.

I can save Jelt.

Hark stared at it, waiting to feel relieved. He'd risked everything for this, and now he had it. Why did his lungs feel so full and so empty at the same time? The book was heavy as lead in his hands, and the thought of climbing back up the hill suddenly seemed exhausting.

No, I can't, came the thought unbidden. *I can't. I can't save him.*

Outside, the gull cries erupted in a sudden uproar, as if they were trying to drown out the thought. *No, no, no, no!* they seemed to be shouting. It was only when Hark heard a crunch of footsteps outside that he realized why the birds had been disturbed.

Hark leaped for the other door, opened it and slipped through into darkness. He closed the door behind him, just as the main entrance creaked open.

For a few moments he stayed perfectly still, his ear pressed to the door. From within the office he could hear a male voice speaking quietly and the sound of one or more people moving around. Hark could just about catch some of the words.

". . . sticking to the same story . . . claims she knew nothing about any . . . if we did, it might send a strong message to her gang . . ."

This sounded rather ominous, but at least the new arrivals didn't appear to be talking about him. However, they didn't seem to be in a hurry to leave, either. He heard a scrape of chair legs, as if someone had pulled one up to sit.

If they're going to settle in for a good long chat, then I need to find another way out of here, he thought.

He looked around, blinking hard to acclimate his eyes to the dark. A little light seeped in from eight small glass windows set in the roof, showing him a shadowy, cluttered room, far larger than the office, probably taking up the rest of the warehouse.

There was a strong odor in the room, one that Hark recognized. It was the nerve-tingling, rotten, salty reek of Undersea water. There were other scents too: the vinegar tang of pickling, the smell of oil, and the queasy after-stink of scare-lamps.

To the left, crates and casks were stacked against the wall, next to barrows and a couple of small dock cranes, their chains and hooks glinting dully. To the right, trestle tables were crowded with delicate silvery tools, bottles of brown and black liquids, and huge glass lenses clamped to marble countertops.

In the center, filling most of the room, was something huge and irregularly shaped, just visible behind a wall of sailcloth screens. Hark padded over, too curious to resist. Very carefully, he moved aside the nearest screen so that he could see through.

The object within was twenty feet long. It lay upon a rough wooden platform, like the sort Hark had seen sometimes in a marketplace so that fresh fish could be laid out without dumping them on the ground. *Catch of the day*, thought Hark madly.

It was a nightmare of chitin, iridescent glass, and pallid flesh, constructed with horribly meticulous symmetry. From its upper part jutted a dun-colored tube filled with concentric rows of blunt teeth, like a lamprey's mouth. Great, serrated claws with a mottled shell extended on either side, resting on iron supports. Wires and copper pipes glinted between plates of barnacle-studded armor. Pale sacs of fluid sagged against the thing's flanks.

At the center of it, connected to a dozen snaking glass tubes, was a foot-wide gray slab of flesh with a dark, curling slit in its surface. It was the Hidden Lady's gills.

But . . . Vyne's supposed to be working on a submarine! She said she was!

Or had she? Now that Hark thought back, he couldn't recall her ever using the word "submarine."

At last Hark understood why the Vigilance League had chosen an unpopular island for their new base. He understood why they had hidden their project away and defended it with armed sentries so that nobody knew what they were building. He knew why Vyne hadn't wanted him or anyone else to come into the village.

They weren't working on a submarine. They weren't making something for people to ride in at all.

They were building a god.

Hark was still staring mesmerized at this creature when the god-heart chose to beat.

The dark slit of the gills suddenly closed and clenched. Yellow liquid surged through the surrounding glass tubes, drawn by a violent suction. A shudder passed through the shadowy hulk on the platform. Armor rattled. One great claw jerked clear of its support and fell to the stone floor with an echoing crash.

Hark leaped backward, blood banging in his ears. He could hear sounds of confusion and uproar in the office. As the adjoining door was thrown open, he darted into the little fort of screens. Through the sailcloth of the screens he could see the brilliance of a purple scare-lamp.

"There's someone in there! I saw him! Over there!"

He fled around the side of the great sprawled shape, hoping to hide behind it, but in vain. Running steps approached, and then several pair of hands dragged away the screens and cast them aside. He was spotted, he was cornered, he was blinded by purple light. He was grabbed by the arms and hauled out of his corner, into full view.

"I'm supposed to be here!" he shouted, deciding to give his last wild gambit a fair chance. "I've got a note from Dr. Vyne! I'll show you!"

The two men who had seized him changed their hold so that he could reach into his belt pouch and pull out the note. When the third man stepped forward, Hark realized that it was the Leaguer captain he had met before. The captain stared at him in recognition, then snatched the paper out of Hark's hand and read it with a frown.

"Doctor," he called out, "do you have an explanation for *this?*"

Dr. Vyne walked into the room, a small bone saw in her hand. The note was thrust into her hand, and her eyebrows rose.

"You said I should come here if I had news!" said Hark frantically.

"I never said you should come right into the camp," Vyne pointed out without apparent anger. "In fact, I told you specifically not to do that. It's a shame that you misremembered something so important. Your memory's usually so good."

Hark could see her looking at him once again with her skeptical, analytical eye, and then noticing the scattered screens behind him and the exposed monstrosity.

"Oh, Hark," she said. "You *really* shouldn't have seen that."

"I won't tell anyone!" he said quickly. "You know I won't!"

She sighed and shook her head. *No*, said her smile. *You won't.*

Different people turned against you in different ways, Hark had always known that. Some did it angrily. Some did it calmly, or sadly, or coldly. And some, it turned out, wore a rueful, self-deprecating smile when they became your enemy.

The smile faded as Vyne noticed that one of the great claws had fallen onto the stone floor. She scowled and strode over, then stooped to examine it, running a gentle finger over the claw's armor in search of cracks.

"Hark!" she exclaimed accusingly. "What have you been doing to my god?"

As if in reply, the god-heart pulsed once more. Again the gills convulsed and drew in sickly gold liquid through glass veins. The hulk rocked and shuddered. Wires broke free, and a metal band snapped loose, shooting a rivet across the room.

Vyne turned to stare at Hark.

"Search him!" she shouted.

Hark struggled as hard as he could, biting and kicking, as he was wrestled to the ground. All of Quest's warnings about the heart returned vividly to his mind—the return of the gods, an eternity as the slaves of monsters. Far too late, Hark tried to smash the swaddled god-heart with his elbow. All was in vain. The captain pulled the sling out of Hark's sleeve and tugged off the cloth. He held up the heart, peering at its perforations in bemusement.

Vyne took it from him and handled it reverently, her eyes wide with undisguised hunger.

Chapter 33

"THIS IS WHAT THAT GIRL DESCRIBED!" EXCLAIMED the captain. "A white, pulsing ball of godware!" He still looked suspicious, but he seemed to be catching some of Vyne's enthusiasm.

"It's exactly what we've been looking for," whispered Vyne. "The 'core' mentioned in the archive scrolls! A reverberator. A source of vibrations to imbue the rest with life, change, motion . . . and it's active!"

She walked over to her creation and peered at it intensely.

"Look at this!" Her smile was almost childlike in its brightness. "The gills have started to meld with the glass tubes I inserted! The reverberator is triggering mutations, just as I hoped! With this, we can get all the parts to accept each other!"

She turned to Hark.

"Where did you get this? How much do you know about it?"

Hark stayed mulishly silent, and Dr. Vyne's smile faded.

"Well, let's see how it interacts with the rest." Hands shaking with excitement, the doctor leaned across the great construct and pulled wires loose from a device like a tiny accordion. She removed the contraption and laid the heart in its place, nestled against the Hidden Lady's gills.

"Don't!" shouted Hark. "You'll bring it to life!"

"Well, I certainly hope so." Vyne began tethering the heart in place with wires and straps. "I had been tuning a special instrument in the hope of producing the right vibrations, but this is much, much better! With this at the center, we might create a self-sustaining system. Now, come on, my beauty, give us another pulse . . ."

A few seconds passed, and then the heart obeyed. Again the great hulking shape convulsed, but this time more violently. The armored plates rose, as if the thing were drawing a breath, and for a moment Hark thought the whole nightmarish mass might slowly rear up. The next instant it subsided with a clatter of chitin and a groan of metal. A glass valve cracked. There was silence, except for the faint sound of ichor dripping onto the floor.

"What's wrong with it?" asked the captain. "Why did it stop moving again? Why does it keep breaking things?"

"I don't know!" snapped the doctor, who was hastily working to stop the ooze in the cracked flask from leaking away. "I'll need to make the bonds stronger. And . . . I think we'll need better quality Undersea water to feed into the gills—a lot more of it, too."

"You don't know what you're doing!" yelled Hark.

"I have a doctorate in practical theophysics!" retorted Dr. Vyne. "If anybody can understand this, it's me!" She pushed her hair out of her eyes with her forearm. "I *will* solve this, but I need to concentrate! Everyone out of here!"

"What about the boy?" asked the captain.

"I'll want to question him later," said Vyne, without looking up, "so don't shoot him more than you have to."

She didn't even glance at Hark as he was carried bodily out of the warehouse.

Hark was manhandled through the village, still kicking out at anyone close enough. He was in a blind, vengeful, desperate rage now. Everything was lost, so he might as well cause as much damage as possible. He hardly felt the blows he received in return.

Two men carried him to one of the wooden shacks. One of them lifted a heavy bolt and opened the door, and the other threw him inside. He lay on the floor, hearing the door slam behind him and the bolt drop back into place.

Carefully, he sat up, feeling his lip and cheek sting. Pain was fine, he didn't mind pain. He deserved it. His mind was on fire.

I wish I'd smashed the heart when Quest told me to. Or when I first thought about it, that night on the beach.

But I didn't. All of this is my fault. That heart was doing no harm where it was, lying on the seabed. But I brought it up with me and gave it to Jelt. If I hadn't, none of this would have happened. Jelt wouldn't be a monster. Those men he killed on Wildman's Hammer would still be alive. Then I brought the heart here. *And now Dr. Vyne has what she needs to bring her homemade god to life, so that's it. No more hope. Just an age of nightmares that never ends.*

There had been times in the past when Hark had felt stupid or worthless, but never before had he wished he could wipe himself off the world like an ugly smear. He wanted to be nothing. He wanted all his years of life not to have been. All he could do was sit there, numb with exhausted misery, hating himself.

His skin tingled as though the eyes of an angry universe were fixed on him. It took him a while to realize that he *was* being stared at, but by someone rather smaller.

The other figure was pressed against the back wall of the shack, perfectly still, her large, bright eyes wide and wary. A little light filtered in through a hole in the roof, allowing him to see her tied-back hair, angular features, and mottled freckles.

It was Selphin, alive but not as well as the last time he had seen her. She looked tired and drawn, her dark hair dank with neglect.

"Selphin!" exclaimed Hark in shock. "What are you doing here?"

Selphin shook her head urgently and threw a meaningful glance toward the door. However, Hark's head was filling with a jumble of memories—the frantic search for Selphin, the mysterious armed men emerging from the shadows on Wildman's Hammer.

"You double-crossed us all!" he hissed. "You—"

Selphin scowled furiously and raised a finger to her lips. She grimaced, pointing to the door, and this time Hark understood. Perhaps the guards *were* listening in. He started to notice other details, the blanket rumpled on the floor, and the wooden plate and water jug nestling in a corner next to a chamber pot. Evidently Selphin was as much a prisoner as he was.

I know you went to the League behind everyone's backs, he signed. *You told them about the relic, so they'd attack us and take it!*

Selphin gave an angry, little shrug and glared at him unapologetically.

Nobody listened to me! she answered. *I had to do something! I had to protect myself and my crew!*

Every inch of her was tensed. She was bracing herself for a fight, Hark could see. Looking at her, however, Hark realized he had no fight to give her. He was acting out a remembered anger without really feeling it. All of his rage was turned on himself. He didn't seem to have any extra for anyone else.

I don't care. He exhaled, and delivered the sign with an exhausted flick. *I don't care.*

When he continued to show no sign of hate-filled frenzy, Selphin gradually relaxed her battle-ready posture a little.

How long have you been here? he asked.

Four days, came the answer.

It had been five days since he had last seen her, diving into the frenzied waves. If she had been a prisoner for four days, the rumored sightings of her at the Pales must have been false.

Why are you a prisoner? Hark signed. If Selphin had given the Vigilance League such a valuable tip, why had they locked her in a dark shack?

The League didn't trust me, replied Selphin, her signs bitter but matter-of-fact. *They thought I might be sending them into a trap. They said they wanted to keep me prisoner until they had the relic, just to be sure. I said yes. Then your friend killed lots of them. The League decided it* was *a trap after all. They kept me for questioning.* She shrugged and gestured at her cramped prison.

Hark wasn't surprised by the Leaguers' anger. They must have lost a dozen of their number that night.

How are my crew? The signs tripped off Selphin's hands as if she had been aching to ask this from the start. Her eyes were wide and concerned.

She was probably worried that some of her gang had been caught up in the carnage on Wildman's Hammer. Then why risk double-crossing everyone in the first place? Hark was about to give an acidic reply, when he remembered how the attacking Leaguers had pulled their blows at first. Somehow she had persuaded a group of hardened fanatics that they didn't want to rush in with their blades drawn. Maybe the rumors of Selphin in the Pales had been deliberately spread to make sure the smuggler gang were elsewhere looking for her.

I don't know, he replied. *They're safe as far as I know.*

Does your friend know I went to the League? asked Selphin, and Hark could see a glisten of fear in her eyes. Evidently she meant Jelt.

No, he reassured her.

Selphin chewed her lip but continued looking steadily at Hark, so he knew the conversation wasn't over.

What's wrong with your friend? she signed at last.

The relic, Hark began, then stopped himself. *Everything*, he signed instead.

He could feel himself starting to shake, even though it wasn't that cold. There was something hard in his throat, and it tasted like old metal. His lungs were tight and his joints felt loose and his eyes hurt. Something hot was leaking down his cheeks.

Everything is wrong with my friend. Hark's eyes blurred, and he could hardly make out his own signs. *It isn't the relic making him a monster. It's him.*

Jelt . . . kills people.

There it was, the truth at last. The only way was forward.

Jelt doesn't have to, but sometimes he just does it. I don't even know how long he's been like that. Probably years. I've been trying not to know. I felt like, if I knew for certain, somebody would die. The old Jelt. My friend.

He looked at Selphin, willing her to understand.

My friend Jelt was amazing, he signed. *But he's gone. He's been dead for years. All that's left of him is in my memories.*

And there's this other Jelt . . . Hark shook his head. *He's all I've got. He's still my best friend, the only friend that matters . . . and I hate him. I hate him. I needed to save him, I needed him to be safe and alive and well, so I could walk away and never see him again.*

It was the impossibility of this that had descended upon Hark as he stood in the office with the gray book in his hands. He had realized suddenly that Jelt would never be safe and well enough for him to walk away. However hard he tried, he could never, ever save Jelt, because Jelt would never allow it.

Hark wiped his face, feeling like his insides had been ripped out.

I tried to save him, he signed. *I came to steal some secret papers to make him better. I got caught. The League have the relic now.*

Good riddance, Selphin signed emphatically.

No. Hark shook his head. *It's bad. Really bad. They're doing dangerous things with the relic.*

So were you. Despite the barbed response, Selphin's eyes seemed a little more sympathetic now.

Worse things, said Hark, in no mood to argue. *They could destroy everything.*

Chapter 34

HARK STUMBLED THROUGH A QUICK EXPLANA-
tion of Vyne's work with the Vigilance League, the makeshift
god twitching in the warehouse, and the doom of mankind. By
the end, Selphin's eyes were wide. She gave a small snort of
incredulous laughter.

You really did *make a mess of things*, she signed. *Worse
than me.*

Oddly enough, it made Hark feel slightly better. He had been
expecting the smuggler girl to stare at him with fear and horror,
as though he were a Jelt-like monster. "Make a mess of things"
seemed like the sort of mistake a human being might make.

She scratched the back of her neck, frowning intently.

Does anyone know you're here? she asked. *Will anyone
come if you don't return?*

Only Quest knew where Hark was, and Hark sincerely hoped
that the old man wouldn't try to storm the League's village by
himself.

One old man knows, he signed, *but he's sick. I don't think
he's coming. We're alone.*

Just us, then. Selphin scowled, then looked up at Hark,
fiercely expectant.

That glance seemed to jolt something in his head. He had
been so devastated by the thought of the looming apocalypse,

and his part in it, that he'd lost track of one very important fact. It hadn't happened yet.

It was true: Hark and Selphin were alone. Nobody was coming to rescue them or stop the gods from rising again. They were the only people who knew about Vyne's creation. If they didn't do anything to prevent this calamity, nobody would.

They were trapped, they were helpless, the odds against them were impossible. And yet . . .

You'll do it if you have to, Jelt was always telling Hark, with his customary smirk. The memory drove a barb of anger and hurt into Hark's heart. He'd hated the way that Jelt forced him into situations where he had to perform miracles on demand. But the truth was, he usually *had* managed to achieve them.

Jelt had always been bitter medicine, and now he was poison. However, he was still forcing Hark to become bigger, bolder, smarter, and tougher than he thought he could be.

I'll do it because I have to, thought Hark. *Somehow I'll stop the gods from rising.*

Can we get out of this shack? Hark signed.

Yes, Selphin answered. *There's a secret door. I just stay in here because I love it.*

Hark rolled his eyes and made an entreating gesture. Selphin relented.

There's a heavy bar on the door, she explained. *I tried to get wood splinters through the door crack to lever it up, but they snapped. I made some holes in the walls. They're good for spying, but I couldn't loosen the planks. When they bring me my food now, there's always three of them, because I bit someone's nose.*

Hark turned out his own pockets and belt pouch, to see whether he had anything useful to contribute. His captors had searched him, but they'd stopped when they found the heart. Hark found that he still had his bandages, handkerchief, comb, some string, a piece of chalk, and other oddments. Among them he saw a silvery gleam: He still had his tuning fork.

He picked it up and tentatively tried inserting the handle into the door crack, to see whether he could use it to lift the bar. However, the crack was too narrow. The chalk and the comb didn't fit into the gap, either.

Pry nails out, signed Selphin, eyes narrowed.

Hark tried using the fork to lever out one of the nails that held the wall planks in place, but it soon became clear that the metal was too supple. If he kept going he would bend the tines irrevocably, without shifting a single nail.

Stab the guards in the eye with it, then, Selphin suggested.

You're feral, signed Hark, but he felt his spirits rise a little. Captivity and interrogation didn't seem to have crushed the smuggler girl's nerve. *You've been spying on them?*

Selphin nodded. She beckoned and showed him a small crack between the planks in the wall next to the door. He could see that she had picked splinters away from the edges of the planks to make the crevice wider, and for the first time he noticed her broken fingernails. When he peered through, it gave him a view of the warehouse, a few other buildings, and the hill behind. Another similar crack on the seaward side offered a squint of the jetty, the rugged little fishing boat, and the black withersteel armor of the *Abysmal Child*.

What have you seen? he asked. If they wanted to escape, they needed as much information as possible.

There are sixteen men in the camp, she told him, *and sometimes the woman who bought you. The boat brings supplies. The big submarine has been here all the time. There are two lookouts up on rocks above the village, and one on the jetty.*

Do they light lanterns at night? he asked.

No big lanterns, came the answer. *Some of the guards carry scare-lamps.*

If the camp wasn't lit at night, it might make it easier for Hark and Selphin to sneak away. On the other hand, it meant that soon the shack would be dark, and it would become harder for the two of them to sign to each other.

When they bring us breakfast or come to question us, signed Selphin, *we stab them with your fork and we run to the warehouse. Then we smash your relic before they can stop us.*

It didn't sound like a tactic that would save the world, but it was oddly heartening to have any plan at all. He hoped that they could come up with something better before morning.

Can *we smash it?* asked Selphin as an afterthought.

I hope so, answered Hark.

What is it? Where does it come from? continued Selphin.

It's the heart of the Hidden Lady, Hark explained. It still felt unchivalrous sharing such a secret.

How do you know? asked Selphin, brow furrowed.

My old priest friend told me, explained Hark.

How does he know? persisted Selphin, brow furrowed.

This was an excellent question. How had Quest been able to recognize the heart? He had only ever seen the Lady when she was alive, hadn't he? Her torso had never been recovered. How could *anybody* know what her heart looked like?

I don't know, Hark signed back. Evidently Hark had not plumbed the full depths of Quest's secrets, even now. He was starting to wonder whether he understood anybody at all.

As the darkness settled in the shack, Selphin spread her blanket over the floor and curled up on one side of it. She didn't explicitly invite Hark to share it, but she left enough room for him.

He lay down on the other end of the blanket, staring up at

the dark roof of the shack, and tried to come up with a plan. Exhaustion had other ideas, however. His thoughts lost their shape and their way, like wanderers in fog, and sleep drew him into a kindly numbness.

Hark was woken hours later by a nudge in the small of his back. He started, confused in the darkness by the sound of the sea, the chill, and the absence of the dormitory smells. He was cold, stiff, and hungry, but he couldn't remember why. Then memory drenched him like cold water.

A faint glimmer of moonlight seeped in through the cracks in the walls and under the door. He could see Selphin standing over him, the faint light catching the edge of her cheek and putting twin stars in her eyes. She pointed urgently to the nearest spy hole in the wall.

He staggered groggily to his feet and put his eye to the hole.

The village lay before him in utter stillness, save for the dimming and blooming of the moonlight as clouds sailed across the sky. All the windows in the village were dark, except those of the warehouse, which still glowed with a purple light. He could see nothing unexpected, so he turned back to Selphin, shook his head, and shrugged. Her hands moved, but it was too dark to make out her signs, so he shook his head again.

Selphin reached out and took hold of his hands. He felt her turning them, arranging the fingers, and then slowly moving them. Her hands were smaller than his and a little cool, with calluses on the palms and fingertips. After a few seconds he realized that she was slowly guiding his hands through signs.

Nearest building, she signed with his hands, then released them.

Hark looked through the crack again, this time staring toward the building opposite the shack. Now that he knew where to look, he could see a figure-shaped patch of darkness pressed against the shadowy wall.

After a while it stirred and flitted swiftly to another building, where it held itself against a different wall. Then it moved to the next building. It was a little too tall to be human, and its outline was slightly wrong.

The Jelt-thing *had* been stalking him down the hill, just as he feared. Now it was flattening itself against building after building. He could only guess that it was trying to detect the sustaining pulse of the god-heart.

The dark shape turned, and he could just about see its head twitching this way and that. Then it began loping toward the shack.

Hark took hold of Selphin's hands and quickly moved them through one hurried sign.

It's coming!

Both of them froze. Hark could hear something outside the shack, a very faint, dry rustling that made him think of dead insect wings and the windblown husks of crab shells. Selphin's gaze flicked to one wall, and he guessed that she had noticed some faint tremor in the planks that his eyes were not sharp enough to catch.

Hark imagined the Jelt-thing pressed against the other side of the wall, alert for any noise or vibration. It must be mere inches away, and Hark was suddenly terrified that it would sense him, recognize him, *smell* him . . .

Eventually the stealthy noises receded, but it was a long time before Hark and Selphin dared to move, and even longer before Hark could get back to sleep.

When Hark was woken a second time, it was considerably less gently. A sudden kick in the ribs made him curl defensively, covering his face. Someone grabbed his shoulder and shook it. He peered out between his fingers.

The spectral, predawn light was seeping into the dark of the shack. Selphin was bending over him, her hair tousled, her eyes still puffy with sleep.

They're taking the god away! she signed urgently.

Hark scrambled to his feet and pressed his own eye to the crack in the wall.

The big doors of the warehouse were open. Very slowly, with reverent care, ten men were carrying Vyne's nightmare out into the early morning light. Poles had been slotted through the wooden platform to make it portable.

The inert god didn't look any less chilling in the stark, gray light. It lay there in state, its glass and steel glinting. Sailcloth slings now supported its great claws. A large oilskin was draped over the pale flesh and metal piping of its innards.

The whole convoy looked like a weird funeral procession. The "bearers" all seemed to be dockyard scum, with knife-cut tattoos. A few better-dressed men stood around like mourners, two of them skinny and scholarly, the others rich enough for crisp uniforms, none of them quite the same.

Thankfully, the god was still playing its part as corpse. Vyne did not seem to have brought her makeshift deity fully to life yet.

Hark pulled back from the spy hole.

Are they taking it onto the boat? he signed.

Selphin shook her head.

They're getting the submarine ready, she replied. *I saw them carrying air-bottles, god-glue, breather boxes, and supplies. They're loading it up for a trip.*

Hark tingled with frustration and panic. He stared around him at the heavy wooden walls, as if he could glare them into smithereens. If such methods worked, however, he reckoned Selphin would have broken free days ago.

Instead, he slammed both his fists against the door. Next to him Selphin jumped, presumably feeling the shock wave through the wood.

"Let me out!" he shouted in desperation. "I'll tell you about the relic! I'll tell you anything you want to know!" He readied the tuning fork, holding it so that it was flush against his forearm and hidden under his sleeve. If this bluff made them open the shed door for a moment, just a moment . . .

Nobody answered. No footsteps approached. The door did not open.

He glued his eye to the crack again. The Leaguers carrying the god were paying no attention to his cries. They were probably too far away to make out the words. A couple of the better-dressed men were closer to the shack and casting glances his way.

"I'll tell you where I found the relic! There's more godware there!"

The two men whispered avidly. Then one of them shrugged and shook his head, turning back to the god-parade. They could make Hark tell all he knew in the fullness of time. They knew he wasn't going anywhere.

All the Leaguers shared the same expression of rapt calm. Something immense was happening, and they were a part of it. Hark could almost feel their doubts and disappointments dropping away from them, leaving something pure and certain. *They* were immense now, bigger than everyone who had ever made them feel small.

The procession was just moving out of sight when Hark was startled by the sound of raised voices from the direction of the harbor. Selphin, who was peering through the crack on the seaward side, gave a little intake of breath. She turned to Hark and signed frantically.

Something happened! People are running around on the jetty!

Through the tiny spy holes they could just see a small group of men, gathered around a brown bundle of something lying on the jetty. One of them was the captain. He seemed to be giving orders, and the little huddle soon dispersed. Something had happened, but it was no longer happening. The loading of the sub continued with even more haste than before.

The gray light was ripening to pale gold, the sea color warming to a pleasant blue. Selphin frowned suddenly.

Your hands are shining, she signed. She grabbed his wrist and pulled his right hand into the shaft of light from the hole in the wall.

The little beads of god-glass winked from the long scar. Hark had forgotten about them. He turned his hand this way and that, counting the beads. How much god-glass was in them altogether?

I have a plan for getting out of this shack, he signed. He didn't like it much, though. He wasn't sure it would work, and he was completely sure it would hurt.

While Selphin kept watch, Hark tried to get the bits of god-glass out of his hand. He first tried letting the tuning fork ring next to his knuckles, in the hope that he could squeeze out the beads of glass as they softened, but this just made them squirm deeper under the scar tissue.

He had no choice but to dig the beads out of his knuckles and no time to do it gently. The sharpest thing he had was the tines of the tuning fork. He kept his hand curled in a fist to keep the skin taut and make the little blobs of glass bulge, but it was still hard to force the metal edge into his own flesh. Tears of pain kept welling in his eyes. He had to blink them out in order to see straight.

Occasionally, Selphin would turn around to sign a bulletin to him, with increasing urgency.

They're checking ballast, inspecting oars.

They're lowering the god into the rear hatch!

Everyone's getting into the submarine now. I think they're all leaving! Hurry up!

Hark's knuckles were a mess, but he had twelve little beads of god-glass laid out on Selphin's wooden plate. He struck the tuning fork against a wall and heard its tingling whine settle into a high, pure note. When he rested the tip of its handle on the floor next to the plate, the note became louder.

The little spheres of glass softened and spread slightly, like wax beads starting to melt in the sun. By pressing them with the back of his fingernail, Hark was able to squash them.

Over and over he struck the tuning fork, then nudged and rubbed at the softened god-glass. At last it was spread thin, a lumpy, glossy smear like a snail trail. Using a corner of his sleeve to grip it, Hark carefully lifted it off the plate, a slender, mottled, ragged blade of glass.

They're closing the hatch! signed Selphin. *Quickly!*

Hands shaking, Hark slid the blade of glass into the crack between door and jamb. Its unevenness rasped against the wood, but he managed to force it in. Then he slid it upward until he felt the weight of the bar resisting it.

"They've cast off!" Selphin whispered aloud, the noise startling after their silent exchanges. "They're rowing away!"

Hark forced the blade upward and felt the bar lift. He pushed at the door, and it creaked open a few precious inches.

A quick peer through the opening. No guards waiting outside. Hark slipped out through the door, Selphin a step behind him. No sign of musket-wielding Leaguers outside the warehouse, or on the jetty, or up on the lookout points . . .

Hark and Selphin hurried around the edge of the shack and stared out at the sea, where the *Abysmal Child*'s long, jet-black shape was leaving the harbor. There was a hiss and hush of ponderous valves closing or opening and a throaty sound of water gushing through pipes. Nose first, the great submarine was dipping beneath the waves at its leisure, the froth of the surf closing over its long, coal-black back.

What had Hark expected to do, if he escaped the shack? Leap into the water and grapple the *Abysmal Child*? Punch a hole in its hull, perhaps?

Hark stood there, watching the waves resume their dance and pretend that they had not just welcomed the doom of mankind into their secretive embrace. He might have stood there longer if Selphin had not suddenly grabbed his arm.

He looked around and discovered that not all the Leaguers had left on the submarine. There was one still there, standing on the jetty. He had probably just leaped down from the boat. He was quite young, with a sailor's tan, and good-natured creases in his cheeks. He was the kind you might see in any bar, happy to arm wrestle but dazzled-looking if girls talked to him. You could make them laugh, that sort.

Hark's untamed mind still wanted to understand this man, to find a way to win him over. He almost couldn't comprehend that the Leaguer was leveling his musket at the pair of them and tensing to fire.

The shot, when it came, was a disappointing rap, like a cane hitting a desk.

Hark flinched, but there was no pain. Instead he saw the

young man jerk, twitching his head to a quizzical angle, and then very slowly fall over. His musket hit the jetty with a crack, and Hark realized that it wasn't smoking. The shot had come from somewhere else.

Looking past the fallen man, Hark noticed again the brown, cloth-covered object sprawled at the far end of the jetty. It wasn't a bundle at all; it was a figure. It had pushed itself up onto one elbow, and now it collapsed to the boards once more. A tiny curl of smoke wisped from the pistol in its hand.

Hark sprinted down the jetty, past the fallen Leaguer, toward the sprawled, brown-clad figure at the end. As he drew closer, he could see it more clearly. The small, ornate pistol drooped from one hand. The other hand clutched at the figure's side, where a great, damp blot of darkness was spreading, spilling redness over its fingers.

The bundle was Dr. Vyne.

Chapter 35

"IS HE DEAD?" ASKED DR. VYNE.

"I think so," said Hark, managing to keep his voice steady.

"I've never killed anyone before," the doctor remarked. "We surprise ourselves with the things we can do." Her face was haunted-looking and very pale.

"You're hurt," Hark blurted out, not knowing how to feel. He could now see the ugly tear in the coat from which the blood was spilling. It looked like a stab wound. "Who did that?"

"The Vigilance League captain," Vyne said, with a shadow of her usual wry smile.

Selphin ran up to join Hark. Evidently she had stopped to pick up the dead man's musket. Now she stood scanning the village and the hill behind, looking for the next threat, the gun leveled and ready. It looked very long and unwieldy in her hands.

"There are more Leaguers in the camp somewhere," Selphin said in a quiet, urgent tone. "We need to get off this jetty."

She was right. Here they were exposed and likely to get cornered if their enemies reached the waterfront. Even as Hark thought this, though, his gaze was drawn back to Vyne's blood-soaked flank.

He dropped to his knees and scrabbled in his belt pouch for bandages. He forced a pad of clean dressing into her hand and held it against her wound.

"Press that as hard as you can," he growled. "Can you stand?"

"What are you doing?" exclaimed Vyne in surprise. "There's no time for that!" She gripped his sleeve and stared up into his face. "Hark. You need to get out of here *right now* while you can! You need to get word to the governor somehow—tell him that those maniacs are taking the god-project to the Undersea! Thousands of people will be in danger if he doesn't do something!"

Hark's heart sank like a stone. The League weren't just moving their god to another base, they were taking it to the very place where it could grow in strength and become unstoppable.

"Why do you care?" he snapped. "That's what you wanted, too, isn't it?"

"Of course not!" Vyne actually looked shocked. "It was never supposed to be *let loose*! That would be insane!"

"I can see more Leaguers behind the bellows house!" said Selphin, crouching down next to Hark. "Some of them have muskets. They're moving along behind the buildings—they're cutting us off!"

Hark glimpsed one of the Leaguers, sprinting from behind one building to the next. Once they had a decent sniper point, they could shoot at the jetty and reload, shoot and reload. Selphin, on the other hand, only had one shot.

"Hark," said Vyne firmly. "You need to run *now*. That's an order!"

She was right. If he and Selphin fled straightaway, maybe they could escape through the village before they were cut off. Lady's Crave had taught him all he needed to know about running.

The last four months, however, had trained new instincts into Hark. Every graze he'd washed, every sore he'd soothed with ointment, every swelling he'd packed with ice had left a tiny, indelible mark on his mind. Without him even noticing it, other people's injuries had become his problem. They called to him like an itch or niggling pain.

"I don't follow your orders anymore," he said.

There was only one other escape from the jetty. Hark caught Selphin's eye, jerked his head toward the boat, and gave her a questioning look. She scowled, then gave a curt, unhappy nod.

"Can you help me lift her?" he asked Selphin.

Vyne looked startled as they heaved her unsteadily onto her feet. They had to support most of her weight as she hobbled toward the fishing boat, stumbling and gasping.

There was a crack—a full, loud musket crack this time—and a nearby jetty board jumped in its socket, spitting a little shower of splinters.

Another crack stung the surface of the water with a tiny flash of white foam.

"Quick! Into the boat!"

Hark guided Vyne up the gangplank, wincing each time her feet slithered. As soon as she was aboard, she collapsed on the deck. Selphin followed and took up a crouched position, aiming her musket at the shoreline to discourage attack. Hark untied the moorings, then leaped aboard as well. He pulled up the gangplank, then hurried to loose the mainsheet.

As Hark hauled on the halyard, he could hear the Leaguers on the shore yelling in anger and dismay. Another musket fired, and Hark flinched, his skin tingling apprehensively.

"Something's happening!" Selphin called out suddenly. "They're not shooting at us!" A moment later: "There! On the hill!"

Hark looked over his shoulder, in time to see a dark shape racing down the hillside toward the village. He knew it instantly by the way it moved, leaping ten feet at a time. It was the thing that had been his friend.

Another musket was fired, smoke drifting on the wind, as the yells grew shrill with panic. Hark saw the Jelt-thing jerk, a little cloud of dry stuff bursting from its shoulder like thistledown. It changed course and leaped into the cover of the crags.

As well as the Leaguer's frantic yells, Hark could hear a deeper voice roaring the same word again and again. The voice was so guttural and grating, Hark barely recognized the word as his own name.

As Hark pushed across the boom and saw the sails swell, it felt like air in his own lungs. The first stealthy motion of the boat toward the sea was slow, and he willed it, begged it to go faster. Then the creep became a glide and gathered momentum. The jetty was skimming past them, then receding behind them. The edges of the harbor fell back on either side. Looking back, Hark could see the Leaguers' village shrinking with distance, out of musket range.

For now, the Leaguers and the Jelt-thing were busy with each other, but soon one side would triumph. Whoever won would want to pursue the stolen fishing boat; he had no doubt of that.

He cast a quick glance across at Selphin, who had put down the musket and was working the ropes with fierce competence. Her jaw was clenched, and Hark wondered how much will-power her composure was costing her. Hark was also finding it hard to concentrate. His hands performed their tasks mechanically, but whenever he thought about the *Abysmal Child*, moving unstoppably through ever darker seas, his mind filled with a deathly numbness.

Hark and his companions were not safe. Nobody was safe.

The escapees skirted the northwest corner of the island in their stolen boat, and then ran due south along the coast, with the wind behind them. They picked up pace quickly, and for now there was no sign of pursuit. Hark bandaged Vyne's wound, and Selphin found some bread, cheese, and ship's biscuits stored below deck. Hark ate half of his share ravenously, then saved the rest to give to Quest later.

That was your friend again, attacking the camp, signed Selphin during a quieter moment. *Why didn't he attack earlier?*

Hark had also thought it strange. A wistful part of him still wondered if Jelt had attacked to save Hark, when he was cornered by enemies. But Jelt hadn't broken cover while Hark was being shot at on the jetty, or when the Leaguers were closing in. He'd only charged down the hillside when . . .

He saw me get on a boat, signed Hark, his heart sinking. *Maybe he thought I was leaving the island, and panicked. I've escaped him by boat before.*

You're sure he can't follow us? asked Selphin.

Jelt had escaped from Wildman's Hammer somehow. Now Hark thought of the Marks he had glimpsed, so much like Vyne's dragonfish sketches.

No, he admitted. *I'm not sure.*

They both threw a brief glance back the way they had come, where the gleaming lace of their wake streaked the freshening sea.

Where are we going, anyway? signed Selphin, with her usual bluntness.

I don't know, Hark replied. *The doctor wants us to get word to the governor on Lady's Crave.*

Good, Selphin responded promptly, her brow clearing. *We'll go to Lady's Crave. I want to tell Rigg about the League and warn the gang.*

Hark's gaze crept to Dr. Vyne again. Her eyes were closed now, her face drawn into a continual wince.

Traveling to Lady's Crave would take hours, he signed. *The doctor might die on the way.*

Selphin gave a conflicted grimace.

You like saving terrible people, don't you? she signed. Her large eyes were not unsympathetic, though. *Will the message to the governor stop the League?*

I don't know, admitted Hark. He needed to prevent a new age of gods, and he wanted to save Vyne from bleeding to death. He really hoped he wouldn't have to choose between the two.

Talk to your crazy murder-doctor, answered Selphin. *Find out what she knows, then we'll decide what to do. I'll take care of the boat and keep lookout.*

Hark had to call the doctor's name several times before she opened her eyes.

"Hark." She blinked, and her eyes seemed to come into focus. "You *must* take a message to the governor, for everyone's sake. He's the only one who might be able to stop a live god slaughtering innocent people. I can make it worth your while. I've got a notebook and pencil—I'll write him a letter, and tell him that I'm setting you at liberty for the rest of your indenture."

Hark gaped at her, knocked off-balance. It wasn't fair of her to dangle a hope that like in front of him.

"I don't believe you!" he blurted out. "How can I believe anything you say? You would have let the League kill us! You helped them build a god! Why? And why do you suddenly want to stop them? How can I trust you?"

"I told you, I never expected it to be released!" protested Vyne. "As far as *I* knew, the plan was to keep the construct restrained and mindless forever! We would give it a supply of Undersea water and feed it materials so it could absorb them, and then trim off new growths. It would be an endless supply of godware, with no need for people to risk their lives in deep-sea salvage subs!"

"That's all right, then," said Hark bitterly. "Nobody could object to that, could they? In fact, I can't imagine why you all hid the project away on a cursed island and decided to kill anybody who found out about it."

Vyne grimaced a little, and not just from the pain. Hark had made his point. She had made hers as well, though. Hark could see why Dr. Vyne would be tempted by an infinite quantity of the most precious stuff in the Myriad.

Hark glanced across to Selphin, hoping that she was able to lip-read some of their conversation, but she was not even looking his way. The boat seemed to be demanding all of her attention. He would just have to tell her everything later.

"I didn't want the governor to find out what we were doing," Vyne admitted. "I thought he might be angry enough to take my museum away from me. But I failed to realize quite how insane the League were. That only became clear to me last night.

"After you . . . after our last conversation, I spent hours trying to get the construct to animate sustainably. It jerked whenever the reverberator pulsed, then fell back dead, every time. By the early hours, I suspected that there wasn't enough fear for it to breathe. *My* suggested solution was that we acquire much bigger tanks of higher quality Undersea water and try again. The captain's suggestion was that we pack the god into the *Abysmal Child* and take it down to the Undersea.

"I told him it was a mad idea. The whole point of our plan was to make sure that our god-construct remained safely confined and under our control. At about this moment I realized that this wasn't the point of *their* plan at all. They had no intention of farming the god. They wanted to bring it to life and release it in the Undersea. That's why they had the *Abysmal Child* waiting in the harbor."

"Why?" asked Hark, though he already had some suspicions.

"They think it's for the good of Myriad." Dr. Vyne sighed. "They think the time of the gods was a golden age, when we

Myriddens were great." She gave a wan smile. "They say we were the monarchs of the seas. They're terrified of foreign ships, and they think the return of the gods will keep us . . . safe."

"Safe," Hark echoed hollowly.

"The gods may have been vast, terrifying abominations, but at least they were local." Vyne gave an incredulous shrug. "So . . . the captain and I had a disagreement . . ."

". . . in which he stabbed you," completed Hark.

"Not straightaway. I realized that I was alone in a nest of fanatics, so I pretended they'd talked me around. They seemed to believe me, but afterward they watched me very closely whenever I was near the god-construct. They didn't stop me wandering near the *Abysmal Child*, though."

Vyne reached into her pocket and pulled out another tuning fork from her collection, slightly smaller than the one in Hark's pocket.

"I was trying to make a hole in one of the portholes," she said. "If the sub sank in the harbor, then at least it wouldn't reach the deeps. Unfortunately, the porthole was rather well designed, with two layers of god-glass tempered differently so that no single note could soften both of them. I developed that technology myself." She grimaced. "Irony. Anyway, they caught me pushing my hand into the glass." She glanced down at her bandages ruefully. "So they made a hole in me instead."

"If we did get a message through to the governor, what could he do?" asked Hark, trying not to panic.

"He can get his subs and ships ready and armed," Vyne said with quiet ferocity. "He can prime the cannons on the coasts. If our project *does* come to life in the Undersea and rise up, he can be ready to blow it to pieces before it gets too large.

"Otherwise, it *will* get large, Hark. Quite quickly, I'm afraid."

She sighed and looked embarrassed.

"You might say I built it to be hungry," she continued. "I wanted it to be an abundant source of godware, so I augmented everything that would allow it to eat, absorb, and grow. If we let it start devouring ships and subs, it will soon be too big and strong to face. But right now I know its weaknesses. If I can warn the governor, he can destroy it as soon as it rises!"

For a moment Hark's spirits were buoyed by her words, but then they sank again.

"That won't happen," he said. "It won't leave the Undersea till it's bigger. Much bigger."

"I think the Leaguers will want their god on the surface as soon as possible," said Vyne.

"That won't matter!" Hark's conversations with Quest rushed back into his mind. "If the Leaguers animate a god, it won't do what they say! It'll be hungry, and it'll be next to a big, crunchy submarine full of stupid people. So it'll eat them all and roam around the deep until it's digested them and everything else it can find. By the time it rises up, it'll be completely different, and *huge*."

He remembered Quest's descriptions of the greatest gods, too vast to be reasoned with, blindly following their hunger and instincts. Now there was not even a priesthood ready to appease or distract the god and stop it from sliding up onto land, devouring all in its path.

"It'll be unstoppable," he whispered. "Once there's a living god loose in the Undersea, everything's hopeless. We need to stop the League *before* they can release it!"

"There's simply not enough time!" exclaimed Vyne miserably. "If the governor's subs were closer, it *might* be possible. The *Abysmal Child*'s slow, and I have some idea which route she's taking. The captain was talking of heading to the Embrace. The shortest route there is past the south end of the Entreaty Barrier. After that . . ."

"After that there's no way to tell which way they've gone," Hark finished despondently, and was surprised to see Vyne give a small, lopsided smile.

"Ah," she said. "Well. Their sub might be leaving a few traces behind it. My tuning fork didn't make a hole in the porthole, but I *may* have accidentally melted the god-glass cover of their front aurora lamp."

Aurora lamps were expensive cutting-edge technology, using fluids from phosphorescent deep-sea jellyfish, combined with a trace of luminous ichor from the glands of certain gods.

"If I'm right, then that lamp is leaking luminescence," said Vyne. "There might even be a trail."

It was the first glimmer of hope Hark had felt since the *Abysmal Child* had descended. It was so fragile that he was almost afraid of it. Hark could imagine the luminous trail left in the water, floating wisps of glow unraveled by every fin flick, every surge in the swell . . .

"How long would a trail like that last?" he asked.

"Not long enough," said Vyne with miserable bluntness. "It'll take us hours to reach Lady's Crave. Even if the governor believed us right away, his subs wouldn't be here before evening."

"There is one sub close enough, isn't there?" Hark said slowly. "A really fast sub . . ."

Vyne was already shaking her head.

"The *Butterfly* was exhausting to pilot, even when I was in full health! And now . . . Hark, I don't know how long I'll be conscious. I'm really rather cold. I'm not a medical doctor, as I've told you, but I know that's not a good sign."

"I'll come in the sub with you," said Hark. "I'll help you." The words were out before he even had time to think.

"That's an unhinged idea!" exclaimed Vyne. "Look, I'd probably pass out or . . . *die* . . . before we were even out of the cave! What would you do then?"

"I've watched you drive it!" Hark insisted, though he wasn't sure how much this would help. "Anyway, what choice do we have? You'll just have to . . . not die!"

"Always my preferred option," murmured Vyne. She did not, however, look hopeful.

Chapter 36

SELPHIN STOOD AT THE FRONT OF THE BOAT, the sea spray chilling her to the bone. She was very aware of the chop and thrash of the waves on either side. Every time the boat flew lightly off one wave and hit the next, she felt the impact like a fist in her gut. Once upon a time she would not even have noticed it.

She wasn't fooled by the waves—she knew what they were under their gleaming skin. She didn't just *remember* her nightmare swim from Wildman's Hammer, she could still *feel* it. She could feel the ruthless drag of the water, as wave after wave reared up to strike her gasping face, blocking her view on all sides. She could feel each icy crash that drove her under, and she couldn't see, couldn't breathe, could only thrash while unseen rocks raked her limbs.

Each time a wave glinted mockingly in the sun, she wondered whether she had escaped at all. It was as though the sea had *let* her crawl, bruised and weeping, back onto the shore. Now it waited mere feet away for a chance to seize her again.

Hark was still busy aft, talking to the crazy doctor who had bought him. He was facing away from her, but she had a view of the doctor's face. Since Selphin was keeping the boat running and standing lookout, however, she was only reading tantalizing fragments of what was clearly an important conversation.

You better not agree to anything stupid, Sanctuary boy, she thought. He obviously had a history of doing the wrong things for the wrong people.

Selphin turned her attention back to the sea behind them. There was no sign of a pursuing sail, but her instincts were tingling. She stared into the wind, past the long streak of the boat's wake, beyond the parade of headlands, rendered gauzy by a mist of spray. In the far distance, there was a tiny flash of foam as something broke the surface.

A school of flying fish? It was possible, but she did not think so. She would probably have seen the telltale silvery glitter. A dolphin or a seal, perhaps? Selphin stared out to the sea, looking for irregularities and breaks in its natural music. She had a feel for her great enemy, a sense of its rhythms and whims.

Another flare of foam, still distant but slightly closer. For a second, the curve of a dark back was visible. Bigger than a seal or a dolphin.

Still she waited, wanting to be certain. It could still be a young whale astray from its pod and too far inland, breaching to take a breath . . .

The third time, there was no mistake. It was too narrow to be a whale, and as it plunged beneath the surface, she thought she glimpsed two legs instead of a tail.

Selphin stamped on the deck to get the others' attention, the way everyone did on her mother's boats. Hark and the doctor both looked up.

We're being followed, Selphin signed.

Are you sure? asked Hark.

Yes, she signed. *One person swimming fast. Very fast. Underwater.*

Hark went pale.

Can we outrun it? he asked.

The boat had the favor of the wind and was managing a good rate of knots. Every time Selphin had seen the pursuing shape, however, it had been closer.

No, she signed.

Will it catch us before we reach the third headland ahead? asked Hark, then pointed.

Selphin narrowed her eyes, trying to reckon the distance.

I don't know, she signed back eventually. *Maybe. Why?*

There's a cove beyond the third headland, Hark signed back. *In a cave, there's a submarine. It's crazy and dangerous and it screams. But it's fast enough to chase the Leaguer sub. I can help the doctor drive it.*

Heart and soul, Selphin wanted to push on for Lady's Crave. She wanted to see that beautiful, ugly double-humped silhouette appear on the horizon, with the greasy streak of smoke from the glue factory's chimney. She wanted to sprint through the docks, and find her crew alive and well, and let them cuff her and scream at her and maybe never forgive her.

If they pushed on toward Lady's Crave, however, whatever was chasing them would catch up with them long before they reached it. Besides, they had to seize any chance to stop the Leaguers. What was the point of going home today if her beloved island was god-food tomorrow?

Tell me everything, she signed.

Chapter 37

HARK QUICKLY TOLD SELPHIN ABOUT HIS CON-
versation with Vyne.

What is she doing now? asked the smuggler girl. Vyne was
huddled over her notebook, scrawling on a torn-out page with
a pencil.

Writing a message to the governor, he answered. *We should
send that, too, just in case.* If the *Butterfly* plan didn't work,
which seemed likely, someone needed to warn the governor
what was coming. *You could take the note to Lady's Crave,* he
suggested. Selphin was clearly aching to go home. *You can run
to the harbor and find a boat to take you.*

Maybe, she signed back, looking unhappy and conflicted. It
was a less enthusiastic answer than he expected.

You don't have to, signed Hark, unsure what was wrong. *I can
give the note to my old priest friend. He's waiting at the cove.*

As he mentioned Quest, Hark felt a flood of shame and dread.
He would have to tell the old man that he *had* let the heart out
of his possession, it *was* on the way to the Undersea, and that in
fact it had been plugged into a ready-made god-body.

He realized that Selphin was staring at him.

The old priest is at the cove? she asked, her eyebrows rising.
Is he good at running?

Hark saw at once what she meant. They would reach the
cove before their pursuer caught up with them, but it would not

be too far behind. They would not have much time to get an elderly, sickly man and a badly wounded woman off the beach.

As their destination cove finally came into view, Hark looked across and saw the shack, as expected. There was, however, an unexpected figure in yellow robes standing outside it. Hark had no time to react to this, however, because the boat was already committed to the turn, at a reckless speed.

The cove wasn't really a natural harbor, so they made a slight hash of their approach, running in too quickly, then yawing desperately to avoid rocks. They beached themselves on the shingle in the shallows and settled at a tilt.

The Sanctuary attendant flinched back against the shack, looking startled. He was a strongly built young man who had been at Sanctuary only six months longer than Hark.

"Dr. Vyne!" whispered Hark, tugging at the doctor's sleeve. "There's a Sanctuary attendant on the beach! You need to talk to him! He'll listen to you!"

Vyne did not answer. She was still breathing, though with obvious difficulty. There were dark shadows around her eyes, and when he nudged her she showed no signs of waking.

"Hark?" The junior attendant had spotted him. "Where have you been? Kly's *raging*! He's going to rip your head off!"

Hark took a deep breath as his plans somersaulted, tumbled, and tried to right themselves. He furtively slipped the doctor's ring of keys from her belt and hid it in his own belt pouch, before standing up.

"Help!" he yelled at the top of his lungs. "Help us! Dr. Vyne's hurt—she's been stabbed! You need to take her to Sanctuary!"

"What?" asked the young man, looking overwhelmed. "Who stabbed her?"

"Leaguers! I can't explain now—you need to take her to Sanctuary right now or she'll die!"

"But . . ." The attendant looked back at the shack. "But Quest is in this hut! We've been looking for him all night! I saw him on the beach, but now he's barricaded himself in there somehow—"

"I'll deal with that!" Hark insisted. "He listens to me!"

The promise was enough. The young attendant waded out into the shallows, and Hark and Selphin carefully lowered Vyne into his arms.

"Go! Quickly!" Hark knew he was pushing his luck, giving orders to someone higher up the pecking order. However, he knew that at any moment their negotiations might be interrupted by a sleek dark shape with razor-tipped limbs . . .

Struggling a little under the doctor's weight, the yellow-clad figure hurried over the rocks in the direction of the harbor. Before he was out of sight, Hark had dropped over the side of the boat into the shallows, where the breakers buffeted and dragged at his legs. Selphin splashed down behind him and staggered but kept her balance. She still had the Leaguer musket held above her head to keep it dry.

Belatedly, Hark remembered the note to the governor. He hadn't claimed it from Vyne. Everything had happened too fast.

"There's a letter in her notebook!" he yelled after the distant attendant, hoping he could hear him. "It's for . . . Kly! Show it to him, he'll understand, he'll know what to do!" Any number of Sanctuary attendants might be League sympathizers, but Hark was completely sure that Kly wasn't.

Clothes sodden, Hark hurried up the beach to the shack and pounded on the door.

"Quest! It's me, Hark! Open up!"

There was a faint shuffling of steps from within.

"You're sure it's safe?" Quest's unmistakeable tones inquired.

"Nothing's safe!" admitted Hark. "But we have to go!"

The door opened. Quest's red-rimmed eyes peered over the muffling of his clothes.

"Who is your small friend, and why is she armed?" asked the old man.

"Selphin's . . . on our side. We ran into trouble . . ."

"What kind of trouble?" Quest's forehead furrowed deeply. "Tell me you still have the heart!"

Hark couldn't tell him that. He felt his face crumple miserably and saw realization dawn across Quest's features, followed by devastation and despair. There was no anger or resentment in the old man's expression, and that somehow made it harder to bear.

"I'm going to stop them!" said Hark, filled with a sudden surge of desperate resolve. "The Leaguers are taking the heart to the Undersea—they *want* a new age of the gods. I won't let that happen, I promise! But right now we have to get off this beach!"

There was a wordless cry of warning from Selphin, who was pointing out to sea. Something dark was approaching the cove with frightening speed. It undulated and split the waves like a dolphin, but the shape was wrong, the ridges down its back were wrong, the things it trailed were wrong.

"Run to the door!" shouted Hark. He guided the startled Quest up the slope to the cliff door, closely followed by Selphin. As he wrestled with Vyne's ring of keys, out of the corner of his eye Hark could see Selphin facing the beach with her musket ready and bristling with as much terror as defiance.

"Stay back!" Selphin yelled, her voice cracking. "Stay back, stay back!" He had never heard her voice sound so raw and uncontrolled.

Hark risked a frantic glance at the beach and regretted it. A glistening head and torso had emerged from the waters and was moving toward the shore. Water poured out between its teeth, its too many teeth . . .

He desperately fumbled key after key into the lock, his ravaged knuckles stinging.

This key? No. This? No . . . maybe . . . no. Oh please, one of you!

A key that seemed too small suddenly lodged in the lock. Hark twisted it in panic and heard something click. A fraction of an instant later, a gunshot a foot away nearly made him jump out of his skin.

Selphin was screaming something at the top of her lungs, but he could no longer tell what. He flung his weight against the door. It opened, and he fell through into the waiting darkness. The other two shoved in after him, bumping into him in the dark. With panicky force Hark slammed the door behind them again.

"Lock it!" Selphin was shouting. "Lock it!"

He couldn't find the keyhole in the dark. His desperate fingers did find a bolt, however, and he wrestled it into place. A moment later, he felt the door jolt violently, as something slammed into the other side. With shaking hands, Hark found two more bolts and threw them, then felt for the keyhole and locked the door. Another blow from outside hammered the door, and there followed a roar of frustration.

Dr. Vyne's scruples had room for improvement, but she did have a nice line of good, solid doors. Right now, this seemed like a highly redeeming quality.

Selphin only calmed down once Hark had found and lit a scarelantern. The hand-hewn cave filled with purple light and the smell of singed unease.

It came out of the water, she signed hastily. *It had hundreds of teeth. I told it to stay away. But it leaped out and ran for us, so . . . I shot it. I shot it. I hit it in the hip. It fell down and squirmed. Then it started to get up again . . .*

Selphin had dropped her musket outside after firing it. She was now hugging her own arms defensively. Hark couldn't tell if she was bruised from the recoil or just shaken, and knew better than to ask.

That shot gave us time to escape, Quest signed rather slowly and stiffly. *Thank you.* Hark was startled to find that Quest knew sign language, unlike the other Sanctuary priests. Then he remembered that the old man had still been out in the world long after the Cataclysm. *What* was *that creature?*

Hark exchanged a glance with Selphin.

My friend, he signed reluctantly. *The one I thought I could save.*

Quest gave a heavy sigh. "I am sorry, Hark."

The roaring beyond the door had ceased. Hark imagined the dark, scaly figure lurking silently on the other side.

Is there another way out of here? Selphin asked abruptly.

No, Hark admitted. *Only the submarine.*

But we can't use that anymore! signed Selphin. *We don't have Dr. Vyne!*

Submarine? asked Quest.

Hark inhaled deeply, then took the explanation at a run.

"Dr. Vyne and the League were working together to build a god. She thought they were just going to keep it in a box and trim bits of godware off it, like fleecing a sheep. But the League want to set it free and bring back the age of the gods. She found out their plans, so they stabbed her. They put the Lady's heart in their god, but it wouldn't come to life properly, so they're taking it to the Undersea in a submarine so it can breathe more fear. Downstairs is a secret, fast submarine Vyne designed herself. She was going to pilot it, but she passed out. So . . . I'm taking it out and going after the League."

He felt his face heat up with panic as he said the words.

"Show us this submarine," said Quest.

Hark led them down the winding stone steps until they came to the cavern where the *Screaming Sea Butterfly* bobbed in the dark water.

"It looks like the accursed offspring of a jellyfish and a sting-ray," said Quest after a moment. "You say you know how to pilot this . . . error of judgment?"

"I've ridden in it with Dr. Vyne," said Hark, aware that this wasn't exactly an answer to the question. "You change the sound and it makes the wings flap. It's loud, so you have to wear a helmet . . ."

"Anything else I need to know before we go?" Quest asked.

"What?" exclaimed Hark, horrified. "But . . . you're ill!"

"Have either of you ever been to the Undersea?" demanded Quest, his voice gaining force. "Do you have any idea what it is like down there? The switchback currents? The great waves where Undersea meets sea? The creatures that live down there? Trust me, you need me. There is room for three in there . . ."

Selphin stamped her foot for attention and waved at Hark until he looked at her.

What's the priest saying? she signed. *He wants to come? You can't let him come! Priests worship gods! He won't want to stop the League making one!*

This priest is different, signed Hark.

How? Why? demanded Selphin. *Why should we trust him?*

He's my friend! signed Hark in frustration, then realized that this was a poor argument, given his past record with friendships. *And he's right! We need someone who knows about the Undersea!*

That just means he can send us off course or get us killed! signed Selphin fiercely.

He warned me about the gods! Hark protested. *He tried to break the heart!*

How did he know it belonged to the Hidden Lady? Selphin returned to her earlier question, her signs expansive and exasperated. *He knows something about all of this that he's not telling you! Why are you so stupid?*

"Quest," Hark said slowly, "how *did* you recognize the Hidden Lady's heart?"

"There is no time for this!" Quest's face was contorted with anxiety.

How many times had Quest sidestepped or deflected questions? Quest was like a dry rose, a tightly folded knot of old secrets. Every papery petal you pulled away revealed more. Even now, Hark knew that there were more layers. He couldn't say how many or what lay at their heart.

Hark needed to know, before they went into the dark together. Selphin was right.

"I want to trust you, Quest," Hark said quietly. "But I can't just follow people blindly anymore. How did you know it was hers?"

There was a pause, during which Quest breathed deeply and raggedly. Then he gave Hark a haggard, complicated smile. It was the smile of one who sees that a long game is over and who realizes that he is very tired of playing it.

"I knew," said Quest, "because the Hidden Lady showed me her heart. And because I tore that heart from her when I killed her."

Chapter 38

"YOU . . . KILLED HER?" HARK REPEATED STUPIDLY.

You couldn't! signed Selphin, looking flabbergasted. *She was a god!*

The Lady with her drowned-looking beauty and her impossibly long spider-crab legs, hidden in a forest of her own snaking, weed-like tresses. The Lady with her mysteries, and secrets, and otherworldly cleverness. The mistress of Lady's Crave, a teller of tales older than the oaks . . .

Quest turned to Selphin.

May I explain in speech? he asked. *My sign is slow and not good enough.*

Selphin gave a little frowning shrug and turned up the scare-lamp to full brightness. Quest blinked as the purple light shone onto his face.

"The Hidden Lady was a lonely god," he began. "That was her weakness. She told me her secrets. She had found a way to move her heart out of her core, up her neck and into her hair. She even showed me. It took a long time, and it hurt her, but she could push her heart to the end of a hair tendril—like a ball in a stocking."

Why would she put her heart in her hair? demanded Selphin.

"She was lonely," said Quest again. "She was desperate. We priests spoke with her, but our lives were too small, warm, and brief. She wanted to talk to her own kind, who had seen and breathed the abyss long enough to understand her. But she did not dare get too close to them."

Hark noticed Selphin looking uncertain and hastened to explain.

Heartbeats, he signed. *The gods felt each other's heartbeats from a distance. It made them go crazy and forced them to fight each other to the death.*

"When she was still a young god," continued Quest, "the Hidden Lady heard the Gathergeist singing in the deep. She realized it was another young, clever god and wanted to talk to it, but she could not risk feeling its heartbeat or letting it feel hers. She knew that would overwhelm their reason and force them to fight.

"So she learned to move her heart.

"With the heart at the end of a hair strand, she could hold it at distance from her body. Holding her heart out behind her, she approached the Gathergeist, close enough to call out to it. The Lady told it what she had done, so it imitated her and moved the chain containing its heart farther away from her. They could speak that way, without sensing each other's hearts.

"They did not talk often. It was dangerous to be so close and to leave their hearts so vulnerable. Sometimes years would pass without them speaking, but it was enough to hold off their madness."

"They were . . . friends?" Hark knew immediately that this was the wrong term.

"No," said Quest. "They were each other's . . . storykeepers. However, after the Gathergeist ate the Swallower and doubled in size, it felt its mind dulling."

Big gods lose their minds, Hark explained to Selphin.

"The Gathergeist was able to tell the Lady of that last fight, but after that its mind guttered and went out. The Lady hid from the Gathergeist as it swam toward Siren. Afterward, she was alone again. She asked me to help her . . ." Quest was trembling slightly. "She asked me to find another intelligent god and lead them close enough to talk to her. I lied. I told her I had arranged it. She moved her heart to a hair tip, waiting to hear the new god approach. I cut the heart away. Fled with it. Left her to die."

Quest's brutal frankness was too much for Hark.

"Why?" he blurted out, feeling an ache like grief. "Why did you do it?"

Despite all Quest's bitter words about the gods, he had seemed to respect the Hidden Lady. Hark had sensed a strange intimacy—not the physical closeness of lovers, nor even a romantic friendship, but a meeting of souls nonetheless.

"She had to be destroyed," answered Quest. "Her mind was dying, leaving only a monster. And I needed her heart."

"What for?" asked Hark, then immediately felt that he knew the answer. "You needed to heal someone!"

"Not someone, no," answered Quest. "I needed her heart so I could heal the Myriad from an ancient sickness. I needed it so that I could kill the gods. All of them."

Hark and Selphin stared at the old man before them.

The Cataclysm. Quest was talking about the Cataclysm. The event that had reshaped the Myriad, left hundreds of orphans, wiped ports off shorelines, and scarred a million minds. Everyone over thirty-five remembered where they had been when the Cataclysm happened.

Now Quest stood there calmly, face livid in the purple light, and told them that he had planned it.

"I joined the priesthood to be near a woman who did not love me," Quest went on. "But I stayed in the priesthood to find a way that the gods might be destroyed. I watched them for twenty years, to discover whether they could die.

"I learned they fell apart without enough fear to breathe. If a god was too far from the Myriad for too long, its heart failed and it died. A god called the Fourfaced was swept by storm far out to sea, then chased a pod of whales a hundred miles. It died, and whalers from the continent found its body. The priests kept it secret.

"At first I thought I could lure the gods away from the Myriad to their deaths, one by one," Quest went on. "Some gods could be lured a little distance. The Cardinal followed bright lights. Dolor liked colored boards. Wanderer would chase a dead whale dragged behind a boat. But they would turn back when their bodies started to fail.

"Then the Lady showed me her heart. I realized that if I could cut it away still beating, I had something no god could resist. Gods would chase another god's heartbeat even to their deaths.

"It would take too long to lead each of them out to sea with the heart, one by one. There were more than forty gods, scattered over a thousand miles. If I took too long, the priesthood would catch me or new gods would rise.

"I needed a much quicker way of killing them, and I found it."

In Hark's head, the pieces started to come together.

"You led them to each other!" he said accusingly. "You used the heart to bring them together, so they would fight and eat each other!"

"Yes," confirmed Quest. "A group of us in a fast ship dragged the heart in the water. We made the gods fight, then led the winner to the next god, and the next. When a god had eaten many others, and grown so vast it was causing tidal waves, we led it far out to sea to die. Then we returned, went to another part of Myriad, and did it all again, and again."

The apocalyptic sea battles, still recounted in taverns or whispered of on deathbeds, had all been part of a carefully constructed plan. Kalmaddoth's battle with the Red Forlorn, the Silver Cataract's ravaging of the Dawn Sister, the shrieking rampage of the Gathergeist . . .

People died! Selphin signed sharply. *Hundreds of people died from the waves and the gods going crazy!*

"Yes," replied Quest. "Maybe even thousands in the end. The friends who helped me all died, too, during our mission. The last god to die was the Gathergeist, and it dragged down our ship with its last strength. My comrades were lost, and so was the heart."

Hark felt shattered and shaky. Quest, his wise, secretive ally and confidant, had deliberately triggered the Cataclysm. The answer to the greatest secret of the age had been curled in his frail fist for thirty years.

"You look angry and upset," said Quest, watching Hark in his usual shrewd way. "Are you grieving for the innocents lost? Or are you still thinking of the Lady? She killed thousands, mostly on whims. The island of Twice is so named because she rose up on two different occasions to devour all its inhabitants. Was she more tragic than they were?"

Hark felt himself redden. It was true: Quest's betrayal of the Lady still stung him to the core. He realized that he had been thinking as though her pain, loneliness, and death were somehow bigger and more important than anyone else's. *Hypnotic*, Quest had called the gods. Even though Hark had never seen the Lady in life, he had been hypnotized by the sinuous allure of the stories. What was she, though, when you dissected the thought of her?

"You must not love them," said Quest gently. "It is easy to love power, because power tells you it is majesty and beauty and greatness. But the gods were monsters. Do not even love their memory. Hate me if you like for the human deaths I caused. I tried to avoid them, but I knew the risks. I am not a good man. But the gods are dead."

Hark looked at Selphin, who scowled heavily.

If he's telling the truth, he's a monster, too, she signed.

A monster who kills gods, Hark replied.

The smuggler girl glared at him or at some thought beyond him.

Let's go, she signed suddenly and angrily. *All of us. Let's go now.*

By the scare-light Hark could see that her jaw was set, her face ashen pale.

Are you sure? He signed back.

Just open the hatch! She signed rapidly. *Do it quickly!*

Do it quickly before I change my mind, said her expression.

Chapter 39

ONE BY ONE, ALL THREE SCRAMBLED INTO THE *Butterfly*. Hark and Selphin had to take the seats so they could operate the pedals. Hark didn't like asking Quest to squeeze into the gap between the seats, but there was no choice.

Hark quickly checked the air rack and breather boxes behind the seats. There were three full air-bottles. The soda ash was fresh and the soak powder dry. He pulled the hatch closed, and as before, the outside world was fogged by the faintest rainbow haze.

There were only two helmets. Selphin watched her crewmates buckle them on with an acerbic eye.

You both look like mushrooms, she signed. Hark noticed, however, that she was taking care to look only at her companions or at the ceiling of the cave. She was breathing quickly and keeping her gaze away from the dark water below and on either side.

We're going down, he signed, as best he could without elbowing Quest.

She nodded curtly.

He pulled a handle gently and hoped. The water enveloped them, plunging them into darkness. Too late, Hark realized why Vyne had put the front light on first.

He remembered her lighting the lamp by turning a wheel. The first wheel his groping fingers found caused a shrieking, white-cold musical note to shudder the sub. The second made the sub lurch backward a foot so that it jolted against the stone ledge.

Quest was trying to sign something. It was barely visible and was probably some variant of *Are you sure you know how to drive this thing?*

Thankfully, the third wheel caused a glimmer to appear in the lamp.

We have to pedal now, Hark signed, and then realized that Selphin had her eyes tightly closed and was gripping the sides of her seat. When he tapped her arm she opened her eyes, and he repeated the signs, but he wasn't sure at first whether she had understood it. After a few seconds she gave an unsteady nod.

He turned the pedals and felt them move with more ease once Selphin joined in.

Now I just have to remember the rest of the controls, he thought. *These steer left and right, I think—yes!*

One step at a time. One difficult and potentially fatal step at a time.

The water grew lighter as they emerged from the cave. The underwater light was even more beautiful than before, dimly jeweled by the morning sun. Shocks of weed danced like green and amber flames.

A dark shape swooped at the *Butterfly* from a distance, undulating with unbearable grace, and buffeted the glass sphere. Hark yelled aloud, and his was not the only scream. The next moment, his brain understood what he had seen: the whiskered face, the paw-like fins tucked against its body, the silvery glisten of its oily dark pelt.

Selphin burst out laughing. *Seal*, she signed. *Hunting a big glass fish.*

Hark laughed, too, his heart still banging. He couldn't put

things off anymore. The real Jelt might be noticing the disturbance in the water even now. Hark tucked the bellows under
his arm, and gave it some experimental squeezes.

I'm turning on the scream, he signed, so that the others
could brace themselves.

Hark turned what he thought was the screaming wheel, and
the sub lurched backward again. A forward jet of water blasted
a couple of anemones off their rock and made the pipefish scatter. Hark swore violently. He was now perspiring as much from
embarrassment as effort.

The next wheel *did* release the same pure, rending scream
as before. Its note slowly waned to a dusky murmur, but when
Hark squeezed the bellows under one arm, the note returned.
This is just a giant pipe organ, Hark told himself, staring at
all the stops, pulls, and levers. *I just need to work out how to
play it.*

He pulled out one of the stops, and the single note rose to a
piercing wail that he could feel in his teeth. The wings on either
side were now drooping, and the sub's nose was dipping. The
Butterfly was drifting downward toward the ragged rocks fifteen
feet below.

In a panic, he pushed the stop back in again, and the sound
dropped to a bass rumble. The wings whipped up so sharply he
was afraid that they might snap. He needed to make the wings
flap, so if he pulled the stop in and out . . .

The *Butterfly* yodeled sickeningly, as though he were tortur-
ing her. The wings jerked up and down, buckling weirdly as
they did so and making the sub dip and rear. Hark felt sick. This
wasn't how Dr. Vyne had steered it at all! She had made the
wings ripple like silk. How had she done it?

He remembered the straps of her helmet hanging loose and

the grimace of pained concentration on her face. She must have left it unfastened so that she could hear the notes a little better.

Reluctantly, he pulled loose the buckle of his helmet. The pressure of the padding was released very slightly, and the *Butterfly*'s sound slid into his brain like a knife. He felt as though his skull was shuddering and shaking his brain to jelly. He released the bellows, but the note seemed to go on and on. It screamed the way the sea screamed, without reason or forgiveness. It was a white sound, everything was white, he was lost in the white . . .

Something in the white darkness was shaking him by the collar. It slapped him twice, then shook him again.

Hark gradually recovered his ability to think. The world was still a loud and painful place, but now the ululating scream had settled into a long, piercing trill that didn't melt his brain. He groggily opened his eyes and found Selphin leaning across him so that she could get the bellows under one arm.

Stop us from crashing! she signed frantically, hampered somewhat by the bellows.

The glassy wings *were* rippling slightly now, propelling the sub forward. However, this was taking them directly toward a jagged-looking rock the size of a house. The *Butterfly* was also listing relentlessly to starboard.

Hark grabbed the steering controls and turned sharply to port. Selphin dropped back into her own seat, and Hark tucked the bellows back under his own arm. The tilt started to right itself slightly, possibly because Selphin was no longer on Hark's side of the sub.

The *Screaming Sea Butterfly* wheeled slowly to the left, turning away from the rock face, but Hark could see that her starboard wing would pass perilously close to it. He could feel his stomach muscles tensing, as if that would help the wing flinch back. He didn't want to see its supple curve torn to limp pulp like jellyfish flesh . . .

The iridescent wing tip skimmed past the surface of the rock, so close that it broke off one pockmarked sponge. Its passing stirred little flurries of silt and strands of mossy weed. As the sub glided clear of the rock, Hark remembered how to breathe again.

Hark looked at the controls. Several of them had been moved from their previous positions. Two of the stops, side by side, had been pulled out to an equal extent. Hark glanced again at the rippling wings. It was a feeble quiver, but it was a good start.

How did you manage that? Hark signed to Selphin, who was also recovering her breath.

She gave an expansive, bewildered shrug and pointed at the controls.

I pulled things out and pushed them in! A lot! She put out one hand, and briefly stroked the glass wall of the sub. *I could feel the vibrations*, she explained, and shrugged again.

There was a compass in front of Hark, making it possible to navigate the *Butterfly*. After a quick debate, they took a west-southwest course toward the edge of the Entreaty Barrier's net.

Even though the seating arrangement allowed all three of them to see each other's hands, the cramped conditions made it harder to sign with full arm motions. Hark wasn't used to having purely sign conversations this rapid with multiple people, and he struggled to follow the conversation. Selphin's signs were clear, fluid, and expressive, but Quest's were more stilted and limited, his face often creased in concentration rather than reflecting his meaning as it should. It didn't help that Quest had clearly learned sign language on Siren, so some of the signs he did know differed from those used on Lady's Crave.

Hark brought the sub up to a depth of ten feet. Here the water was still bright with slices of dancing sapphire. The swell tugged at her, but she was slippery and sliced through the will of the water the way the fish did. Hark started to feel that odd giddy excitement the *Butterfly* had given him before.

By gently tweaking the controls, Hark found ways to change the scream so that it increased the ripple of the wings. The sub skimmed along faster, and then faster. He couldn't make it dart and swoop the way Vyne had, but at least it wasn't tilting, plummeting, or jerking its wings like a convulsing gull.

For now, there was no sign of Jelt, but Hark didn't believe for a moment that he had given up his pursuit. He would certainly have heard the *Butterfly* leave and perhaps even seen its glassy shape skimming away underwater.

The seafloor was slowly dropping away beneath them, rugged with shadowy crags and ravines. Mackerel exploded in silver from behind the timbers of a shattered rowing boat. Bream and glum-faced groupers darted for cover as the *Butterfly*'s shadow skimmed over them. The sea was five fathoms deep, then six, then seven, the bottom growing murkier.

Hark glanced at Selphin. Her jaw was clenched again, her breathing shaky and shallow.

Sorry, he signed discreetly, so that Quest couldn't see. *I know you didn't want this.*

Selphin gave a lopsided grimace.

I told you, I don't want a stupid death, she signed back, her motions a bit nervous and jerky. *I don't want to drown for no good reason. But saving the Myriad isn't stupid.*

Even in clear water on a good day, there is only so far ahead you can see. A fine mist in the water fogs everything distant. There are tiny particles of things that have lived and things that have not, all on their own individual voyage.

So it was that the great net of the Entreaty Barrier approached the *Screaming Sea Butterfly* by stealth, like an enormous predator. At first it was only an indistinct hint of darkness somewhere ahead. Gradually the huge, shadowy net of chains became visible in the distance, blurry with the marine mist. Hark slowed the *Butterfly* as they approached.

Seen from a distance, the net seemed to hang still, like the web of a vast spider. As the sub grew closer, however, Hark could see that the whole momentous net was swaying slowly seaward, then snapping back with surprising force. It looked graceful, like the billowing of weed in a swell, but Hark knew the lashing of the great chains could knock you unconscious or smash in the side of a diving bell.

The square holes in the mesh were five feet wide. The links were a span broad, and their metal all but invisible, choked and shaggy with life. Limpets and barnacles clustered next to pink sea squirts and anemones.

Sway and snap, sway and snap. The net extended to the left and right, no end in sight in either direction. Hark turned the sub to the left, to follow the net south.

The air had been growing stuffy, and Hark noticed himself feeling groggy, so he released a little air from one of the copper bottles in the rack. He let out a little more as they skimmed parallel to the net, trying to stay out of its way.

A few minutes later they found where the net ended in a rocky spire that rose up to break the surface. Hark navigated around this island. There was no sign of the *Abysmal Child*'s passing.

Hark turned off the lights.

The darkness was a shock, even though he could still see

a reasonable distance in the blue-gray twilight. It was the disappearance of the submarine that was startling. When Hark couldn't see the cockpit or his friends, he could imagine for a moment that he was quite alone in the deeps, drowning without feeling it.

There was still no sign of a luminescent trail, not even the slightest gleam.

Hark's heart plunged. Of course, the search for such a trail had been a long shot, but if they couldn't find it, there was no backup plan. He scanned the darkness until his eyes ached, then reluctantly put on the lights again.

As he did so, Selphin suddenly tapped his arm and pointed ahead.

Almost beyond the reach of the sub's lights floated a great, indistinct cloud of jellyfish, like spectral parasols. Halfway down its bulk was a darker patch where only mangled, ghostly shreds floated. Something large appeared to have carved through the middle of the fluther, tearing their soft, translucent pulp and leaving a great gash in the cloud.

Hark exchanged an excited glance with Selphin. The gash was of the right size to have been caused by the *Abysmal Child*.

It looks like they went that way! he signed.

They are taking the old route over the . . . ! Quest signed. The last sign was not one used on Lady's Crave, and the priest seemed to notice his companions' confusion.

West, he simply signed instead.

The *Butterfly* left behind the Entreaty Barrier and its momentous net, and Hark set a course west.

Through the glass, Hark could see the sub's lights carving out pale scoops in the dim water. Ahead, the seafloor dropped steeply, in a thirty-foot cliff. At the cliff's base extended a broad, deep plateau. It was barren-looking, too low for kelp or weed, and yet it held a forest of sorts. The light from the *Butterfly* glinted on jostling turrets, upward-jutting oars, broken hulls, and skewed propellers.

It was a submarine graveyard, extending beyond the reach of the light.

Little barrel-shaped skimmers bared their timber bones, their leather long since eaten away. Vast salvage vessels slumbered half buried, never to wake. Diving bells lay on their sides, shelter for dark, darting shoals.

All these vessels had dared the sea, full of ambition, warmth, greed, and camaraderie. The Embrace had chewed them up and spat them out again on its doorstep, as a contemptuous warning. Hark wondered how many of the broken subs had come here to salvage from this very disaster-scape. He remembered what Selphin had said about "stupid deaths."

Gazing ahead and below them, Hark could see a great, double-peaked pillar of rock rising out of the submarine graveyard. It was two houses wide and taller than Sanctuary.

To the pillar, Quest signed.

As Hark guided the sub downward, he started to see the plain of wreckage differently. From a distance, it had looked frozen, its stillness eerie. Now he became aware of countless flickers of motion. Red scales flashed behind a porthole as some bigeyes flinched away from the light. A large spider crab crept over the debris slowly with its long, brittle-looking legs. On every turret and hull, thousands of soft polyps and wispy feelers would be feeding off the current.

Hark loved that about the sea. It was always dangerous, as the plain of wreckage proved, but life always found a foothold, or sucker-hold, or roothold, on anything it could.

Quest winced and stretched, turning his head this way and that to work out the stiffness in his neck.

Are you all right? Hark could not help asking, at a moment when he felt safe releasing the controls. Quest might be the mastermind of the Cataclysm, but he was also a frail, unwell friend who appeared to be in pain.

Quest froze where he was, staring backward through the glass ceiling.

There is something behind us, he signed.

Hark twisted to look back but could see nothing in the darkness behind, apart from a brownish school of large cod. Selphin peered back as well, then met his eye and shook her head.

Was it him? she asked Quest. Hark could guess who she meant.

It is hard to be certain, signed Quest. *It fled the light.*

Down here, the press of the water would surely crush the life out of any creature not suited to such depths. Yet Hark couldn't shake the dread that it *was* Jelt out there, still chasing Hark to recover the god-heart. Jelt didn't know that the heart was now embedded in a god-construct and entombed in the hold of a completely different submarine.

He could still be there, just beyond the light, suggested Selphin, reassuringly. *He could be following in the dark.*

Chapter 40

THE GREAT PILLAR APPROACHED, UNTIL HARK could make out the crevices in its red rock and the rubble around its base. He slowed the sub and turned off the lamp again.

The darkness was denser than it had been before.

After a second or two, however, Hark's sight adjusted, and what he noticed was the livid blueness of the darkness. He had heard deep-sea salvage mariners tell him of the strange brightness of the light in the depths. The rock pillar ahead was still indistinctly visible.

A rapid double tap on his arm. Hark turned the light back on.

Port side! Selphin signed. *Halfway up!*

Hark turned off the light again and saw what Selphin had already seen. Adrift in the water, on the port side of the pillar, was the tiniest wisp of floating light.

Hope hammered painfully in Hark's chest. He flicked the lamp on again to steer around the pillar, then turned it off once more. Selphin's sharp eyes quickly spotted another drifting strand of glow, already fraying. It was to the west-southwest and slightly downward. Dr. Vyne had been right—there *was* a trail they could follow.

Beyond the pillar was another precipice, falling away into darkness. The *Butterfly*'s little lamps could not penetrate to the bottom.

The Embrace, signed Quest. *Things will become . . . strange. We are still above the Undersea, but where the Undersea is high, the ordinary sea is mad. Creatures from the deeps are found higher. Light is lost sooner. All is treachery.*

They found another glowing trace, then another. To follow the luminous trail, they had no choice but to keep turning the light on and off.

Hark realized that he was feeling sick and that his head ached. The first air-bottle was now light and empty, so he released a little air from the next in the rack.

He hadn't yet found a way to expel air from the sub. He'd heard of mariners who released a lot of air into airtight subs during a journey and then fell back with bleeding ears and eyes when they opened the hatch on the surface. However, he was more worried about the rate at which they were getting through their bottled air.

It had been getting steadily colder. Now, when Hark touched the side of the vessel, the chill of the glass was almost painful. If it had not been for the soak-powder box, the walls would have been clouded with moisture.

Selphin sat very still as they continued on and downward, the lamplight reflected in her large eyes. Her fingers picked and picked nervously at the leather of her seat.

Are you all right? Hark signed to her discreetly, while Quest was looking elsewhere.

I'm not going to panic, she signed defiantly. It was not exactly an answer.

I know, Hark replied, feeling a twinge of respect. Selphin continued watching the darkness with wary, haunted eyes.

The creatures they passed were stranger now. Once they were passed by dozens of tiny round blobs of translucence, bobbing through the darkness. They were snails, with delicate, see-through shells, flapping little fleshy wings to fly through the water.

Sea butterflies, signed Quest. *We are moving deeper.* He looked grimly tense and seemed to be trying to analyze every shift in the *Butterfly*'s trajectory, like a soldier sensing an enemy's movements in the dark.

The Undersea is restless, he signed. *Look out for . . .* The last sign was unfamiliar, perhaps a term used only on Siren. Seeing their incomprehension, Quest tried a few other signs instead. *Fountain . . . Plume . . . Shooting upward. If you see it, move away from it fast, or we will be sucked down.*

Soon we will see the Undersea's surface, Quest added. *Enter it fast and cleanly. Do not let the great waves catch us, or they will roll us. We would be half in the sea, half in the Undersea. That would be . . . bad.*

Would that kill us? asked Hark.

Worse, signed Quest, *but you do not want to know.*

It was getting harder to follow the trail of leaked lamp fluid. There were other gleams in the darkness now. One small, drifting hint of radiance suddenly turned around and showed its teeth, then winked out and was gone. Another undulated softly away, yellow and green light shimmering hypnotically in its jellied body.

Selphin suddenly thumped Hark on the arm, hard, and pointed. A split second later the sub was swept backward as if an invisible wave had hit it. Staring where Selphin pointed, Hark could see what Quest meant by "plume."

In the distance, at the furthest range of the light, he could see a vast, cloudy column thrusting its way upward, up past the level of the sub and ever up. It billowed clouds of silt and shell fragments. Green and yellow lights flickered in it, like lightning in a storm cloud. Dark, oily-looking bubbles floated up amid the debris, slowly flexing and gleaming with a purple iridescence.

Quest had told Hark to steer away from any plumes. But the sub was already being swept away from it, wasn't it? Even now, the plume was vanishing from view as the *Butterfly* was driven helplessly backward. Hark felt panicky at the sight. They would lose the trail and be completely lost in the abyss. He needed to push forward, not back!

He fought his instincts and overcame them. He had to trust Quest. Heart thumping, he grabbed the wheel he had initially triggered twice by accident, the one that had made the sub lurch backward. He pushed in the stops that were rippling the wings, and twisted the wheel hard. The sub jerked backward so fast it nearly threw him out of his seat.

Something changed in the water. Their backward race slowed to a juddering putter, and then the water abruptly reversed its pull. The *Butterfly* was no longer racing with the current—it was fighting against it. It was losing. The relentless sweep of the water was pulling it forward, toward the unseen plume.

Onshore, Quest had mentioned "switchback currents." Hark had heard the term before and seen submariners' faces darken at the mention. Now he was battling one in the dark.

He could see the dim, brown smudge of the great plume ahead now, but it was no longer really a plume. It was a huge, downward vortex, with a twist of darkness at its heart.

Hark kept the wheel twisted to its full extent, but he could feel it losing its strength. Whatever emergency water jet had thrust them backward was apparently not infinite. The *Butterfly* was drawn closer and closer, until he could see the glitter of mangled fish whirling inside the pillar.

Then the current slowly eased its terrible grip. The spiral

of darkness faded, and the column of debris lost its shape and floated loose. The *Butterfly* drifted into a fog of silt, fish bits, and wood splinters.

Quest was making approving signs, and Selphin was gingerly climbing back into her seat. Hark spent a few seconds gasping lungfuls of their precious air and staring out at the drifting debris. Then he remembered the controls, turned off the wheel, and got the wings' ripple working again.

We've lost the trail! exclaimed Selphin.

The plume destroyed it anyway, answered Quest. *No matter. We are close now. We must descend. Go carefully. Watch for the waves. They may be very, very large.*

Keeping the lamp on, Hark persuaded the *Butterfly* to descend. It started to give off unnerving ticks, audible even through the helmet. The god-glass sphere of the submarine was holding out against the pressure but was evidently not enjoying it.

Below was blackness and more blackness. Above, the only hint of light was a twilight grayness, an ache in the eye rather than true light. The *Butterfly* carved itself a halo of radiance in the void, and that was all that really existed.

Hark became aware that far down below, the darkness had a texture. There was something in motion, glistening and somehow blacker than the darkness. It was the surface of a second sea, moving with oily, implausible slowness, mauve lights gleaming on its smooth, gliding hummocks.

The waves don't look that big, thought Hark as they descended. The moment he became aware of the thought, he looked around himself apprehensively. He understood his own luck too well.

He noticed a distant motion in the darkness, a glint. For a moment he thought it was another luminous flicker from a creature of the deeps. Then he realized that it was the light shining off something oily and black, a vast, monstrous wave two houses high . . .

Hark frantically yanked at the controls, trying to rise, then settled for crazily spiraling upward, like a buzzard riding a thermal. The great glossy mass rolled by, mere feet below them, and left the little sub seesawing in the turbulence behind it.

The wave rolled out of view. A little later, another wave half its height glided past in an entirely different direction. Hark stared down, finding it hard to breathe.

It was as if some unkind fate were punishing him for his stories. At the Appraisal, he had told a tale of trying to help a sick, confused, old woman, and he had found himself looking after sick, confused, old priests. He had lied to Rigg about being struck by a gigantic Undersea wave, and now . . .

You'll do it if you have to, said the insistent voice in his mind. It wasn't Jelt's voice anymore, though. Now it sounded more like Hark's own, and the tone was different, more encouraging. *You have to dive down without being caught by the waves, so you will. You will.*

Hark looked around for the next wave and saw it. His breath caught in his throat.

Something was rolling in like a vast, glossy, purple-black wall. It was higher than a cliff, and Hark couldn't even see its top. For a panicky moment, he wondered whether it even had one. He had to raise the *Butterfly* up—up! But they wouldn't rise in time to avoid the wave, even if the sub spiraled so tightly that the wings fell off.

No, said a mad little part of his brain. *That isn't how you do it.*

He had to enter the water quickly, cleanly. The wave itself was rippling and turbulent, but just ahead of it, the surface was as smooth as a seal's back.

Hark yanked at the controls, hearing them protest. He mangled them back into the misguided position he had managed at first. The piercing noise of the sub stopped undulating and changed to the terrible unbroken scream that made his teeth ache. The wings folded down, trembling, and the *Butterfly* rolled forward so it was pointing on a downward diagonal.

Then Hark forced the stops back, setting the wings on full ripple, and plunged toward the Undersea, just ahead of the wave.

Hark couldn't tell how many people in the sub were screaming, or if his own scream was making any noise. He could see the great, inky wave rolling in with impossible speed. Too fast. It would catch him. He ramped up the undulation and increased the sub's velocity.

The smooth, glossy expanse in front of the wave sped toward him, and Hark braced. He expected a physical impact, like hitting the surface of the real sea from above. Instead, it gave easily as the *Butterfly* smashed into it.

Purple fireworks exploded before Hark's vision. His ears and eyes ached, and for a moment he felt like every single tiny part of him were floating away from the rest. There was no Hark, only terror, lightness, and a strange peace.

Then he was blinking the blots away from his vision and trying to remember who and what he was. There were metal sticks and wheels under his hands. Everything was dark and light. A rocky spire ahead was very eager to meet him and was rushing toward him.

Hark tugged at the controls and persuaded the *Butterfly* to wheel away from the great spire, which he could now see sprouting from a great plateau of boulders. Was that the sea bottom, though, or a cliff? Which way was up? *Was* there an up? For a moment, Hark didn't know.

Then he looked the way he had come and saw the underside

of the divide between sea and Undersea. It billowed like a vast cloth of deep purple silk, glittering all the while with a poisonous iridescence. He could see the underbelly of its vast waves, every crinkle and undulation picked out in silver.

He could see. He could see everything. His vision was no longer limited to a halo of murky light. He could look down at the landscape of the sea bottom, with its rock spires and its plains of rubble and pale silt. Everything was purplish dark yet seemed as vivid and clear as daylight air.

The girl next to him was waving at him and signing rapidly. He couldn't remember what the hand motions meant. She was pointing at the old man, who was slumped and sick-looking, his eyes closed.

Who were they? They were his friends. If all three of them survived, they would be his best friends. They would know who he was at the bottom of the sea.

Selphin and Quest, he reminded himself, starting to recover his senses. *Selphin and Quest. We're in the Undersea. And I think Quest's hurt.*

He blinked hard to clear his head and focused on Selphin.

. . . still breathing, she was signing. *I can't see blood.* She reached past Hark to retrieve the current air-bottle and released a little of its contents near Quest.

Quest slowly seemed to come to but didn't move from his slumped position. His chest quaked as he breathed. The priest looked around him at the purplish vista, then directed one of his small, wry smiles at Hark. It was an exhausted smile, and Hark was afraid that it might be a farewell.

Stay with us! Hark signed furiously. *We need you!*

Quest raised one hand and managed to touch a finger to his forehead in a tiny, half-mocking salute. *Aye, Captain.*

It hadn't occurred to Hark that he *was* the captain. He'd never been captain of anything in his life. He hadn't even been captain of his own life. Yet here he was.

He took a deep breath and looked around him. They were in the Undersea, but time and air were running out.

The *Butterfly* was still thirty feet above the sea bottom, with a good view across it. In the distance, he caught a glimpse of motion. Something large and dark was gliding slowly between the rocky spires. It was too large to be a shark and too slender to be a whale. Oars twitched, filament-fine in the distance.

It was the *Abysmal Child*.

Chapter 41

IT TOOK ONLY A MOMENT FOR HARK TO POINT out the *Abysmal Child* to his companions.

No sign of the god, signed Selphin, her face tense.

Still in the hold, Quest signed feebly. *If it was free, we would know it.*

Hark blinked. A glistening line seemed to have been drawn around Quest and Selphin, as though to make it clear that *these* two objects were important. His mind felt like an open wound, his thoughts tender and exposed, but he was starting to recover a little now.

Selphin, as usual, came out with the most important and awkward question.

What do we do now? she asked.

Let's hide before they see us, Hark signed. *Then make a plan.*

He set the *Butterfly* on a slanting descent path and halted it when a rock pillar hid it from the *Abysmal Child's* view.

Hide? asked Selphin doubtfully, and gestured at her surroundings. *Screaming submarine! They've heard us already. They've seen us already.*

They'll hear something, Hark signed back. *They probably don't know what. They may not have spotted us, either. We're small and hard to see.*

It was one thing to notice the large outline of the *Abysmal*

Child, its black metal distinct against the pale silt seafloor. Spotting a much smaller glass submarine against the coruscating underside of the Undersea's surface would be a lot harder.

The *Butterfly*'s scream sounded holy and terrible, and not remotely like a submarine. Someone hearing it for the first time was unlikely to guess what it was, or where it was, for that matter. Many sea creatures could sense the direction of underwater sounds, but people couldn't. To human ears, underwater noises were generally loud, strange, and from everywhere at once.

Selphin rubbed her eyes with the heels of her hands, then blinked hard.

Everything looks strange, she signed. She was gazing out through the glass wall of the sub. Hark looked out in the same direction.

A shiver was passing through the seabed, as if it were a living thing. The rock pillars were quavering and shifting. Some pushed upward, becoming a few feet taller, while others sank farther into the seabed. The purple dark-light was fluctuating around them, flickering like flames. He could feel the light's coolness against his mind, the way sunlight warms the skin . . .

Hark realized that Quest was tugging hard at his arm.

The Undersea will enchant you, the priest signed, ashen-faced but icily calm. *Concentrate! Does the* Butterfly *have weapons?*

Hark stared down at the controls and forced himself to think. He was fairly sure he knew what all of them did now.

The Butterfly *has its scream*, he signed. *That can knock you out like a cudgel.* It probably wouldn't be so loud outside the sub, but he still didn't envy anyone nearby without ear protection. *There's nothing else.*

Would the scream melt their god-glass? asked Quest, frowning in concentration.

Hark shook his head. Vyne had told him that the *Abysmal Child*'s windows were of specially tempered glass that no single note could melt.

Our scream might stun the crew for a bit, he signed. *But that wouldn't change anything. It wouldn't help us get in the hold to destroy the heart.*

Can we ram them? suggested Selphin, then winced and shook her head. Hark didn't much like the idea, either. The little *Butterfly*'s solid inner sphere had a decent chance of surviving collision with the bigger sub's withersteel hull, but the glass wings and tail seemed softer when in motion. If they were torn to shreds, the *Butterfly* wouldn't be a sub anymore, just a glass globe with slowly suffocating people inside.

If we damage the Leaguer sub but do not destroy it, signed Quest, *Undersea water will get in, and bring the god to life.* That thought dampened the discussion for a few moments.

We could wait until they bring the god out, signed Selphin slowly. *Then ram the god.*

Hark exhaled slowly. It was the best plan they had yet, even though it involved throwing themselves at a god in an experimental submarine.

We'd need to be quick, he signed. *Knock it apart before it can glue itself together properly.*

Quest was shaking his head.

Not enough, he signed. *The heart would escape. We must destroy it!*

Hark didn't like where logic was leading him. He was fairly sure his companions wouldn't like it, either.

The Butterfly *rams the god*, he signed. *I go outside the sub and smash the heart.*

There was a pause while the implications sank in. Undersea

water was breathable and wouldn't crush you to a pulp like the water in the deeps of the real sea. You could never be sure how it would affect you, however.

There's only one hatch, signed Selphin. *If you open it, the sub fills with water. No more air.* She was right. This plan meant all of them breathing Undersea water until they reached the surface again, if such a return were even possible. Selphin put a hand over her mouth, and her breaths became shallower and shakier.

One can breathe Undersea water for a long time, Quest signed, and Hark remembered that he was speaking from experience. *One does not always get Marks.*

Selphin was glaring at Hark, making calculations. Then she scowled and thumped the arms of her seat hard.

You can't go! she signed angrily. *You need to stay, to pilot the sub! I'll go out!* She folded her arms hard and was clearly gripping them to stop them shaking. He remembered her adopting the same pose just after shooting Jelt.

Hark felt an unexpected rush of affection for Selphin and her proud, stubborn courage. She had braved her fear of the sea to come all the way to the Undersea, and now they were talking about flooding the *Butterfly*, which clearly terrified her. He couldn't ask her to fling herself up into the Undersea, as well.

After we ram the god, we won't need anyone piloting the sub, he pointed out. *Just someone pumping the bellows, keeping the* Butterfly *screaming while I grab the heart.*

Selphin's panicky scowl relaxed a little, and after a few moments she nodded.

What are the Leaguers doing now? asked Quest. Hark edged the *Butterfly* forward so that he and his friends could peer.

The scenery outside was no longer palpitating. The *Abysmal Child* had settled on the seafloor and raised her many oars aloft.

Several figures in metal diving suits were now visible outside her. Some floated while others walked on the silt, their feet stirring up grayish clouds. They appeared to be unscrewing the side of the hull.

They're opening the hold! signed Quest urgently. *There is no more time!*

Hark guided the *Butterfly* downward so he could attack at a flatter trajectory and avoid slamming the sub straight into the seafloor after ramming the god. Selphin yielded her seat to Quest, so that he could make use of the seat belt, and clambered into the narrow gap behind the seats. There she hastily sealed and strapped the breather boxes and secured the air-bottles in their rack, before wedging herself in and bracing.

Hark's god-glass knife had melted during the journey, fusing with the fabric of his belt pouch. It wouldn't be much use for destroying the god-heart, so instead he tucked a heavy wrench into his belt.

The dun-colored seafloor was closer now. It bewildered the eye, appearing to move in a gentle, roiling motion. With a shock, Hark saw that thousands of white, spindly starfish were blindly writhing over each other in the bone-pale mud. Disturbed silt rose in little clouds, then eddied to form shapes and patterns. Letters, these were letters, and he would be able to understand them if he thought hard enough, if he *felt* hard enough . . .

Two people were jabbing him painfully in the arm. He started and looked around apologetically.

There were shapes, he signed. *I wanted to understand them.*

They would tell you only of fear, Quest replied.

That was right; Hark had been forgetting. The Undersea was where all the fears of the Myriad ran, like rainwater into the sea. Every scintillating drop of it was aglow with human terror.

When the Undersea water comes in, signed Quest, *breathe the water in quickly, but remember that you are breathing fear. Do not believe what it tells you.*

Hark took a deep breath, exchanged signals with his companions, then carefully slid the *Butterfly* out from the pillar to get another view of the *Abysmal Child*.

He could see the Leaguers more clearly now. They wore cylindrical diving suits of a sort he had seen before, with holes for the arms and legs and windows in front of the face so they could look out. One of them was lying on his side, knees drawn up, hands over its faceplate. Perhaps Hark wasn't the only person struggling with the mental effects of the Undersea.

Two other figures were cradling what looked like copper air-bottles in the crook of their arms. Hark guessed that these were probably attached to wind-guns. The Leaguers were prepared for attack.

Six more figures in diving suits emerged from the long, black oblong of the gaping hold, carrying a wooden platform, on which rested an enormous and familiar bulk.

Immediately it was impossible to look anywhere else. The god-construct no longer looked like a patchwork of parts. Now it had a horrible harmony. The strange dark-light glisten Hark had seen for a moment around his friends snaked all over the vast figure, as if the entire Undersea had turned its attention to it. This was where the monstrous thing belonged.

The shape heaved and arched, and Hark could imagine the fear in the water, the terror of countless minds, being sucked into the thing's gray gills.

Now.

Hark pulled the *Butterfly* out from behind the rocky pillar, and ramped up her ululation. The little sub swooped down and raced toward the awakening god.

Hark saw the Leaguers reel back from the full force of the *Butterfly*'s scream. They dropped to their knees, some letting go of the platform, others losing their grip on their wind-guns.

The floating, glistening mass of the god-construct loomed before Hark as he sped toward it. He felt the god-heart pulse, sending a shimmer through the air and a shudder through the *Butterfly*.

Then the glassy nose of the *Screaming Sea Butterfly* crashed into the Leaguers' makeshift god. The impact threw Hark forward against the controls, his seat belt nearly cutting him in two. The front of the sphere was suddenly dark, obscured by splattered ichor, flabby sacs pressed against the glass, and one great, sprawling claw. A second impact jolted him over sideways, yanking his neck.

Hark spent a second half-stunned before realizing that he didn't have time to be. The *Butterfly* was still screaming and stirring up the seabed. He could hardly see anything through the glass and didn't know whether the collision had successfully knocked the god apart.

Behind him, Selphin was clutching her head, her face contorted in a rictus of pain. She didn't seem to be bleeding, thankfully.

There was no time—no time to ask if she was all right, if she needed anything. So he tapped her arm and signed the only question he could.

Ready?

Her eyes widened with utter terror and panic, and she nodded. Before he could think about what he was doing, Hark yanked the lever to open the hatch.

Neither of them were ready.

As the hatch gaped, Undersea water surged in with terrifying speed. One minute Hark was sitting in the cockpit with his hand on a lever, the next minute the water hit him like a vast icy fist.

It knocked the wind out of him, and as he gasped in another breath, the water was somehow already up to his neck. Then that last trace of air was gone, too, and he was floating, struggling, his belt still binding him to his seat, his mouth clamped shut reflexively.

His eyes were stinging, and everything was indistinct and purplish. Shapes and outlines slithered out of focus. Hark wasn't ready to breathe in the Undersea. He wasn't ready. He wasn't ready for any of this. But he had to be. He gathered his will, opened his mouth, and took a breath.

All his instincts recoiled as he felt the water rush into his mouth and nose and sting his throat, then choke his lungs. He couldn't breathe. His chest convulsed. His limbs flailed, wanting to fight his way back to air, even if he had to swim all the way to the distant surface to do it.

It didn't matter that he knew he wasn't drowning. It didn't matter that he could feel the strangeness of the Undersea water numbing his lungs instead of chilling them. At the same time he *knew* he was a shipwreck victim sinking under the weight of his clothes, he *knew* he was a child fallen overboard, too young to swim, he *knew* he was drowning in a broken diving bell. These terrors were not his, but they were in his eyes and throat and lungs. He was full of them, choking on them.

Remember you are breathing fear, Quest had told them. *Do not believe what it tells you.*

Hark fought back. He wasn't drowning, it wasn't true. He was breathing. He took breath after breath, feeling the numbing tickle of the water through his throat. It tasted the way the scare-lamps smelled.

Selphin had drifted upward and was flailing in panic, just as Hark had, moments before. If she was experiencing what he had, she was living all her worst nightmares—a thousand ways for the sea to kill her, crammed into one moment. Her wide eyes were on Quest, though, who was leaning forward to sign to her, holding her gaze calmly and steadily.

Hark wanted to stay but couldn't. There was no time. He unbuckled his seat belt, then pushed the hatch fully open. He dragged himself up through it and looked around, dazzled by the dark-light.

The *Butterfly* had come to a halt against the side of the *Abysmal Child*, with a messy splat of god-construct sandwiched between them. It looked like Hark's ramming swoop had taken off the construct's left claw, along with some machinery and oozing glands.

Looking back at the *Butterfly*'s wake, Hark could see the rest of the god-construct sprawled on its back a few yards away. The impact had not knocked it to pieces, as he had hoped. The bulk of it was intact, but a ragged hole had been torn out of its left side. Yellowish fluids dissipated into the water in misty curls. The flesh containing the gills looked misshapen now, like a slab of gray dough someone had punched. All of this would probably heal, though, once the god-heart started to beat.

Around the god-construct, Leaguers lay sprawled or curled, some of them vainly clutching at the metal casing around their heads. In their diving suits they couldn't even cover their ears.

Where was the heart? Hark swam over to the god-construct as fast as he could.

There! The white orb was hanging from a tangle of soft, translucent pipes. As he drew near, it pulsed, and for a moment it seemed to blaze black. A blinding shimmer rippled out from it through the water.

He kicked hard and lunged for it. His fingers closed around it . . .

. . . and then something large and dark hit him like a runaway horse, shoving him aside and knocking the wind out of him. He gasped, then rallied and righted himself. To his horror, he saw that the heart was gone. It had been ripped away, leaving the soft, fleshy pipes ravaged and floating free.

Before he could recover, Hark was grappled from behind and wrestled down onto the soft seabed on his back. A wind-gun was pointed in his face. A metal-suited Leaguer was leaning over Hark, shouting something at him in an angry, panicky way. All around him, other Leaguers appeared to be getting up. Why weren't they incapacitated anymore?

The nearest man snatched the helmet off Hark's head and sound returned to Hark's world.

"I said, don't try anything!" the Leaguer with the gun shouted again, his voice echoing inside the metal shell. The face behind the suit's glass plate looked as startled and frightened as Hark felt, which wasn't reassuring. Frightened people sometimes panicked and killed.

Now Hark could tell why the Leaguers were recovering. The *Butterfly*'s scream had waned to a faint gurgle. Why weren't Hark's friends pumping the bellows?

Then he noticed that the rest of the Leaguers were paying Hark no attention at all. Instead, they were staring upward.

Twenty feet above them was a single floating figure. Hark's heart sank as he saw the round, colorless eyes, the long-hinged jaw, the preposterous clustering of teeth.

It was Jelt. In his hands, he gripped the heart of the Hidden Lady.

"Give that to us!" called out one of the Leaguers. The top of his diving suit was unscrewed, exposing his face to the water. It was the captain who had stabbed Vyne.

Jelt looked mangled, half his chest badly dented like a rotten fruit. His flesh was gray and ravaged-looking, scattered with dark, leprous-looking scales. A chunk of his shoulder was missing, and there was a deep, round wound in one hip.

As Hark watched, Jelt placed the heart against his own chest. He began forcing it into his own flesh, with a rictus of effort and pain. There were cracking and popping sounds.

"Jelt, don't!" shouted Hark, the water tickling the inside of his throat as he did so. His voice sounded unusually loud.

The world shuddered and shimmered as the god-heart beat. Jelt's scaly flesh crept over the heart and closed around it. The relic had found its home.

Chapter 42

JELT. OF COURSE IT WAS JELT.

Hark would never be rid of him. However hard Hark tried, however high he climbed, Jelt would always be there to pull him down. Even if Hark gave in to desperation and plunged down to the greatest depths, the depths beneath the depths, Jelt would find him there, too.

The heart beat again and again. Each pulse sent a great ripple through the dark-light. Hark felt it pull at his bones and blood.

Jelt convulsed. The hole in his shoulder was closing, fine dark scales sliding over the new flesh like silk. The wound in his hip was healing, too, and filling with gray, misshapen pearls.

"Don't fire at it!" yelled the captain. "You might hit the heart!"

The captain looked around frantically, then noticed Hark on the seafloor with a gun trained on his head. The man did a double take, then recovered.

"You up there!" he shouted hoarsely at Jelt. "Look! We have one of your friends!" At a gesture from the captain, the Leaguer with the gun dragged Hark upright so that Jelt could see him better.

"Friends?" It was Hark's turn to be confused. Then he started to understand. The captain had seen Jelt swoop down and rip the heart out of the construct, right after the *Butterfly* had rammed it. No wonder he thought Jelt was working with the *Butterfly*'s crew.

The Jelt-thing stopped jerking and looked down at Hark. Its pale, dull eyes were like coins worn slick and meaningless by the waves.

"Hey, Hark." Somehow the Jelt-thing sounded close, as if speaking next to Hark's ear. "Didn't see you there. Thought you'd be waiting for me by the cairn on Nest about now. Isn't that what you promised?" The voice had a fluttering rasp, like something eating a live moth. Yet the bitter mockery was still unmistakably Jelt.

"You need to take that thing out of your chest!" bellowed Hark. "It'll kill your mind!"

"Actually," Jelt continued, in the same dangerously offhand tone. "I don't think you can be Hark. The Hark I know wouldn't run off and leave me to die, would he? So I guess these people can fill you with as many holes as they like. Save me the bother."

Hark could see a dart poking out of the wind-gun aimed at his face. He'd always liked those darts, he remembered. The feathers made them easy to spot when they washed up on the beach, and you could sell the metal. You just had to be careful with the sharp, sharp tips.

There was more yelling and confusion from the direction of the *Butterfly*. Selphin was being dragged out of the sub by force. She was lashing out at her captor's heads with a copper air-bottle, perhaps in the hope that it would rupture and explode. It was wrestled out of her hands, and a few moments later Quest was also ushered out of the sub at wind-gunpoint, without his helmet.

"I know what you are!" the captain called out to Jelt. "You're the monster from Wildman's Hammer—the one that killed a dozen of my men. You're ruthless, but I doubt you will sacrifice your allies." His hair floated up to form a haze, showing a bald spot that had previously been hidden by his shiny hat. "You all came a long way to steal that heart. Braving the Undersea takes camaraderie."

"Camaraderie?" Jelt rasped out a bitter laugh. "That little snake stole the heart from *me*! I've been following him to get it back!" Hark could almost feel the gaze of the dull-penny eyes again. "Do you know what it was like swimming all that way, Hark? Do you know how cold and dark it was? Do you know how it feels when the water's crushing you, and your ribs break, one by one?"

The captain gaped at Jelt. Hark could almost see the man dismantling his wrong conclusions and putting them together in a different arrangement.

"Swimming?" he repeated in hushed, incredulous tones. "You came here without a submersible?" Hark didn't like the captain's expression. Previously it had shown only a stern desperation. Now he was gazing at Jelt with fierce awe. "How did you become so strong? Was it the blessing of the heart?"

"So what if it was?" retorted Jelt, with the same tone of sour nonchalance. He was regarding the captain with more interest, however.

"We should never have been enemies," the captain declared. "Stay with us. Work with us. Let us make you greater still."

"Didn't you just say I killed a dozen of your men?" asked Jelt sardonically.

"Of course you did," the captain replied simply. "That is what gods do."

Even though Hark couldn't see the other Leaguers' faces, he could hear some of them muttering to each other in tinny consternation. This whiplash change of direction had taken them by surprise, and they didn't sound happy about it.

Jelt, on the other hand, now looked keenly interested, the snaking appendage under his chin flicking like a cat's tail.

"You people don't seem to be kneeling," said Jelt. It was almost an order.

"You are born to be a god," said the captain, holding his nerve, "but you are not one yet. After you don your mantle and assume your true might, *everyone* will kneel."

"Mantle?" asked Jelt.

With a sense of inevitability, Hark saw the captain gesture toward the sprawled god-construct.

"It is a body for a god," the captain said. "Given life, it will have gills to draw strength from the souls of thousands, eyes that can see in the deepest darkness, and claws strong enough to cleave steel. I see now that you were always meant to wear it. We made it for you without even realizing it."

It was simple, horrible, and inspired. The god-construct had been torn in two, and the League no longer had Vyne on hand to reattach everything skillfully. Adding Jelt would solve all those problems. Quest had told Hark that humans were the god-heart's "favorite clay." It would mold him into whatever it needed to bond the pieces.

"Well, get it ready, then!" demanded the Jelt-thing. "And don't let anyone point guns at me, or you'll be losing more men!"

The Leaguers shambled into clumsy, unwilling motion. A couple went to retrieve the claw from behind the *Butterfly*, pale starfish writhing under their boots. Other Leaguers fetched god-glue from the sub and knelt by the damaged god-construct.

"What are you doing?" shouted Hark. "He killed your friends! He didn't have to, he *wanted* to! I know, I was there! And now you want to give him god-powers?"

"Don't listen to him!" snapped the captain. "This moment is the greatest test of your courage and loyalty! Don't falter now!"

Hark exchanged a desperate glance with Selphin. Both had

wind-guns pointed at their heads. There wasn't much either of them could do without getting shot. Charging toward Jelt or the god-construct would be suicide.

All Hark could do for now was keep talking. He didn't have much hope that Jelt or the captain would listen to him, but he had to try. Besides, they were not the only people present.

"Listen to me!" he shouted. "If you don't stop this, we're all going to die!"

He turned to the thing that had been his friend.

"Jelt, do you know what happens if you *do* merge with that big heap of godware? The heart will glue you into that body, so you'll never escape. It'll bend you and melt you, till everything fits. And do you know what happens to a god when it grows? Its mind starts to die. It forgets everything and becomes a big, dumb fish. A big, *hungry* fish. If your mind dies, *you* die, Jelt!

"Do the rest of you know what happens after that? Do you think you'll still be making deals with him? You won't, because he won't understand you. *And he'll be eating you.* Is that what you want?"

A few of the Leaguers had halted in their tasks, listening to him.

"It is all true," said Quest, his voice carrying with steely clarity. His frailty had a certain majesty here, with his brown robes billowing and his blanket spreading like a cape. He looked like an ancient sage or prophet. "I was of the priesthood. I have talked with great gods and seen the mindlessness behind their eyes."

The Leaguers who had stopped to listen to Hark and Quest were clearly getting the sharp end of the captain's tongue. They hesitated, looking daunted, then carried on reassembling the god, patching leaks and tears. They laid out the torn-off part of the god next to the rest, with a person-sized gap between them.

"Oh, come on!" erupted Hark. "You can't all be crazy! Some of you must want to live! Some of you must care about your dead friends!"

The Leaguers all looked like automata, in their metal capsule bodies. But there were men underneath the suits, all with their own memories, hopes, mistakes, and triumphs.

"Well, I'm just going to keep talking," Hark said, "because maybe one of you is a little bit sane. One of you doesn't want to die. Maybe there's more than one of you thinking that way right now, and you don't know it because you're in those suits and can't see each other's faces.

"You joined the League to be part of something that mattered. Saving the Myriad, right? You got secret missions, you were in this special band of brothers that knew things. Then you found out about the *really* secret plan, and it scared you, but by then you were in so deep you couldn't back out. You just had to believe that you'd made the right choice.

"Now you're here. You're in deeper than deep, every kind of deep, and you can't see a way out. You think you can't change your mind anymore. But you can. You always can. You have to, or we're all going to die. All the people you're trying to protect will die or live in terror forever. The gods were monsters, and they *never* cared about any of us!"

"Carry on!" snapped the captain. "You over there—shoot that boy if he keeps talking!"

Hark bit his tongue. The captain had silenced him too late. *They've already heard me*, Hark thought. *They can't un-hear me. My words are in their heads now.*

One of the Leaguers suddenly set down his flask of god-glue.

"I don't like this," he declared abruptly, in a Lady's Craver accent. "We shouldn't be doing this."

"This is what we came here to do!" blazed the captain. "Everything we've done for the last six months has been for this very moment! If you are losing your nerve, step away from the god."

"This wasn't the plan!" protested the rogue Leaguer, as he was pushed away from the construct. "*That* thing"—he pointed at Jelt—"wasn't in the plan. And you didn't say anything about being eaten!" The louder his objections, the more clearly he seemed to be outlined by glistening light.

"Enough!" the captain snapped. "The mantle is ready."

"Don't try anything stupid," warned Jelt, as he descended toward the god-construct. Other voices were being raised, however.

"Hold up! What's the hurry? Why can't we hear what those people have to say?"

"You didn't say this was a suicide mission! I've got kids!"

There were still four Leaguers standing by the captain, defending the construct as Jelt lowered himself down between the two halves. As the captain helped guide Jelt's limbs into the works and attached soft, glutinous tubes to his skin, some of the others charged forward.

"I said, stop what you're doing!"

"Get back—I'll fire!"

Metal suits collided and gonged as the Leaguers fought each other. Somebody yelled as a dart hit his leg. One of the rebels barged his way past the defenders, grabbed at a fistful of the construct's tubular innards, and tried to yank them loose.

Amid all this confusion, the god-heart pulsed. For a second it was the black-white center of everything, a hole and a tiny sun at once. Hark saw the Leaguers jerk and felt the beat like a kick in the chest.

Jelt howled.

Hark had guessed what would happen. He'd even described it. However, it was much worse than he'd imagined. Jelt's limbs were sinking into the works of the construct, like soft wax sliding down a hot knife. The heart beat again, and again, and Hark saw Jelt's limbs contort and stretch. Skin crept over metal and glass like a pale lichen.

Pulse followed pulse followed pulse. The heart had been waiting for this chance to fashion a truly suitable vessel. It was strengthening sinews, locking plates of chitinous armor, sliding parts into place. The new god slowly reared up, a faint glisten slithering all over it. The god was the center of the world, a vortex of power and hunger, sucking everything else toward it. The seabed was shuddering, too, as though with excitement.

One of the Leaguers leaped toward the new god, in one long, drifting bound. He swung an axe down into its back with a meaty *thock!*

A great claw lashed out. Suddenly the axe-wielder was floating in two pieces, his body and metal suit neatly severed, blood blooming in the water like a giant rose.

"I warned you!" It was recognizable as Jelt's voice, but only just. The vowels were guttural and groaning, the consonants a deep, reverberating buzz. "You lied to me! You tricked me! You never told me it would feel . . ."

The other Leaguers were yelling, backing away or turning to flee. The captain, inevitably, stood his ground.

"I did not lie to you!" he shouted. "Everything I have done was to bring you into the world!" He dropped to one knee as he had promised. "Everyone kneel and show your fealty!" But the captain's hold on his men had been broken. Most were fleeing back into the *Abysmal Child*.

Jelt's long, whiplike barbel lashed out at the captain's head.

It was an apt blessing from the new god. Hark flinched and looked away. He hadn't liked the captain, but he hadn't wanted to see him die.

Because he had turned his head, Hark was looking in the right direction to see Selphin swimming rapidly toward him. The man pointing a gun at Hark didn't know she was there until she grabbed him from behind and slapped a fistful of mud across the window of his suit.

Hark seized his moment and grabbed the wind-gun, wrestling it out of the man's hand. Selphin shoved the man away, and he lost his balance and fell over sideways, arms windmilling as he floated down to the silt.

"Thanks!" Hark said quickly, when Selphin's eyes were on his face. He stooped to snatch his helmet.

They swam over to Quest, who was sheltering under the wing of the *Butterfly*, also unguarded. The shuddering of the seafloor was shrugging silt and small stones onto the little sub's wings. If they didn't get it moving soon, there was a danger that it might get buried.

Hark pulled himself in through the hatch and floated down into the driver's seat. He put on his helmet and waited as the others piled in. Only then did he realize that Selphin was signing to him.

No scream! she signed. *The scream's broken!*

Hark stared at her in bewilderment, so she reached over, grabbed the bellows, and squeezed them hard. Small bubbles erupted from the machinery, but there was no scream. He tugged off his helmet as Selphin squeezed the bellows again. They made a sloshing, rubbery, glugging noise, and nothing else. A fresh shoal of bubbles twitched and danced their way upward, mocking his panic.

The *Butterfly*'s crew had all known that their lungs could

use Undersea water instead of air. None of them had wondered whether the little sub's pipe-organ innards could do the same.

Pedals! Hark signed.

Quest pulled the hatch shut, everyone crammed themselves into place, and Hark and Selphin began frantically pedaling. The *Butterfly* grated a little against the side of the *Abysmal Child*, then shuddered away from it. Hark could feel bumps and vibrations as the tail propeller dragged in the mud and bounced off rocks.

For now, the Jelt-god was not following the *Butterfly*. Looking back toward the fight, Hark could see why. Somebody in the *Abysmal Child* had brought the great sub's harpoon guns to bear on the god. As he watched, a harpoon sank into the monstrosity's flank, then was tugged loose by a great claw. He didn't know how long the rebel Leaguers could hold off the angry god like that, but at least they weren't all kneeling in a neat line ready to be eaten.

It's a god! It's alive! signed Selphin. *How do we destroy the heart now?*

We must, answered Quest. *The god is still new. It will be stronger later.*

Through the smeared glass, Hark could see that the underwater landscape was restless again. They passed a huge rock pillar that was pulling itself farther out of the seabed, like a claw sliding from its sheath. Its emergence sent a heap of rubble bouncing with lethal laziness through the water. The boulders idly chased the *Butterfly* for a bit.

Can we shoot the heart from a distance? asked Selphin.

Hark thought of feathered darts slowed by water. They would be very effective against ordinary human flesh at close range, but he doubted that they could get through Jelt's god-hide if fired from afar.

He shook his head.

We need to get close, then, Selphin signed.

The last person who had tried to attack the Jelt-god at close quarters had ended up in two pieces. If they wanted any chance of striking at the heart, they had to do it by stealth.

Hark stopped pedaling, and Selphin followed suit, looking at him curiously. He took a deep breath.

I think I can distract him, Hark signed, gripped by cold certainty. *If Jelt sees me swimming away, he'll follow me.*

Hark wasn't an expert on gods like Quest was, but Hark knew Jelt. The roaring god out there wasn't Jelt, but it was built from him. It had been made using a monster that had once been a murderer that had once been a boy called Jelt. Perhaps it still had some of his memories and instincts.

I'll hide over there, signed Hark, and pointed at a rocky outcrop with a cleft down the middle. *In that crack.*

"But that is very dangerous," Quest protested.

"I don't know what else to do!" said Hark.

You're sure he'll follow you? asked Selphin.

If he still thinks like Jelt, he'll want to eat me, explained Hark. *It's . . . been that kind of friendship for a while.*

You are not allowed to choose your friends anymore, signed Selphin, and Hark couldn't quite suppress a smile.

"Here—take these!" Hark handed Selphin the wind-gun and his wrench. They didn't look like a particularly impressive god-killing armory. His hands were shaking, and hers weren't much better. "I . . . I'd better leave the sub here."

With every passing moment, the new god would be knitting itself together more strongly. It would also be attacking the Leaguers. That was the problem with working out what made people tick; sometimes you were left understanding them and not wanting them to die.

Hark flipped open the hatch. There didn't seem to be anything more to say.

He did think of something a minute later. *I think I've gotten a lot better at choosing friends*—that would have been the right thing to have said. But by the time he thought of it, he was already swimming as fast as he could for the rocky outcrop, hoping to make progress before an angry god noticed him.

Chapter 43

HARK WAS NEARING THE OUTCROP WHEN HE heard a thunderous cry, as if a tempest were calling his name.

Twenty feet away. The crack looked narrower now. Was it too narrow? Fifteen feet . . . ten feet . . . five . . .

Hark reached the crevice and wriggled in sideways. It was barely more than a foot wide, its bottom choked with rubble. The two rock faces were bruisingly uneven, and he scraped and scratched his face and arms as he squirmed farther and farther into the cleft.

The whole outcrop shivered and shifted. Dust and fine rubble flowed hazily down past him, filling his mouth with the taste of sand. Somewhere outside the crevice, something roared Hark's name so loudly that the rock vibrated against his back.

A long, black cord lashed out along the cleft toward Hark, its tip glowing yellow-white. It came within a foot of him, making him flinch, then withdrew. He crouched a little to make himself a smaller target. Hark was in the middle of the cleft and probably as inaccessible as he could make himself.

Looking back the way he had come, Hark could see a great shape obscuring his view out. Something large was pressed against the crack, staring in at him.

"I can see you, Hark," said the Jelt-god.

. . . . .

Through the smudged glass dome of the *Butterfly*, Selphin saw the outcrop approach. It did so slowly, because she was doing most of the pedaling. The sub wasn't so much gliding as bouncing along the seafloor.

The great, dark mass of the god was pressed against the edge of the crack. She hoped it was watching Hark and not digesting him. The god was all wrong, a malfunctioning mix of too many creatures. At the same time, a dark part of her mind knew that the god was exactly as it was meant to be. Its grotesque mosaic of gray flesh, glass, and metal was somehow inevitable.

It was also incomprehensible. Selphin didn't know what she was looking at or whether it could look back at her.

"You're the god-killer," Selphin said aloud to Quest. "What are all those . . . bits?" She didn't dare let go of the controls, even to sign one-handed. There were too many erupting pinnacles and playful boulders she might need to swerve around.

The old man signed answers to her in bits and pieces, whenever he saw her looking his way.

The red shell was impenetrable. The round hole on its back was an extra mouth. When the hairs around its edge sensed movement, the whole mouth would lunge out, drag in its prey, and bite. The only good news was that the god's rear cluster of eyes had been split and damaged by the dead Leaguer's axe. Quest suspected that these would heal soon, but for now the axe was still embedded in them.

"Can it still see us if we creep up behind?" Selphin wanted to know.

Probably less well now, suggested Quest.

"Where do you think the heart is?" asked Selphin.

When we are close, we can look for the shine of the heartbeat, signed Quest. *Then we will know where it is.*

The "we" was not lost on Selphin. She realized that the crazy old man was intending to come with her. Then again, why not? It was time to throw all stakes on the table.

The god had called to Hark by name, so it was still capable of speaking. There was still some of Jelt's mind left.

"I really did mean to meet you at that cairn," Hark called out.

"You mean all kinds of things," the Jelt god rasped. "I don't care how well you 'mean,' Hark. You stole the heart and left me to die!" The words ended in a roar.

Of course Hark could defend himself. But this would be his last conversation with Jelt, one way or the other. He wasn't going to play the old games anymore.

"Yeah, I guess I did," he admitted shakily. "I'm sorry things ended up this way."

"You're only sorry because you're trapped in a crevice like a blob of clam meat!" the voice hissed ominously. The comparison made Hark sound worryingly edible.

"I can't let you eat me, Jelt," Hark said flatly.

"You're supposed to be my friend!" Underneath the mind-shuddering rumble of the god-voice, something was reaching for the strings of Hark's soul with the deftness of habit. "Do you know what this is like, Hark? I'm being stretched. I'm pulled so tight I think I'm going to snap. But it'll be all right with two of us. We won't have to stretch so far when there's two."

Hark had assumed that Jelt wanted to tear him into gobbets before eating him. Jelt's actual plan seemed to involve swallowing Hark alive and letting the heart warp him into new shapes. This did not sound better.

"I don't want to be twisted up and trapped in a god-body forever," said Hark, loudly and firmly. "Why would I want that?"

"You owe me this!" thundered the shape. The rock faces shuddered again, dropping another fine cloud of dust and gravel around Hark.

"No!" Hark called back, even as grit stung his eyes. "I don't! There are things you can't owe anybody!"

Jelt had saved Hark's life, but that didn't mean Hark *owed* Jelt his life. Maybe you couldn't ever owe somebody your life, not really. You couldn't let anyone else decide what you did with it. You had to live it yourself, as truly as you could.

"Don't be an old coward!" persisted the Jelt-god. "I'm giving you the chance to be part of something big! You're lucky I'm willing to let you join me!"

Hark was speechless for a moment, then snorted with uncontrollable laughter.

"I know!" he cackled helplessly. "It's a promotion!"

"Don't laugh at me!" snarled the god outside the cleft.

"Oh, why not?" Hark felt giddy with fear and sadness. "We used to laugh, didn't we? For years your jokes have been like punches in the face! But you used to be funny. Life with you used to be . . . fun."

"I grew up, Hark!" thundered the thing outside. "I found out life is war. Maybe I didn't find everything so funny after that. You never want to know about that, though, do you, Hark? You run away when things get ugly. You dump friends when they're no use to you anymore—when knowing them isn't convenient, or fun.

"You know when I was drowning in that bathysphere? I was choking, knocked giddy, and trying to get out, but . . . I noticed this bubble. It was twinkling up away from me. Dancing. It was made of air—air that could keep me alive. But was it staying down there to help me? No, off it went, up to the sky, leaving me behind.

"You're like that bubble, Hark. Shiny and full of nothing. Dancing on up and leaving me to drown."

It wasn't fair—nothing Jelt said was fair—but it made Hark's heart ache. Was that really how Jelt had seen him all this time, as a maddening, bright thing that could keep him alive but that was always dancing farther away from him?

"I can't save you, Jelt," said Hark, his eyes stinging again. "I'm sorry. I'm so sorry. But it's too late. You're . . . you're dead, Jelt. You died in the bathysphere. You drowned. I didn't get there in time." Hark had come too far to turn back. "When the winch broke and the chain ran out, I just . . . froze. I don't know how long. I snapped out of it and dived down to save you, but when I got there . . . you were already dead."

The whipcord came at Hark again, out of the dark. It wrapped around his chest, then dragged him off his feet. As it hauled him relentlessly back toward the god, Hark braced against the sides, scraping his hands and knees. His shoulder smacked into a large boulder. He wrapped his arms around it, twisting so as to wedge himself as best he could.

The cord yanked twice, trying to pull him loose. Hark could feel his skin stinging where the cord was tangled around him.

"You did this to me!" hissed the voice, becoming shapeless with rage. "This is *all your fault!*"

"I tried to save you!" shouted Hark, feeling raw and battered. "I thought I had! But your body was dead. The only thing keeping it moving was the heart. That's why you got sick every time you went away from it. That's why your Marks changed you so much. Now your mind's dying, too, because you stuck yourself in a god. You're talking to me at the moment . . . but it's getting harder, isn't it? Soon something will be swimming around, eating people—a big, dumb, hungry fish. But it won't be you.

"So I can't let you eat me, Jelt. Maybe I *am* a bubble, wanting to dance off and live my own life. But I don't want you to vanish, either. You were my friend, my hero, my *brother*, and soon I'll be the only person who really remembers you. Once I'm dead, you're gone, too. Not even a memory left.

"I'm not your friend anymore, Jelt. I'm your storykeeper."

"You don't want to know the stories I could tell," came the savage, guttural whisper.

"Yes," said Hark. "I do."

"Really?" rasped an inhuman throat, in a voice full of human scorn and pain. "You want to hear a story about what *really* happened that night on the Rattleguise mudflats? Do you want to know what I was being paid to do, while I was away from Lady's Crave? What about that old scavenger from the shack on Nest? Do you want a nice story about what happened to him? No, you never wanted to hear! You don't want to know anything that means you have to grow up!"

Hark rested his forehead against the rock wall. There was enough truth in those words to hurt.

"I want to know those stories," he said. "Yes. Let's start with those."

The *Butterfly*'s bounces were stirring great billows of silt from the seafloor. Glancing over her shoulder, Selphin could see them drifting, obeying the pull of a slight current. She abruptly changed her course, aiming to the right of the outcrop, and then swung the sub into a few great zigzags.

When she stopped, panting for breath, Quest tapped her shoulder.

What are you doing? he signed.

We need all the cover we can get, answered Selphin, gesturing toward the great clouds of brown haze that were drifting to engulf the outcrop.

Selphin tied a cloth around her nose and mouth so she wouldn't breathe the silt clouds. Quest donned one as well. Selphin slung the wind-gun over one shoulder.

All stakes. It helped that the coruscating waves above, the shivering plain, and the restless rock pillars didn't seem real. It was a dreamscape. Selphin could tell herself that it wasn't water they were drifting in, it was just . . . slow air. Then she wouldn't have to think about the sheer, black, unimaginable weight of water above that flexing, purple divide, or the distance that separated her from real air.

Most of all, she wouldn't have to think about what the *Butterfly*'s broken scream meant. The little sub was flooded, so there was no air to fill the ballast tanks and help the *Butterfly* rise. Loss of the scream meant they couldn't use the little sub's rippling wing power to get home, either. It meant never seeing Lady's Crave again. Or Coram, or Sage, or Rigg.

She would fight to save them all, though, even if they never knew she had.

Hark listened to the stories he had hoped never to hear.

He heard about the first clumsy, stupid murder two years before, after a drunken argument late at night on Jelt's little boat. The other man split his head open on Jelt's wildly swung boat hook and went into the water. He didn't come up. Jelt threw the man's belongings overboard, too, then returned to harbor and walked all night to get his head clear.

Jelt thought he'd gotten away with it. He tried to forget the whole thing. It was just one time, and not his fault, and an accident mostly. But the memory was always there, something rotten at the bottom of the barrel, tainting all his other thoughts.

The man he'd killed had been seen getting on his boat, and the rumor had reached dangerous people. It was all right, they told him. They knew who the witnesses were, and would make that problem go away for him. And in exchange they'd tell him which of their problems *he* should make go away.

He wasn't a killer for hire; it was just an exchange of favors. Sometimes when he was in trouble, he just had to go away for a bit and do a few favors for some people so they'd deal with *his* trouble. It was just the way the world was, Jelt explained. You couldn't ever be prey. You had to be one of the hunters.

Hark listened and started to understand.

Jelt couldn't bear the thought that he had done something horribly wrong that could never be fixed. Of course he hadn't, he was *Jelt*. So what he had done was fine, better than fine, a sign of his strength, strong will, and fitness to survive. He had to believe that, even if it meant twisting his whole character out of shape and plunging into a deeper darkness. He was a hunter, a *hunter*, and he had to prove that to himself, over and over. Beneath every word, Hark sensed Jelt's despair, loneliness, and savage loathing for everything.

Hark should have been horrified, but he had used up all his horror. Instead he felt intense sadness.

He barely noticed the silt clouds drifting overhead.

Selphin swam through the haze of silt, the wind-gun slung over her shoulder. Grit got in her eyes, and the cloth nuzzled her mouth every time she breathed in. To her surprise, she was grateful for Quest's frail grip on her arm. Without the contact, they would have lost track of each other quickly.

She hated not being able to see very far. It made her feel helpless and disorientated. Of course, this was the result of her own plan working well.

Another pulse slammed into her, with a flash of mauve darkness.

Close now, signed Quest, his gestures just visible in the haze.

Soon Selphin could make out details of the god's vast, indistinct bulk ahead, the pale smudges of pulpy sacs and the round hollow of the mouth. It was hard to think this close to the god. Selphin felt like it was sucking away her thoughts, the way a passing whale drags smaller things into its wake. The writhing dark-light around it made her eyes and mind ache.

The next pulse nearly stunned her. For a few seconds afterward she couldn't remember where she was or what she had seen. But there were bright smudges on her retina. She had seen the flicker at the start of the shimmering ripple.

It's behind the mouth! she signed.

The two swam toward it cautiously. The mouth's long funnel was lined with tapering teeth. The curved bristles around the outside flexed slightly like grass in a breeze.

Selphin had only one dart. She needed it to go deep. Pulling out a bent coin, she flicked it forward through the water.

It floated toward the conical hollow . . . and then suddenly the entire mouth gaped wider and lunged forward toward the coin. The throat at the back of the mouth opened to show a dark tunnel, and Selphin fired down it.

The throat closed again. There was a swirling disturbance in the water, and the great mass in front of her jerked and shivered. Hairs bristled, scales tightened against each other, tiny stingers emerged.

Another pulse pummeled through the water. She had not destroyed the heart. And now the god knew they were there.

Hark was startled when Jelt broke off mid-account, with a roar of rage.

"You little snake! This was all an act! You were just waiting for your friends to attack me!"

The whipcord around Hark's middle tightened again, until he thought his ribs would break. It pulled with new intensity, and now the boulder against which Hark braced started to move, grinding along the base of the cleft toward the god.

Quest gave Selphin a piercing look of entreaty.

The wrench, please! he signed urgently. *Quickly!* He held out his hand.

Selphin suddenly realized why he had come with her. He had never believed shooting a dart would work. He was planning to lunge right into the mouth and smash at the heart with his dying strength . . .

There had to be a better plan, but there was no time to think of one. The god would attack at any moment. Selphin stared helplessly at the wind-gun, now a deadweight in her hands.

No. She was thinking about everything wrong. She hurriedly unscrewed the copper bottle from the barrel.

She wasn't holding deadweight. She was holding a heavy stick and a bomb.

Plunging forward dangerously, she launched the heavy bottle toward the gaping maw. The mouth lunged outward, bit down on the copper bottle, and pulled back. She saw the copper buckle under the pressure of the sharp teeth. Then the metal punctured, and Selphin shielded her face from the shock wave as the bottle exploded, its compressed air escaping in a great eruption of bubbles.

When she looked again, the conical mouth was mangled and torn. There was a hole at the back of the throat. Through it, Selphin could see a tangle of soft, fleshy-looking tubes, connected to something round and white.

It was the heart.

Selphin launched herself forward, jamming the gun barrel

lengthways into the gaping, mangled mouth to prop it open. She shoved her free hand deep into the hole, feeling sick at the clammy contact with her shoulder. Her fingers closed around something cold and round. She felt the perforations bite into her hand. It welcomed her skin. It wanted her bones. It had plans for her flesh.

She felt it move beneath her fingers as she tightened her grip.

"You never cared about me!" roared the Jelt-god. His voice was changing, the vowels becoming longer and more groaning, the consonants a distorted buzz. A human mind was guttering and going dark.

The rage was still there, but now what Hark heard most clearly was the pain.

"I always cared, Jelt!" yelled Hark with all his might, even as the whipcord threatened to cut him in two. "Even when I hated you, I cared!" The sides of the cleft scraped him as he was pulled helplessly along. "I always *will* care, as long as I live! But you should have let me go, Jelt! For both our sakes!"

As those words tore from his throat, Hark felt something change. Later he could not say what. The roaring ebbed and ceased.

The whipcord stopped dragging him through the cleft. It was still wound tightly around him, but its grip gradually became less vicious. At last it was exerting only a gentle pressure, like an arm wrapped around him.

Very slowly and deliberately it released him. Then it went slack, and the light in its tip dulled. Hark lay there dazed, staring at it.

"Hark?" A different voice echoed down the cleft. It sounded like Quest.

Hark painfully wriggled all the way out of the cleft, feeling like he had been peeled.

Sprawled against the side of the outcrop was the body of the god. The great bulk was a thing of patches and tatters again, moving with the sway of the water and nothing else. There was nothing in it Hark could recognize as Jelt, no body to bury or mourn over. All that remained of Jelt was carried in Hark's head, in his trove of stories, precious as gold and bitter as hemlock.

Amid the ruins of the body, he found Quest and Selphin, both looking muddy and exhausted.

In Selphin's hands rested a battered and cracked-looking god-heart with a few thin tubes winding off it.

"Is it dead?" Hark croaked.

"I think so," said Selphin grimly, "but I'm going to make sure." With shaking hands, she laid the pale, beautiful heart on a boulder and smashed it repeatedly with the butt of her gun until it fell into shards.

The *Abysmal Child* had gone. Unless the unpredictable terrain had swallowed the great sub, it looked like enough Leaguers had survived to crew her and depart.

Hark couldn't blame them. The Undersea, never docile, was becoming downright excitable. Some of the rocky spires were changing their angle and leaning dangerously. Crevasses opened in the seafloor, then closed again with a shudder. Perhaps the Undersea didn't like it when people killed its brand-new god.

The *Butterfly* lay not far from the rocky outcrop, its glass now heaped with fine mud and splatters of goo. It looked as exhausted as its crew felt.

"She served us surprisingly well," said Quest, looking at the little sub. "I take back what I said about her being an 'error of judgment.'"

By using the past tense, Quest had admitted what they all knew. The *Butterfly* had brought them to the Undersea, but without her scream she could not take them back.

Good view, Selphin signed, gesturing curtly at the insane vista. *Next time we'll bring a picnic.*

The Undersea *was* spectacular. Not many people would see a view like that, and fewer would live to tell the tale. Hark suddenly couldn't bear the thought that the three of them would *not* live to tell the tale.

One more try, Hark signed, and opened the *Butterfly*'s hatch.

Yes, signed Quest, without much sign of hope. *Of course.*

Hark was exhausted. He was bruised, battered, scraped, squeezed, and stung by strange ichor. There was nothing he wanted more than to lie on the seafloor and just let himself go numb. But instead, he climbed into the sub and dropped down into the driving seat.

He started pumping the bellows under one bruised, stiff arm and tweaking at the controls. There were more bubblings and sloshings, and the works spat out more bubbles.

Selphin climbed in, too.

You have a plan? she signed. She was wincing and frowning as if she had toothache, and Hark realized that she was trying very hard not to hope.

"Not really," he said. "You know me. I'm stupid. When something doesn't work, I keep trying it, anyway."

His lungs hurt, and they seemed to keep shuddering weirdly. He thought about the dead god that didn't look like Jelt, and his eyes stung.

He sniffed hard and squeezed the bellows again. This time only one bubble came out of the machinery. One silver bubble, dancing callously upward. Hark thought of Jelt drowning, really drowning in the bathysphere. Spending his last seconds of life looking at a bubble and thinking of Hark abandoning him.

Hark squeezed the bellows again, and there were no bubbles. None. Jelt, floating drowned in the water. Only a faint breathy sound from the bellows.

The Undersea drank his tears, the way it drank everything it could. Hark heaved on the bellows again, one last useless time.

A moment later he was reeling over, clutching his ears, and desperately scrabbling for a helmet. The timbre was different from the earlier screams but still very loud.

"It's working! Everyone, get in! The pipes *can* use Undersea water, they just couldn't while there was still air in them!" Now Hark thought about it, lungs didn't seem to cope well with a mix of air and Undersea water, either.

Quest clambered in, and everyone hastily made ready. While their doom seemed inevitable, there had been a mood of numb calm. Now that there was a tiny chance of survival, everyone's panicky sense of urgency returned. They still had no air in the sub to help them rise, but at least now they had propulsion. With luck, the *Butterfly*'s wing ripple could drive her upward, the way a bird's flapping wings bore it into the sky.

Hark set the wings to a ripple, adjusting for the new timbre of the scream, then guided the little sub off the seafloor. One of the wings was kinking slightly, making it harder to steer. He took the *Butterfly* up in an ascending spiral, watching the undulating "sky" above all the while.

The waves and eddies were too wild this time for him to predict the pattern. All he could do was to aim for a flattish patch, and hope.

When the *Butterfly* flew screaming into the divide, it was grabbed and shaken like a rattle. Only Hark's helmet prevented him from being knocked out against the glass wall. There was sudden inky blackness and a feeling that somebody had taken Hark's mind and soul in a fist and squeezed them to the size of a raisin.

Everything was spinning. Or was it? It was too dark to tell. Hark reached out a heavy arm and groped until he found the light.

The sub *was* spinning. Hark leveled it out just in time to dodge a towering Undersea wave.

The *Butterfly* tried to spiral upward, but another petulant current sent her rolling again through the blackness. Every time Hark worked out which way was up, a stray current grabbed them, twisted them, buffeted them. They were a wounded mouse in the mouth of a great, black cat. It was an angry black cat, with a mouth so large it could swallow cities.

Then the cat got tired of the game. The *Butterfly* was sent tumbling and smashed against something so hard that Hark was flung up out of his seat, breaking his seat belt. As he floated back down again, he saw where they were.

All around were ruined turrets, rusted portholes, the hulks of diving bells. The Embrace had chewed the *Butterfly* up and spat her out on the submarine graveyard. It had chewed hard. One wing had been torn off, and the other was a mangled rag of its former self. The rear propeller was bent at an angle. Neither Selphin nor Quest appeared to be conscious.

Even as the hopelessness of the situation sank in, other bits of debris fell down around the *Butterfly* and started to bury it.

Hark pumped the bellows again, and the *Butterfly*'s solitary scream rang out across the corpses of its fellow submarines. All he could do was send out a noise to get attention. It was a forlorn hope. Nobody was likely to be looking for them, and there was no reason for anybody to guess that the strange wailing was a cry for help.

He heaved and heaved on the bellows, anyway. He didn't know how long they had. Eventually the lamp would fail, and other debris would cover them, and then they would never be found.

It was getting harder to stay awake. Perhaps the Undersea water they were breathing was losing its goodness, like air. Sometimes he found himself lying across his seat, not knowing how long he had been unconscious.

Clink, clatter, clink! More debris falling on the sub. He opened his eyes.

No, debris was being moved *off* the sub. Someone in a heavy diving suit was pulling pieces of metal off the *Butterfly*. They stared in, and with a sense of unreality, Hark recognized Rigg's face glaring at him.

You, she mouthed, pointing at him. *Are. Dead.* She emphasized this by drawing a line across her throat.

It seemed like a long way to go just to threaten somebody. This was Hark's last thought before he passed out.

EPILOGUE

AS IT TURNED OUT, THE *BUTTERFLY* WAS ONLY found due to Vyne and Kly.

When the junior attendant staggered into Sanctuary carrying the injured Vyne, he threw the whole building into confusion. Thankfully, a lot of Sanctuary's staff had medical training. While they were attending to Vyne's wound, she woke up and loudly shared a lot of explicit terms that she had certainly never learned during her doctorate.

Meanwhile, the junior attendant remembered Hark's words about Vyne's letter and passed the doctor's notebook on to Kly. As Hark had hoped, Kly realized that the scrawled, bloodied note addressed to the governor was very, very important.

It also wasn't signed. Kly realized that if he didn't get Vyne to add her signature and seal, the governor might not believe it was from her, so he decided that he had to speak with the doctor before he left. It was very lucky that he did so.

Dr. Vyne was, by this point, very worried. She had missed the keys from her belt and guessed that Hark must have taken them. Since she had already confessed her worst misdeeds in the letter anyway, Vyne told Kly about the imprisonment of Hark and Selphin, the escape from the Leaguers, and her fears that even now Hark might be trying to drive the *Screaming Sea Butterfly* without her.

Alarmed for Hark's safety and keen to find Quest, Kly ran down to the cove where Hark had last been seen. He found the abandoned boat and a cliff door that had been torn off its hinges. There was no sign of Hark, Quest, Selphin, or the submarine.

He did, however, encounter what he believed to be a visiting scavenger gang from Lady's Crave. Naturally, he asked whether they'd seen the fugitives and gave their names and descriptions. Since they were actually members of Rigg's gang, the mention of both Hark and Selphin aroused their intense interest. Kly refused to explain why he was asking after them, so the smugglers bundled him into their boat and took him to Rigg.

Kly spent the next hour being yelled at and threatened by an angry smuggler matriarch who wanted to know where her youngest daughter had gone. Once he realized that she was Selphin's mother and not hell-bent on murdering the girl, he started answering her questions. He admitted that Selphin might be en route to the Embrace in a dangerous, screaming submarine.

Rigg released Kly and let him head to the governor with Vyne's note. By the time the governor had agreed to talk to Kly, Rigg was already readying her most durable submarine and attaching a salvage-dragging harness to it.

Rigg and her crewmates heard the *Butterfly*'s scream long before they found the sub. It is hard to tell the direction of a sound underwater. However, one can sometimes work it out, with enough stubbornness, just by cruising around to find out where the noise gets louder.

Fortunately, Rigg was very, very stubborn.

The crew of the *Butterfly* were submerged in Undersea water for eight hours altogether. By the time they were tipped out on a Nest beach like so many gasping fish, their skin was pale and their hands and feet wrinkly as walnuts.

Quest terrified everyone by nearly dying on the spot. His lungs had been gently adapting to the Undersea water, and the change back to air was a brutal shock to his system. His convulsions convinced Rigg to take him and his crewmates to Sanctuary for treatment.

Hark spent the next week only intermittently conscious. On the first day, somebody asked him a lot of questions. He answered them, in the hope they would go away. Later, he realized that the questioner had been Kly and that Kly had been kind and very patient.

Hark felt unbelievably heavy whenever he tried to sit up. He couldn't swim through the air, and he didn't know why. Sounds were too raw and breathy, colors too bright. When he looked out of the window, the sky didn't look quite real. He kept closing his eyes and opening them again, expecting to see a vast, billowing coverlet of purple, silver, and ink.

Hark hadn't believed that he would see the surface world again, and now he couldn't believe that he *was* seeing it. His mind was still down in the deepest deeps.

A month of the cleansing baths, special ointments, and a gruel-based diet gradually brought him back to himself. The mauve tint in his eyes faded, and his skin returned to its natural color. Better still, he recovered his curiosity about the world outside his own head.

Dr. Vyne had been arrested, he discovered. The museum had been locked up, and Kly was running Sanctuary under the governor's orders. The governor had apparently made it clear that Hark and his friends were to receive the best treatment but that they should be cloistered from contact with anybody else until they were well.

"Don't let them talk to anyone yet," had been his exact phrasing.

Hark also discovered that, even after all the baths, he and his crewmates had been left with some permanent Marks.

Hark had a curving zigzag of pale skin that traveled across his scalp, from the peak of his forehead to the nape of his neck. It looked like a young snake, and the hair that grew from it was white.

Gripping the Hidden Lady's heart had left little dents in Selphin's left hand, where the edges of the perforations had dug into her skin. They covered her palm and the underside of her fingers. The pattern looked a bit like lace.

Quest had to keep breathing the fumes from scare-lamps, or his lungs went into spasm. It altered his voice, which now left an uneasy residue on the mind like the scare-lamps themselves. He spoke less and less each day, however, and slept more and more.

Hark knew that Quest was dying.

"You can't leave yet!" Hark blurted out one evening in the old priest's sickroom.

For a few days he'd had a desolate suspicion that Quest was quietly casting off his moorings and waiting for a wind to carry him away.

"I see!" said the priest. "Thank you for telling me."

"I mean it!" said Hark. "You . . . you haven't given me all your stories. You're the only one that knows the Hidden Lady's tales, and the ones she heard from the Gathergeist. You can't go until you've passed them on. You're their storykeeper."

"You have a point," said Quest, sounding surprised. "I should tell you those tales. After all, you have already heard the worst of them—I have no reason to hide the rest."

So Quest did not die the next day, or the next, or the next week, or even the week after that. Hark came every day to hear the tales of the gods, and then the tales of the priests, and at last, simply the tales of Quest. Hark even started to hope that if he just kept asking questions, teasing out stories, then Quest would never leave at all. Stories would somehow keep Quest alive, but less horrifically than the heart had sustained Jelt . . .

Hark wondered how lonely Quest had been all these years. He shared some common ground with the other priests, but beyond that lay his own private quicksand and hidden forests. He had been an infiltrator among them, his fellowship with them a lie.

It took a while for Hark to understand the soft, cryptic smile that Quest wore when he talked of his past. These were boxes of memories he had not allowed himself to open for many years. Now at last he did, and he found their colors still fresh. He was looking at them one last time as he gave them away.

As time went by, he talked more and more of Ailodie. Ailodie before she became an acolyte. Ailodie as a troubled young priest. Ailodie changing, becoming someone else . . .

In the end, Hark couldn't help asking. The gap in the story was too large, too aching.

"What happened to her?" He bit his tongue, battling his suspicion, then gave in to it. "She didn't . . . she didn't become Moonmaid, did she?"

"Moonmaid?" Quest stared at him in astonishment. "No, no! She never changed *that* much! She isn't at Sanctuary. I am afraid I will never see Ailodie again."

"She didn't die in the Cataclysm?" This thought was even

worse. It would have a cruel poetry, like something from an old ballad.

"No!" Quest corrected him swiftly. "She lived, she thrived, she is probably still out there on Malpease. I will not see her again, though, because she despises me. You see, after the Cataclysm she was the only person I told about my part in it. She was horrified. She said I had no right to gamble with so many people's lives. Besides, she took oaths very seriously and considered our priestly vows utterly binding."

"But . . . you did it partly to save her, didn't you?" said Hark. "Did you tell her that?"

"Yes, I was stupid enough to make that clear, and arrogant enough to think she would fall into my arms out of gratitude," Quest remarked wryly. "Of course she didn't! Why would she? She hadn't *asked* me to murder her divine patrons and kill hundreds of people for her sake. No, she went off and married someone else."

"That's not fair!" exclaimed Hark impulsively.

"Of course it is!" replied Quest, with a little snort of mirth. "I didn't see it that way at the time, but I do now."

"But—"

"She *married*, Hark! She had the children she always wanted, the children she thought she couldn't allow herself while she was a priest. Whatever my selfish young dreams, I did love her. I wanted her to be happy. I suspect now she probably is. If so, then *I have won*."

Hark was suddenly aware of the ways people changed, and the ways they didn't. On the one hand, Quest clearly had the same steely will and subtlety as his younger self. There had been time for him to mellow, though, and reflect.

"She was right, anyway," said Quest. "I *did* gamble with countless lives. For thirty years I have been wrestling with this and trying to decide whether I did the right thing. I have even tried to guess how many more would have been killed by the gods or murdered as sacrifices over the last thirty years, if I had not done what I did . . . but that is self-deception. You cannot justify an atrocity with mathematics. Is a terrible deed ever worth it for the greater good? I am sure those Leaguers thought so when they were building that god. Am I any better than them? I cannot say. All I know is that I could not bear to do *nothing* about the gods, and I could not think of anything else to do."

Hark remembered admitting that "nothing" was the worst thing he had ever done. He suspected he'd done worse than that now, though he'd managed to undo some of it.

He also remembered Quest's own words about change.

What aspects of yourself would you fight to protect, as if you were fighting for your life?

"Look," Hark said, "I don't know if it was right! You shouldn't ask *me*, anyway. I make really stupid decisions. But I'm glad the gods are dead. I'm glad we're making windows and bridges and medicines out of them. I'm glad we're free, even if we do stupid things with the freedom sometimes. Maybe sometimes there *isn't* a right thing to do. Maybe there's just lots of wrong answers, and you have to pick one you can bear—something that doesn't break who you are. Maybe if you hadn't tried to kill the gods, you wouldn't have been Quest anymore."

"Perhaps," said Quest gently, and smiled a little, as if the thought were a kindly one.

A few hours later, Quest, the arch-traitor and mastermind of the Cataclysm, left the world quietly in his sleep.

We have to tell everyone the truth about everything, signed Selphin, a few days after Quest's death. *It can't hurt your priest friend now.*

Selphin's recovery had taken longer than Hark's, because she had been close to the god-heart for several beats while it was empowered by the Undersea. Even now she was pale under her freckles.

Hark and Selphin's conversations had changed. One of them would launch headfirst into the subject in their mind, the way you did with old friends. They had both fought a god in the Undersea. Nobody who hadn't could quite comprehend them anymore. Their mutual understanding was a relief to both of them, like countrymen meeting in a foreign land.

We should talk to the governor first, Hark replied.

He won't see us, Selphin signed doubtfully.

She was wrong. The governor responded to their message within a day. Three days later, the pair of them were on Lady's Crave, drinking tea with him in his private residence.

From a distance, the governor had always looked very imposing, in his brightly colored coat with his white beard cut to sharp edges. Meeting him face-to-face, Hark was surprised to find that he looked a lot like a squirrel—an old, fat, clever squirrel, with a mean mouth and a tolerant eye. He wore velvet, as a governor should, but his good boots were scuffed with use, and Hark fancied he was carrying pistols under his coat.

"I was already hoping to talk to you both," the governor said, and then smiled at them with narrowed eyes. "What *are* we going to do with you?"

This was ominous. It made them sound like problems to be solved.

"Give us both lots of rewards?" suggested Hark hopefully. "And . . . set me free from my indenture?"

"Mmm," said the governor, and gave a twinkle that could have meant anything. "Well, I think we can get rid of that indenture of yours. I'm confiscating all of Vyne's possessions right now, and that includes you. In her note, she did *ask* for you to be set free, anyway."

"What's going to happen to her?" asked Hark. He still hadn't untangled his feelings about Vyne. She was callous, irresponsible, and definitely a little crazy. For her own selfish reasons, however, she had opened up his life and shown him new possibilities.

"Is that the voice of misplaced loyalty?" asked the governor. "Don't worry, she's far too useful to drown in the harbor as a traitor. I'll need to keep an eye on her, though, so . . . I've decided to put her up for indenture for the next fifteen years, then buy her myself at the Appraisal."

"Someone else might bid for her," said Selphin. "The League, or someone worse." She had been speaking aloud and lip-reading since entering the governor's house, rather than asking for the conversation to be in sign. Hark hadn't asked her why, but he suspected that it had something to do with pride and the intimidating nature of the occasion.

"Oh, they won't," said the governor, and ate another honey cake. "So . . . your rewards." He looked shrewdly at Selphin. "I'm sorry, but you can't keep the submarine."

"Submarine?" Selphin looked confused.

"I can't let your gang keep the wreck of the *Screaming Sea Butterfly*," said the governor pleasantly. "Your mother sent you here to ask for that, didn't she? I'm sorry, but she needs to hand it over. It isn't salvage if there are living crew aboard when it's pulled up. The sub belonged to Vyne, so I'm confiscating it with the rest of her property."

Selphin was slowly shaking her head.

"I'm not in my mother's gang anymore," she said flatly.

This was news to Hark. He had noticed that Selphin seemed sullen and out of sorts.

"She found out I betrayed the gang," she continued, in the same cold, matter-of-fact tone. "So she disowned me. I'm not a member of her gang or her family. You'll have to talk to her about the submarine." Selphin kept her eyes clear and defiant but her voice wobbled toward the end.

"I see," said the governor, frowning slightly. "I'm sorry to hear that." Oddly enough, it sounded as though he meant it. "Do you want me to talk to her on your behalf?"

"No," said Selphin, almost before he had finished the question. Hark had to bite his tongue to stop himself saying anything.

"So why *are* you here?" asked the governor.

Between them, Hark and Selphin told him about the true nature of the gods, their human core, and the great, mad beasts they had become when they grew too large. They told him about Quest and the way in which he had caused the Cataclysm.

By the end, they had the governor's undivided and decidedly startled attention.

"Are you sure of all this?" he asked, but did not sound scornful. "You heard it all from a single old priest, who is now dead?"

"He wasn't confused," Hark said quickly. "He was clear as ice. And I bet there's more proof in the Sanctuary archive."

"We want to tell everybody," said Selphin, firmly, as if she could overwhelm the governor's money, power, and status by strength of will. "Everybody in the Myriad."

The governor pursed his lips and thought for a long while.

"That . . . is a lot to take in all at once." He sighed. "I shall try to be honest in return. Do you know what rumors are flying around already?"

Both shook their heads.

"Everybody knows that the League tried to raise a god," said the governor. "The League has some powerful enemies now. We governors don't agree on many things, but none of us want giant, mutant crabs turning up and taking our islands away. The League's reputation is mud—they won't find it so easy to recruit or get funding after this. Also, everyone knows that the newly raised god was killed by Lady's Cravers. *That* news spread like measles. It's an open secret that the two of you were involved. Many people assume I had something to do with it, too. Of course, I've officially denied having a secret god-glass submarine fleet for the defense of Lady's Crave against all human and divine attacks."

"So now everyone thinks you *have* got one," said Hark promptly. "Are you going to build one? Is that why you want to keep Dr. Vyne alive?"

"No, definitely not." The governor chuckled. "The *Butterfly* is a typical Magdala Vyne project. Dazzling execution, *terrible idea*. The sound knocks people out! It melts nearby god-glass! The sub's almost impossible to pilot, and the wings rip like jelly! No, I really don't want a fleet of those. But"—he raised a finger—"an *imaginary* fleet of them could be incredibly useful. I don't think anybody will be attacking my islands any time soon, do you?"

"The other governors might try to build their own, if they think it's possible," pointed out Selphin.

"I'm sure they will! They'll spend time and money on sound-powered god-glass submarines, before finding out how impractical they are." The governor was visibly trying not to laugh. "Then *they'll* deny having elite secret fleets, so everybody will assume they've got them too. Think of that! Dozens of imaginary god-glass submarine fleets, strung out along the Myriad, protecting it!

"The League thought we needed new gods to protect us from invasion," he went on. "But I think our new reputation as god-killers will be a much better deterrent, don't you? Would you want to invade a people who have mastered mysterious technologies and can kill a full-blown god at four hours' notice?"

Hark was starting to see his point.

"What I am saying," the governor explained, "is that I am managing the spread of numerous rumors right now. The fascinating information you have just given me will fit in rather well with them. But it would be better if you let *me* circulate it. My reach is greater than yours, and I have been doing this for a long time. I am very good at it."

Hark looked at Selphin and raised his eyebrows. She shrugged.

"All right," he said.

"I'm glad that this turned out to be such a pleasant conversation," said the governor, helping himself to another cake. Hark wondered how unpleasant the conversation might have become if he and Selphin had given the wrong answers.

The governor probably wasn't a good man. It would probably be better to have a ruler who didn't sell people or bend his own laws. For the moment, however, this man was perhaps just the best of the wrong answers available.

Since neither Hark nor Selphin had really considered what they wanted as a reward, the interview ended shortly after. Selphin blurted out something about money or passage to one of the continents. Hark surprised himself by stammering that he still wanted to learn to read and asking if he could keep his job at Sanctuary for now.

"Why don't you both think about it for a while?" the governor said as he showed them out. "There's no hurry."

Selphin was tired out after lip-reading such a long conversation, so she headed back to the boat. Hark suspected that she was also finding it painful to be on her precious Lady's Crave, now that she had lost her home there.

He promised to meet her later. Then he went in search of Rigg.

Hark asked the right people and found the smuggler captain. She was with Sage and Coram, up on the hillside above the harbor, not far from the place where Jelt had first introduced them. Rigg saw him approach and held up a warning finger.

"You," she said, "need to stay out of my way, or I'll regret letting you live." She started to turn away.

"Rigg," Hark called out, "I want to talk to you about Selphin."

She turned to glare at him. Hark had the strangest feeling that she had grown shorter since their last meeting. She seemed to be looking at him differently now, as well. Perhaps it was because of the snaking white mark down the middle of his scalp and the halo of rumor hovering around him. Maybe she also sensed that he wasn't so afraid of her now.

She was dangerous, of course, but there were different kinds of fear. He'd dodged mighty waves on the surface of the Undersea. He'd been squeezed almost insensible by a god. Now he looked at Rigg and saw a human being—angry and loyal, loving and cruel, stubborn as granite.

"There's nothing to say! She betrayed the gang!" snapped Rigg.

"She spotted a threat to the gang and tried to deal with it!" Hark retorted. He had brought that threat to the gang, and maybe he would pay for that, but he would worry about that later.

"She should have dealt with it by talking to me! She didn't even tell me there was a relic!"

"You'd have locked her in a room with it, wouldn't you?" Hark charged on, before she could interrupt. "I saw what that heart did to my friend Jelt by the end. Selphin was right to want it far away from you all. All right, so she found a way of saving you that she knew you'd hate. So what? Isn't that exactly what you were trying to do to her?"

There was an intake of breath from Sage and Coram. They looked like an audience at a bearbaiting.

"That's different, you cocky little vermin!" Rigg glowered at him. "I'm the leader of this gang! And I'm her mother!" Pause. "I *was* her mother," she corrected herself.

"You'll always be her mother!" Hark could sense it properly now, the savage, unquenchable love beneath the battle of wills. "You're just like each other! You're both carved out of the same freckled rock! Stubborn, proud, angry all the time . . . Rigg, she *is* you."

"There are codes!" snapped Rigg. "What would people say if I took her back now?"

"They'd say, 'We'd better not mess with that gang; even the kids kill gods before breakfast,'" replied Hark.

Sage gave a muffled snort. It was the first time he'd seen her show any sign of humor.

Rigg turned to glare at Sage, but the scarred woman responded with a sequence of signs. Hark couldn't understand all of them and guessed that the crew had developed some private slang.

He got the gist, though.

You won't lose face, Sage was signing. *You'll look weaker if you let her go.*

Rigg showed no sign of buckling, but when did she ever? *You could wreck a ship against that face*, thought Hark. Yet she was letting Sage talk. Perhaps she was even glad that somebody was trying so hard to talk her out of her decision.

Sage glanced at him occasionally. There was a sign she used now and then, a bit like that for an eel, but in a snaking motion over her head. Eel-over-head? Hark caught Sage's nod toward him as she repeated the sign and remembered the snaking pattern on his scalp.

It was his *name* now, he suddenly realized. He had a sign

name. He'd never had one—a lot of people who weren't sea-kissed never got one. You had to be given one by a sea-kissed. But now he had one. He felt a huge surge of surprise and pride. It made him feel more real.

The only sea-kissed whom he could imagine wanting to name him was Selphin. If Sage knew a name that Selphin had invented, then that meant the two of them were still talking to each other. Selphin still had friends in the gang. Rigg would be tough to convince, but it looked like he wouldn't be doing it alone.

"When did you grow a spine, anyway?" Rigg growled at Hark.

"Eels always have spines," he answered. "They just bend a lot."

Deals were made stealthily, as was the way on Lady's Crave.

Rigg suddenly acquired a brand-new skimmer sub, some diving equipment, and a licence to dive for salvage in certain prized areas. Such things weren't as exciting as a god-glass submarine, but at least they didn't come with the lasting enmity of the governor.

She also reacquired her youngest daughter. Anyone who talked as though there had ever been a rift between the two of them received blank, menacing stares from the rest of the gang until they agreed that they must have been mistaken. Selphin could be seen striding with Sage and her sea-kissed friends through the harborside, reveling in her ominous celebrity.

To the lasting confusion of her mother, Selphin could also sometimes be seen swimming in the shallows.

"I just told her that I wouldn't make her go in the sea anymore," complained Rigg. "And the next day . . . this!"

She's like you, Sage told her, echoing Hark. *Force something on her, and she'll fight you till the world burns. Best let her do things her own way.*

Meanwhile Selphin stood hip deep in the water of the sheltered bay, watching the sparkles on the little waves as they butted her playfully and passed her by to chase their foam up the beach. She dragged her lace-patterned left hand through the top of the waves. There were so many colors in every wavelet, so many gleams like chipped gems. Foam glistened and fizzed cold against her palm.

She took a deep breath and was full of the moment and the sky. There was so much—the terns and the gulls up above, the slick red backs of the crabs racing for the pools, the giddy little boats tipping their red sails out in the distance, the shacks up the hillside, the scavenger gang watching to make sure she wasn't there to forage . . .

I beat you again, she told the sea, her beloved enemy. *We saved everyone from you, and we survived. I'll keep beating you, you'll see. I won't let you kill me. But you can't make me live in fear of you, either.*

With her toes, she gripped the shingle of her beloved island. Her gang was hers again, and the warmth of that belonging was like the sun on her skin. Things were not the same as they had been, and they never would be. Selphin's crew-family could no longer see her as the little kid they had watched grow. Now their affection was mixed with the same wary respect they showed storms, whirlpools, and Rigg. Nobody talked about Selphin as Rigg's successor, but Rigg and Sage had taken to beckoning her over when they discussed plans for the gang's expansion.

Perhaps there were worse fates than becoming a smuggler queen. Selphin smiled up at the sky, knowing that Lady's Crave was hers, hers, *hers* . . .

There had been a long debate about how much the old priests should be told. Could they bear to hear that their carefully guarded secrets were spreading through the Myriad? Or that Quest, their friend of decades, had been a traitor in their midst? While the staff agonized over this issue, somehow the priests managed to hear about it anyway. Rumor is like sand: Once it starts blowing around, it is very hard to keep it out of anywhere.

Some of the priests were bitterly distressed by the news. Others took refuge in denial and refused to acknowledge it.

After the initial shock, sorrow, and rage, however, many of them started to talk. For decades their oaths and habits of secrecy had kept their tongues under seal. Now that all was lost, they had nothing more to lose.

In particular, they talked to Hark.

He had been nervous about returning to Sanctuary. After all, he had fled its halls after driving most of the priests to frenzy with the god-heart. Besides, he knew that he was different now. He was no longer the same desperate-to-please boy who had pretended to be cheery and harmless, to keep everyone off guard and at arm's length.

The other Sanctuary staff didn't know how to treat him. He was no longer indentured, he was Marked, and rumor hung above him like a storm cloud.

The priests, however, opened up to him like flowers. They saw the weaving white mark in his hair, and perhaps even the Undersea reflected in his eyes. There was an unspoken under-standing. He and they were bruised veterans from the same war, even if they had not been on the same side.

The stories tumbled out.

Hark heard about the time Entreater-of-the-Torrent prevented Kalmaddoth from devouring everyone on Maddothmain by talk-ing to it nonstop for nearly two days and finally persuading it to swim off in pursuit of the moon's reflection.

He heard about the youthful, passionate affair between Call-of-the-Air and Fifth Lament. Once, they had even smuggled wine and sweetmeats down in a bathysphere with them and enjoyed a romantic interlude, fairy-lit by phosphorescent creatures of the deep.

Wailwind turned out to have a daughter, whom he had kept at a distance so that he would betray none of the priesthood's secrets as his wits faded. Now Hark saw them together, rebuilding their bridges one invisible brick at a time.

Moonmaid was the real revelation. She was enraged by Quest's treachery and even more furious that his accounts might shape forever how people saw the priests. She was determined to set the record straight, so she kept cornering Hark to pelt him with jagged anecdotes. Her personality still struck Hark as cold, but he learned that she could also be interesting and clever, with a ruthless eye for character.

Best of all, the priests felt free to talk and reminisce together, now that they were less fearful of being overheard. Once, to his astonishment, Hark saw Moonmaid and tiny Seamist both laughing so hard at some shared memory that he feared for their health.

In the evening, Hark went to Lady's Crave. He headed to one of the old taverns where the salvage crews and submariners drank, the sort where storytelling always started by moonrise. It was an inn where Hark had gone when he was a little kid, to hear stories of the gods, and smuggling runs, and missions to the deep, and faraway lands. He had hung around on the edge of the crowd or wriggled in under a table, straining to hear some of the story, like a stray cat prowling for scraps.

This time, he didn't have to elbow a space in the tavern.

The crowd shifted and made room for him, the way they did for friends and dangerous people. They no longer saw him as a skinny Shelter kid or Jelt's sidekick. They saw a teller of stories strange and true, with his adventures written across his scalp. A space was cleared for him on a bench.

Hark had arrived halfway through the telling of a tale, as he had so many times before. This time, however, he didn't feel confused or left out. No stories were complete anyway. They were all really just parts of a bigger tale that could only be told by many different voices and seen through many different eyes. There was always more of the story to learn.

The story was being told through a sea-kissed song. The "singer" was magnificent, creating silent music through her sway-ing as she signed, the expressions of her face ever shifting and expressive as the sky. A drummer held the beat, but everyone in the tavern matched it by stamping on the floor in time, send-ing an ever stronger vibration through the timbers. It was the heartbeat of the story, and everyone could feel it through body and soul. It filled Hark with a feeling of kinship and strength.

It was a story of doomed lovers on a salvage mission to the Undersea, and Hark could tell that the singer had really been to those deeps. She showed him anguish, beauty, and terror, and every moment was mesmerizing.

Stories, stories. He had always been a storyteller, of sorts— eager to entertain, or win people over, or get something he wanted, or play the hero for a bit. Now other people's stories were the treasures he prized. He was a storykeeper for gods and heroes.

Once he could read and write, he would travel, he realized. He would leave Sanctuary and sail all over the Myriad. He would collect stories everywhere and save them before they could fade away from everyone's memory. You could keep people alive forever through stories.

"What about you?" someone called to Hark, after the sea-kissed song ended. "Are you telling us one tonight?"

They wanted to hear the true story of the Cataclysm, or the Gathergeist's strange dealings with the lantern wraiths of the deep, or the priests' daring theft of the Dawn Sister's gelatinous tresses while she slept. Of course he would tell one of those true tales tonight, while the audience listened, spellbound.

For now, however, he was aware of others in the crowd, still mustering the courage to raise their voices. The old woman with tattoos from three submarines along her thin arm. A polite middle-aged man with a continenter medal pinned discreetly under his collar. A young man Hark recognized, looking nervous and rueful without his Leaguer uniform.

Hark could see the stories they yearned to tell glimmering in their eyes. They could be coaxed out, with a little effort.

"In a while," Hark answered, "I'm listening for now."

ACKNOWLEDGMENTS

I would like to thank: Ella, a young reader who contacted me to ask whether I would ever consider including a deaf character in one of my books, triggering a small avalanche in my brain that resulted in the invention of the sea-kissed, after which she generously became my expert consultant; the other members of the Young People's Advisory Board of the National Deaf Children's Society (Amber, Adam, Cam, Esther, Francesca, Ida, Jayden, Jovita, Lily, Lucy, Molly, Mollie, Lucy, Reuben, Rhodri, Sam, Sarah and Zain) for all their incredibly useful input; My sensitivity readers (Jane Newman, Judith Tarr and Kayleigh Goacher, plus Ella, Jovita, Francesca and Ida from the YAB); Rosie Eggleston; my editor Rachel Petty for not screaming when I handed her a first draft slightly bigger than the moon, and for helping me hack it down to something book-sized; my agent Nancy Miles; Martin for putting up with a crazed, feral, semi-nocturnal author-girlfriend in deadline crisis for months; Rhiannon Lassiter for preternaturally clear-sighted feedback; *Ships Beneath the Sea: A History of Subs and Submersibles* by Robert F Burgess; *Half Mile Down* by William Beebe; *The Deep: The Extraordinary Creatures of the Abyss*; *The Incredible Record-Setting Deep-Sea Dive of the Bathysphere*; *Being Deaf: The Experience of*

Deafness, edited by George Taylor and Juliet Bishop; *Inside Deaf Culture* by Carol Padden and Tom Humphries; *Deaf Culture Our Way: Anecdotes from the Deaf Community* by Ry K. Holcomb, Samuel K. Holcomb, and Thomas K. Holcomb; and last of all, every scuba instructor and dive leader who has shown me the strange glories of the deep.

ABOUT THE AUTHOR

FRANCES HARDINGE IS THE WINNER OF THE 2015 Costa Book of the Year for *The Lie Tree*, one of just two young adult novels to win this major UK literary prize. She is the author of several books for young people, including *Cuckoo Song*, *Fly By Night*, *Verdigris Deep*, and *A Face Like Glass*. She lives in England.